LOVE'S TROUBADOURS

LOVE'S TROUBADOURS

Karma: Book One

A Novel

Ananda Kiamsha Madelyn Leeke

iUniverse, Inc.

New York Lincoln Shanghai

Love's Troubadours

Karma: Book One

Copyright © 2007 by Madelyn C. Leeke

iUniverse books may be ordered through booksellers or by contacting:

iUniverse
2021 Pine Lake Road, Suite 100
Lincoln, NE 68512
www.iuniverse.com
1-800-Authors (1-800-288-4677)

Because of the dynamic nature of the Internet, any Web addresses or links contained in this book may have changed since publication and may no longer be valid.

This is a work of fiction. All of the characters, names, incidents, organizations, and dialogue in this novel are either the products of the author's imagination or are used fictitiously.

Author Photo—Copyright © 2007 by Leigh Mosley

ISBN: 978-0-595-44081-8 (pbk)
ISBN: 978-0-595-88404-9 (ebk)

Printed in the United States of America

For the Divine Spirit, my ancestors, Rayes Deno Moss, and Andrew G. Peace

God is love, and those who abide in love abide in God, and God abides in them.
1 John 4:16

Aham Prema—I am divine love.
Sanskrit Mantra

Love is capable of uniting living beings in such a way as to complete and fulfill them for it alone takes them and joins them by what is deepest in themselves. All we need is to imagine our ability to love developing until it embraces the totality of men [and women] and the earth.
Pierre Teilhard de Chardin
Visionary French Jesuit, mystic, paleontologist, biologist, and philosopher (1881-1955)

Preface

Love's Troubadours was inspired by a speech given by American playwright Lorraine Hansberry in February 1964. She spoke to a Harlem-based group of aspiring young, gifted, and African American writers about the power to love in America. In her remarks, Hansberry referred to African Americans as troubadours, the descendents of people who used the power of love to live through and overcome despair and insurmountable odds. She went on to urge the audience to seek wisdom from African Americans because of their capacity to love.

I first read about Hansberry's speech in *Salvation* by bell hooks in 2001. *Salvation* discusses how African Americans have used the power of love to transform their lives and communities. hooks' writings called me to question how I could use my gifts as an artist and writer to promote love as a healing tool in the lives of individuals and communities in America. I answered that question by writing and self-publishing the novel you are about to read.

I began working on the novel in 1997. That same year, many of the characters introduced themselves to me while I attended Essence Magazine's Music Festival in New Orleans. They traveled home with me and into my daily life. From 1998 to 2000, I wrote bits and pieces of the characters' stories. In 2001, I stepped out on faith with the creative support of Rayes Deno Moss, and committed to writing a novel manuscript entitled *Ask The Troubadours Who Have Come From Those Who Have Loved*. Deno provided a much needed male voice to the project. Our collaborative efforts created a series of stories narrated by a cadre of male and female characters. We completed a final manuscript on January 23, 2003. A few days later, we mailed letters of inquiry to several agents. Deno made his life transition on February 6, 2003, two days after his 41st birthday. He was buried on

Valentine's Day in his hometown of Wilmington, Delaware. While reading Deno's obituary to his family and friends at his funeral, I realized that he was truly one of Love's Troubadours.

Deno's life transition created tremendous healing and growth opportunities in my life. I was forced to face my fear of writing a novel on my own. This fear was one of the major reasons I invited him to co-write the original manuscript. In addition, I learned how to sit with the grief and suffering that comes from losing a dear friend. With the presence and support of the Divine Spirit and my angels, ancestors, editor/brothalove friend Wayne P. Henry, and sacred circle of family and friends, I mustered the energy to surrender my ego and write from my heart. Prayer, meditation, affirmations, yoga, chanting, reiki healing touch, acupuncture, music, painting, collage-making, wire sculpting, journaling, walking, running, and weight training also helped me stay the course.

I solicited feedback on the manuscript from agents, writers, family, and friends in 2003 and 2004. During this process, I was encouraged to expand the characters' emotions and experiences. As a result, the original manuscript gave birth to four new manuscripts. In 2005, I became overwhelmed with writing, especially when it came to expanding novel excerpts that contained Deno's words. They were the only written evidence of his creative spirit. I didn't want to change anything. I needed to preserve his soul on paper. So I decided to focus my energy on developing a manuscript about a female character that was closest to my heart.

In 2006, I decided to shorten the name of the novel series to *Love's Troubadours*. Today, it is a healing fiction series about people learning and living as they love. I define healing fiction as stories about people who discover their own power and choose to use it to uncover their hidden wholeness. As they travel this journey, they learn that they cannot control life. They also learn that their hearts are adaptable despite what occurs in life. They come to know and apply the universal truth of maintaining an adaptable heart which helps them understand, accept, and transform their lives according to the natural flow of the universe.

Love's Troubadours—Karma tells the story of Karma Francois, a thirty-something Oakland-born BoHo B.A.P. (Bohemian Black American Princess) with Louisiana roots and urban debutante flair. She is a daddy's girl from her head to her toes; HBCU graduate (Historically Black Colleges and Universities, Morgan

State University); and sorority sister (Sigma Gamma Rho Sorority, Inc.) who is accustomed to living extremely well. Karma is a natural woman with a unique style. She could easily pass as the twin sister of Celia Faussart, one of the Afropean sultry hip-hop songbirds commonly known as Les Nubians. Passing would probably be her first choice since her relationship with her twin sister is emotionally distant. Reddish brown locs crown her head. She sees the world through cocoa eyes. Her skin is the color of burnt sugar. The French call it caramel, a contrasting force of salt and sugar. And like caramel, Karma's personality is a contrasting force of salt and sugar. She epitomizes the Sanskrit meaning of her name: the total effect of a person's choices, actions, and conduct during her lifetime.

The book begins with Karma's life in an uproar. Her life, relationships, and museum curator career that she struggled to build in New York City no longer exist. They have crumbled before her, leaving no viable options to rebuild. Relocation to the Nation's capital, Chocolate City D.C., has offered Karma a new home in a condominium owned by her relatives. Denial, depression, and debt have become her roommates. Lack of full-time employment opportunities has forced Karma to craft a gypsy existence as a Jill of Many Trades: yoga teacher, art consultant, and freelance curator. Unable and unwilling to appreciate these trades as gifts, she chooses to wallow in a pool of lost identity. One can hardly blame her given the family drama, secrets, and pain she is forced to endure, understand, and accept. All of it deepens her pool wallowing into a near drowning affair.

For the first time in Karma's life, she must see herself for who she really is. When she looks in the mirror, she sees a woman who has made choices in her relationships that dishonor her personhood. They make her question whether she loves and accepts herself. With the prodding and support of a therapist, Karma reluctantly begins the long arduous journey of seeking to transform the total effect of her choices, actions, and conduct during her lifetime. She discovers who she is, one of Love's Troubadours.

Acknowledgements

We are all connected and interdependent. We are all one. This truth has carried me throughout my life. It was a constant reminder as I gave birth to this book. This book was created with the love, prayers, support, positive energy, wisdom, creativity, and inspiration of the Divine Spirit, Mary, Jesus, Erzulie, Oshun, Oludmare, Yemanya, Obatala, Shango, Oya, Ogun, Elegba, Auset, Ausar, Ma'at, Sekhmet, Het Heru, Seshat, Amitabha Buddha, Kuan Yin, Shakti-Shiva, Ganesh, Lakshimi, Sarasvati, Vach, Kali, Durga, and Krishna; my angels, ancestors, spirit guides, and master teachers; and the folks listed below.

Rayes Deno Moss, my brothalove friend and guardian angel

John and Theresa Leeke, my parents

Michael and Lu, Mark, and Matthew Leeke, my siblings

Marcie and Jordan Moss, Deno Moss' wife and daughter

Diane Hicks, Deno Moss' mother-in-law

Deno Moss' family and friends

Wayne P. Henry, my editor and brothalove friend

My sacred circle of family and friends

Tre Roberts, my cousin and graphic artist

Thomas E. Roberts, Sr., my uncle and proud member of The Monday Club

Reverend Carolyn Francis, my therapist

Henry L. Jackson, my prayer partner

All Souls-Insight Meditation Community of Washington Sangha, my meditation community

Shirley Jagdeo, my Reiki Master and Teacher

Gloria, Marisa Alonzo, Yael Flusberg, Faith Hunter, and Debra Mishalove, my yoga teachers

Don Diggs, my acupuncturist and Ayurvedic practitioner

Tracy Mickens-Hundley, Daphyne E. Williams, Kamaria Richmond, and Karen Crump-Wilson, my sistalove friends who read novel drafts and provided their female insights

Jason Randolph and Keith Sykes, my brothalove friends who read novel drafts and provided their male insights

Marcia Duvall, Karen Sallis, and Sandra Butler-Truesdale, my Trade Secrets family

Leigh Mosley, my photographer

Lauren and Aislee Smith of Tax Concepts, LLC, my attorneys

Michael Bush, my accountant

Judy Weathers, my financial advisor

My inspirational sheros and heros: my great great grandmother Millie Ann Gartin, the original Black American Princess—my great grandmother Eunice Ann Thomas Roberts, my grandfather John Leonard Leeke, my grandmother Frederica Stanley Roberts, Swamini Turiyasagitananda Alice Coltrane, Ohnedaruth John Coltrane, Swami Satchidananda, Lorraine Hansberry, Rumi, Paramahansa Yogananda, bell hooks, Rutgers University Women's 2007 Basketball Team, Ruby Dee, Diahann Carroll, Jasmine Guy, Afeni Shakur, Thich Nhat Hanh, Jan Wills, J. California Cooper, Pearl Cleage, Oprah Winfrey, Maya Angelou, Susan L. Taylor, Marcia Ann Gillespie, Angel Kyodo Williams, Joyce Meyers, Rev. Michael Beckwith, Rickie Byars-Beckwith, Kasi Lemmons, Sting, TKS Deskachar, Nischala Joy Devi, William and Camille Cosby, Sharon Gannon, David Life, Krishna Kaur, Gurmukh Kaur Khalsa, Rabbi Daniel Schwartz, Rev. Rob Hardies, Rev. Shana Lynngood, Ken Yamaguchi-Clark, Rev. Scott Alexander, Thomas Ashley-Farrand, Malcolm Jamal Warner, Saul Williams, C's Little, First Sunday Family, Shondra Grimes, Debbie Allen, Phylicia Rashad, Emily Dickinson, Sylvia Eng, Anand Shantam, Moshe Wise, Shanti Norris, Scott Stoner, Rachel Remen, Michael Lerner, Lori Malachi, Sharon Malachi, Gail Gartin, Madelyn C. Grace, Jackie Brown, Brenda C. Coleman, Peter Hundley, Marcus and Thomas Hundley, Haley Brown, Marie A. Butler, Tim'm West, J. Scales, Jill Barrett, Marie-Denise Simon, Toni Asante Lightfoot, Fred Joiner, Judith Harris, Willard Stanback, Assata Shakur, Mara Brock Akil, Audre Lorde, Frida Kahlo, Carol Mosley Braun, James Baldwin, Paul Robeson, Claudette Perry, Connie Razza, Zora Neale Hurston, Langston Hughes, Imani Uzuri, Tricia Rose, Mark Anthony Neal, Yvette Lee Bowser, Queen Latifah, Erika Alexander, Kim Fields, Jean Toomer, Sharon Salzberg, Tara Brach, Grace Ogden, Janis Ellis, Isabelle Allende, Veronica Chambers, Joan Morgan, Jervey Tervalon, Deepak Chopra, Catherine Ponder, Lama Surya Das, MN8, Susana Baca, Hugh Byrnes, Don Miguel Ruiz, Jodine Dorce, Jewell Parker Rhodes, Darlene Nipper, Venus and Serena Williams, Tiger Woods, Margaret Burroughs, Pema Chodron, Alice Walker, Toni Cade Bambara, Ntozake Shange, June Jordan, Thulani Davis, Monique Greenwood, Caroline Shola Arewa, Marianne Williamson, Amel Larrieux, Eric Roberson, HKB FiNN, Wynton Marsalis, Madame C.J. Walker, Suze Orman, Stephanie Stokes Oliver, Iyanla Vanzant, Gwendolyn Brooks, Useni Eugene Perkins, Haki R. Madhubuti, E. Ethelbert Miller, Ron Gault, Charlayne Hunter-Gault, David Baker Lewis, Judge Robert Duncan, Katie K.White, Eric Butterworth, Myrtle and Charles Fillmore, Shirley Servis, Terry Cole-Whitaker, Garlynn P. Jones, Monique Ruffin, Selma Hayek, Amma, Sri Sri Ravi Shankar, Ernest Holmes, Mother Teresa, Osho, Barbara Chase-Ribaud, Luisah Teish, Toni Blackman, Kwame Alexander, Kevin Powell, William Jelani Cobb, Kara Walker, Chris Ofili, Thelma Golden, Dorothy Poinsette, Marie Laveau, Tanya F. Lewis, Agnes Roseboro, Corine L. Green, Rashe L. Hayes, Brenda Dancil

Jones, Rocky Jones, Carol Brantley, Toni Dutton Butler, Argentine Craig, Sandye J. McIntyre II, Father Neal Ward, James Neelon, Angela Bassett, Courtney Vance, Jada Pinkett Smith, Vanessa L. Williams, Lynn Whitfield, Shirley Chisholm, Luberta and Frederick Mays, Reginald F. Lewis, B. Smith, Sandra Gettings, Belinda Rochelle, Briane E. Reed, Renita J. Weems, Anna Julia Cooper, Renee Stout, Helene Fisher, Eraka Rouzorondu, Lois Mailou Jones, Michaela Angela Davis, Mari Evans, Jill Scott, Les Nubians, Roberta Flack, Cicely Tyson, Nikki Giovanni, Barbara Jordan, Angela Davis, Suzanne de Passe, and so many more folks....

2005-2006 Flow Yoga Center fellow teacher trainees

kg yoga clients and supporters

Smith Farm Center for Healing and the Arts

Howard University Hospital patients and staff

All Souls Unitarian Church, People of Color Sangha—Insight Meditation Community of Washington, Unity of Washington, DC, St. Augustine Catholic Church, and St. Joseph Catholic Church

My 16th and U Street Starbucks Family: Marques, Ashanti, Keith, Kalvin, Ricky, David, Eddie, Dominique, Teirra, Khadijah, Imani, Janelle, Janai, and Malcolm

Owners and staff of Mocha Hut, Love Café, Cyberstop Café, Whole Foods Market on 14th and P Streets, Safeway on 17th and Corcoran Streets, CVS on 17th and P Streets, Blockbusters on 17th Street, Adams National Bank on 17th Street, Health Bar, Teaism, 18th and U Duplex Diner, HR57, Utopia, Cada Vez, 24/7 Café, Jin (formerly Mangos), Café Luna, Simply Home, The Diner, Rice, Bua, Wild Women Wear Red, Habitat, Pulp, Busboys and Poets, Java Green, Dupont Optical, City Kinks, Ann Taylor Loft on Dupont Circle, and Results Gym

My Blogspot, Myspace, and Yahoo Group Friends

My teachers at Kenmoor Elementary School, Kenmoor Junior High School. Elizabeth Seton High School, Morgan State University, Howard University School of Law, and Georgetown University Law Center

Sigma Gamma Rho Sorority, Inc.

Staff who wrote incredible articles in the following newspapers and magazines: Washington Afro-American Newspaper, Washington Post, Science of Mind, Daily Word, More, O, Heart and Soul, Essence, Latina, Black Enterprise, EBONY, Jet, American Visions, American Legacy, Sister2Sister, Port of Harlem, Upscale, Honey, Black Issues Book Review, Complex, Black Men, Yoga Journal, Ascent, Yoga International, Yoga + Joyful Living, Fit Yoga, Town & Country, Tricyle, Shambhala Sun, Homes of Color, Real Simple, Cosmopolitan, Glamour, Elle Décor, Martha Stewart Living, Dwell, Metropolitan Home, Artnews, Self, Today's Black Woman, and Prevention

Artists, writers, composers, singers, and musicians whose work kept me focused during the novel writing journey (too many names to list)

iUniverse staff

Everyone who has crossed my path or will cross my path in this creative journey … you know who you are.…

Readers of this novel: may my words bless you in the ways that you need.

Thank you all. Be love, love light, and live as the spirit of life!

Namaste,

Ananda Kiamsha Madelyn Leeke
Washington, DC

P R O L O G U E

▼

"You show me the path of life. In your presence there is fullness of joy."

—Psalm 16:10

A salty oat cookie and large clay mug of chai tea kept me company as I sat writing in my journal on the second floor of Teaism, an Asian-inspired teahouse located a few steps from Connecticut Avenue on Dupont Circle. My sistalove friend Ma'at introduced me to this shrine of tea a few months ago. I fell in love at first sip. Since then, I have been using it as my urban retreat center for unscheduled moments that invite me to pause and reflect on life. This morning, I felt one of those moments coming on as I was teaching my yoga class in Malcolm X/Meridian Hill Park.

As I looked at my students practicing *Adho Mukha Svanasana* on their mats, I giggled about how my life resembled this inversion pose last year. With all of the ups and downs that I experienced in 2000, I can definitely say that I received each and every benefit from living in downward facing dog: a deeply stretched back to carry a load of emotional issues that I was unwilling to claim; an open heart to embrace the lessons learned; a stimulated brain and nervous system to help me identify, understand and accept my choices; and improved memory, concentration, hearing, and eyesight to assist me in navigating my life and making better choices with increased wisdom.

More thoughts about the people I met and decisions I made raced through my mind. It was overwhelming. It felt like what the Buddhists refer to as monkey mind. The mind of a person who is not in the present moment and is stuck in a mental state that jumps from thought to thought. After a few seconds, I took a couple of deep breaths, made a mental note to spend time at Teaism after church, and returned to my role as yoga teacher.

Right after class, I headed home to shower before going to Sunday service at All Souls Unitarian Church. As I walked up 16th Street to church, I listened to Alice Coltrane's *Journey in Satchidananda* on my CD walkman and made a mental note of how I would spend my time. First, I planned to order the vegetable bento box, chai tea, and salty oat cookie. After eating the contents of the bento box, I decided I'd stare out the window and people watch. When I got bored with that and my stomach settled, I figured that I'd munch on my cookie, sip my chai tea, read the April issue of O Magazine, and write in my journal. I didn't have a plan for what I would write. I imagined that the words would flow freely onto the page. They would express whatever my soul needed to say.

When I arrived there, I noticed that most customers were sitting outside of the turn-of-the-twentieth century neoclassic building. They seemed to be enjoying the spring weather that the month of April often brings. I hoped their presence meant that the upstairs area was almost if not, completely empty. After I paid for my entrée and tea, I climbed the stairs to the second floor. Seven other people were sitting on banquettes and small Asian stools at handcrafted mahogany tables. That scene made me happy. A corner seat by the window caught my attention. I walked over and made it my home for the afternoon.

Forty-five minutes after I finished my meal and reading several magazine articles, I reached into my purse and pulled out my journal, CD walkman, and Eric Roberson's *Esoteric* CD. Eric's music kept me company as I wrote in my journal.

On days like today I find myself hearing the majestic voice of Nina Simone sing ever so eloquently to Lorraine Hansberry about how young, gifted and Black she was. I can't help but think that I am precisely what she was. When Momma called me yesterday morning, I told her how fantastic I felt. She exclaimed, "*Cherie,* I am so happy that you are filled with joy. It makes a mother feel magnificent to know that her child is grounded and has a reason for living."

I dropped out of the conversation for a few minutes. My mind got stuck on the phrase, reason for living. It made me think about a quote by Hansberry that discussed her reason for living. I can't remember the words verbatim, but I think that Hansberry's reason for living was grounded in her belief that life has within it goodness, beauty, and love. In this moment, I can say that I totally agree. Had you asked me last year, my response would have been very different. The pain in living that I experienced cut so deep that no matter what I tried to do to uplift my spirit, it remained. With each passing day, it seemed to grow stronger. Sometimes life became so difficult that I couldn't even enjoy breathing, meditating or practicing yoga. My gifts from the Divine Spirit couldn't event bring me peace. And the harder that I prayed, the farther peace seemed to move from my soul. I felt restricted, squeezed, and painfully bound. My state of mind experienced a severe limitation of possibilities to act and understand. I was living in a state of *dukkha*, a Pali term that refers to suffering. I found myself wanting to check out of life. I was simply unwilling to withstand the suffering any longer.

Suffering helped me understand that to live, you must suffer. My own experience taught me that it is impossible to live without experiencing some kind of physical or psychological suffering. All human beings have to endure sickness, injury, tiredness, old age, death, loneliness, frustrations, fear, embarrassment, disappointment, anger, and loss. It sounds pessimistic, but it's not. It gave me a gift of truth that I can overcome suffering by living in the heart of love. Living in the heart of love first begins with me finding comfort and security in receiving the Divine Spirit's unconditional love. The next step involves me learning to love and accept myself as I am. I'm still working on this step. It's a life long process.

All of these revelations helped me wake up to my higher self. They also gave me a deep sense of gratitude for the path I have walked, the lessons I have learned, and the love, prayers, positive energy, and support I have received from the Divine Spirit and my family, friends, and therapist. When I came back to the conversation, I told Momma how grateful I was for the support that I received from everyone. She responded with an unexpected sermon that all mothers are entitled to deliver from time to time. "Last year was a hard one for you, Karma. By the grace of God, you made it through. I think at some point you made a decision to rely on the life of Christ within as your source of healing and continued renewal. That was your place of surrender. You discovered your own ability to have faith. Your choice to surrender and have faith let God know that you needed direction on how to live. With God's wisdom, you were able to make changes that benefited your soul. You became a spiritual warrior by doing what the Biblical scribe in Ephesians 4:24 instructed us to do: clothe yourselves with the new self, created according to the likeness of God in true righteousness and holiness. That was and remains a miracle filled with a lifetime of joy for me."

Momma's expression of joy multiplied my own. Last night, one of my favorite cousins, Cane, expressed the same sentiment while we were eating dinner at The Islander, a family-owned Caribbean restaurant on 12th and U Streets, NW. "Cuz, did you know that you're my shero? I'm really proud of how you've pulled your life together. The whole family is."

Our dinner was the perfect prelude to MN8's concert featuring Eric Roberson at the 9:30 Club. The dinner was nice, but Eric was the highlight of the evening for me. Why? Because this uncompromising musical genius from New Jersey is a visionary and poster child for authentic music in a time when it is so easy for artists to surrender their creative voices and freedom of expression for the dollars that lie behind the doors of major recording companies. In short, Eric reminded me of what it takes to tell your truth and live it. And we all need that kind of reminder on a regular basis because it is so easy to lose oneself, get sidetracked, emotionally confused, overwhelmed, hurt, angry, and stuck in a long episode of pain.

All week long, I looked forward to seeing Eric perform tracks from the *Esoteric* CD. Track 13 entitled *Woman* was beginning to hold a special place in my heart after frequently experiencing joy in the company of a certain person. My new-found joy was just the tip of the iceberg of celebration. Cane was probably the only family member that could see my life had dramatically changed since I arrived in Chocolate City a year ago.

We were always close as children, but lost touch as we grew up and went our separate ways. Me moving to D.C. last year offered us both an opportunity to rekindle our friendship, but neither of us pursued it. I don't know the reason why Cane didn't, but mine was simple. I was drowning in my own personal pool of emotional confusion and pain without any life jacket, goggles, or floating devices. My definition of self was pinned to a profession that burst into flames. Nothing was left except the ghost of who I thought I had become: a chic New York City cosmopolitan careerist.

My financial outlook was bleak. Debt had become my first, middle, and last names. Career options with a salary and benefits to accommodate my current lifestyle were nonexistent. The freedom to call my own shots and determine my own destiny had shriveled up like a raisin in the sun. I was left eating humble pie in an apartment owned by family in a city I didn't choose to live in.

To make matters worse, I was faced with high family drama ... the life changing kind that comes from parental indiscretion that can't be swept under a table or hidden in a closet in a back room or attic. It was sandwiched in between the fallout from my choices in relationships with men as partners, lovers, and friends.

An unhealthy pattern had formed in my life. It painted a picture of a woman who volunteered for the starring role in a soap opera drama that could easily win a daytime Emmy. I was playing the role of a moth throwing herself into flames. I was intent on destroying myself in the process. No one could save me except God and myself. Fortunately through God showing me the path of life, I was able to learn how to swim out of the confusion and pain, and into the fullness of joy. My soul was my pilot throughout this entire journey to the land of joy. And it was precisely this joy that Cane detected during a conversation we had at the annual Baptiste Kwanzaa celebration on New Year's Day in Annapolis. Since then, we have been spending time together, laughing, talking, and sharing. Like my brother Ohnedaruth, Cane is becoming one of my closest male confidantes.

At the concert last night, Cane teased me, "you are the queen of esoteric." Smiling, I took it as a compliment for being one of Eric's biggest fans. The word followed me into the next morning and disturbed my peace so much so that I looked up the definition to see if Cane's compliment had a double meaning. According to the good people who publish Webster's Dictionary, esoteric is an adjective that means confidential or private. Okay now I see what Cane was trying to say about me. His compliment echoed some truth about my personality and the ability to fully disclose and communicate my vulnerabilities. However, if anyone ever discovered my journal entries from the past year and read them from cover to cover, I'd no longer be able to sit on my throne of esotericism. All my business would be out on the street for all to read, debate, and judge.

The thought of that happening used to scare me, but now after umpteen hours of therapy and many months of healing work, my soul is standing ajar and ready to welcome the ecstatic. This state of being is the reason I can now say that it wouldn't matter if someone read what I wrote. What would matter is if they learned something that could be used in their lives to help them or another person move through and grow beyond fear, anxiety, emotional scars, and obstacles that all human beings face on a regular basis. I'd write them a short note that would say,

Dear Beloved Readers,

My life journey isn't a secret. It's an open book for you to explore. I pray that you are able to witness the path of life God showed me to take to become who I am today … Karma, one of Love's Troubadours. A woman who understands, accepts, and demonstrates that the first and most important love affair she can have is with Creator. The second is with herself. The third is with her divine mate, partner, lover, and friend. The fourth is with her family and friends. And the fifth is with everyone and everything in the universe. May my journey be a light that helps to illuminate God's fullness of joy in your life. May you accept and live out your divine inheritance as God's people learning and living as they love.

Be love, love light, and live as the spirit of life!

Karma

PART I

▼

The worthies of the past ages all sought the truth and did not deceive themselves. They were not like moths throwing themselves into flames, destroying themselves in the process.

—Ta-sui

CHAPTER 1

▼

"What is my strength that I should wait? And what is my end that I should be patient."

—Job 6:11

Yesterday, I woke up in the middle of the night sweating. An ocean of tears followed. The clock registered three thirty-six a.m. My psyche was attacked by the same nightmare that has repeated itself for the past several months: my life in living color. This time I was left with a question. Who am I? After the tear storm stopped, I tried to hide under my covers to avoid answering it, but it repeated itself until I turned on the light and reached for the handmade journal that my therapist Francis convinced me to purchase.

I wrote the question in big black letters across the pages of my journal.

Who am I? My birth certificate says that I'm Belle Violette Francois, the daughter of Eugene Jerome Francois and Hyacinth Belle Baptiste Francois. My family and friends say I'm Karma, a nickname my father gave me as a child. When I look in the mirror, I see that I'm a woman with long reddish brown locs who sees the world through cocoa eyes. My skin is the color of burnt sugar. The French call it caramel, a contrasting force of salt and sugar. But who am I really? If I knew I guess I wouldn't feel like a victim of identity theft. Not the typical kind where someone takes your identity for financial gain. I'm talking about a new and improved kind where life robs you of your hard-earned professional identity and leaves you with nothing more than a pile of ashes and never ending suffering.

Do I sound bitter? You bet your sweet ass I am. My life was supposed to be a certain way. I did everything I was supposed to do. And just when I was about to cash in on all of my hard work, I lost everything. I feel like an IDP, an internally displaced person who has been forced to leave her cosmopolitan life in New York City as a result of a human-made disaster called termination of employment. I've been deprived of my livelihood, network of friends, and access to personal services such as my yoga classes at Ta Yoga House; shiatsu massages at Artista Salon; manicures and pedicures at Perfect Polish; appointments with my loctician at Khamit Kinks; chocolate martinis on Fridays at Soul Cafe; Salsa dancing at S.O.B's; and shopping sprees at Carol's Daughter, Ann Taylor Loft, Eileen Fisher, and Moshood.

I miss my life. I miss it dearly like a child longs for its mother or a lover mourns the loss of a lover. I do indeed miss my life. I miss who I used to be. At least I had some sort of identity back in New York City. The last time I was there was December 1999. My best friend and neighbor, Branford and I were scheduled to have an early dinner before we attended *All Rise,* an evening-length twelve-part composition commissioned and premiered by the New York Philharmonic with the Lincoln Center Jazz Orchestra and the choir of our alma mater, Morgan State University. The emotional landscape of our lives was rapidly eroding. We were both nursing the wounds of recent breakups. His two year marriage to Sinclaire, a woman he had known and loved since childhood … a woman who had recently kicked him to the curb when he admitted his true sexual identity as a man who has emotional relationships with women and sexual relationships with men. My eight-year on and off relationship with Madison, a narcissist that I could never find the will to leave. Four months prior to my breakup, Daddy died suddenly of a heart attack and my vocational calling became the casualty of a violent institutional drive-by shooting engineered by the political mafia within the Walden Museum of American Art's ivy tower.

The blues had become my national anthem. Billie Holiday was my patron saint. A shadow of darkness cast itself upon my life, leaving me weak, worn down, and wondering how I was going to make it. The only certainty I could grasp was an inner knowing that I didn't have the strength to wait on the Lord for any answers. Anger and fear consumed me. They gave birth to a question that I didn't have the strength to wait on for an answer: what is my end that I should be patient?

By default, I accepted that mine was a perpetual cycle of suffering. So I dwelled in it as I witnessed the lease on my spacious two-bedroom apartment expire. Memories and mementos of my cosmopolitan New York City life were packed in clearly marked boxes and mismatched luggage. They were headed south in a U-Haul destined for a much-needed safe haven in the Nation's capitol. Things were moving so fast that I couldn't keep up. I was in the world, but not of it. It felt like I was melting away. I needed something to bring me back to myself, but I didn't know what it was.

As I crossed 62nd Street, a group of college students from Columbia University mistook me for the twin sister of Celia Faussart, one of the Afropean sultry hip-hop songbirds commonly known as Les Nubians. When I denied any ties to these Afrosoulicous sisters from Bordeaux, France, they taunted me with comments that I was hiding from fame. How I wish! No matter how I protested, they insisted on believing that I, a newly unemployed spendthrift museum curator with less than a hundred dollars in my Citibank checking account and an American Express gold card bill of nine hundred dollars waiting to be paid on my King Louis XV mahogany writing desk, was escaping a glamorous high profile life as a world renowned entertainer.

They were right about one thing. I did want to escape my current existence and rewind it back to the year before my father's death, breakup with Madison, and monumental fall from grace at the Walden. That would have been 1998, the era of my own personal version of Camelot when all things were possible and ART-news, America's oldest and most honored art magazine, profiled me in its November issue feature article on *The New Guard: Shaping the Art World*. With one internal restructuring, Walden officials erased me from the face of the new guard. I lost my job because I was politically aligned with the wrong person. My carefully planned career of ten years in the New York art world came to an abrupt halt. As I sought to understand the meaning behind this unsettling turn of events, colleagues advised me not to take my termination personal, but how else could I take it after climbing the ladder of success to the position of Curator and Director of Branch Museums. Was I supposed to lie down and relinquish a decade of hard work that started from humble beginnings as a curatorial assistant with two college summer internships at the Studio and DuSable Museums, a part-time gig as an administrative assistant in the education department at El Museo de Barrio, and a Bachelor of Arts in art history and African American Studies with a minor in Spanish from Morgan?

Some colleagues argued that I was caught in the crossfire between my boss, Sebastian and Walden's Board of Trustees. After the Board appointed a new director, Sebastian was forced to resign. Rumor had it that his resignation was prompted by a series of philosophical clashes on emerging artists' exhibitions and the recruitment and promotion of employees of color. It was easy to believe this rumor in light of Sebastian's commitment to excellence, diversity, and building an art collection that personified America's rich multicultural legacy. During his fifteen year tenure, the halls of the Walden were transformed from a plain vanilla ice cream cone with a smattering of colored sprinkles to a twenty-one flavor extravaganza of professionally competent staff and undiscovered artistic treasures mined in America's communities of color. Sebastian's commitment brought me to the Walden. He discovered me at El Museo del Barrio and offered to serve as my mentor and guardian angel. Within the Walden, I was his cherished protégé. He became the one person I could count on to navigate the museum's political terrain and absorb any negative drama directed my way.

Memories of bold, groundbreaking exhibitions dominated by cutting edge work created by emerging artists discovered in the midst of risk taking adventures filled my head. The high of it all carried me from year to year. No matter what was happening in my life or relationship with Madison, I could rely on my rich passionate career as a source of happiness. So when those Columbia students hounded me on the corner, I found it impossible to deny their request to sing a few lyrics from Les Nubians' album, *Les Princesses Nubiennes*. Their excitement transported me back to a world that had become my queendom. Feeling the momentary glory of my royal throne, I cleared my throat and whipped out my best alto impression of the first lines of *Demain*. They seemed pleased with my afternoon charade. I walked away secretly wishing that I had the power to click my heels like that chick Dorothy and wake up in my former life with old my job and all the trappings, privileges, and accoutrements that were part and parcel of my existence as Karma Francois, the aggressively bright, bold, determined, and passionate rising star with no end in sight.

Sitting in my new surroundings I now know that there is no chance of that happening. My bourgeoisie bohemian lifestyle with a brownstone apartment on

Edgecombe Avenue in Harlem's Sugar Hill has been downsized to a one-bedroom condominium apartment previously occupied by my cousin Colette and owned by her parents, Aunt Josephine "Jo" and Uncle Charles, Momma's brother. Although my new residence is located right smack dab in the middle of the northwest corridor of Chocolate City's historic U Street, it doesn't feel like a neighborhood to me. It is missing the most important ingredient, my sacred circle of friends who are back in New York City.

Melancholy sadness keeps me company as I recall how wonderful it was to live five blocks from Madison who owned a brownstone with his brother, Michael. Whenever Madison and I were feuding, I had two places that I could visit for a pick me up. Branford was a block away and my nail artist, Tracy and her husband Peter and their two darling sons Marcus and Thomas lived directly across the street. And when I needed to kick back and drink margaritas with my Beta Tau Chapter line sisters of Sigma Gamma Rho Sorority, Amy and Marie-Denise, all I had to do was walk around the corner. I even had two fabulously cool co-workers, Gabriella and Stephanie from the Walden sharing a cozy brownstone on Convent Avenue. On the third Sunday of each month, we'd get together and religiously dish the dirt on whatever was going on at the Walden and feast on Sylvia's famous soul food. It was our ritual after attending Mass at St. Thomas the Apostle Catholic Church. All of these wonderful people got along famously. Throughout the year, we would gather in each other's homes and celebrate birthdays, anniversaries, and a host of multicultural holidays. Even though we all promised to stay in touch, my fear that my move to D.C. would affect the closeness of our relationships wreaked havoc in my head.

Anxiety from future changes to cherished friendships was just a drop in the bucket of my life transition. My career as a curator has been reduced to a shameful gypsy existence with no health insurance and three part-time jobs as a yoga teacher at Our Womanist Spirit Center; freelance curator at Howard University's art gallery; and a seasonal consultant to a wealthy, charismatic, and demanding West Coast patron from my Walden days that I'd prefer to fire, but can't because I need every dime I can earn. Wearing these three hats has made me what one of my favorite artists, Adrian Piper, calls a Jill-of-All-Trades. Unlike her, I'm not proud to wear any of them. One hat as an art curator is sufficient for me.

Family and friends constantly remind me that I should be grateful for having these blessings, but my ego and pride fiercely resist and mourn the loss of my former identity. American Express, Visa, MasterCard, Discover, and a host of other small creditors are on my ass for their money because I'm behind in payments. My credit rating is dropping by the minute. My finances are beyond tight. My emotional well being wavers in between anger and depression. I appear to be on the brink of a nervous breakdown. My head tripping and crazy work schedule have eliminated any viable opportunity for a budding romance. And the only thing that I know for sure is that my head is just above water because of a life jacket that I call Francis, my therapist.

CHAPTER 2

▼

"I have no peace, no quietness; I have no rest, but only turmoil."

—Job 3:26

The second week that I was in D.C., Momma shamed me into paying a courtesy call visit to my Aunt Jo. I put it off as long as I could for fear that she would see right through me because that woman is a Howard University trained psychologist. She could always read my emotions better than anyone I know. So one Friday afternoon, I took a deep breath, put on my best fake me out smile, and walked a few blocks to 16th Street and Riggs Place. I counted each step trying to turn an eight-minute walk into a forty-minute journey so I could rehearse my mental script. As I approached Aunt Jo and Uncle Charles' house, I looked up at the attic and remembered the many summers that my twin sister Violet and cousin Cane played make-believe. This house has always been our second childhood home. Aunt Jo was working outside in the front yard on her flowers. She greeted me with a quiet joy that I always wished my own melodramatic mother would display from time to time.

In her deep southern Mississippi accent, Aunt Jo replied, "Honey girl, you are a sight for sore eyes. How are you darling?"

Doing my best to put up a good front, I smiled as hard as I could, "Just fine. Just fine Aunt Jo."

"Karma, sit on the steps for a few minutes. I need to finish trimming the cherry blossom tree at the end of the yard."

I was grateful for a few minutes to collect myself. "Take all the time you need."

Aunt Jo was an understated diva. Her grayish locs were neatly piled on top of her head surrounded by a piece of indigo fabric. She managed to make her denim overalls fashionable with a simple white t-shirt and a chunky turquoise necklace and bracelet. A set of small turquoise chunks decorated her ears. Her feet were dressed in her classic white Keds.

Twenty minutes later, Aunt Jo appeared and invited me inside for some herbal tea in her sage-colored kitchen. She rummaged through a collection of CDs sitting in a wicker basket on the counter and popped one into her CD boom box. The familiar sounds of Tuck and Patti echoed from the speakers. Then she opened a kitchen drawer, pulled out a white candle, three sticks of incense, and a cigarette lighter. Her short blue black fingers flipped the lighter and used it to light the candle and incense. The aroma of jasmine began to fill the air. Unbeknownst to me, she was setting the stage for an atmosphere of truth telling.

The room was uncomfortably silent. The only thing I could hear was Aunt Jo pouring spring water into the glass tea kettle sitting on her stove. She placed a wooden box of herbal teas on the kitchen table. Spoons, honey, napkins, and two containers of unsweetened applesauce followed. How in the world did she remember my childhood favorite snack? It is beyond me! I opened the wooden box and selected a raspberry zinger tea bag. Aunt Jo selected a lemon tea bag. The tea kettle sounded the alarm that the water was hot and ready for pouring. Aunt Jo handed me a large multicolored mug with pictures of Kemetian women dancing on the front of it. I dropped my tea bag in and let it seep for a few minutes before adding three teaspoons of honey. My hand slowly stirred the spoon in the tea cup. I was hoping to buy more time in the land of uncomfortable silence, but Aunt Jo put an end to my hopes when she gently touched my hand and looked deep into my soul.

"So Ms. Karma, tell your aunt how you are making out."

Trying desperately to read from my mental script, I answered, "Doing just fine. I can't complain."

"Honey, it's okay to complain if you want to. You are going through a lot of changes now."

"Actually, I'm doing fine."

"Are you sure?"

"Yes, ma'am."

My pride would not allow me to expose the pain and shame that I was keeping bottled up inside. Aunt Jo let me pretend for a good hour before she unleashed her famous quiet candor. In her words, she said that I "was exhibiting many of the symptoms of depression—sadness, loss of energy, and feelings of hopelessness." She told me that it was normal for me to feel depressed, sad or blue about losing my job and having to leave New York City. Aunt Jo suggested that I enlist the support of a good therapist to help me navigate this major life transition. As she hugged me, she handed me her therapist's business card. I glanced down at the name Francis Alleyne, quickly stuffed the card in my purse, and promised to think about using it.

Another three weeks passed by. One Saturday morning Aunt Jo paid me an unexpected visit. She noticed my weight loss. That's when she threatened to contact my mother, "*la grand dame of control*," Hyacinth Belle Baptiste Francois in Oakland if I didn't agree to talk to someone. To avoid Momma's melodrama, I bowed to Aunt Jo's deference and allowed her to schedule an appointment with Francis.

Aunt Jo accompanied me to my first session with Francis. Her office was located in Metropolitan Baptist Church on 12th and R Streets, NW. Since it was so close to my apartment, Aunt Jo and I walked. While we walked, Aunt Jo explained that Francis was a licensed minister and therapist. My facial expression registered deep-seated hesitation. Aunt Jo made me promise to keep an open mind about the session in exchange for her promise not to disclose my sessions to anyone, not even Momma or Uncle Charles. I felt safe with her as my confidant.

My session with Francis was launched with a compliment about her nails. She had long, slender raisin brown fingers. As Francis touched her short, neatly coiffed Afro, I noticed her fingernails were covered with an incredibly stunning design created by intricate brushwork reminiscent of a Monet masterpiece. The design itself was circular and set in gold on a canvas of fire engine red nail polish. The swirling detail of the emblem centered in the middle of each nail made me think of my own nail artist, Tracy and her talented staff at Perfect Polish on Lenox Avenue. In an instant, my smile turned into numbed homesickness. Francis looked over her eggplant reading glasses. Her acorn colored eyes drew me in. She made me feel like she had eyes inside of my head. Francis noted the shift in my disposition and quickly asked me what I was thinking. Not wanting to reveal myself, I clammed up. We sat in silence for thirty-five minutes. It astonished me to see Francis allow the silence. Much to my surprise, I found myself speaking.

"Your nails remind me of New York City and my own nail artist and friend. Whenever I needed a pick me up or my nails or toes done, I could call Tracy at Perfect Polish. We'd sip on champagne with strawberries in crystal flute glasses while listening to one of our favorite pieces of classical music by pianist, Awadagin Pratt. We'd do the girl thing—gossip, bitch and moan, and then purge whatever was causing us stress. Now that I'm in a new city, I dread the idea of having to find a new nail artist."

"Is finding a nail artist the only thing you dread?"

"No. Finding a circle of friends, satisfying job, and making a life are probably my top three dreads. I hate the fact that I am being forced to start my life over again. In many ways, I feel like God is punishing me. And the thing that hurts the most is that I don't know what I did to deserve all of this pain."

"Let's stop there and go back to a few things you mentioned. First, I need you to know that God is not punishing you. Second, you didn't do anything to deserve your current life experience. Third, this experience is here to teach you to grow. Fourth, I am here to help you navigate it. Perhaps you can start looking at your current life experience as an opportunity to grow. I am not certain how long it will take you to reach this understanding, but you will. In the meantime, I'm here to support you. With that said Karma, our time is almost up for today. I would like to invite you back for another session next week if you are open to it."

"Before we talk about another session, I need to know how much your fee will be because my income is limited right now."

"I offer clients my services on a sliding scale. How much do you earn per year?"

Embarrassed to admit the pitiful patchwork of a salary, I started nervously twirling one of my locs. After a few seconds, I looked up at the ceiling and said, "I don't really have a feel for what my annual salary will be this year."

"Okay, give me your best estimate for a month."

"I make about nine hundred dollars after taxes."

Looking down at her chart, Francis says, "You'll have to pay five dollars. How does that sound?"

"That sounds fair to me."

"I have an opening on Thursday evening at five thirty."

"I can make it."

"One more thing. I have some homework for you. I want you to write three things each day that express what you are grateful for. You will need to bring them to our session."

Shrugging my shoulders, I pulled out my notebook and wrote the instructions down while mumbling to myself how can I be grateful when I have no peace, no quietness, no rest, only turmoil?

CHAPTER 3

▼

"Call if you will, but who will answer you?"

—Job 5:1

When I went to my next session with Francis, I hadn't completed my homework. I simply didn't think I had anything to be grateful for. Within ten minutes of the session, Francis ended it. "I don't see a need for us to continue if you aren't serious about doing the work. It's really a waste of both of our time."

Stunned by her response, I sat like a mischievous child who knew she needed to go stand in the corner, but was too scared to move.

Francis continued, "When I agree to work with clients, I take my commitment seriously. I expect my clients to do the same."

Her words summoned a response in me. "Honestly speaking, I just didn't have anything to be grateful for. That's why I didn't do the assignment."

"Now you're giving me something to work with. I hear what you're saying about not having anything to be grateful for, but I wonder how you would feel if you walked in the footsteps of someone like Job. Your assignment for next week is to read the entire Book of Job. After you finish it and if you still find that your life is far worse than Job's life, then I will understand where you are coming from.

However, I suspect that after reading Job your list of gratitude will flow like a river."

"Okay, I can do that."

Handing me a worn copy of the New International Version of the Bible, Francis remarked, "I'm going to make it even easier on you and give you a Bible and more time to read. Our session today is over. Let's meet again next week at the same time."

I quietly nodded my head in agreement.

"Are we on the same page, Karma? I'm talking about our joint commitment to work through this life transition you are currently experiencing."

Uncomfortable emotions entered and prevented me from readily commenting. I sat staring at the ceiling for several seconds.

"Earth to Karma."

"Yes, we're on the same page. I'm here to do whatever it takes."

Francis stood up from her chair and motioned that I stand with her. "Okay, let's move forward. Why don't we close with a prayer?"

Joining my hands with hers, I answered, "Fine with me."

"Gracious and Good God, we thank you for this day and opportunity to center ourselves in your one power and presence. We give thanks for all the blessings that you have bestowed upon us and are sending our way. We are grateful for all of these blessings. We lovingly embrace the opportunity to work towards the complete restoration of Karma's spirit. We surrender our will to your will, knowing and trusting that you are guiding us in your ways and that all things are working for Karma's highest good. We say Amen."

"Amen."

Francis hugged me and walked with me into the hallway that led to her office. I thanked her for her patience and went on my not so merry way.

When I returned home, I decided to start my new reading assignment. I made it through five pages before the first twinges of a migraine headache appeared. I tried to persevere through the reading despite my not being able to connect the dots of Francis' rationale for having me read the story of Job. By the time I got to the fifth chapter, I couldn't take the pain any longer. I called out to the ethers for help. Silence was the only response. It reminded me of the past year and the attempts that I made to call out to God and not receiving any response. So I got pissed and abandoned my efforts and view of the raspberry-colored kitchen from the breakfast nook located in the rose-colored living room. I walked into my bedroom and was met with high voltage hues of more pink splattered on each wall. Interwoven shades of fuchsia, bubblegum pink, and watermelon seemed to shock the Euro style beech wood platform bed that Madison gave me last year for my birthday into the farthest corner of the small room. I shut my eyes on Colette's poor attempt to create an atmosphere of feminine mystique and prayed that a new paint job was a day away. I couldn't really be mad at Colette. After all, the girl is a social worker with no artistic bone in her body. I still couldn't figure out why every inch of this tiny matchbook apartment was painted in a rainbow of shades belonging to the pink family. First glance would make you think that she was an AKA, but her fierce pride would broadcast her true identity as a Sigma Gamma Rho legacy that just happened to be in love with the color pink.

As I lied down on my eggplant comforter, my nose caught a whiff of the assorted flowers sitting on the nightstand in the cylindrical glass vase that Aunt Jo left behind last week. They were a bouquet of pink blooms—alstroemeria, carnations, lilies, and daisies. Each one was cut short and perfectly arranged in Aunt Jo's signature style. She gave them as a gift with the hope of uplifting my spirit. Unfortunately, the only thing they did was take up space.

Not wanting to sit in the room alone, I looked to the television for temporary comfort and escape. My body vegetated in front of it for the remainder of the evening. The next morning, I decided to skip a day of work from my gypsy employment experience. When I went to use the telephone, I noticed that I had several messages. I must have been in a deep zombie-like trance last night because I didn't recall the telephone ringing. Two messages were left. One was from Momma reminding me about my cousin, Charlie's wedding in two weeks. The other was from Branford. He was faithfully conducting his daily check up to ensure my sanity.

CHAPTER 4

▼

"For my thoughts are not your thoughts, neither are your ways my ways, declares the Lord."

—Isaiah 55: 8

What a difference a day makes! The migraine headache disappeared. Skipping work must have helped. Now that I am more relaxed, I guess I better call Branford and Momma back before I start my reading assignment. I chose the easiest call first—Branford.

"Well, well, Ms. Belle Violette Francois is in fact alive."

I hate when Branford calls me by my full name. It reminds me of Momma. He knows that I prefer to be called by my nickname. Daddy gave it to me when I was a little girl. It happened the day that I bugged him to take me to his yoga class. After the class, Daddy and I went to get ice cream. While we were eating, he told me that I reminded him of his life's karma. Momma was his cause and I was the effect of their love. After that, he called me Karma. I took an instant liking to it and haven't changed it since.

"Yes, Negro, I'm alive."

"Why I gotta be a Negro?"

Laughing, I responded, "Cuz' you are?"

"Well, *Mademoiselle Negresse*, I thought we had an agreement that I would check in with you on a daily basis. What happened yesterday?"

"I know Branford. I'm sorry for not returning your call. I came home from my therapy session and got a migraine headache. Before I knew it, I had fallen off to sleep."

Kidding me, he replied, "Likely story! You know you had a hot date."

"Yeah right!"

"Well, anyway, I wanted to make certain that you were going to be in town during the last weekend of June."

"Why?"

"Before I tell you why, answer my question."

"I'll be around, I guess."

"You guess?"

"Well it depends on what you have in mind."

"Randy is coming to town and I thought it would be great if we all hooked up and hung out."

"So Mr. Playboy is going to grace us with his presence."

"Yep, he's gonna be staying with some woman he's been dating. She lives in Arlington."

"But of course. Where are you staying?"

"Like I need to even ask. With you."

"What if I'm not up to it?"

"Well, then that's too bad because I am coming any way."

"You know after fifteen years of friendship you'd swear I could get rid of you."

"No chance sister!"

"So how's therapy coming along?"

"Let's just say it's coming. I have to read the Book of Job."

"Sounds intense."

"It is. Look I gotta call Momma back before I start my reading assignment. I'll talk to you tomorrow."

"Alright, until then."

I moved on to the next call. Thank goodness for the three-hour time difference. Hopefully, I can avoid a conversation. Momma is probably out doing something with Aunt Nina. I quickly dialed the phone number. As luck would have it, there was no answer. The voice-mail clicked on. So I left an upbeat message. "Hi Momma. Got your message yesterday. Sorry I didn't call you back. All is well. Just busy teaching back to back yoga classes and working on a new exhibit at Howard."

I wondered if she would be able to see through my white lie of a message. Probably not, but at least I made the call and could now go incognito for the rest of the day. The Book of Job called my name. I decided to start at the beginning. So I opened to the first chapter and read,

There was a man in the land of Uz, whose name was Job; and that man was perfect and upright, and one that feared God, and eschewed evil. And there were born unto him seven sons and three daughters. His substance also was seven thousand sheep, and three thousand camels, and five hundred yoke of oxen, and five hundred she asses, and a very great household; so that this man was the greatest of all the men of the east. And his sons went and feasted in their houses, every one his day; and sent and called for their three sisters to eat and to drink with them. And it was so, when the days of their feasting were gone about, that Job sent and sanctified them, and rose up early in the morning, and offered burnt offerings according to the number of them all: for Job said, It may be that my sons have sinned, and cursed God in their hearts. Thus did Job continually. Now there was a day when the sons of God came to present themselves before the Lord, and Satan came also among them. And the Lord said unto Satan, Whence comest thou? Then Satan answered the Lord, and said, From going to and fro in the earth, and from walking up and down in it. And the Lord said unto Satan, Hast thou considered my servant Job, that there is none like him in the earth, a perfect and an upright man, one that feareth God, and escheweth evil? Then Satan answered the Lord, and said, Doth Job fear God for nought? Hast not thou made an hedge about him, and about his house, and about all that he hath on every side? thou hast blessed the work of his hands, and his substance is increased in the land. But put forth thine hand now, and touch all that he hath, and he will curse thee to thy face. And the Lord said unto Satan, Behold, all that he hath is in thy power; only upon himself put not forth thine hand. So Satan went forth from the presence of the Lord. And there was a day when his sons and his daughters were eating and drinking wine in their eldest brother's house: And there came a messenger unto Job, and said, The oxen were plowing, and the asses feeding beside them: And the Sabeans fell upon them, and took them away; yea, they have slain the servants with the edge of the sword; and I only am escaped alone to tell thee. While he was yet speaking, there came also another, and said, The fire of God is fallen from heaven, and hath burned up the sheep, and the servants, and consumed them; and I only am escaped alone to tell thee. While he was yet speaking, there came also another, and said, The Chaldeans made out three bands, and fell upon the camels, and have carried them away, yea, and slain the servants with the edge of the sword; and I only am escaped alone to tell thee. While he was yet speaking, there came also another, and said, Thy sons and thy daughters were eating and drinking wine in their eldest brother's house: And, behold, there came a great wind from the wilderness, and smote the four corners of the house, and it fell upon the young men, and they are dead; and I only am escaped alone to tell thee. Then Job arose, and rent his mantle, and shaved his head, and fell down upon the ground, and worshipped, And said, Naked came I out of my mother's womb, and naked shall I return thither: the Lord gave, and the Lord hath taken away; blessed be the name of the Lord. In all this Job sinned not, nor charged God foolishly.

My first thought was how could someone praise God after losing so much? I know I couldn't. This Job fellow and I are completely different. I can't see any reason why he should be grateful. It's beyond my understanding. In a moment of frustration, I closed the Bible and stared out the window. I sat in silence for a few minutes. Then I heard a still small voice inside me say, "Of course you can't understand Job's ability to praise my name, but you will one day. Just know that my thoughts are not your thoughts, neither are your ways my ways." Before I could say anything, my telephone rang. I quickly answered it. It was Momma returning my call. I was happy to hear from her. That still small voice spooked me out a bit. She babbled on and on about her current passions, an advocacy campaign to convince Pope John Paul II to elevate Pierre Toussaint to sainthood and the perfect wardrobe for Charlie's June wedding weekend. I zoned out half way through the wardrobe discussion. Talking with Momma was rarely a two-sided event.

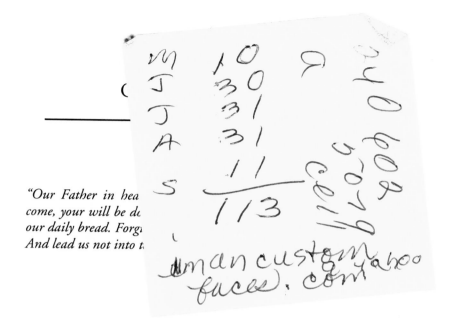

"Our Father in hea
come, your will be d
our daily bread. Forg
And lead us not into t

Branford was scheduled to arrive the day that I was supposed to meet with Francis. This would be the first appointment I actually kept since I decided to take a break from therapy. Washington weather in early June can be tricky. The weatherman on WHUR predicted early morning showers, but so far none have appeared in the royal blue sky. Perhaps the warmth of Mr. Sun has chased them away or maybe the weather report was just damn wrong.

It was such a nice day that I took my time walking to Francis' office. As I approached 13th Street, my chest tightened. A part of me was reluctant to enter the building. Fears of attack for not being able to make a gratitude connection with the Book of Job flooded my psyche. It took me back to sixth grade and the terror that I felt standing at the blackboard in Mr. Neelon's math class. Knowing that I couldn't make heads or tails of the ninth grade algebra problem, but he forced me to work it through. I hesitated for a few seconds after I stepped inside the building. If I left right now, Francis wouldn't even know I was here. As I considered my escape, a voice caught me by surprise. It was Francis. She was walking with one of the other reverends. This must be a sign that I need to go to therapy.

This time, Francis tried a different approach. She didn't mention the Book of Job or my running away from therapy. She proceeded like everything was fine and just let me talk. I appreciated her not chastising me. She lit a frankincense incense stick and purple, white, blue and pink candles. Before starting our session, she had me close my eyes and remove my shoes. I uttered one of my favorite Hindu mantras that Daddy taught me: *Om Shanti Om*. It was for peace of mind. We practiced several breathing exercises before ending in a short prayer. Afterwards, I felt at ease and relaxed enough to share my mixed emotions about spending time with my family at Charlie and Millicent's wedding and running into Laurence, Millicent's brother and my former lover.

This would be the first time that my family had been together since Daddy died. It would also be the first time that I actually saw Laurence since we hooked up two summers ago. We spent three months enjoying conveniently late evening champagne and strawberry soirees in his suite at the Waldorf Astoria. That's when I was living the life of a single urban femme fatale … doing what I wanted, when I wanted, and with whom I wanted. I was down for anyone and anything that invited adventure. Laurence covered both well.

He never disclosed his marital status, but then again I never asked. All I knew was that he was a refreshingly handsome stranger fifteen years my senior. His French surname *Delacroix* and gingerbread skin that decorated the body of a Mandinka warrior made me wonder if we shared Louisiana roots. I'm sure if we talked long enough and did some research our pedigree trees would meet at some fork in the road, but that wasn't a priority. Our priorities were pure, commitment free sex, and late night companionship.

Our conversations revealed Laurence to be a devoted son to his elderly parents. He was a committed corporate lawyer who traveled on a weekly basis to service client needs in the tri-state region. Laurence and I shared a passion for Cuban musician and composer, Omar Sosa. He had magical feet that could dance the hell out of any woman. When he stepped on the dance floor and whipped out his salsa, meringue, and tango repertoire, I had no choice but to follow.

Our paths crossed one afternoon at the Walden. I remember my somber state as I walked along the amber lit walkways and the echo of my footsteps on the polished hardwood flooring of the museum's fifth floor. My mind was in such disarray after having yet another shouting match with Madison. This time he claimed I owed him money for the things he purchased for me as gifts. The anger in his voice let me know that we were finally over. I sought comfort in one of my favorite galleries containing the work of Alexander Calder. His wire art always made me forget my troubles.

As I turned into the gallery, I bumped into this strikingly handsome man. He was apologetic, even though the fault was mine. I composed myself, assured him that nothing was broken, and finally looked at him. I had been so caught up in my own drama that I didn't even look at who I was accosting with my clumsiness. He was slightly older than the men I usually found attractive. His temples had the slightest hint of gray. It played well with his tightly curled hair. His eyes were a very stable and lightfast greenish blue with limited hiding power. Laurence's cheekbones were high and structured in a regal manner. And that smile … that smile that widened across his lips.

My apology led to a conversation on Calder's work. We both discovered that we loved Calder's wire sculptures, especially the one that depicted Josephine Baker. The mere mention of her name generated an hour discussion on Blacks in Paris. That conversation resulted in an evening drink followed by an expensive dinner at Chez Josephine. The more we talked, the more we acted on the chemistry that our connection produced. He invited me back to his hotel suite. I accepted. The Cuban eclectic music of Omar Sosa shook up the night. We drank, danced, and dove into white cotton sheets with reckless abandon. No questions were asked. Just fun-filled passion. The less that I knew, the better. Laurence was nothing more than a summer tryst.

Laurence resurfaced last month when I attended Charlie and Millicent's wedding shower. As I was flipping through her engagement photo album, I saw her wedding announcement from the Washington Afro-American newspaper. Photos from the engagement party featured Laurence standing between Millicent, his wife, and their two teenage sons. Yeah, that's just what I need to run into an old lover and his whole family while experiencing the grandeur of Momma. Witnessing her larger than life personality unleash itself as Violet trails behind her playing the role of the dutiful daughter puppet, while flashing her new engagement ring from that fool Ramses that she has decided to marry, would be a lot for me to bear. Oh let me not forgot that wedged in between this madness would be

Momma's endless attempts to introduce me to all the single, available bachelors that she managed to interview and invite to the wedding on the sly. I thought about just skipping the event, but I couldn't do that to Charlie. He's always been one of my favorite cousins. My only saving grace in this train wreck waiting to happen was Branford. I invited him to accompany me to the wedding knowing full well that Momma, Laurence and a multitude of other distractions would be crammed into the emotional space of my life that was now the size of a thimble. I needed to see Branford though. I needed to be in the comfort of the air that he breathed into my life. His presence alone should ward off some of the madness like garlic to a vampire in search of fresh blood.

After I finished rambling, Francis fired away, "So would it be safe to say that despite your feeling uncomfortable about seeing a former lover and interacting with your mother and sister, you are grateful for Branford's friendship in your life?"

"Of course, I am grateful for him. We've been through what seems like everything monumental in life. College … relationships … breakups … death … career changes … everything."

"Touchdown. You do have something to be grateful for. Now how bad is your life compared to Job?"

"I guess not that bad."

"That's all I wanted you to begin to see."

"Francis, that was kinda smooth how you got me to admit my gratitude."

"*Au contraire*, my dear Karma, I didn't do anything except listen. You just shared from your heart. That's all."

Dreading, I asked, "So I guess we have to talk about the Book of Job now?"

"Not unless you want to."

Perplexed, I answered, "I thought that was my assignment."

"Your assignment was to use it as a catalyst to explore gratitude. I'm not certain if reading the text helped you, but you had a gratitude breakthrough when you admitted that you were grateful for Branford's presence in your life. And the goal was to get you thinking about gratitude so that you could see that your life has some bright spots. Do you think your life has any?"

"It does. So where do we go from here?"

"That depends on you. Do you want to continue meeting on a regular basis?"

"Well, it couldn't hurt."

"Then you tell me what works best for your schedule."

"You probably want me to come once a week."

"Forget about what I want. What works for you?"

"That's a switch."

"I've learned that it pays to be very open and flexible with clients."

"Clients who run away from therapy."

"Well, them and all of the rest."

"Okay, then let's try and meet every other week."

"Great. Same day and time two weeks from now."

We hugged and closed in a prayer that I offered. "Thank you God for this session and counselor. I am grateful for her presence in my life. Amen."

As I was walking home, Branford called on his cell to let me know that his cab was about two blocks away. He wanted me to meet him as the car pulled up. He arrived as I opened the door of my apartment building. We always had great timing. When his cab pulled up I didn't think that he would ever stop stepping out of the damn thing. All six foot four inches of his two hundred and ten pound frame managed to squeeze in the back seat with relative comfort. The cream linen suit and pale orange shirt was loose and breezy, but still clung to the defined features of his arms and chest. Somebody's been working out! I knew that I would try and hijack the shirt. It had my name written all over it. His dimples almost disappeared in the deep mahogany of his face as he smiled at the sight of me waiting for him to arrive. I noticed that he cut his hair. It had the short, fine appearance of the skin of a peach.

When we entered my apartment, Branford removed his blazer. I could see the imprint of his muscles through his shirt as he remarked on the very pinkish nature of my new home. That actually aroused me. How could this be happening? I knew the boundaries of our friendship and his sexual identity would circumvent any possibility of us hitting the sheets. His inquiry about the sleeping arrangements broke the dam that served as a barrier of protection against the unexpected temptations of my flesh. I resisted the naughty voice inside my head. Despite my efforts, she kept coaxing me to say, you're sleeping with me big fella. She wouldn't let up. And that's when I could easily see myself saying that line with reckless disregard for any boundaries. Where was the good sense that Momma gave me? Somehow it arrived as I opened my mouth to say, "Go ahead and put your things in my bedroom. I'm gonna sleep on the air mattress."

"We can't have that Ms. Karma. I'll take the floor."

"No really, Branford, take my room. You're my guest."

"Oh so now I'm a guest. Okay, homegirl, I'll play along with your hostess routine. Just remember that when I start to get on your nerves."

Staring off into space, my logical self disappeared. Naughty Girl emerged and invited herself into my thoughts. "I'd play the hell out of Ms. Hostess if you let me."

"Karma, did you hear what I said? Where are you anyway?"

"I'm sorry Branford. I just started day dreaming."

"About what?"

"Nothing worth mentioning."

"Okay, so you don't feel like sharing. I won't take it personal."

"That's good to know."

"By the way, my cousin Randy and I made plans for us all to meet at the Mexican spot down on 18th and Florida Avenue. It starts with the letter T. You know it, right?"

"You mean El Tamarindo."

"Yep, that's it. We should be there at sevenish or thereabouts for margaritas and dinner. Randy wanted to drop by Republic Gardens afterwards. So wear your dancing dress and shoes. It's salsa night."

"If we have to be there at seven then we have about an hour to relax before we need to get dressed. What are you wearing?"

"The same thing I am wearing now, but I am going to take this shirt off before I wrinkle it more. What about you?"

I lost track of the conversation as Branford began unbuttoning his shirt. My mind and eyes were distracted by the prominently displayed deltoid muscles in his shoulders, pectoral muscles along his upper chest, and the washboard worthy abdominal oblique muscles that caused me to gasp with great excitement when I made eye contact with his stunning six pack. The visual impact of his body's stellar appearance invited Naughty Girl to return. She nicknamed him Buff Brotha. What has he been doing to himself? More importantly, what is he doing to me? How can he be looking so yummy? Catch yourself girl. Maybe I'm just acting out cuz' it's been a long time since I was intimate with someone. Whew wee!

"Karma. Did you hear what I was saying?"

"Oh yeah, what I am wearing is a surprise."

"Make sure you won't hurt anybody with your curves."

His comments are so hard to resist, but I gotta …

"I won't."

"Karma, I'm gonna take a little nap before we head out."

"Okay, old man. I just need to get a few things out of my bedroom closet before you lay down."

"Who's calling who old? As I recall, you are nineteen days older than me. You got any Belgian Beer in the refrigerator?"

"Is my name Karma?"

"That's my girl. You always know how to hook a brotha up."

While Branford was in the kitchen, I selected a white silk-blended Marilyn Monroe-inspired halter dress and the strappy white three-inch Bandolino sandals that I wore last summer. I hung the dress in the linen closet before entering the bathroom to begin my beauty regimen. Aveda products stared at me as I made a mental note of which ones I would use to transform myself into lusciousness. The deep cleansing herbal clay masque was a must. The Echinacea, English kaolin clay, hyssop, and red clover would do a terrific job of absorbing excess oils from my skin. I sprinkled some of the Chakra II Attraction bath cleanser in my bath water. It filled the tub with a striking aroma of myrrh, olibanum, opoponax, and rose. The combination of scents hypnotized me and sent me into a calming trance. I lowered myself into the tub and closed my eyes. The soothing waters massaged my limbs and relaxed my mind. Time stood still for a few minutes until erotic thoughts of Branford and I arrived on the scene. Unable to stop them, I gave up trying to fight them off. Naughty Girl was finally happy. My fingers explored the inside of my vagina in the way that I imagined Branford would. Just before I reached a climax, Branford knocked on the door.

In a loud, pestering voice, Branford yelled, "Hey. I gotta go to the bathroom like yesterday."

Fumbling for my towel and feeling like I had been caught with my fingers in the cookie jar, I answered, "I'll be out in a second."

"Make it a half of a second. I gotta go."

My bathrobe was nowhere in sight. Anxiety kicked in. How could I avoid temptation walking around half-nude with these crazy thoughts? The only thing I could think to do to calm down was to say, "Our Father in heaven, hallowed be your name, your kingdom come, your will be done, on earth as it is in heaven. Give us today our daily bread. Forgive us our debts, as we also forgive our debtors. And lead us not into temptation, but deliver us from evil." As I opened the door covered in my mustard cotton towel, Branford stood shirtless in his russet boxers. For my sake, I hoped that the last part of the prayer had already kicked in.

CHAPTER 6

▼

"Watch and pray, that ye enter not into temptation: the spirit indeed is willing, but the flesh is weak."

—Matthew 26:41

Grandmere always said prayer changes things. And that's exactly what happened. My lustful thoughts about Branford simmered by the time we met Randy and his date, Marisol, at El Tamarindo. They were picture perfect. A bronze version of Matel's Ken and Barbie dolls. When they stood up to greet us, Randy paused before removing his right hand from Marisol's shoulder length honey blond streaked hair. I noticed that his left hand found it difficult to stop fondling Marisol's curvaceous buttocks. His face was filled with the teenage innocence of an altar boy caught doing something wrong. It was a scene that I secretly hoped Branford and I could reenact.

I can't say when the shift in my thoughts occurred, but it was probably in between those two chocolate martinis. They really chilled me out. Maybe it was the fact that I was able to have a reasonably intelligent conversation with Marisol. She defied Randy's typical twenty-something, eye-candy token bimbo. Marisol was elegant in a Nina Simone kinda way and appeared to match Randy wit for wit. Branford teased that I only took interest in Marisol when I learned that she was a manager at the MAC store in Georgetown. Part of me hated to admit that I was seeking a hook up on lipstick, but what is a girl to do when she is on a tight budget. We capped the evening off with salsa dancing at Republic Gardens. The fellas couldn't even hang with Marisol and I. We put them to shame after the first hour and replaced them with new partners. The man I danced with reminded me of Laurence. His skill, ease, and passion were intoxicating. I tried not to think of Laurence since I would be seeing him in the morning at the wedding, but thoughts and images of our adventures popped in and out of my mind. They even followed me home and into my dreams.

The next morning, Branford and I walked to St. Augustine's to attend the first part of Charlie and Millicent's wedding. An early Catholic service at eleven o'clock to honor Millicent's devout Catholic father. A mid-afternoon Hindu ceremony to honor Millicent's mother and Indian relatives, and a wedding reception done up in the grand Creole style of the Baptiste family. Family rumor has it that the date was selected based on astrological charts that Millicent's mother and a Hindu priest reviewed and analyzed to find a time. Millicent's father and step-mother vehemently objected to this process and raised a big stink over the date. Thankfully, Charlie and the rest of the Baptiste family didn't mind. I can't even begin to imagine all of the ins and outs that Millicent has had to navigate between her African American Catholic and Hindu roots. Cane told me that Charlie was secretly worried that the day would turn out to be a circus since there is still bad blood between Millicent's parents. It was a nasty divorce that ended with full custody awarded to their father. Somewhere during the divorce proceedings, Millicent's parents hooked up and produced her younger sister. Millicent learned of her younger sister several years after her mother left D.C. for London. Now if that ain't some soap opera madness I don't know what is. But then again, my family can't talk. At least, Charlie and Millicent both have something in common ... soap opera family drama history. Hopefully, it won't repeat itself in their family.

Tension and stress were already building in my shoulders as I thought about my own impending drama ... Momma's theatrics, Violet's one-woman puppet show, and a possible confrontation with Laurence. How weird is all of this? I wanted to turn back around and go home. Had Branford not been here, I swear I would have followed through on my thought. Instead, I braved the few steps leading to the church sanctuary. When I walked in, I noticed that the historic African American church was decorated with hanging ivory metal baskets holding sunset colored fresh flowers of calla lilies, lilies, tulips, roses, and berries, with hydrangeas marking the pews. The altar was adorned with large bouquets of calla lilies. It was clear that Aunt Jo's personal touch was on each and every arrangement. They were floral masterpieces filled with Millicent's favorite flowers. A woman should always have her favorite flowers on her wedding day.

Thanks to Cane's investigatory work, I was able to find a nice print of *Nude with Calla Lilies,* Millicent's favorite painting by Diego Rivera. The frame shop on 17th Street did a wonderful job framing it in a one-inch clamshell black matte frame with a brilliant white top mat. It would be waiting for her and Charlie to hang in the appropriate place in their new Lake Arbor home after they returned from part one of their honeymoon. They would celebrate part one at the Hillside Inn in the Pocono's. It was nostalgic for the couple since it was where Charlie proposed a year ago. Part two of the honeymoon would be the generous gift that Millicent's father gave them. A honeymoon package to Paris, Cannes, London, Milan, Venice, Rome, and Madrid. A woman couldn't ask for more.

Millicent was a wonderful addition to our family. Like me she was passionate about art. Millicent carried none of her father's bourgeois pedigree tendencies. We have enough of that madness from Colette, Momma, and Violet. Every family has a limit. We exceeded ours years ago.

One of Charlie's Alpha Phi Alpha frat brothers from his Morehouse days escorted me down the aisle. Branford trailed behind humming the wedding march and teasing me that my turn was coming. This guy was at Morehouse when Violet and Colette were at Spelman. He used to attend Charlie's summer beach parties at Highland Beach back in the day. I couldn't recall his name. Damn that really gets on my nerves. His family even had a home near Uncle Charles' home. When it was obvious that I had forgotten his name, he reminded me that it was Julian.

If memory serves me correctly, he used to dig Colette. For a split second I wondered what he ever saw in Ms. Ice Princess number two with Violet being number one of course. Colette's my cousin and all, and I love her, but some of her drama is over the top. Most times, I think she should have been Violet's twin. How I gladly give her my title if she only wanted it. Thanks to Aunt Jo, Colette has been forced to balance her Ice Princess stuff with a down to earth attitude. Her choice in a career as a social worker for The Women's Collective is a perfect example. I know her down to earth demeanor is what enables her do-good work with the women living with HIV/AIDS who come into her office on a daily basis. She's definitely complex. It must be her Gemini rising acting out. Who knows?

In any event, Julian informed me that he was seeing Colette and that he was working his way to becoming a partner in his daddy's architectural firm. That bamboo-colored Brooks Brother Negro was exactly the kind of pretentious man I could see her with. A match made in *bougie* heaven! I pretended to be thrilled when in fact his news didn't much matter to me. He kept talked about the July 4th event his family was having down at the beach and extended an invitation. I nodded like I was planning to come when I knew I wouldn't be anywhere near that scene. My escape route presented itself when Branford made it clear that we were together with a gesture of reaching for my hand as he entered the church pew. We were together, but not together, if you know what I mean.

As I was getting comfortable in the pew next to Branford, I heard the unmistakable confident, bass of Laurence's voice. It was almost like the strings of a cello being played with the slow even stroke of its bow. He was gliding up the aisle with the wedding photographer giving commands like he was Colin Powell. Damn that man knows how to give up sexy flava. I dropped my head as he walked by, hoping he would not see me in my bright canary yellow, sleeveless wraparound, silk shantung shirtdress. Why did I have to wear such a bright color? My small maneuver seemed to work until Laurence stood in front of the altar and pulled me into his direct view. A rush of uncomfortable emotions surged from a buried cauldron. He walked over as I tried to wipe the sweat from my lower lip. Composure was nowhere to be found.

In his infamous gentlemen quarterly style, Laurence greeted me, "*Enchante, Mademoiselle Francois!*"

I tried to hide my flustered feelings. "Good to see you too!"

Branford reached out his hand to greet Laurence. I quickly offered an introduction. "This is my friend, Branford."

"Pleasure to make your acquaintance. My name is Laurence, brother of the bride."

Branford remarked, "Good to meet you too."

Laurence bid me adieu with a flirtatious smile and wink. "*Mademoiselle François*, do save me a dance at the reception. There's much to discuss, *n'est-ce pas.*"

His French flirting was always a turn on. He was obviously doing it on purpose, but little did he know that I wasn't falling for his bag of tricks. I know too much now. He's married which makes me automatically disinterested. And save him a dance? No chance. He's exactly the kind of danger I am trying to avoid. So I sat silently with a polite smile on my face. That was the only response I was willing to give.

Laurence hadn't been gone more than forty seconds before Branford initiated his version of the Spanish Inquisition. His curiosity surprised me. "So *Mademoiselle Francois*, what was all that about?"

"Oh, he's just an associate."

"Sure you right and I'm the Easter bunny. Cut the bullshit, Karma. What's the deal with you and homeboy?"

"There's no deal."

"No deal, my …"

"Why are you so bothered anyway?"

"No reason, just being nosey?"

"Nosey cuz' you might be interested yourself?"

"Now you know even if I was interested, I wouldn't try and pick someone up at your family's wedding."

"So are you?

"Am I what?"

"Interested?"

"The only thing I am interested in is finding out why Mr. Man has ruffled your feathers."

"He's nobody."

"Yeah right, come on Karma. What's all the secrecy? He must be something since you won't even tell your best friend."

Getting ticked at his line of questioning, I gritted my teeth and said, "An associate."

"Don't even try to play me, Karma. There was some strong tension between you both. I know what I saw."

"And what did you see? Don't bother answering. You didn't see anything."

"Okay, Ms. I don't wanna say nothing, but I know what I saw. Brotha was digging on you kinda hard. That kind of digging ain't from friendship. It's some straight up you used to be my woman kind of digging."

At this point, I was ready to let Branford have it. Why does he know me so well? I can't hide anything from him, but I really didn't want to have to reveal the connection that Laurence and I shared, especially not today … and not after my battle with my own lustful thoughts. "Look, Mr. Nosey. Laurence and I met while I was working at the Walden. We had a couple of friendly lunches. That's it. Nothing more."

"Are you sure that's all you had cuz' it seems like y'all had each other?"

"That's it. Let's drop this subject."

"Okay Ms. Belle Violette Francois, it is dropped for now. We'll revisit this subject later."

Oh no we won't. I am not about to share the details of my affair with a married man. Why is he so damn interested in Laurence? Branford and I sat in silence for what seemed an eternity. The appearance of Momma and Violet broke our silence barrier. As usual, Momma sauntered into the pew with *haute couture* high drama. Her lips were dipped in fire red compliments of Chanel. Momma's wavy black hair was pinned in her signature chignon and hidden underneath a royal blue wide brimmed hat. Her hat matched her silk clutch and V-neck sleeveless dress that draped nicely on her perfect size eight frame. As always, Momma's Napoleona complex from being five feet was enhanced by four inch black patent leather sling back shoes. She wore one of my favorite jewelry collections that Daddy purchased while he was in Tanzania. He loved to tell us the story of how he discovered the stones that made up Momma's tanzanite necklace, earrings, bracelet, and cocktail ring in the foothills of Mount Kilimanjaro. Momma enjoyed boasting that Daddy thought she was more precious than tanzanite, a gemstone that was a thousand times rarer than diamonds. I loved staring into the kaleidoscope of colors that tanzanite offered the human eye: indigo, lilac, periwinkle, royal blue and violet. They dazzled Momma's tapioca pudding skin.

Violet trailed behind Momma wearing what appeared to be a Talbot's Barbara Bush-like suit, flesh tone stockings, and Ferragamo black kidskin spectator pumps. She was prim and proper with pearl earrings, a simple gold watch, and a two Carat princess cut engagement ring. Violet's processed cocoa brown hair was tightly secured in a ponytail with a gray bow. Her face was nude with the exception of her horn-rimmed bifocals. It was hard to believe that she was Momma's daughter.

The rest of the family showed up one by one. The first two pews were knee deep in family. The remaining pews were filled with Charlie's Alpha frat brothers, friends, colleagues, and Baptiste family friends and neighbors. In total, we took most of the pews on the groom's side. It was heartwarming to see all these folks turn out for Charlie. Millicent's side of the church paled in comparison. Her mother was dressed in a saffron colored sari. It complimented her cashew skin and dark black hair. She sat in the front row some distance away from Millicent's stepmother. Laurence and his wife and two teenage sons were seated next to her. A dozen aunts and cousins sat in brightly colored saris in the second row. There was a small entourage of what looked like her father's family and some of her college friends in the third and fourth rows.

The ceremony began with the processional. J.S Bach's *Prelude in C* introduced Charlie, his best man Colin and groomsmen Cane and Chase as they lined up on the altar in their black tails tuxedos. The two bridesmaids and maid of honor gracefully sauntered into the church in burnt orange strapless, full-length A-line silk shantung dresses with tie sashes. They were carrying simple, but elegant bouquets of calla lilies. The maid of honor slightly resembled Laurence. She must be the baby sister. I confirmed my thoughts with the wedding program.

A soloist from the choir sang a beautiful rendition of the *Ave Maria* as Millicent made her grand entrance on her father's arm. Colette told me that Millicent had gone to New York to have her wedding gown designed by Cassandra Bromfield, an upcoming wedding designer featured last year in Essence Magazine. Millicent's curvaceous figure complemented the ivory silk shantung strapless, full-length A-line gown. Her tiara veil and strand of pearls added the final touch to her special day.

In a matter of forty-five minutes, the bride and groom became man and wife. A receiving line made up of both families was formed in the back of the church. As we approached Laurence, Branford gave him the evil eye. Laurence returned it. Their body language reminded me of two bullies on a playground ready to rumble over somebody else's toy. I certainly was not trying to be either of their toys. Ignoring them both, I greeted Laurence with a hardy hello and friendly European-style kiss on both cheeks. Laurence whispered, "So who is your bodyguard?"

I tried not to laugh as I responded, "My friend."

"Not for long."

I backed away when he uttered his last remark. It felt like we were beginning to fall back into a pattern I had no intention of repeating. As I turned away from Laurence, I accidentally backed into Branford and almost fell. Lucky for me, he reached out and caught me. His tight grip held my waist and pressed my nose against his chest. His manly scent tormented my flesh and brought me right back to the place I thought I had escaped the night before. Branford was wearing my favorite citrus cologne for men, Raks by Andre Barnwell. It felt like he and Laurence were conspiring to drive me crazy.

Plagued by a double whammy of demonic lust, I searched out a haven. My sister appeared out of nowhere and offered the only escape. Having no other choice, I took it and landed in the middle of a frying pan popping with hot grease. Our conversation was a lecture dripping in dating wisdom that she garnered on the way to becoming a successfully engaged woman. That conversation lasted all of fifteen minutes. Why it lasted so long I don't know? Perhaps the double whammy of Laurence and Branford wore me down and made me vulnerable to Violet's foolishness. Reason returned and inspired me to plan my next escape. The bathroom was where I thought I would find at least ten minutes of peace before facing Branford again, but Momma appeared from the neighboring stall and proceeded to fry me worse that Violet ever could. With nowhere to go, I stood still. The only thing I could think to do was pray for two miracles. The first would relieve me from the temptations of my flesh for my best friend Branford who only sleeps with men and Laurence, a married ex-lover. The second was a get out of jail free card from Momma and Violet's verbal torments. When a vision of an open bar at the wedding reception appeared, I knew my prayer had been answered.

The taste of last night's chocolate martinis reappeared on the tip of my tongue. It was enough to calm me down and surrender to Momma's presence. Somehow the nodding of my head in what appeared absolute agreement got her to the finish line of whatever she was talking about. We peacefully walked back into the church as the picture perfect mother and daughter ready to take the family photo. I was content with the vision of alcoholic libation. It was becoming my peace of mind for the next hour and half as I prepared to endure the presence of four evils … Laurence, Branford, Momma, and Violet.

CHAPTER 7

▼

"Cast all your anxiety on him, because he cares for you."

—1 Peter 5:7

Decorated in a riot of color and creativity, the Federal Room in the Capital Hilton located on the corner of 16th and K Streets, NW, played host to Charlie and Millicent's vibrant Hindu wedding and reception. Red was the dominant color. The wedding program indicated that it symbolized auspiciousness. The ceremony took place under a canopy called a *mandap*. Banquet tables with gold chairs and white linen tablecloths were arranged on both sides of the *mandap*. A red carpet marked the aisle that Charlie walked down towards Millicent's mother. He bowed to her mother and greeted her with a coconut. She accepted his gift, placed a garland in his hand, and escorted him to the *mandap*. Millicent's aunt and cousins greeted him with a song and dance that included rice tossing. After the performance, Millicent's aunt carried a plate that held a lighted lamp and conducted a ceremony called *grahashanti*. It means peace with the planets. She asked that each planet bestow blessings on the new couple's life. Charlie's fake smile let me know that he wasn't thrilled about this ceremony and the wedding costume he was wearing. That's when I realized that love makes you do a lot of things you wouldn't otherwise do.

Momma, Violet, Branford, and I sat at a table next to the Baptiste peanut gallery consisting of Colin, Chase and Cane. Throughout the ceremony, they acted like six-year old boys giggling about how silly Charlie looked wearing a white turban, long white shirt extending to his knees, matching leggings, and sandals. I actually thought Charlie's white ensemble made his fried chicken brown skin look regal as he waited for Millicent to join him. The peanut gallery's laughter came to an abrupt halt at the sight of Millicent. Wearing a red and white silk sari draped modestly over her graham cracker colored skin, she walked towards Charlie beaming with an inner radiance. The Mehndi designs that decorated her hands were readily noticeable. She was carrying a garland in one hand as Laurence escorted her to the *mandap*. The sight of him awakened my *Naughty Girl* thoughts. I was distracted by Momma whispering in my ear about how unique it was to see Millicent's mother wash Charlie and Millicent's feet with milk and water. Momma explained that this solemn ritual was called *kanyadan* and used to purify the couple's new life together. For once I was grateful for one of Momma's interruptions. It brought me back to the present moment.

In the next phase of the ceremony, Millicent and Charlie held their hands out with palms raised upright as Laurence placed his open palms over theirs. Millicent's mother poured water over Laurence's hands. The sound of the water and Laurence's facial expression brought me back to a disturbing space ... our evening showers. How I wish Momma would say something now to distract me. No chance this time. She was all caught up in the pageantry of the event. I was left with my memories as I pondered how the mere sound of water could bring me back to the summer spent at the Waldorf. The more that I tried to fight them off, the longer they lingered. An unexpected case of panty wetness set in as the Vedic priest announced,

"We have come together to wed Millicent Lakshimi Delacroix, daughter of Sarasvati Rangarajan and Delano Truman Delacroix to Charles Augustin Baptiste, Jr., son of Josephine and Charles Augustin Baptiste, Sr. Today they begin the foundation of their marriage upon the earth, in the presence of the sacred fire and the radiant sun, among their family and friends."

The bride and groom sat facing one another under the *mandap*. A choir of Millicent's cousins sang what appeared to be Hindu chants. An invocation to the Hindu god and goddess, *Ganesha* and *Sarasvati* was done. Millicent and Charlie's hands were tied together with cotton thread and wound several times as the Priest recited a prayer for harmony that sounded like one of Daddy's favorite mantras *Om sahana vavatu* ... something or another.

Following the priest's prayer, Charlie and Millicent exchanged beautiful garlands as they thanked God for the gift of life, loving parents, and caring siblings. Their parents stood and gave thanks for their children. Charlie and Millicent followed with a request for blessings in their journey together as partners in life. Millicent's mother answered for everyone by reciting one of the most precious wedding blessings I have ever heard.

"We bless you that your married life is always divinely centered and harmonious. May your lives be filled with happiness. May you fill others' lives with joy. May you have a long life with good health. May you have a spiritual, loving and healthy family with spiritual, creative, intelligent, strong and loving children. May you be loving and caring parents. May you be like two wings of a bird, unified at all times and in all situations. May your union and life be as bright as the sun, gentle as the moon, and vibrant as the sea. May you be kind and gentle to yourself, each other, the helpless, the old and the weak. May you always rely on your spirituality as your source of strength. May you be strong and hold your heads high through all of life's challenges. May you be generous, giving more to each other and the universe than you take. May you always live in harmony with the universe and do good work to elevate the love vibration of all life."

After she finished, Branford gently touched the small of my back and remarked, "Wasn't that absolutely beautiful?"

His touch set off a wave of sensual tension. I felt like I was being attacked from all sides. Laurence first and now Branford. Trying to prevent another panty wetness episode, I quietly moved my chair closer to Momma. I politely smiled back in agreement, and tried to direct my thoughts anywhere other than where they were. Branford moved his chair closer to me. That's when my anxiety reached its threshold. Instead of casting my cares on the Lord like the scripture encourages, I focused on casting them on three chocolate martinis. When will this damn ceremony be over? Neither I nor my panties can take much more of this!

CHAPTER 8

▼

"Have mercy on me, O God, according to your steadfast love; according to your abundant mercy blot out my transgressions."

—Psalm 51:1

My current reality was one that I wished I could escape. And this is why. Sitting closer to Momma in an effort to avoid Branford was a monumental mistake. As soon as the ceremony was finished and before the dinner was served, Momma launched a nuclear attack. She began with whispers regarding my status with Branford and his apparent eligibility and good breeding. All I could say was that we were friends. Dissatisfied with my response, Momma increased the volume of her voice and invited Violet, Branford, and the other guests sitting at our table into our conversation about the possibility of Branford becoming her son-in-law. Embarrassed beyond belief, I took my famous approach of withdrawing and walking away from confrontation. Branford followed me to the bar where I ordered the first of several chocolate martinis. He tried to get me to talk, but silence prevailed as I guzzled martini number one. After fifteen minutes another martini became my best friend. By now, Branford had tired of begging me to talk. So he retreated and circulated among the guests. Feeling relieved, I ordered martini number three. The bartender tried to have a conversation with me, but I told him all I wanted to do was sip my cocktail in peace. I happily sipped it and ate mixed nuts until I was ready for martini number four.

By the time I ordered martini number five, the cocktail police arrived on the scene to chastise me about becoming a lush at my cousin's wedding. Seeing Momma and Violet with frowns that would not end was my clue to mix and mingle with the guests. I got to stepping so fast that I bumped into Laurence by accident. My mishap gave Momma and Violet an opportunity to catch up to me. They were one table behind me when I took Laurence's hand and walked back to the bar. What possessed me to do that? I guess the need to escape from Momma and Violet. I tried to play off the tingling sensations running up my arm and down my back as we held hands. When we returned to the bar, Laurence brought life to these sensations when he jokingly asked if my panties were wet. I tried to look disgusted. He bypassed my fake disgust and bestowed unwanted comments about the shape of my behind. Without even blinking an eye, I drank my cocktail and ordered another one before heading to the ladies bathroom.

Surely my blatant disregard for his presence would convince Laurence to leave me alone, but it didn't. He followed me into the hallway. A part of me wished he hadn't. The other part that was dominated by pure animal lust was open to whatever was about to occur. Lust flooded my consciousness. I slowed my step giving him a chance to catch up. Lust is such an overwhelming experience. The word itself doesn't begin to capture its deadly power. You'd think the folks at Webster's would have a caveat emptor warning in its dictionary entry. I could see it now. It would read: a noun with an etymological past from England and Germany. Strongly connected to the Latin word lascivious with roots in the word wanton. Defined by a portfolio of equally dangerous words that one must be careful when to role-play in the real world. Words like pleasure, craving, eagerness, enthusiasm, delight, personal inclination, and wish don't do the definition justice. Phrases like unbridled sexual desire and an intense longing are more likely to paint a realistic picture of the word's true meaning. The best way to understand the word's meaning is by examining its juicy fruit synonyms such as aphrodisia, eroticism, lickerishness, or passion. These words may set you and yours on fire. So beware. Use protection. Enjoy the ride.

The three words aphrodisia, eroticism, and lickerishness described what I knew Laurence and I were about to do. It would be an aphrodisiatic experience that would transcend our previous erotic history of sexual exploits that always left us both in a state of lickerishness. Enough of my wordsmith masturbation. It's time for the real thing.

Before I could grab the knob on the bathroom door, Laurence's hands were resting on my waist. Trying to play the role of the utterly disgusted woman, I barked, "Get your hands off me."

"Stop acting like you don't like this when you know you do."

Knowing my resistance would get us both hotter, I belted out, "Did you hear what I said?"

"Your mouth is lying. Your body is saying you want me."

"Don't flatter yourself."

"Karma, passive aggressive doesn't suit you well."

"Laurence, leave me alone"

"Oh so you wanna play it that way? Okay I'll play along. Look that's not what I wanted to hear."

"I'm not playing it any way. Just get your hands off me."

Removing his hands from my waist, he smiled with arrogance painted on his lips as he said, "*Mademoiselle Francois*, you know you can't resist my touch?"

"Oh the **hell** I can't."

"I doubt **that** ... I hear passion in your voice."

"Wrong ... it's disgust."

"Stop fooling yourself woman. You know I can do all kinds of things to you. Do you want me to remind you?"

"Look Laurence that was a long time ago ... plus you are very married with two children."

"That never stopped me before."

"Well, it is enough to stop me."

Coming closer, he stared at me, "Well, we will just have to see."

Moving a step back, I interjected, "Look, I don't want to make a scene here."

"Then stop running."

"I'm not trying to play any games with you."

"Well, what makes you think I'm trying to play games with you?"

Placing my hand back on the bathroom doorknob, I said, "That's it. I am going to the bathroom. So why don't you go back inside the reception and find your wife. Just leave me alone."

Laurence stood there in silence as the bathroom door closed. I found comfort in the couch in the lounge area. Quickly gulping down my martini in a manner that Momma would rate déclassé, I realized that I might have played my hand in the wrong way. Perhaps I was really trying to save myself from myself. How deep is that? Maybe I was checking myself on wanting be with a married man. Maybe I was afraid of crossing the line into a place of no return. Perhaps my conscious was trying to prevent next day regrets. Kicking off my shoes, I had to admit that it was frustrating to feel things for Branford when I couldn't do anything about it. At least with Laurence, there is a mutual attraction that allows me to feel something and have it returned. Now I know I need help. What's wrong with me? Look at me making up reasons why being with a married man is the best option for me since I don't stand a chance with my best friend. As I closed my eyes, I felt that my life was sinking to an all time low.

When I awakened, Laurence was sitting next to me. I tried to put some distance between us by getting up. He followed, grabbed me from behind, and started gyrating against my buttocks. I could feel his penis hardening. His hands began fondling my breasts. His touch was irresistible. I secretly didn't want him to stop. My verbal protests disappeared as we moved into a bathroom stall. The design itself offered privacy. Each stall was created like its own mini room with doors covering the length of the stall. No one could look over or under the stall and discover us. Laurence lowered his pants and boxers. He pulled a condom out from his front pocket and prepared for entry as I hoisted my dress up to my waist. He pressed me against the stall and mounted me from behind. Within seconds, we were back to our old habits except this time I couldn't play ignorant that I was getting my groove on with a married man.

Our bathroom episode lasted all of five minutes before a herd of women converged in the bathroom. Luckily we were in the last stall. We quieted ourselves and quickly redressed. When the room became silent, I gently opened the door and surveyed the common areas. The coast was clear. As we both hustled out of the bathroom and back into the lounge, Laurence tightly grabbed my buttocks and cupped both cheeks in his hand. I pretended to be bothered. He dismissed my fakeness and invited me upstairs for round #2. I followed.

The suite he reserved was freezing from a blasting air conditioner. Despite the cold, we managed to sweat ourselves into what seemed to be a sauna on the floor. Carpet burns filled my back from mission style sex. When I complained, Laurence picked me up and brought me to climax on the bed with me on top. Our afternoon romp lasted an hour before we both realized that our lust had gotten the best of us. As the brother of the bride, he needed to return to the reception. We popped into the shower only to begin again. Twenty minutes later, we returned with some semblance of normalcy. When Laurence asked me if he could call me, I hesitated. He gave me his card and left the decision up to me. While I knew that what happened could not happen again, the mere thought of what occurred excited me. So I tossed his card into my purse as I walked back into the reception.

The guilt from committing adultery followed me like a skunk's stench. Wanting nothing more than to seek the Lord's mercy, I headed to the bar to blot my transgressions. Before I could order, Branford bum rushed me with Gestapo-like questions regarding my absence. Surprisingly, he bought my excuse about clearing my head from Momma's drama by taking a walk down K Street. Momma caught us talking and decided not to miss another opportunity to embarrass me. Branford blocked her attempt by politely yet forcibly telling her we were leaving since I was tired and he needed to get back to New York. She had no other choice but to let me go. Once again, Branford stepped up to the plate like a boyfriend ready and willing to be my knight in shining armor. As he hailed a cab, I realized that I needed to stop thinking of him in this manner. My only dilemma was how.

CHAPTER 9

▼

"Do not arise or awaken love until it so desires."

—Song of Songs 2:7

A green World Cab Association with the number 333 painted on the passenger's door in white lettering was parked in the driveway of the Capitol Hilton. Branford opened the backdoor expecting me to get in. Intent on avoiding any sexually tense moments with him in the backseat, I opened the front door and planted my derriere in the passenger seat. The driver's appearance immediately captivated my attention. He was a dead ringer for Ethiopia's great emperor Haile Selassie. The driver politely smiled and asked for our destination. Unable to respond due to my martini-induced intoxication, Branford supplied the information. Seven minutes later the cab arrived in front of my building. Branford paid the driver as I walked up the steps and opened the front door. I turned around and saw him standing at the bottom of the steps. I asked, "You coming in?"

"Actually, it's a little early. So I am going to head down 17th Street to grab a drink. I'll be back a little later."

Knowing Saturday night on 17th Street and Branford's fondness for my neighborhood's male residents, I pretended to act like the good platonic friend I have always been. "Have a good time."

Climbing the steps to my apartment, I wondered if he could see beneath the thin veneer of my masquerade. Probably not since he thinks we are the happy inhabitants of Planet Platonica. This platonic friendship is about a b-i-t-c-h. You'd think I wouldn't be so affected given my adulterous sexcapades with Laurence earlier this evening. Multitasking man drama has become my obvious forte. It is a skill I hate to claim. From a purely rational point of view, I shouldn't entertain thoughts of what could happen between Branford and me. What the hell! I can only imagine him telling me one of those famous platonic let down stories peppered with a truth I didn't want to hear ... I dig men more than women.

Before I ventured any further, I rummaged through my purse and pulled out Laurence's business card. His cell phone number was written on the back. I walked over to my phone in the kitchen and dialed his digits. Before the third ring, I hung up and chastised myself for crossing yet another line of unacceptable behavior. As I walked down the hall to my bathroom, I started thinking about the madness I was getting myself in by entertaining an affair with Laurence while having feelings for Branford. My thoughts were ambushed when the telephone began ringing. When I walked back to the kitchen to answer it, I heard Laurence's voice on the other end. Without hesitation, I did the healthiest thing I had done all evening, which was hang up the phone. I wondered how he got my telephone number. I know it's that damn caller id. That's how. Sometimes technology can be a pain in the ass!

The phone rang again. This time I let the answering service catch it. It was Laurence. As he rattled off a menu of fantasies that he proposed we turn into reality, I saw his piano-key smile seducing me through the phone. He played a seductive game of memory lane when he recounted our summer fling where we both explored anal eroticism. His descriptions of him eating my shaved vagina and tongue fucking me until I came and couldn't take it anymore were so detailed that I actually considered calling him back to set up a meeting. I contemplated offering him his favorite pleasure ... me rimming him with my tongue and inserting love beads in his anus. The thought of cosigning on the dotted line of a dangerous liaison stopped me cold. Panic set in. It was the kind I had when I first lost my job at the Walden. What was I doing with my life? Not sure, I dialed Francis' message service. Regret about my fling with Laurence and unexpressed feelings for Branford dominated my convoluted message. After I left the message, I realized that Francis was still on vacation. It would be at least two weeks before I heard back from her. What's a girl to do now without her therapist? Who else can I talk to? Branford was definitely a no go. My girlfriends in New York were probably out on the town. So I turned to my journal.

Chicken scratch notes poured out rapidly. When I read them back, they sobered me up quicker than a cup of Turkish coffee.

What makes a married man with a wife and two children cheat? Greed. Selfishness. In an ideal world, there should be absolutely no reason to cheat, but I know better. And who am I to judge given the fact that I was guilty too? What makes a single woman cheat with a married man with a wife and two children? Human nature. Weakness. Sadness. Rejection. Poor self-esteem.

Branford. Is it love? Hate to admit it, but yes in the worst kind of way. No outlet. Stuck. Backed up. Not fair. Not sure. Laurence. Is it lust? Damn skippy. Wrong? Hell yeah! Run like hell. Nothing good can come of it. Plus he would only be a bad substitute for what you are really aching after ... Branford. Rejection before it comes is what? Absolutely uncomfortable. And when it comes ... It is deadly. This one would hurt even more if I pushed the envelope and tried to awaken love. It would hurt when he apologized with his truth ... I like men. We both like men. That's the problem. Why do things have to be so hard for me? Why can't this equation work for me? The why's are just prolonging the inevitable ... What are you going to do? Be silent. Sit in my own pain. How long? Not sure. What's gonna get me through? Time. Time. Time. Time. And more time. You just gotta wade through this one kiddo. Wade through is what you gotta do. Time.

When I finished underlining the word time for emphasis, I closed my journal and walked into the kitchen to make a cup of Turkish coffee. While I waited for the coffee to brew, I checked my AOL e-mail account and discovered three messages in my in box. Two were spam. The third was from Serengeti, one of the owners of the Our Womanist Spirit Center. We were slowly forging a friendship. She was writing to invite me to the Center's monthly spoken word series called Sapphire Sista Cypher. The theme was "Wisdom in Mercury's Retrograde." At the bottom of the e-mail she included a short explanation of the retrograde. I chuckled as I read my astrologically correct friend's words.

It's here. The mothership of energy affecting communication, contracts, and negotiations has landed. I do apologize for the delay in getting this news to you.

What you need to know is that on June 23 at three thirty two a.m., the planet Mercury went into retrograde. A retrograde occurs when a planet appears to move backwards in space as viewed from the earth. When this happens in Mercury, you gotta be extra careful about making major decisions, purchases, and signing contracts. Most astrologers advise to wait until Mercury turns direct to focus on these matters. I think y'all should put a halt on all matters until Mercury turns direct on July 17 at eight twenty a.m. As many of you sistas know, I have been living according to these astrological principles since 1982. And let me tell you, it works. I learned the hard way. When I didn't follow these principles during a Mercury Retrograde, situations that I initiated would not hold and would even reverse themselves or there would be major errors involved. From trial and error, I learned to follow these phases as a way to avoid conflict. The other thing I wanna mention to some of you vocal sapphires is to watch your tongue during the Retrograde because what you say may be misunderstood by others. Watch out for problems with technical things, mechanics, and communications including computers, telephone, and computer networks. You should expect delays, breakdowns, and problems in these and related things. That's it for now. Be astrologically wise and careful during this period.

The event sounded like it would get my mind off of my man drama. So I made a mental note to go. As I closed my lap top, the door to my apartment opened. It was Branford. Out of nowhere, I decided to try and set the stage for an intimate discussion by offering him a cup of coffee. He declined and began complaining about the absence of excitement on 17th Street. I desperately searched for an opening to spill my guts, but none appeared. Before I knew it, Branford had finished his conversation and was excusing himself for the evening. I was left standing with my freshly brewed coffee and the memory of Serengeti's e-mail about Mercury's Retrograde.

That night, I slept with a pit in my stomach, tossing and turning while wondering if I should have shared my unexpressed emotions. Serengeti's e-mail message kept coming back in my head as a reminder. This pattern of thought persisted through out the night, offering me little solace or peace of mind. When the new morning arrived, the pit remained in place. Before I could move through my morning routine, Branford gathered his things and departed with a friendly goodbye. As we hugged, I could feel the emotional distance starting to set in. The kind of coldness that one feels as a result of an unpleasant break up came over me. What was the remedy? A forecast of separation revealed itself in my mind's eye. I embraced it as my swan song of salvation knowing that it was best not to awaken love until it so desired.

CHAPTER 10

▼

"How long must I bear pain in my soul, and have sorrow in my heart all the day?"

—Psalm 13:2

As July's infamous humidity wreaked havoc on the lives of Washingtonians, I tried to keep busy with my newfound routine. Meditation, yoga, and journaling in the wee hours of the morning. Teaching the seven a.m. gentle yoga class at the Center, Monday through Friday. Working on the fall gallery series at Howard University, Tuesday through Thursday. Most days, I moved through the pain in my soul and the sorrow in my heart by releasing my emotions on the pages of my journal. The Sapphire Sista Cypher convinced me that I wasn't the only woman in Washington with heartache. Being in the company of women facing similar challenges inspired me to continue journaling and attending the monthly Cyphers.

After my first Cypher, I surprised myself when I accepted Serengeti's invitation to an evening of Thai cuisine with some fellow sista poets at Bua Restaurant on 17th and P Streets. Resistance was my first response because my interactions with women haven't always been positive. Despite the fact that I had close relationships with several women from college and my New York days, I had more luck with men as friends. My reservations were also tied to the madness that I experienced from a backstabbing sister and controlling mother. Despite my baggage, I took a leap of faith and listened to that still small voice inside me. The voice reminded me of Serengeti's kindness. So I gave the sista poet gathering a chance.

A multi-cultural collage of seven urbanistas reveling in the spectrum of our feminine creativity sat comfortably around a long table at Bua on a hotter than July Thursday evening. Some of us could easily pass for the sepia version of those *bling bling* Prada wearing glamour girls from Sex and the City. The rest of us were an interesting mix of colliding colors, patterns, and textures. Our styles fell somewhere in between ghetto fabulousness and bohemian exquisiteness. Fashion designs from Trade Secrets, Stef 'n' Ty, Denise Goring, Moshood, The Tibet Collection, Ann Taylor Loft, Target, Filene's Basement, and Eileen Fisher enhanced our womanly curves in all the right places. Belts, baubles, and a bonanza of diamonds, fresh water pearls, gemstones, Swarovski crystal rondels, glass beads, vintage, and African- and Asian-inspired jewelry and accessories dazzled our outfits.

The waiter kept coming back to our table to take our order, but we were knee deep in a discussion regarding Black women's fiction. We all agreed that fiction allowed Black women to see images of themselves that were not regularly portrayed in mainstream media. However, our differences separated us into three camps. Serengeti, Kalahari, Ma'at, and I were members of the first camp. Serengeti pompously described us as people who appreciated "literature with beautiful language and richly layered themes depicting African American life." She even listed the names of certain authors such as Ann Petry, Nella Larsen, Zora Neale Hurston, Dorothy West, Paule Marshall, Alice Walker, Ntozake Shange, Toni Morrison, Gloria Naylor, and Jewell Parker Rhodes. I confessed that I had only read works by Alice, Ntozake, and Jewell, but also enjoyed Chick Lit, the contemporary literary genre that relays easy breezy Cover Girl lipstick tales of the perilous terrain that imperfect career women find themselves in and the impact it has on their psyche, weight, search for love in relationships, career, and wardrobe. Ma'at, Greer, and Yamuna chimed in with a passionate Amen. In a matter of seconds we were now the official members of the second camp: Chick Lit readers. Our conversation about authors such as Sandra Kitt, Sheneska Jackson, Donna Hill, and Tajuana Butler dominated the discussion. When we raved about the storylines and our impressions of Helen Fielding's popular British book, *Bridget Jones' Diary*, Serengeti got on her high horse and criticized us.

"I don't understand how you can enjoy those Easter egg pastel-colored books with retro images of martini glasses, trendy purses, and spike heel pumps that most women in the real world would not even be caught dead in. Tell me what do you sistas exactly get for the money that you spend on mind candy with plots involving upwardly—mobile, designer clad, paper doll characters engaged in day-time television drama in urban scenes? Don't bother answering the question because the mere fact that you read that deathless prose is a smack against all of the gains made in the feminist movement. Your preference for this trash threatens to flood the market in women's reading."

I wanted to interrupt her, but what good would it do. As a self-proclaimed champion of high culture, she obviously didn't get the humor we found in reading stories about women that made us laugh without having a panic attack over what it says about women as modern feminists. So I joined Ma'at, Greer, and Yamuna in disregarding her comments. That's when I learned that sometimes you have to ignore Serengeti. Like most of us, she was a complex woman with a multitude of layers and conflicting interests such as feminism and capitalism. Harmony was restored to the group when we all discovered our love for erotica. Sunee, the quietest one in the bunch, shared the titles of her three favorite books. We burst into laughter and sounded off a chorus of hallelujahs because we each owned copies of *Erotique Noire, The Bluelight Corner,* and *Dark Eros* in our personal libraries.

Having ended our discussion on a unifying note, we returned our attention to the menu and gave the patient waiter our order of spicy entrees: *Pad Thai* without eggs for Serengeti, *Pad Thai* with eggs for Ma'at, *Panag Gai* for Kalahari, *Wang Keow* for Greer, tofu with string beans and chili paste for Sunee, *Gong Pik Pow* for Yamuna, and tofu and mixed vegetables with curry peanut sauce for me. While we were waiting for the food to arrive, Serengeti stood up and gently tied her shoulder length blondish brown Cassandra Wilson-like locs into a ponytail so that they would not interfere with her eating. Then with the regal elegance of a shapely five-foot even toffee-colored Charleston debutante, she stood and raised her fork like it was a scepter and dubbed us the official Sista7 group. Her actions got the attention of the rest of the second floor patrons. All eyes were on her as she proclaimed herself Sista7's queen of metaphysics, astrology, and numerology. Dramatization was definitely her forte. Her facial expressions and body language signified a confident empress. At one point we all stood and high-fived each other as she outlined our Sista7 manifesto.

"Love, creativity, peace, abundance, wisdom, joy, and wholeness make up our DNA. Because we are divine, our hearts are tuned to authenticity. Our life experiences amplify who we are. They tell our stories in our words. They set us free to live and create in our unique way. We are our own affirmation. Competition with others ceases to exist. We are about the business of being ... of loving self and others ... of serving those in need ... of shining light into the universe. And if folks fail to grasp our essence, then so be it. We aren't concerned or left questioning the nature of our source because we know from whence we came. It is this knowing that allows us to remain sane. So we give thanks to the Almighty known by many names for blessing us with the gift to walk the Earth with love and without fear or shame in the bodies of magnificently bold, bright, beautiful, and brilliant colored women in a plethora of groovy shades."

By the time Serengeti completed her impromptu speech, every patron was on foot offering her a standing ovation. Naturally we joined in.

Her partner, Kalahari, a plus size Spanish speaking woman with a Grace Jones hair cut and skin the color of the reddish brown landscape sweeping across the desert she was named for, stood next to her smiling peacefully like the Black Madonna of the Andes in her native Peru. They looked so cute together ... almost the same height. It was obvious that she was the quiet one in their union. Kalahari's silence didn't stop Serengeti from christening her "queen of calm before the storm" and showering her with praises for being the glue that kept them together as a couple and family. Serengeti pointed out that we all shared a Northern California connection since she grew up in San Jose with her Houston-born and bred mother and step father, Kalahari in Richmond with her Afro-Peruvian musician parents and two brothers, and me in Oakland with my Louisiana Creole, control-freak, fashionista mother, Buddhist bohemian academic father, and twisted twin sister.

Greer, the host of the Cypher, stood next to Kalahari. She was about five inches taller with a coke bottle figure, friendly disposition, and skin the color of an acorn. Greer was a homegrown sista. Born and bred in the heart of Anacostia on Good Hope Road. She sported an auburn colored hair cut similar to the one worn by Halle Berry in the movie, *Boomerang*. Greer was the first sista that I met in D.C. who was a practicing Buddhist. When we first met, her passion and commitment to her Buddhist practice and Insight Meditation Community of Washington, D.C., reminded me of Daddy's practice and dedication to his Berkley spiritual community during the last ten years of his life. Serengeti pronounced her queen of feng shui since she volunteered her interior design services as a workshop consultant at the Center. She showed women how to harmonize their home with use of the ancient Chinese art of placement.

Sunee was standing directly across from Greer. They were the reason we didn't have to pay a cent for our meals and beverages. Sunee was the cousin of Greer's fiancé, Niran. She helped manage Bua. Sunee was a four foot eleven, petite, soft-spoken, golden honey-colored woman with jet black curly hair cut in a bob. Her radiant skin color, nose, and lips were evidence that one of her parents was of African ancestry. I later learned that Sunee's spirit and gift of massage matched the meaning of her Thai name—good. Since Sunee worked at the Center as a masseuse, Serengeti appointed her queen of the magic touch.

Leaning on Sunee's shoulder, Ma'at blew congratulatory kisses to Serengeti. Ma'at was a striking cappuccino thick beauty with a matching thick Afro puff bun sitting on top of her head. She often joked that her Afro puff added at least three inches to her five foot four height. Originally from Trenton, New Jersey, Ma'at came to D.C. from Philadelphia a few years ago after she left the Ausar Auset Society and divorced her husband. She worked as a reiki practitioner with Yamuna in a new age wellness center in Philly. When she settled in D.C., Yamuna helped her get a part-time gig at the Center. Now they work together two times a week.

Yamuna was by far the most eccentric member of the group. She stood right next to me. I liked the fact that she didn't claim a surname. Her teak-colored facial features resembled Eastern Europe. She was one of Greer's homegirls. They grew up together as neighbors and childhood best friends. Long black Senegalese curly braids cascaded down the back of her perfect five foot eleven runway model frame. Yamuna was the Center's ayurvedic healer. Serengeti declared her queen of sacred river healing. She later confided in a side conversation that she was born in St. Petersburg, Russia. Her Afro-Russian heritage began when her mother traveled to Russia on a Fulbright Scholarship after graduating from Howard University with a Master's Degree in Biology in the early fifties. While she was there, she met, fell in love, and married Yamuna's father, a Russian Jew, and later died of ovarian cancer. Because her father was grief stricken, his parents decided that it was best to send nine year old Yamuna back to D.C. to live with her grandparents. When she graduated from high school, she got a scholarship to University of Pennsylvania, but dropped out in her junior year. She took up massage therapy and started working as a private masseuse. While she was living in Philadelphia, she met and married her husband. When they moved to California, she said goodbye to her birth name and renamed herself Yamuna, a Hindu name that means sacred river.

Last but not least, Serengeti designated me queen of hearts. I couldn't figure out why. When I asked, she told me that the meaning would be revealed in time. Her mysteriously vague statement didn't bring me any closer to understanding her name selection. As I sat in silence, I realized that we never had a conversation about my love life. And even if we had, my love life would definitely put me out of the running for this title.

Our conversation ceased when our entrees arrived. It was a clear indication that everyone was satisfied. When we came up for air, we were ready for our drinks. Our drink order revealed that we shared a fetish for martinis that made me feel right at home. The interesting thing was that each of us had our own signature drink. Serengeti was all about the traditional martini. It was mixed with one and one-half ounces of Ketel One vodka from Holland and three-fourths of Bossiere dry vermouth, and shaken not stirred with two olives. I couldn't help but agree with her taste in vodka. We both boasted of Ketel One's exceptionally smooth, creamy, sweet taste. Kalahari ordered a Bloodhound martini consisting of one ounce of Bombay Sapphire dry gin, one-half ounce of dry vermouth, one-half ounce of Chambery Fraise, one-half ounce of sweet vermouth, one-half ounce of strawberry liquor, and one large imposing strawberry. It sounded absolutely delicious. Greer requested a dry martini … two ounces of gin and one-fourth ounce of vermouth. Sunee selected a Gibson martini that was a dry martini with a cocktail onion instead of an olive. Ma'at ordered a pear martini made with two ounces of Vodka, one-forth ounce of pear puree, one-fourth ounce of rosemary simple syrup, and a pear slice. Yamuna insisted on having a Marsala martini … three-fourths of dry gin, three-fourths of vermouth, and three-fourths of Florio dry marsala. I stuck with my favorite, Chocolate martini … one and one-half ounces of vodka, one-half ounce of Godiva chocolate, and one-half ounce of Vanilla Schnapps.

While we waited for the drinks, the group went around the table and gave life updates. Serengeti kicked off the sharing circle with her plans to increase funding for the Center in 2001. Kalahari talked about the pressure and guilt trip from her brothers about visiting their elderly mom who is suffering from Alzheimer's. Greer happily shared her plans for her Valentine's Day wedding. Sunee discussed the challenges she was having with convincing her aunt and uncle that she was not interested in co-managing the family's restaurant. Ma'at didn't have much to say. I could tell she was holding back, but no one pried. Yamuna confessed that she was seriously considering a move to the Chicago area to pursue her dream of becoming a naprapathic doctor at the National College of Naprapathic Medicine in two years when her son, Solomon, graduates from high school. When it was my turn, I just smiled and said all was well. I just knew my response would provoke questioning, but no one pried. They let me be.

An hour and thirty minutes later, Serengeti and Kalahari announced their departure. They needed to get home to their toddler daughter and relieve their babysitter. Since Yamuna lived a few blocks from them on Alabama Avenue, they agreed to give her a ride home. From our conversations, I learned that Greer, her fiancé, and Sunee shared a three-bedroom condo two blocks from me on 14th and U. Ma'at lived at 14th and Swann. We all decided to walk home together. Before we said our evening farewells, we stood in a circle and gave each other a group hug. I quietly thanked God for allowing me to connect with such wonderful sista poets.

In the following weeks, Sista7 made a habit of gathering at Bua on Thursday evenings. I always joined them and said relatively nothing during our time together. Mostly I observed how these six women interacted. It was clear that they had forged a bond of friendship that covered a vast terrain. Serengeti, Kalahari, and Yamuna were what I would call inner sanctum friends who welcomed each other into most parts of their lives. They all attended All Souls Unitarian Church together and shared common values along with a proven record of trustworthiness. Greer and Yamuna were what I would call historian friends because they have known each other since second grade and managed to maintain a connection that helps them remain grounded. From what I noticed about Ma'at, Sunee, and Yamuna, they were always engaged in conversations about their healing work at the Center. I'd call them new sisters on the block friends since they provided each other with new perspectives in their work. All of these ladies had the potential to be my inner sanctum friends, but for now they were my friends in transition who were helping me become comfortable in my new life. They were also helping me understand the healing power of maintaining regular contact with female friends. Gratitude was the only emotion I could express for being able to witness their commitment to consistently showing up for each other to provide support, solace, laughter, and a realistic perspective.

During the last week of August, I almost backed out of a Sista7 gathering because so much was going on. Branford had been blowing up my home phone and e-mail account with repeated messages. Laurence stopped by my apartment on several occasions without calling. His behavior bordered on stalking. He never succeeded in gaining entrance or penetrating my vagina because I never let him in. At one point, I almost considered asking my cousin Chase to see if he could use his authority as a policeman to convince Laurence to leave me alone, but I was too embarrassed to get him involved. Besides, knowing Chase, he would have told Colin, Cane and Charlie who would have tracked Laurence down and gave him a proper beat down. The truth was my Baptiste male cousins were stone crazy when it came to protecting the women in our family.

My strategy for both men was complete avoidance. It worked on Laurence. He eventually left me alone. Branford was a different story. He committed the cardinal sin when he called Momma and complained that he hadn't heard from me. That just made matters worse. She put me on her personal speed dial. When I wouldn't respond to her calls, she sent Aunt Jo to visit me. I pretended to act like I was just busy with life, but Aunt Jo didn't buy it. Instead of playing Sherlock Holmes, she gently offered a listening ear. I declined and told her that I had been talking to Francis about my challenges. That was a bold face lie. She could easily confirm it if she called Francis. My guess was that Aunt Jo wouldn't bother. I was safe from her learning about my decision to take a break from therapy again. And what difference did it make if she found out? I am a grown woman with the right to temporarily discontinue therapy. Why am I even tripping? Francis would never breach client confidentiality. The truth is that I just didn't have the energy to deal with the analysis and questions about my choices and emotions surrounding Branford and Laurence. Journaling was the best I could do. Besides Francis seemed to understand where I was coming from when she called me to schedule an appointment.

My little white lie seemed to ease Aunt Jo's concern. Just when I thought I was home free, she told me I needed to call Momma before she got on the next plane from Oakland. Before I made the phone call, I wrote out my points of discussion in my journal so I would not be steered off track by Momma's questions. By the time I was finished, it was too late to make the call. I promised myself to do it the next day, but life got the best of me.

The next day turned into another day and before I knew it Momma was buzzing me to let her into my apartment building. I pretended not to hear her voice when I picked up the phone. And then I committed the ultimate sin in Hyacinth Belle Baptiste Francois' bible of appropriate and respectful conduct for daughters. I hung the receiver up. Unfortunately, my sin did not stop the control-freak queen. One of the neighbors gave her access to the building. They clearly were not aware of her ability to create hurricanes of epic proportions.

She pounded on my door and threatened to begin a yelling match if I didn't open it. Not wanting to cause a scene, I opened the door and greeted her in my silk blue and silver floral Chinese vintage cheongsam that Daddy helped me pick out the last time we went shopping in Chinatown. Hurricane Hyacinth was wearing a black two-piece ready to wear ensemble by Cuban designer Narciso Rodriguez. I hadn't seen her in it since she returned from her trip to Milan in 1998. Momma adored this outfit because it made her feel beautiful, graceful, and sensual ... all of the things that Daddy seemed to be most passionate about her. She often joked that her dream was to own three hundred and sixty five days worth of Rodriguez's designs because they made her feel good and flattered her body in ways that would work magic on Daddy. We all knew she wasn't joking! Momma was definitely her own fashion icon. She wore what she wanted when she wanted. That's one thing we both shared in common. Compared to her classic approach, I was more bohemian. Today she sported her Mahnolo Blahnik's Carolyne black slingbacks, Hermes Kelly bag, Cartier's tank watch, three-carat diamond stud earrings, and a gold diamond eternity necklace that Daddy gave her two years ago on their anniversary. One thing was missing: her wedding band.

Consistent with her hurricane reputation, she launched her attack with a hint of politeness that put me on notice that she was not to be toyed with, "Karma, now what in the dickens is going on with you? And what's with you hanging up on me? Why did I have to catch a plane all the way from Oakland and interrupt my week?"

"It's good to see you too, Momma. How long are you in town for?"

"Don't try to skirt the issue. I am in town as long as it takes to get my daughter to tell me why she will not answer my phone calls or talk to her best friend."

"Really Momma. You are such a drama queen. Everything is just fine."

"Don't you dare patronize me. Your father used to try that when I knew something wasn't right. I know my intuition. And it is telling me something is wrong."

"Well, this time, your intuition is off."

"That's not what your Aunt Jo told me."

"And what did she tell you?"

"You were having some challenges getting settled into your life in Washington."

"That's natural don't you think given the last year of events."

"It might be natural, but I want to know what's bothering my baby girl."

"First of all, I am a grown woman. If I wanted to tell you, I would tell you. Why do you have to always pry into areas that you have not been invited into?"

"Miss Smarty Pants, I know how old you are. I am your mother. That means that you will always be my daughter. And because of that fact, dear one, I don't need an invitation to know what is wrong with a child I birthed."

"Would you just stop with the guilt trip. I'm just not in the mood for your drama."

"My drama. This is yours. If you simply returned my phone call, I wouldn't have to come clear across the country to confront you."

"That was your choice to waste your money flying out here. I am not Violet. You can't control me."

"Why do you always have to turn my concern into some drama about me controlling you? Throwing up her hands in frustration, she exclaimed, "Damn it, you are your father's daughter. I can't do this anymore. I did it too long with Eugene."

Confused and not really understanding what Momma meant, I answered, "How does this have anything to do with Daddy?"

The tone in Momma's voice changed. It was squeaky as she began crying, "Karma, I'm doing my best to be two parents to you girls as I have always done."

"What do you mean be two parents? We always had a father in Daddy."

"Is that what you think? You don't know the half of it."

"Daddy was always there for me. This doesn't have anything to do with him."

"The hell it doesn't. I got on that plane because I have always been both parents to you and your sister while your emotionally unavailable father was busy pursuing his academic career and sleeping with his yoga instructor."

"What are you talking about? Devi was our yoga instructor since I was a little girl. She was his friend. My goodness she was like an aunt to us and helped me get certified as a yoga instructor. How could she and Daddy have an affair when she was such a big part of our lives? Momma, Daddy would never trip like that."

"*Cherie*, I know it is hard to believe, but it's true. I did my best to conceal your father's indiscretion, but when I learned that he fathered a child with Devi Shankar a few months ago, I couldn't hold it in any longer."

"No that can't be. Daddy wouldn't do that to you or us."

"The truth hurts, but your father and Devi had a son. His name is Ohnedaruth Eugene Shankar. Devi brought him by the house because he wanted to meet you and your sister."

"How old is he? What does he look like? Are you sure he is Daddy's son?

"He's got to be in his late twenties. Your father stamped him with the Francois linebacker body frame, pug nose, lips, and chin."

"So where has he been all of this time?"

"With Devi's brother in London. He's been in Ohio for the past year. I believe he is working on his M.B.A. in organizational management and logistics at Ohio State University."

"So if he's been in the states this long, why are we just learning about him now?"

"That I don't know. Your father is the only person who can answer that question. *Cherie*, I'm sorry the news had to come out like this. I was hoping to tell you and Violet over Thanksgiving when I had more time to collect myself."

"Momma, I don't believe you. This is just more of your drama."

Handing me a piece of paper, Momma angrily responded, "That's your choice. But your brother wants to meet you and your sister. Here is his contact information."

Glancing down at the neat penmanship on the paper, I blurted out, "Ohnedaruth E. Shankar, Jones Tower, 101 Curl Drive, Columbus, OH, 43210. Phone: 614.555.4321. E-mail: oeshankar@osu.edu. Does Violet know about him?"

"Not yet. I'll tell her when I get home."

"So what am I supposed to do now?"

"That's for you to decide. What you do about your brother really doesn't concern me. I am here to find out what's wrong with you."

Pissed beyond belief, I yelled, "Oh so now you drop a bomb on me and expect me to tell you what's happening in my life."

"Don't take that tone with me, Belle Violette Francois. I don't have a lot of energy to beg you to tell me. For the last time, what's happening with you?"

"Nothing."

"Alright, I am not in position to fight you, young lady. It's clear we aren't getting anywhere. I just wanted to see that you were okay and bring you these packages of your father's things."

"Yeah, we never get anywhere."

Handing me three packages, Momma coldly remarked, "You always have to have the last word. Well, have it. Here are the packages. I am going to be on my way. If you need to reach me, I'll be staying at your Aunt Jo's until the weekend. Have a good day, *Cherie*!"

I hate it when she says *Cherie*. It makes me melt into her hands like I was a six year old child. My resistance came down for a minute and allowed Momma to come closer and give me a kiss on the cheek before she opened the door and exited. Minutes later, I sat down on the living room floor staring at the three neatly wrapped packages and the handwritten note from a stranger claiming to be my brother. How could Daddy play around and have a son without Momma knowing about him all these years? Why would Momma stop wearing her wedding ring?

When I opened the first package and saw that it was filled with a collection of Daddy's favorite Faith Ringold prints that he proudly displayed in his office, I wondered what Momma was up to. His passion for Ringold's painted story quilts and other artwork wore off on me. I remember when I was leaving for Morgan and begged him to give me *Love Black Life* and *Soul Sister*. Daddy refused, but promised that I could enjoy them in the comfort of my own home when he died. And now thanks to Momma and her drama, I was doing exactly that.

The second package contained Momma and Daddy's favorite love song CDs by Chet Baker, Ella Fitzgerald and Stan Getz. How could she part with this music? I wanted to know why, but that would only invite her into my life. And that's not an invitation I am seeking to extend.

The third package was filled with Daddy's prized John and Alice Coltrane's CDs: John's *Love Supreme, Ascension, OM,* and *Coltrane for Lovers*; and Alice's *Journey to Satchidananda, Universal Consciousness, Ptah The El Daoud, Eternity, Transfiguration,* and *Transcendence.* They brought back memories of the Sunday afternoons that Daddy and I spent in San Francisco's Western Addition neighborhood. The music of John Coltrane swallowed me up each time I entered the tiny storefront church called St. John Coltrane African Orthodox Church. Daddy tried to expose Violet and I to the church, but she always acted out and complained during the entire service. Eventually, Daddy decided to stop forcing the church on her and let her go with Momma to the local Catholic Church. I guess that's how I became my father's daughter and Violet became Momma's daughter.

Two large, paintings with Byzantine-inspired golden-haloed images of John Coltrane with saxophone in hand adorned the walls of the church. I thought I was hot stuff when I was able to read the scroll in the paintings which contained lines from the liner notes on *A Love Supreme.* The other icons sharing the space were renderings of the Virgin Mary and a dreadlocked dark-skinned Jesus. Before coming to this church, I had never seen Jesus depicted as his true self … African.

I think one of the reasons Momma didn't have a problem with me attending service with Daddy was because the church was affiliated with the African Orthodox Church, a branch of Catholicism. And she really couldn't talk since she dabbled in Voodoo traditions. The music carried most of the service that typically started at eleven forty-five in the morning. Backing up the choir was a house band of musicians including tenor and soprano saxophonists, pianists, drummers, stand up bassists, guitarists, conga drummers, bongo players, and a violinist. Congregants joined in with their own instruments. Daddy used to bring a tambourine for me to shake. We weren't playing any ole' music. It was pure Coltrane jazz. The church was the first place I heard *A Love Supreme* played live. The song itself was the highlight of the entire service. It also included traditional Catholic prayers sung to Coltrane melodies.

Looking back those were magical times with Daddy. Come to think of it. Devi would come with us sometimes. Oh shit! And the house band's name was John Coltrane's Hindu spiritual name, Ohnedaruth. Damn it, Daddy and Devi were probably carrying on right in front of me. That was some funky shit to do in the presence of a little girl. And he had the audacity to name his son after the church band. No wonder Momma packed up all of the Coltrane CDs and their love song CDs. It was too many memories. What did she think I could do with them now that I know our family was based on a bunch of twisted lies?

A few hours later, Serengeti called to tell me that the location of tonight's Sista7 gathering had changed to Greer's apartment. I didn't feel like going given all of the drama from Branford, Laurence, and Momma's revelation about Daddy's indiscretions. The only thing I wanted to do was hide in my bed underneath my comforter and pillows. When I told her that I might not come, she didn't ask me any questions. She just reminded me that I always had an open invitation. Her understanding made me do a complete U turn and show up.

Greer was grappling with the news from her parents that her immediate family would not be attending her wedding because Niran was Thai and they both practiced Buddhism. She was devastated by their decision. I couldn't see the problem they were having with Niran. In the short time that I have known him, he appeared to be a great guy who loved the ground Greer walked on. We were all baffled by her family's response until she explained that they wanted her to marry a good ole' Baptist Black man. When Greer calmed down, she admitted that she wasn't really shocked by her family's response since they never warmed up to Niran in the three years they had been dating. They tolerated him to a degree and always chastised her for meeting him on line at Love@AOL. Greer's missionary mother referred to Internet dating as the Devil's playground and condemned anyone who participated in such sinful activity. That comment alone let us all know that Greer and Niran never stood a chance with her family. The saving grace was that at least Niran's family embraced the couple.

After listening to Greer bear her soul about her family drama and witnessing Sista7's loving response to her, I felt more connected to the group. When it came time for me to give my life update, I opened my journal and read a portion of what had been troubling my heart for the past two months … my feelings for Branford.

Last week, I couldn't stand the pain any longer … the sorrow in my heart had overwhelmed me to such a degree that I gathered all my stuff and got on the first red eye heading east of my past and straight to my next destination. I wanted to fast forward to my next series of blessings, but my past wouldn't let me go. My present was full of tears intermingled with thoughts of why love with him was not possible. My future was blocked. The only safe place I had to rest my weary head was purgatory. It feels like my residence here is permanent. They keep telling me that it is temporary ... for the time being, but no one in this damn place has informed me of my date of release. It is an unknown entity that I struggle with. Why did parts of my soul insist on sending the entire soul into this place of obvious danger? Glimpses of what it was like to be in his presence consume me. We were so in tune with each other on so many levels. The sweetness that we could have shared was impossible. The memories keep coming. How long must I exist in this place of pain and sorrow? It hurts so much that I wanna awaken love for love's sake even though I know it is wrong. My saving grace has been the holy scripture: "Do not arise or awaken love until it so desires." Melancholy sadness always fills the air when I reach this point in my process. Flashbacks of unwise choices that caused expensive pain pop up reminding me that all of my accounts are overextended. My heart is in debt. My soul is in bondage. My mind has been foreclosed upon. I am a fire sale waiting to happen. Today I reread the scripture ... inhaling it as I have come to do. I chant it in the back of my mind so I will never forget that only Creator can bring love near. Not me. Not begging. Not pleading. Not becoming a sacrificial lamb. My prayer is to finally let go and give way to the flow of divine order. Hopefully the echo of scripture will be the wisdom my heart needs to heal itself so the next beloved can appear.

After I finished, Serengeti hugged me and whispered in my ear, "That took a lot of courage to share."

As the tears rolled down my face, the other members of the Sista7 extended hugs. Their unconditional support was more than I was prepared to receive. It was a blessing I hadn't planned for, but definitely needed.

CHAPTER 11

▼

"A new heart I will give you, and a new spirit I will put within you."

—Ezekiel 36:26

Sunee let me borrow two of her Deva Premal CDs: *Love Is Space* and *Essence*. She uses them during her massage sessions. I became a huge fan of Premal's music. Lately, I have been using the chants on the *Love Is Space* CD. My favorite is *Om Namo Narayanaya*. Translated it means, "I offer my respect to the Absolute, the Sustainer of all beings." When I focus all of my energy on the sound and the vibration of this mantra, I can hear it and even feel it in my heart. On the days that I teach yoga at the Center, I work hard at bringing this feeling of inner peace to my class.

Three days ago, I just couldn't do it. All of the pain, disappointment, and anger would not budge. I was stuck. A panic attack occurred in the middle of my Tuesday morning class. Consequently, my yoga students suffered. I ended up taking two days off so I could deal with my stuff. Things really didn't get much better, but I did make a decision to return to therapy with Francis because it was obvious that I couldn't deal with the news of Daddy's son, my feelings for Branford, and the guilt I was feeling about my sexcapades with Laurence without some form of support.

On the first day of Autumn, I woke up, meditated, chanted, prayed, journaled, showered, dressed, sipped on a smoothie, walked to the Center to teach my yoga class, and went back to therapy. Francis' office was different. The four walls had been transformed from a dull taupe to a buttery yellow. Although I was happy with the change, I wondered why she made it. I once read that neutral colors such as taupe, beige, and pale gray send restful messages to the brain and are typically used with mental health centers to de-stress patients. The yellow walls did bring more warmth and coziness to the room.

Francis' outdated furniture had been replaced with a stack of comfortable earth tone throw pillows stacked next to a chocolate leather love seat that faced two matching oversized leather chairs. Mud cloth pillows decorated the love seat. Her desk area looked like it had come straight out of the IKEA catalog. The top of the desk was beech veneer with tinted lacquer. The desk legs were steel pigmented with powder coating. Two beech veneer file cabinets, one bookcase, and a comfortable black swivel chair completed the set. Plopping myself down into one of the comfy chairs, I let out a sigh.

"So this is what makes therapy fun?"

Francis cracked a half smile and said, "You bought the bait."

"Hook, line, and sinker."

"So what's been going on with you?"

"Lots of journaling."

"Care to elaborate?"

Pulling out my journal from my black Phat Farm bag, I answered, "I think my journal entry from this morning best describes where I am. Do you wanna hear it?"

"Definitely."

"It may sound kinda raw."

"Go ahead and read it. I'm sure it's just fine."

"The safest place to hide from pain, anger and disappointment is nowhere. There is no safety in hiding. So why do it? There really isn't any escape. If you think otherwise, you're fooling yourself. Hide where? You can't hide from yourself. You can certainly numb yourself for a period of time. Excessive drinking, drugs, sex, shopping, etc., all fit the bill for this one. When the high is over, all you have left is the same stuff you were hiding from along with layers of work that must be done. So why not get on with it? You know … cease the fantasy island existence and face the inevitable … the work of healing and moving past the pain. Go on and take the plunge. While you are at it, ask the Almighty for a new heart and spirit to carry you into the life you were created to live."

As I closed my journal and looked up, I saw Francis smile as she stood and applauded me.

"Brava. Brava. Brava. You get it. You really get it."

"Get what?"

"That you have to do the work to heal and move forward."

"Yeah, I finally got some of it."

"That's fine too. Getting some of it is a good place to start."

"Well it is about time, don't you think?"

"Karma, you can't measure evolution. Each person's path is unique."

With a hint of sarcasm in my voice, I responded, "Now you sound like one of the Hindu sages."

"That's a compliment, I think."

"Yeah, that's a compliment."

"So what brought you to this enlightenment?"

"A panic attack that I had a few days ago."

"Why do you think you had one?"

"Stress from all of the drama I have been dealing with."

"Drama such as ..."

"I am sure you remember my convoluted voice-mail in June about my feelings for Branford and the whole Laurence fiasco. In addition to all of that drama, my mother recently told me that I have a half brother living in Ohio. His mother was a family friend and my former yoga instructor. She and my father had an affair while I was little girl."

"How do you feel about this news?"

"Shocked, angry, and confused about whether to approach my half-brother. He wants to meet Violet and I. Momma gave me his contact information. I am in conflict. I wish I could yell at Daddy for betraying our family. I am mad at Momma for staying with Daddy after he had an affair. I don't understand how she could allow Devi to remain a part of his life ... our lives ... I feel guilty and wonder if maybe I blocked out the signs of Daddy's affair with Devi since she was around him when we went to church on Sundays. Maybe I saw something and could have warned Momma. Maybe I was so shocked that I blocked it all out. I get this feeling that Daddy never really totally loved Momma and us the way he professed. Maybe it was all an act since he had an affair and a son to boot."

"Let's back up a bit and deal with your guilt. You have nothing to feel guilty about. You were a little girl. What ever happened between your parents happened between them because of their choices. You should not feel responsible for your father's choice to have an affair or your mother's choice to accept the affair. Those were their decisions."

"I hear what you are saying, but I just can't get beyond the fact that Daddy played around on Momma and had this baby with Devi."

"Don't expect to get past this news so quickly. It is shocking. Give yourself permission to be shocked. Have you talked to your sister about it?"

"I can't talk to her."

"Why not?"

"We aren't on the same page about anything."

"This challenge might be an opportunity for you to get on the same page."

"Trust me this is not the time."

"What about your mother? Have you talked to her about it?"

"That's definitely not going to happen."

"Is there anyone in your family that you can talk to?"

"Aunt Jo."

"Okay then. I suggest you try sharing your feelings with her. She could serve as a neutral sounding board."

"I'll do my best."

"That's all I can ask. So it sounds like you and your journal have fallen in love."

"Believe it or not, we have. I write in my journal on a daily basis. It really helps me release my thoughts."

"What motivated you to journal daily?"

"In June, I was invited to attend a poetry gathering at the Center. Listening to other women read from the pages of their journals about emotional challenges helped me see that I wasn't alone in my struggles. Afterwards, Serengeti, a co-owner of the Center, invited me to dinner with a group of six other sista poets.

Our dinner turned into a weekly event that allows us to share bits and pieces of our lives."

"Sounds like you have found a group of supportive girlfriends."

"I guess so."

"So what is the hesitation in your voice for?"

"I like the group and have shared a portion of my drama about Branford, but I haven't embraced them totally. No one in the group pries. They all let me be. If I don't share, there's no drama. If I do share, they surround me with love and acceptance."

"Friendships take time to establish. So take your time. I'm just happy that you have found a group of women that you feel comfortable around."

"Me too."

"Have you talked to your girlfriends in New York City lately?"

"No."

"Why not?"

"I haven't felt compelled to call them."

"Have they tried to contact you?"

"They call and send e-mails periodically."

"That shows they care."

"I know, but I just haven't found the energy to respond."

"I can't tell you what to do, but if you value these friendships, then you need to act like it."

"I know, but I just don't feel like dragging them through my issues."

"You don't have to tell them everything. You could write them a short e-mail to say hello."

"That's a thought."

"So are you interested in setting up another appointment?"

"Definitely."

"Okay, does this time work for you?"

"Uh hum."

"Let's say next week same day and time."

"Done deal."

"I want you to think about reinventing your life and what it would look like if you were able to resolve your feelings for Branford, release your guilt from your affair with Laurence, and accept your father's affair and half-brother."

"That's a tall order."

"Not for a woman who is ready to do the work of healing."

"You got me on that one."

I left my session with Francis feeling like I had made a breakthrough. When I got home, I had time to eat a Caesar salad for lunch and check my e-mail before heading up to Howard. My in-box was filled with messages from Branford, Serengeti, Yamuna, and a host of strangers sending their daily spam. I deleted all of the spam and decided to hold off on reading Branford's message. It's probably filled with pleas to return his calls. Not wanting to go there, I chose to read the messages from Serengeti and Yamuna.

Serengeti's e-mail was another Sista7 astrological report about the equinox and how it signals the beginning of autumn. I never really paid attention to the fact that it represents the point where there is exactly twelve hours of daylight and twelve hours of darkness at the equator. She even included instructions on how to use the celebration as a sacred space cleansing opportunity. It sounded like a good idea so I decided to do it. At the end of the message, Serengeti provided a reminder about the Harvest Moon celebration that the Center was having today. The celebration itself would begin in the courtyard at five p.m. Everyone would be given an opportunity to decorate the Moon altar and make offerings of incense and foods associated with the Moon like melons, grapes and moon cakes. Afterwards, we would wait for the sun to set and the moon to rise before bowing to her light. Incense and candles would be lit immediately after. The celebration would close with a sharing of Moon-inspired poetry.

Before reading Yamuna's e-mail, I quickly typed a reply message to Serengeti that I would attend the event. Yamuna's e-mail was sent only to Sunee and I. It referenced an article written by Connie Briscoe in the August issue of Essence magazine. It was entitled, *Mr. Right.com.* Yamuna was so impressed by Connie's own story of meeting her husband through an online dating service that she decided to prepare an ad in hopes of meeting some eligible single men. Because of Greer's success with Love@AOL, she decided to post her ad on their site. What she needed from us was our support and opinion of her ad. Why would she ask me? We never talked about dating. I didn't even really know that she was actively searching for a boyfriend or people to date. She always talks about her work or son. And I am definitely not an expert in writing online dating ads. Men are not even on my list of priorities.

As I read her ad, I was amazed at Yamuna's courage.

I am blessed to walk the earth as a unique soulfully complex, fun, loving, peaceful, spiritual, and creative woman. I am forty-two years old. I am an Afro-Russian/Jewish American woman who is happily divorced. I am the mother of one truly together teenage son. My spirit, health, creativity, and relationships are my cherished treasures. I work as an ayurvedic healer. Ayurveda is the traditional healing system of India. The word itself means the knowledge and wisdom of life. The meaning is the primary reason I was drawn to study this science of how one develops greater harmony with her environment through all senses at the California College of Ayurveda. This work is one of my life's passions. I have been doing it for over 10 years. I started in this field while living in Sacramento, California. Although I miss northern California, I have enjoyed living in Washington for the past two years. Right now, I am focused on training for the Marine Corps Marathon in October. This is a huge commitment that I am flowing with one day at a time. I am running and walking for the Leukemia & Lymphoma Society in honor of my grandfather who died of Leukemia two years ago. So far, it has been good … a little soreness, but that's par for the course. I enjoy reading, listening to music, going to museums, walking, running, weight training, traveling (just came back from Jamaica), eating Thai and other Asian food, learning how to play chess (need a lot of help), salsa dancing, meditating, and learning new things. Connecting with people is always an interesting process. I am always amazed at how soulfully complex we really are as human beings … It is our complexity that makes us so unique … makes us dynamic … makes us laugh … makes us cry … makes us smile … makes us go hum … What do you think? If you are interested, drop me a line. Know that I will respond in a colorfully complex yet soulfully beautiful way … Have an incredibly beautiful day and weekend! Peace to you.

The only word I could type in my reply message to Yamuna was fabulous. I learned so much from reading her ad. She is truly a dynamic woman who deserves a dynamic man. I wanna be like her when I grow up!

CHAPTER 12

▼

"Now the Lord is that Spirit: and where the Spirit of the Lord is, there is liberty."

—2 Corinthians 3:17

My next session with Francis helped me understand and embrace my anger as an ordinary feeling everyone encounters at some point in life. It's a feeling that should be experienced fully, not resisted or ignored. She explained that anger is lightening in a bottle with the bottle being the human body. When it is not released, it can create health challenges. Francis described anger as an ego problem resulting from having expectations that don't manifest according to our individual plan. The key sources of anger include fear, unhappiness, habit, inappropriate attention, and attachment. They can take the form of betrayal, outrage, frustration, jealousy, resentment, fury, hatred, and verbal and physical abuse. Francis continued by sharing that there are six levels to healing anger: anger, hurt, fear, regret, intention, and love. There are two feelings associated with each level. Blame and resentment are connected to anger. Sadness and disappointment to hurt. Insecurity and wounds to fear. Understanding and responsibility to regret. Solutions and wishes to intention. Forgiveness and appreciation to love. Logically, these levels made sense, but doing the work didn't. That's why I remained silent when Francis asked, "So what is frightening you? And what has saddened you?"

I wondered if I could give voice to my swirling emotions without creating World War III. My silence prompted Francis to remind me what I already knew. "Karma, you can't be healed until you love yourself enough to do the work."

I shook my head in agreement. "I want to heal myself, but it feels like an impossible goal."

Francis took our discussion to another level. "Your goal can be accomplished one step at a time. Look at the goal as a series of baby steps with the first step requiring you to imagine what would happen if you chose not to fully release anger from your body."

My body language automatically shifted to a position of retreat with my arms folded tightly across my chest with my eyes glancing down at the floor. I wish I could hide my uncomfortable emotions from Francis, but I can't. That's when Francis reminded me of something I preach to my yoga students.

"Anger will destroy your peace of mind."

Francis thought she was slick by asking me to demonstrate yoga positions that I recommended to angry students. That was a no brainer. The cleansing or wood-chopper breathing exercise, *Savasana,* and *Siddhasana* were the perfect combination for softening and releasing anger in the body.

I started with the woodchopper breathing exercise by standing with my feet hip width apart, interlocking my fingers, and raising my arms in a straight position. Then I began breathing out through my mouth with a "ha" sound as I bent forward. At the same time, I swung my arms through my legs as if I were chopping wood and slightly bent my knees while pulling in my abdominal muscles to squeeze out all the air from the bottom of my lungs. I breathed in deeply through my nostrils, gently moved my arms over my head, and straightened my back into the standing posture. I felt the air leaving my lungs and being replaced with clean air.

The next demonstration focused on *Savasana.* I sat on the floor with my knees bent, feet resting flat, and leaned back onto my forearms. Then I lifted my pelvis slightly off the floor. With my hands, I pushed the back of my pelvis toward my tailbone, later returning my pelvis to the floor. As I slowly inhaled, I extended my right leg, then the left, pushing through my heels. Next, I released both legs and made certain they were angled evenly relative to the mid-line of my torso. Turning my feet out equally, I narrowed the front of my pelvis and softened my lower back. Laying in this pose felt peaceful. So I stayed in it for ten minutes. When I decided to come out of the pose, I looked up at Francis and saw a smile. Her patience with my unique healing process was a blessing.

Siddhasana was also good for celibacy, something I knew I needed to practice for the time being. I sat with my legs stretched forward. First, I bent my left leg at the knee and placed the heel at the soft portion of the perineum. Then I folded my right leg and placed the heel against my pubic bone. My hands were facing with the palms up and resting on my knees. As I breathed in and out, I focused on keeping my posture straight.

Francis asked me, "How do you feel?"

"Small pieces of anger feel like they are breaking up into particles that I can chew on and release in time."

Francis recommended, "You should take your own advice by using these yoga poses and breathing exercises on a daily basis. You should also consider using a visualization exercise to help you get in touch with your anger. It involves you imagining what would happen if you physically released your anger and lost control."

"I can't do it."

"Why?"

"Because I'm afraid."

"What does losing control mean to you? Why are you afraid to release your anger?"

I couldn't find the words or energy to respond. She accepted my silence and asked me to consider answering the questions as a homework assignment for our next session. It sounded like a reasonable request. So I agreed.

Three mornings and evenings passed before I was able to conquer my fear of answering the questions. Each morning, I chanted *Om Shri Gum Ganapatayei Namaha*, a mantra for removing emotional obstacles such as anger, practiced my woodchopper breathing exercises and yoga poses, and recited a prayer that Daddy taught me.

"This day, Spirit of mercy and love, I offer salutations unto thee. You are omnipotent, omnipresent, and omniscient. You are *Satchidananda*. Existence-knowledge-bliss absolute. You are the indweller of all beings. This day, grant me an understanding heart, equal vision, balanced mind, joy, peace, faith, devotion, wisdom, wholeness, health, and abundance. Grant me inner spiritual strength to resist temptation and to control my mind. Free me from egoism, lust, anger, greed, and hatred. Fill my heart with divine virtues. Let me behold and serve you in all names and forms. Let me sing your glories. Let me abide in you for eternity. *Om Shanti. Shanti. Shanti.*"

Opening my journal is where I stopped. As soon as I cracked it open, I quickly closed it and headed back to bed, hiding underneath my covers. On the fourth morning, I repeated the same behavior except I carried my journal with me. Underneath my covers, I wrote out the answer to the question.

If I physically released my anger at Daddy for having an affair and son with Devi, I would fly to Oakland and strangle Devi for rupturing my perfect childhood. I would go to Daddy's grave and spray paint his headstone red with the word "adulterer." I would cuss at his spirit for not being faithful to Momma. I would shout at the top of my lungs so he could hear how betrayed I felt. If I lost control, I would tell Momma that all of her nagging and bourgeoisie taste pushed Daddy away and into Devi's arms. I would tell Violet that her need to have Momma's approval while we were growing up made Daddy feel like he needed another child to love. I would tell this new brother of mine that his mere presence has caused so much pain that I prefer not to know him. I would blame all of them for creating this madness.

If I physically released my anger at Branford for not being the type of man I could have a relationship with, I would tell him how much he is missing by not being able to appreciate and love me like I wanted him too.

If I physically released my anger at Laurence for seducing me into having a fling with him again, I would cuss him out worse than a sailor for hurting his wife and children in the same way Daddy hurt me.

If I physically released my anger at myself for participating in those sexcapades with Laurence, I would sentence myself to celibacy until I could get my head straight.

My next session with Francis turned into more homework. She asked me to write a letter to everyone who angered me. They were not to be mailed unless I felt comfortable doing so. I wrote letters to Daddy, Momma, Branford, and myself. This process helped me decide to share journal excerpts at the Potluck Cypher. Two days before the event, I submitted my anonymous writing. It was a collage of thoughts expressed in my letters. After I submitted it, I started having second thoughts. The fear of having everyone know my business filled me with anxiety, but it was too late to turn back. Exposure was inevitable. My truth would be revealed. Perhaps if I trusted Spirit and this process, I might be set free.

DJ Fierce's music filled the Center's main auditorium with the sounds of a Latina singer that I was trying to remember. I hate when you know something but can't recall it. Who is that singer? I know her name like the back of my hand. Ma'at, Kalahari, and I were just talking about her last week. She's Afro-Peruvian and from Chorillos, Peru, Kalahari's birthplace. Sarah? No it's Susana. Susana Baca. That's right. Damn that was eating me up. She sings with such emotion and intimacy. Her music is rooted in the richness of the lando, a mix of African and Spanish rhythms. Those highly evocative sounds often baptize me with their slow to mid tempo beats. I gotta find her CD when I get home and play it.

Susana's music complimented the evening's mood and dimly lit, candle-filled auditorium. The makeshift stage sat in the middle of the auditorium surrounded by a semicircle of black folding chairs. They were arranged in four rows. The stage was the home of two bar stools positioned behind a microphone and a table covered with purple and pink Ghanaian Andinkra cloth that contained sixteen symbols: Gya Nyame, Duafe, Akoma Ntoaso, Nkyinkyim, Osrane Ne Nsoroma, Ananse Ntontan, Keerapa Musu Yide, Sunsum, Ohene Aniwa, Nsaa, Nkyimu, Tabono, Nyame Nti, Akoben, Adinkrahene, and Gyawu Atiko. Gya Nyame is the omnipotence of God. Duafe embodies love, feminine consideration, patience, goodness, and care. Akoma Ntoaso symbolizes unity and agreement.

Nkyinkyim stands for change, transformation, and endurance. Osrane Ne Nso-roma personifies femininity, wisdom, humility, and learning. Ananse Ntontan is creativity. Keerapa Musu Yide is good fortune. Sunsum characterizes spirituality. Ohene Aniwa is beauty and vigilance. Nsaa depicts excellence. Nkyimu is skill and precision. Tabono illustrates strength, persistence, and confidence. Nyame Nti describes faith in God. Akoben is readiness and willingness to take action. Adinkrahene portrays greatness and firmness. Gyawu Atiko is bravery and fear-lessness. A basket of sealed envelopes and a gallon of mineral water with a stack of paper cups sat on top of the table.

The first thing that I noticed when I walked into the auditorium was the rain-bow collective of sistas sitting in the audience. They represented a multitude of shapes, sizes, and colors. I settled in the back row closest to the door. My choice was strategic in case I needed to make a quick Pink Panther stage left exit.

DJ Fierce lowered the volume of the music as Greer approached the stage. She was wearing the Sapphire Sista Cypher trademark midnight blue t-shirt and a pair of jeans. I loved the t-shirt's logo. It was a sista wearing an Afro as large as the one worn by Angela Davis, Assata Shakur, Katherine Cleaver, or Elaine Brown back in the day. The word Sapphire was spelled in bold red letters.

"Welcome to the October Sapphire Sista Cypher. My name is Greer Davis. It is my pleasure to serve as your Mistress of Ceremonies for the evening. Before we get started, I wanna take a few seconds to tell the neophytes what this event is all about. The Sapphire Sista Cypher has been meeting at Our Womanist Spirit Center for the past five years. We gather as a monthly collective of women repre-senting all facets of the human rainbow. We come together in love to affirm our spirits and womanhood in creative expression. In this space, sistas speak their minds. They say things that fly in the face of convention. They reveal their truths. They cry, laugh, scream, and shout hallelujah and amen. Our expression is juicy, wild, uncompromising, and untamed. No one apologizes for the way they feel. Some of us are straight, gay, bi-sexual, transgender, Catholic, new age, Baptist, AME, Apostolic, Yoruba, Vodun, Akan, Unitarian, Protestant, Bud-dhist, Hindu, Muslim, Episcopalian, fashionistas, urban professionals, freelanc-ers, entrepreneurs, stay-at-home mommies, working mothers, blue collar, white collar, pink collar, no collar, vegetarians, carnivores, feminists, womanists, demo-crats, republicans, independents, green party members, socialists, communists, etc. etc. No matter what we call ourselves, we are women defining ourselves from moment to moment with new language that moves beyond all identity markers. In this space, we unleash our authentic selves. We invite you to join us as we cast the flame of our lights onto the world."

The audience applauded Greer. She blew kisses and moved the evening's program along.

"Ladies, tonight is Potluck Cypher. Last month we asked folks to submit anonymous writings in sealed envelopes. Tonight, they will be read by several of our nation's finest word mistresses. The first one we're gonna bring to the mic is Original Woman. She hails from Greensboro, North Carolina, and has been writing and performing her poetry in the Dirty South for seven years now. Original Woman is the author of three books of poetry and recently released her first CD, *Cries of Oshun's Daughter Down South*. She is also an assistant professor at Bennett College. Give it up for Original Woman."

Original Woman sauntered across the stage in a white cotton shirt, long denim skirt with a thigh high slit, and five-inch stiletto black boots that elevated her five foot nine inch full-figured frame to towering heights. She moved like she owned every inch of the universe. Original Woman wore a close-cropped Afro with silver hoop earrings dangling against a sable-colored face *sans* make-up. When she reached into the basket for a sealed envelope, I wondered if she would pick mine. As soon as she opened it and began reading, my wondering ceased and became a reality. In a deep raspy voice that reminded me of Me'shell Ndegeocello, she breathed life into my words.

"These thoughts are a collage of unwritten letters that my therapist instructed me to write. My heart and soul have eclipsed into a bitter lemon of sour poison manifesting in my thoughts, words, feelings, and actions as anger, betrayal, frustration, and disbelief. Many days are just plain apocalyptic. Yoga, breathing exercises, chanting, praying, and movement. Sometimes they work, but only for a moment. The emotions are never fully washed away. Journaling stops and starts. I languish. My heart is broken. My soul is splattered across the pages in thoughts that make no sense. Concentration, clarity, and communication with myself are all absent. So I stay lost by choice cuz' if I tried to find me, I'd have to face it all. Walk through the madness. Embrace the apocalypse that my Daddy created when he betrayed my mother, sister, and me by fucking another woman and creating a son … Yeah if I found myself I'd have to admit that my Disneyland family illusion was a bunch of bullshit that my parents carefully orchestrated to conceal the truth … the truth that the love they proclaimed in front of me and my sister was a b-movie filled with my mother's bourgeoisie fantasy world and my father's bohemian Buddhist/Hindu academic nonsense that I bought into hook, line, and sinker. If I really found myself I'd have to admit that my mother drove my father into another woman's arms. Maybe he just didn't have any dick control from the get go which might explain my choice in emotionally unavailable men. Then if I did all of this, and looked at my twisted sister and her need to seek approval from my mother, I might have to admit that I'm just as twisted as she is. Isn't it me who is falling for my bisexual best friend while choosing to fuck the married man at the family wedding? What does it make me? Human. Real. Authentic. Woman in process. Woman who sits across from her therapist every week facing what she is fearful of knowing. Woman struggling to uncover her hidden wholeness. Woman seeking to be well. Woman underemployed. Woman who doesn't love herself? Wait a minute, I do love myself. The evidence is my willingness to work on my issues with a therapist. I'm a walking paradox. Complexity is my favorite cup of tea. Welcome to the prelude … the morning before my poetry awakens. It speaks on many levels. It is language squeezed from the crevices of my soul and the depths of my injured heart. I invite you to partake of a slice of my life in every poem.

Poem #1

This week has been one of great sadness and growth. A friend is dying slowly. It's the old me. The one who pretended to believe only what existed on the surface. When she looked underneath the covers, she had a stroke. By the time the ambulance arrived, she lapsed into a coma. I'm the aftermath. A new truth.

Poem #2

Me as truth. I yell my frustrations, betrayals, and anger until Daddy hears them from wherever his spirit has taken up residence since he last walked this earthly plane. I rant and rave so he will know my pain. Why couldn't you keep your dick in your pants, Daddy? Why did you bring that woman that you had me believing was a family friend into our house when you were fucking her? Momma, why did you let him disrespect you and our family? Didn't you love yourself enough to leave him? Why did you all do this to us? Now I see why Violet might be so twisted and why I pick emotionally unavailable men as partners. It is my family legacy. When will I stop living like a moth, throwing myself into flames, destroying myself in the process?

Poem #3

Me as a sister to a brother I don't know if I want to know. You were born into this crazy bullshit. What legacy do we have to share? But then I can't ignore that you are kin. Blood. We've got the same father. That's got to count for something. I wanna connect and then I don't. My duality is a paradox that you shouldn't have to face, but you probably will since it is mine and I'm your sister.

Poem #4

Drank so much truth serum this week that I think I might overdose if I have to take another swig. The whole damn process got me laid out without the desire to do anything not even wash my ass and go to my gypsy jobs to make ends meet, but I go anyway cuz' I gotta keep moving … living … doing … being … healing …

Poem #5

The goal is cathartic release. When will it be?

Poem #6

It will be whenever I choose to face the fear, embrace, and release the anger, and heal because I love me."

When Original Woman finished she thanked the author for allowing her to read her words. I didn't know how to respond because I was still dealing with all my stuff being out there. I wanted to get up and leave, but my body was glued to my seat. I ended up sitting through the rest of the night in a state of silence, hoping that no one would recognize me in my words. Most of all, I wanted to hide from the truth that my spirit had released. It was located light years away from the freedom I thought it would bring.

PART II

▼

Let Your Soul Be Your Pilot
—Sting, Track 3 on the *Mercury Falling* CD (1996)

CHAPTER 13

▼

"The sun rises and the sun sets, and hurries back to where it rises. The wind blows to the south and turns to the north; round and round it goes, ever returning on its course. All streams flow into the sea, yet the sea is never full. To the places the streams come from, there they return again. All things are wearisome, more than one can say. The eye never has enough of seeing, nor the ear its fill of hearing. What has been will be again, what has been done will be done again; there is nothing new under the sun."

—Ecclesiastes 1:5-9

The confusion surrounding the presidential election in Florida has consumed the consciousness of most Americans. I wish I could add my name to the list, but I can't. Although I cast my vote for Al Gore and sincerely hope that the votes in Florida reflect a win for him, my concerns lie elsewhere in the land of anger, pain, and suffering. The more I try to leave this land, the harder it gets. Barriers to my exit convince me that I have been permanently displaced in a refugee camp for the emotionally unfit. Perhaps my only hope is in receiving a day pass to a place that offers a few hours of peace and calm ... a place that is at least one hundred miles away from my anger zone. Does it even exist? Francis keeps insisting that it does. I think she is trying to fool me into believing that I'll see the pearly gates of this so-called promise land when I peel back the final layer of anger. What a revelation of bullshit! We all know that there's no such thing as a final layer of anything. There's always more to come. To pretend otherwise is just downright stupid. Haven't I been a slave of stupidity far too long? No need to answer it.

Why is it that they say revelation is cathartic? I am here to say that it's not even when it is realistic or done anonymously at an open mic spoken word event. Anyone who falls for this flawed logic is a fool confused by the psychobabble shrewdness of a self-help book or therapist. I count myself as one of the fools. If Francis heard my thoughts right now, she might tell me that I was about to throw myself a huge pity party filled with self condemnation party favors and a chocolate cake with vanilla icing and red lettering spelling out the phrase: I am a victim and love it! To balance out this madness, I would add the music of Susana Baca and dance around the room singing *Se Me Van Los Pies*. Like the title of the song, *My Feet Go*, I'd allow the rich and varied Afro Peruvian rhythms to seduce me into a trance. I'd exorcise the long list of people and experiences that have accumulated in my overdrawn account at the United Bank of Emotional Pain. Screams would emerge from some unknown place in my belly. Before they voiced themselves into existence, they'd have to successfully complete a Jacques Cousteau expedition through my digestive tract to the opening of my mouth. If they got lucky and actually made it, they'd rest on the tip of my tongue before I decided to grant them permission to speak. Depending on how I was feeling, I might let them speak. If I was feeling like I'm today, I'd just swallow the screams and send them back to where they came from.

That was enough introspection for one day. Unanswered e-mail beckoned. I had two messages. The first one was from Serengeti. The subject line caused me to consider deleting the message. Who wants to read some astrological report on Mercury's Retrograde? How can that impact my life? Tempted to delete it, I remembered how sensitive Serengeti is about folks deleting her e-mails. The chick can actually run a status check on all AOL members who receive her message. After she checks, she'll let you know that she knows you deleted her message. So to avoid more drama, I read it in its entirety.

Dear Sista7,

Understanding the current state of politics isn't easy. However, if we look at the recent events under an astrological microscope, we might be able to make sense. Did you know that the phenomena of Mercury's Retrograde on Election Day 2000 contributed to the ballot confusion, the premature media announcements and retractions, and all the recounts that ensued? Now you might be thinking I done lost all my marbles, but wait a second and hear me out. Let's review some key elements of Mercury Retrograde. Mercury moves in apparent retrograde or backward motion for a period of several weeks about three times each year. During these periods, it often delivers mixed-up messages that spell confusion and require the repeating of things. Also, communication and transportation glitches develop. Okay with all that said let's move forward with the most recent Mercury Retrograde on October 18 at fifteen degrees of Scorpio. Did you know that it slowed down significantly and turned direct at 29 degrees of Libra on November 7, Election Day? Its slow pace had an even stronger impact on events surrounding communication. So by the time we got to Election Day and the days that ensued, the worst of Mercury's Retrograde made itself known in how the media and the candidates announced and retracted election results. Added to this madness was the confusion surrounding the counting of ballots in Florida. Where does that leave us? In a state of limbo until Mercury's Retrograde departs on November 23 or 24. That means we are bound to have a peaceful Thanksgiving. Hopefully by then the confusion, recounts, and inclusion of absentee ballots should be resolved. Let this experience be a lesson in how powerful the planets can be in our lives.

Be astrologically wise. Serengeti.

Actually, the message wasn't half bad. Perhaps when the Retrograde is over, I might be able to breathe in a little peace and process my emotional pain better. Oops I forgot I am scheduled to go home for Thanksgiving. Cancel the peace. Being in Momma and Violet's presence is nowhere near it.

Yamuna's message was an update on her dating escapades. Jorge, the salsa dancer, was a no show. He didn't even call to cancel or apologize. Ira, the yoga instructor, seemed to still be in love with his ex-wife. Her date with Ali, the cab driver, was okay, but he seemed immature. David, the plumber, was obsessed with the traditional role that he thought women should play in relationships. You know in the kitchen and bedroom. The only one that made the next round of cuts was Grant, the oncologist. As I read Yamuna's message, it seemed like he might be a good catch.

Grant and I met at Utopia on U Street. He is incredibly cool and intelligent. Witty and very down to earth. More than I expected from a doctor and medical school professor. Did I tell you that he teaches Medical Humanities at Howard's medical school and is coordinating an expressive arts program for the hospital's oncology department? I think you should talk. I can see you working together. Grant was excited to learn about your work at Howard's gallery. The man is something else. He can be eloquent and street all at the same time. Seems like he's in touch with himself and his various personalities. I like that he describes himself as Grant, the down to earth, loving, spiritual person. Dr. Ammons is a no nonsense professional man. "G" is the homeboy from around the way who cusses at the drop of a hat and will wax some ass in chess and on the basketball court. His words not mine. We both agreed that eating healthy and taking care of our body temples are important. He's a vegetarian. Eastern spirituality and philosophy dominate his thought process. He believes in approaching his work from a holistic and traditional medicine perspective. He practices t'ai chi. Born and raised in St. Albans, New York. He is from a nuclear family with both parents still married and living in the house he was raised in. They are former teachers. His older sister lives with her family in Toronto. Grant enjoys traveling. Russia was his last trip. He is a fan of all types of music ranging from reggae superstar Bob Marley to opera singer Maria Callas. What a combination. And the man is sexy. Bald head, oatmeal skin, no facial hair, deep setting brown eyes, thick lips, large hands, and a body built like LL Cool J. We are exactly the same height. He wasn't intimidated by my high heels. There was definitely chemistry between us. So much so that I accepted his invitation to his frat brother's birthday party. It's the week after Thanksgiving. He asked me to invite several of my girlfriends who might be interested in meeting some of his Kappa Alpha Psi Fraternity brothers. Do you want to come? I asked Sunee to come too. Hope you can make it. Happy Thanksgiving! Happiness, Joy, and Bliss, Yamuna.

As soon as I saw the invitation, I hit the reply button and wrote,

Hey Yamuna. I'm glad you and Grant clicked. Thank you for the invitation to the party. Right now, I'm on sabbatical from meeting men. Have fun. I'm headed home to Oakland for Thanksgiving. Hope you have a great holiday. Peace & Love, Karma.

Meeting new men is not the medicine I need to recover from my pain.

Packing to go home for Thanksgiving turned into a weekend struggle. Each time I started, I stopped. The mere thought of going home and staying for five days made me feel like I was stuck in an early morning fog with zero visibility. Simple choices about what to bring escaped me. One option would be to call Momma an hour before I am supposed to arrive and tell her that I missed my flight. Missing my flight might lessen the Francois female drama, but it would not eliminate the heavy emotional baggage I continue to lug around. No matter where I go, it follows me. So why try to escape?

I managed to finally pack my suitcase six hours before my flight was scheduled to depart Reagan National Airport on the morning of Monday, November 20. When I arrived at the airport, I called Momma to confirm my flight plans. She surprised me and said that Aunt Nina and Uncle Gary would be meeting me since she had a client meeting and Violet would be working. Having my godparents meet me would definitely ease the tension of having to spend time in Momma's mega *bougie* land.

Peace Beyond Passion and *Bitter*, two of my favorite Me'Shell N'degeocello CDs, kept me company for most of the trip. Little did I know that the music would provoke six hours of introspection. With nowhere to go, I surrendered to the process. For the first half of the flight, the tracks of *Peace Beyond Passion* played in my ears. Me'Shell's deeper-than-deep voice seduced my ears with lazy bass grooves. Her passion for personal introspection and searing lyrics with messages that explore the impact of race and sex in Christianity make the CD an explosion of unqualified success. And it didn't hurt that she was accompanied by saxophonist Joshua Redman and Wendy Melvoin, Prince's former guitarist.

After the fifth or sixth time of listening to the entire CD, I replayed Track 4. The lyrics of *Ecclesiastes: Free My Heart* motivated me to jot down random thoughts that only a good therapist would dedicate time to decipher. Francis would be so proud of me for taking this kind of approach to my inner thoughts.

The sun rises and the sun sets. I miss it all being consumed by anger and pain. By the time the damn yellow glowing light hurries back to where it rises, my anger emerges running wild like a brush fire mistakenly let loose on an unsuspecting forest of California redwoods. The wind blows to the south, and turns to the north; round and round it goes, ever returning on its course. I am left scorched by flames delivered courtesy of the wind. I try to bathe my anger in the streams since they flow into the sea, but my luck has run out. The streams have returned to the place they came from. A birdie whispers in my ear that the sea was never full. I wonder whether my anger will ever disappear. Will I ever be free, healed from this malcontent and the memory of Daddy's sin and Momma's act of accomplice in the first degree? My pen evaluates the situation and issues a verdict: all things are worrisome more than one can say. I bite the bottom of my lip, pressing the sting of pain into a weariness that forces me to close my eyes and ears cuz' I have seen and heard too much. This one act renders me blind, deaf, mute, and eligible to receive disability. Are things this bad? Hell yeah! They suck, but for God's sake and mine, there has gotta be something new under the sun to free my heart so my soul can breathe in peace.

As I rested my pen on the journal page and breathed a sigh of relief, a Northwest Airlines flight attendant offered me a beverage. I selected ginger ale with no ice. He gave me the entire can. How generous! While sipping my drink, I inserted the *Bitter* CD into my walkman. The first song, *Adam* lulled me to sleep. It was a deep sleep filled with dreams featuring intense dialogue and vivid images. They were haunting and intriguing all at the same time.

The song, *Fool of Me* made me think about my relationship with Madison. It was emotionally charged and filled with scene after scene of me discovering that he had no real interest in me or us. I witnessed how I allowed him to make a fool of me for nearly ten years before I decided to accept the truth and walk away. My psyche drifted into memories of Daddy's unfaithfulness and my rendezvous with Laurence as Me'Shell sang the words of *Faithful*. Something inside me hoped that the message of her song wasn't true. Surely someone is faithful to his mate. I coasted on the subsequent songs until Me'Shell's rendition of Jimi Hendrix's song, *May This Be Love* played. It made me think about Branford and what I wished our relationship could be ... easy, flowing like a waterfall of love between two people. The next song, *Wasted Time* reminded me that my wish would never come true. It made me wake up and face my feelings for Branford. Tears wet my face as I sat drying the stain of unrequited love. It is never pretty. Luckily I fell back to sleep. This time, my headset was off. The next thing I heard was the Captain announce that we were preparing to land in Oakland.

Hearing the name of my birthplace made me think of the way Daddy used to boast about his home away from home on Lagunitas Avenue where we lived in an old Victorian house in beautiful Alameda County. Our family arrived in Oaktown a year before Huey Newton and Bobby Seale founded the Black Panther Party. West Oakland was the first neighborhood that Momma and Daddy made a home in. The close proximity of the Panther Party activity and Daddy's passion for politics convinced him that it was his destiny to join, but Momma threatened to walk out on him and his revolutionary politics. Love will make a man do things he never thought were possible including launching his one-man revolution on Lagunitas Avenue. Violet and I were his first recruits. By the time the Panthers had set up their ten-point platform, free breakfast program, police patrols, and other survival programs, we were miniature soldiers repeating Daddy's Black Power rhetoric that he spewed by day in his history classes at UC Berkley and by night to Momma and us at the dinner table. For him, Oakland always seemed magical. It gave him a sense of himself that Momma could never identify with. For her, New Orleans would always be her home and first city of choice.

To help ease Momma's discomfort, Daddy became Whodini with a pen and authored several books. Two books were made into television movies. He reinvested his earnings in real estate that generated enough revenue to keep Momma living in California with the trappings of southern luxury. The Daffodil Villa, our home, became her showplace. We lived through three remodeling jobs so that Momma could transform our home into an impressive abode influenced by French, Spanish, and Italian home décor.

The interior was covered in seven tones of high gloss yellows. Yellow was Momma's favorite color. Her rationale for selecting such a vivid palette of sunburst colors was to cast a stimulating and blissful mood throughout the home's interior. She convinced us that her use of color psychology in home décor would rescue us from sadness. I wonder if she was trying to rescue her own sadness? Would it rescue mine when I arrived?

I am amazed at that I can see things as an adult that I couldn't see as a child. Perhaps adulthood kills the innocence of childhood. I am starting to feel like it did. My rose-colored glasses have been replaced with Lasik corrected 20/20 vision. Now all I can see looking back at me is stuff I'd rather not see. When Violet and I were small, it was easy to see that Oakland was the place Momma had come to be with the man she loved. Why else would she leave Xavier University in her junior year, elope without her mother's approval, and lose her inheritance of southern luxury? Somewhere between her great sacrifice, our birth, and the mid seventies, when she returned to school at Mills College to complete her undergraduate education, the answer to this question changed.

Momma made us pay for the life choices she made. My payment started when she began working with Aunt Nina and Uncle Gary as a real estate agent. My choices in activities were contrary to what she thought a girl should be involved in. You see, Momma was a third generation Black American Princess turned Queen Mother with an agenda to ensure her daughters follow in her footsteps. Violet went along with the plan. I rejected it and preferred to move through life as a bohemian. Thankfully, Daddy intervened on my behalf and became my savior. I became one more rival for his attention. As years passed, the distance between my parents widened. It was disguised by polite tolerance. Something two southerners born in Louisiana were good at.

Despite the distance and polite tolerance, I can remember there being plenty of displays of affection. Whatever was happening didn't deter them from what Violet and I often called their Saturday morning mating sessions. It would start with the music of Alice and John Coltrane, Chet Baker, Sarah Vaughn, and Ella Fitzgerald. The clock would strike eight. Daddy would appear in his favorite blue candy stripped pajama bottoms and undershirt. Black coffee kept him company as he prepared a breakfast fit for a queen. He'd decorate Momma's sterling silver breakfast tray with French toast, slices of pineapple sprinkled with blueberries and strawberries, a yellow tea rose, and a cup of mint tea. Then he'd serve Momma breakfast in bed, often feeding her as she laughed and giggled like some teenage school girl. Later, she'd feed him with some good loving that would echo through the vent of their bedroom. They'd emerge from the room like young lovers falling over themselves around noon. Damn I wonder how good the sex must have been? It's weird for me to wonder this about my parents, but it must have been good enough to keep Momma married. But then, we all know Momma's devout Catholicism would never allow for a divorce.

As soon as I entered Oakland International Airport, I saw Aunt Nina and Uncle Gary waving at me. They were wearing matching navy blue jogging suits. Aunt Nina is a full-figured woman with ice tea-colored skin and the perfect page-boy hair cut. She has never had a bad hair day! Aunt Nina is shaped similar to actress Della Reese. She is a foot taller than Uncle Gary, a short squatty man with a potbelly stomach and rum-colored skin. They greeted me with their trademark excitement. Momma and Daddy did the right thing in picking them as my god-parents. They always bubbled with a certain *joie de vivre* that would make the saddest person smile and forget her troubles. For a few minutes, they made me forget mine.

When we reached the baggage claim area, my sadness returned. I thought I saw Devi standing by a young man at the next luggage carousel. We had to pass them in order to exit the area. Hoping that she would not see me, I tried to hurry Aunt Nina and Uncle Gary out of the area. Unfortunately, Uncle Gary heard Devi calling me by name and forced me to stop and respond. I turned around and immediately choked at the sight of Devi and what appeared to be my father's son. Oakland had quickly become Blues City.

His eyes met mine. I stood frozen long enough for him to enter my personal space. My worst nightmare was occurring. It was five foot nine inches tall with shoulder length dark brown locs framing a yellow amber face. One glance proved that he was a Francois. We shared the same wide nose with its depressed bridge, poorly defined tip and flared nostrils. Although he had his mother's eyes, our chin, medium-size lips, and matching dimples could easily make us twins. The only thing he didn't have of Daddy's was his towering Paul Robeson-like height.

This man who wanted me as a sister reached out his hand to extend a polite greeting. I pulled back. How could I allow my skin to touch the flesh of bastard skin? Despite my resistance, he continued his attempt to connect. As he uttered the word hello, I saw tears forming in the corner of his right eye. Humanity inserted herself in the midst of family confusion and caused me to search my purse for some tissue. When I discovered two pieces, I offered them as a big sister longing to rescue her baby brother from heartache. Our hands touched. He wouldn't let go. I was lost in these new feelings. Nothing in life had prepared me for feeling an overwhelming sibling concern. How was this possible?

Watching him wipe his eyes made me realize that he and I were the innocent bystanders of choices made by parents who did what they did because that's what they did. Punishing him for others' actions made no sense. Wasting my time with anger and holding onto pain no longer served a purpose because the truth is that I will never know or fully understand why Daddy sinned and Momma went along with him all those years. All I know is that I have a brother. Like it or not, we're family. I can choose to honor or ignore this connection. What will it be?

"Ohnedaruth, it's good to finally meet you. I'm your sister, Karma."

He smiled and hugged me. My prayer for something new under the sun was finally manifesting.

CHAPTER 14

▼

"For I know the plans I have for you, declares the Lord, plans to prosper you and not to harm you, plans to give you a hope and a future."

—Jeremiah 28:11

While Ohnedaruth and I were caught up in the moment, Devi managed to position herself in my personal space. I felt her right hand touch my shoulder. Finding it hard to believe that she would have the audacity to try and comfort me, I pulled away. The anger that I had been holding onto released itself. The target was a four foot ten inch woman. I noticed that she had put on a few pounds. She hid them well underneath a plum stone wash silk ankle-length dress and billowy pants. A plum, lilac, and mauve floral print scarf began to slide down her head. It revealed her mane of wavy black hair. Her olive face reddened as the volume of my voice increased and filled the area we were standing in. People were starting to look. I saw Aunt Nina and Uncle Gary making their way towards me. They didn't look happy, but what they thought didn't matter because I was clear about my actions. My choice to scream my words like a wild coyote was notice that I was definitely making a scene.

"Get your damn hands off me. You. You. You wicked woman. You are the reason that my family was shattered. How could you be with my father and come to our house as a family friend? What kind of person are you?"

Devi tried to explain, "Karma, I'm sorry for what we did. Your father and I were only lovers for a short time. He always loved his wife and family, and never promised me any future. Please believe me that I didn't mean to hurt you all. Your father was a friend to me. And we fell into ..."

Sarcastically, I responded, "Save it. You both chose to hurt our family."

Ohnedaruth forcibly interjected, "*Mum*, go to the car *whilst* I handle this matter."

Devi walked away with her head bowed.

"This is a difficult situation. I am not going to sugarcoat the choices that our parents made. You have a right to be angry. I'm bloody angry too. I missed out on my father, mother, and sisters. *Mum* gave birth to me in London and sent me to live with my grandparents in Lahore, Pakistan. When my grandfather died, my grandmother and I moved to London to live with my aunt and uncle. I grew up thinking that my *mum* was my grandmother. During her funeral, I learned that my mother was *Mum*. That was ten years ago. By the time I came to America in 1998 to study at Ohio State, *Mum* and I had forged a bond. A year later, *whilst* I was visiting her during my winter break, she told me that my father died in 1999. That was the first time I learned about him. It was too late to get to know him. The only thing I could do was visit his grave site. *Mum* forbid me to make contact with the Francois family. Only recently has *Mum* been able to find the courage to connect with your mother so I could meet with you and your sister. So you see life has not been fair to any of us. But now we have a choice in what we do."

"Look, I'm really sorry about what happened to you, but I can't just forgive and forget."

"Karma, I am not *aksing* you to do that."

"Then what?"

"I am *aksing* you to choose acceptance. Accept what our parents did. Don't condone it. Don't pretend that it didn't hurt. Just accept that they were complex human beings who made some choices that hurt and impacted those they loved. If we accept their choice, we will begin to release our anger. Releasing our anger will bring us peace. With peace, we can begin our relationship as brother and sister. That's what I want."

"I don't know. You are asking a lot."

"Life is short, my dear sister. We have already lost our father. Let's not lose each other."

"I'll think about it."

"Can we meet and talk more about this tomorrow?"

Hesitating, I replied, "Yeah, I guess."

Smiling he responded, "I'll take whatever you're giving. Why don't you *ring* me on my cell phone and let me know when and where you would like to meet? My cell number is...."

For the first time, I paid attention to the tone of his British accent. I loved the way he pronounced certain words, especially *aks, whilst,* and *mum.* They sounded so delightful. Regal and charming in a way that I know Violet and Momma might come to adore. Maybe things could work out eventually. Maybe we could start from where we are and begin to bridge the gap.

Pulling out my calendar, I scribbled his number on the last page of November. We smiled at each other and said our goodbyes.

"*Abysinnia*"

Not understanding him, I inquired, "What?"

Chuckling to himself, he replied, "Sorry. Sometimes I forget that America is not the U.K. What a dreadful thing I've done confusing you with phrases that I use with me *bezzy mates* in England. I meant to say I'll see you later."

Hesitating, I responded, "Okay."

Touching his forehead with his right hand, he confidently belted out,

"Absobloodylutely."

Whatever we think our life is gonna be is often different from the plans that Spirit has designed. We hurt ourselves and others when we refuse to surrender to a higher plan that will give us hope and a future. While hugging my brother, I realized that the plan for the Francois family that Momma and Daddy created no longer applied. Ohnedaruth was Spirit's gift of hope, a representation of our family's future. The time had come to discard old hurts and worn out pain. As I walked towards Aunt Nina and Uncle Gary, I realized that my battle had just begun.

Aunt Nina politely asked, "Karma, what was all of that drama about?"

"Aunt Nina, can we talk about it in the car?"

"Yes, but."

Before she could finish her sentence, Uncle Gary whispered in her ear. Whatever he said, she agreed and changed the focus of our conversation.

"You look a bit tired. Let's get you home now. Your mother and sister may be waiting."

On the ride home, we all listened to Uncle Gary's Charles Mingus CD. He and Daddy had a history of arguing about who was the best jazz musician—Coltrane or Mingus. Uncle Gary loved Charles Mingus so much that he named one of his sons after him. We sparred a few rounds of Mingus vs. Coltrane before it ended when he tried to convince me that Mingus' *Fables of Faubus* was better than *A Love Supreme*. It was no contest for me. Coltrane. Coltrane. Coltrane. Our lively discussion distracted me momentarily from my struggle on how to tell Momma and Violet about meeting Ohnedaruth. Surprisingly, Aunt Nina and Uncle Gary never commented on the exchange I had with Devi and Ohnedaruth. I wondered if they knew what was going on. Maybe they knew the whole story. After all, Aunt Nina is Momma's best friend.

As Uncle Gary's black jaguar approached Lake Merritt, I entertained childhood memories. Beyond it being Oakland's crown jewel and America's largest urban saltwater lake, Lake Merritt was our family's special place. I can remember the picnics and Rotary Nature Center outings that Momma and Daddy took Violet and me on. The Center was magical for me. Its surrounding park boasts the nation's first wildlife refuge. Daddy and I always got a kick out of observing species of resident and migratory waterfowl at close range. Momma and Violet couldn't stand the place. They preferred the gardens.

When we pulled up in front of the house, Aunt Nina asked Uncle Gary to get my luggage from the trunk. Before I got out of the car, she cautioned, "Karma, whatever you do, don't share what happened at the airport with your mother. It would only upset her."

Aunt Nina knew our family secret. I wasn't surprised since she was like Momma's sister and my second mother.

"Aunt Nina, maybe it's time we all confronted the truth."

"Trust me when I tell you that your mother has confronted enough truths for a lifetime."

"Why? What other secrets are going to leak out? You can't expect me to act like none of this ever happened."

"I'm not asking you to do that. I am just advising you not to share what happened with your mother."

"So can I share it with my sister?"

"Violet will only tell your mother."

"That may be so, but they both need to know. That's the problem with the family. Nobody talks or tells the truth. I am not going to continue with this sickness."

"Look you're a grown woman with your own mind. Definitely Hyacinth's daughter. So I can't and won't try to tell you what to do. All I can say is that I warned you."

"Thanks for understanding."

"Honey, I hope you know what you're doing."

"Not totally, but I know what I'm not doing which is hiding the truth."

"Give your mother and sister our love."

"You're not coming in?"

"No your uncle and I have another appointment."

Aunt Nina's polite response was coded with the message that she wasn't about to witness one of the worse episodes of Francois female drama. I couldn't blame her.

For a few seconds, I stood on the front porch and said my own version of Reinhold Niebhur's Serenity Prayer.

"Creator help me refrain from creating and/or participating in any Francois female drama. Should the drama appear, grant me the peace of mind, strength, and willpower to successfully navigate it with compassion, understanding, and loving kindness. Bless me with the serenity to change things I can, accept those things I cannot change, and the wisdom to know the difference."

With the prayer said, I took one deep long breath, hoped for the best while expecting the worst as I opened the door. Solid bold black-and-white checkerboard floors greeted me when I walked through the front door of the Daffodil Villa. Beethoven's ballet, *The Creatures of Prometheus* was playing. It was a sign that Violet was home. She is the only Beethoven aficionado in the Francois clan. Momma is strictly a Bach woman. Daddy was a Vivaldi and Handel man. I never had a preference. They all sounded good to me. Coco, Violet's aging toy ivory poodle greeted me at the steps. Violet was three steps behind her. Standing in a pair of brown tweed cuffed slacks and a tan cashmere sweater, she called out my name.

"Welcome baby sister. Ramses will be down to help you with your bags. Momma should be home in a few minutes."

Ramses was just one more added bonus to the Francois female drama. His reformed thug presence and Violet's insistence on referring to me as her baby sister because she left Momma's womb first were two signs that the universe was certainly testing my patience. As Ramses came tumbling down the stairs dressed like Tupac's best friend, I recited my serenity prayer once again and hoped I could follow the Lord's plan.

"Creator help me refrain from creating and/or participating in any Francois female drama this weekend. Should the drama appear, grant me the peace of mind, strength, and willpower to successfully navigate it with compassion, understanding, and loving kindness. Bless me with the serenity to change things I can, accept those things I cannot change, and the wisdom to know the difference."

CHAPTER 15

▼

"For we cannot do anything against the truth, but only for the truth."

—2 Corinthians 13:8-9

I was determined to escape the regular pattern of Francois female drama. So I played the role of cordial daughter and sister who lives out of town until the next morning. This forced me to ignore Momma's soap opera performance at dinner. She worked overtime to make us all believe that she was happy about planning Violet's wedding to Ramses, an obvious social outcast in her socialite circles. Watching my sister acquiesce to Ramses' every bullied whim almost caused me to have cardiac arrest. Momma's silence at the way he crudely addressed and bossed Violet around was disturbing. I wondered how she could ignore blatant verbal abuse in her own home. It was hard to believe that Momma was cosigning Violet's nuptials when it was obvious that it was a train wreck waiting to happen. But maybe it was only obvious to me. Whether it was obvious or not really didn't matter to Momma. She was caught in the rapture of planning Oakland's buppie wedding of the year. She better be glad Daddy died. This wedding would never happen if he was alive. There's no way Eugene Francois would stand by and permit one of his daughter's to volunteer for a life of misery, let alone be disrespected publicly or privately. Somewhere in between the process of Ramses proposing to Violet and her acceptance, he would have intervened and forced a split. Violet always followed Momma's lead, but she was deathly afraid of Daddy. When he disapproved of something that was the end of it. No questions asked. But then again, keeping in mind the latest revelations of Daddy's transgressions, what right would he have to comment about respect for the woman he loved?

The next morning, I woke up feeling like a warrior preparing for Armageddon. Telling Momma and Violet about my airport encounter with Ohnedaruth and asking them to meet and accept him as a member of our family qualified as a potential Armageddon in my book. Given the last conversation that Momma and I had about Ohnedaruth, I knew my chances of avoiding casualties or blood shed, and gaining their peaceful acceptance of the truth were next to none. The odds were definitely stacked against me. I contemplated the notion of trying to break through Momma's high strung, domineering, take-no-prisoner personality and Violet's blanket acceptance of whatever Momma decreed to be law. I felt ridiculous. Despite the likelihood of their acceptance, I still felt called to tell them the truth. The one thing I have learned is that the truth always comes to light. It doesn't pay to hide or minimize it. It must be faced head on because we cannot do anything against the truth, but only for the truth.

There really isn't a proper way to broadcast my news. Unfortunately Miss Manners has yet to publish etiquette on the socially acceptable way to inform my drama-queen, southern belle, socialite mother and sister that I met my father's bastard son and would like us to accept him as a full member of the Francois family. So I was gonna have to wing it with a plan of my own. My plan was to look for an opening in our breakfast conversation, leap at it when it appeared, and bum rush the socialites with my news.

The emotional climate in our family has always been upbeat most mornings. This Tuesday morning followed suit. Momma and Violet were joyfully immersed in Thanksgiving dinner plans. I was distracted by the color of the kitchen. Pink nutmeg paint had replaced apple berry green. Stainless steel appliances, coriander-colored cabinets and bronzed oyster marble countertops invited a more detailed investigation. A painting that looked strangely familiar hung on the right side of the kitchen window. The connection kicked in. It was from *Grandmere's* house. The painting used to be in her rose-colored kitchen. The painter was Sister Gertrude Morgan, an African American folk artist who had a mission house in New Orleans that *Grandmere* used to support. When we used to visit *Grandmere*, I would try to imagine what was happening in all of the rooms painted in Morgan's *New Jerusalem Court, Gloryland St.*

After my cursory investigation, I decided not to question the changes. I didn't want to prolong my news. So I joined the conversation that Momma and Violet were having. They were planning to serve salmon tartare with a delicate cucumber salad and salmon caviar as an appetizer. The main event consisted of a pleasantly plump, juicy roasted turkey glazed with apple cider and stuffed with an ultra rich buttery mushroom and bread stuffing. Side orders would consist of brussel sprouts and butternut squash.

Unlike most traditional Thanksgiving dinners, the Francois family always added its own special twist. This year, we are serving an alternative to traditional cranberry sauce: spicy cherry-ginger chutney. To complete the feast, Momma prepared two autumnal desserts to tantalize her dinner guests' palates: a chocolate-bourbon-prune cake with caramelized pecans and whipped cream; and my all-time favorite, pears poached in citrus juice with a simple, country style home cake. To wash it all down, Momma planned to offer guests her favorite S. Pelligrino sparkling water, hot cherry apple cider, a lovely cherry-flavored Pinot Noir wine from Alsace called Domaine Meyer-Fonne, and Gevalia Kaffe's Expresso Roast coffee.

The feast itself would be served in the dining area. It was already been set up. That was standard practice in our home. Long ago, I learned that a holiday table should reflect the festive atmosphere of the season. Each holiday should have its own fresh, creative idea displayed in the table setting. Managing this task hasn't always been easy for Momma, but thanks to her ingenuity, her Thanksgiving table always looked extraordinary. Momma loves to dress her table with unusual table runners. She usually places several runners across the width of the table. When they are lined up with the dinner chairs, they also make great place mats. This year, Momma is using runners that she found in Chinatown. They're made out of royal blue silk shantung.

Momma's favorite Wedgewood Madeleine classic fine bone china five-piece place setting rendered in distinctive Wedgewood blue and palest cream for an intimate party of ten sat comfortably on the runners next to royal blue raw silk napkins. The intricacy of the acid-etched, 22karat gold, fleur de-lis borders in the china complimented the gold napkin rings. Waterford's Lismore Gold flatware was positioned in the usual manner: dinner forks to the direct left of the plates, making sure the napkins remained on the outside; dinner knives resting to the right of the plates, with the serrated edge facing inward; and soup spoons to the right of the knives. Dessert forks and spoons were put at the top of the plates, with the utensil handles at opposite ends. Momma used her Waterford Lismore Contemporary White Wine glasses and tumblers. The matching footed salt and pepper set was located near the centerpiece, a circular glass container that would later be filled with water and floating gold fleur-de-lis candles.

As they were winding down their conversation, I volunteered to run any last minute errands. It was my way of showing my support of what I envisioned might turn into a ghetto fabulous circus with Momma instructing her in-laws on table etiquette. I'm surprised she didn't have Violet do a training session with them already. When Momma finished dictating the list of errands, I reconfirmed it so she would know I was listening and paying full attention. This was a technique I learned from Daddy. It stroked Momma's ego in a way that made her receptive to what you might want to tell her.

"Okay, Momma, let me read this list back to you to make certain that I haven't missed anything."

"Bon cherie."

Whenever Momma responds in French, she's feeling especially wonderful. So I decided to respond back with a phrase or two. Sweetly, I smiled, *"D'accord ma mere jolie.*

With suspicion in her voice, she stared directly into my eyes. *"Cherie, tu parles francais.* Karma, you must want something."

Trying to fool her, I responded, "No Momma."

"Come on Karma, I was married to your father for more than thirty years. Speaking French to get his way with me was the oldest trick in his book of seduction. What is it that you want?"

"Well, I don't know how to say it."

"Cherie, it sounds serious. Are you okay? You're not ..."

Irritated, I answered, "No Momma, I'm not pregnant."

"I wasn't even thinking about that."

"Yesterday when I was at the airport, I ran into someone we all used to know."

Not having any patience, Violet chirped in, "Get to the point! Who was it? And what's the gossip you want to spread?"

"Violet, it's not gossip. Why are you always jumping in a conversation before you're invited to speak?"

"Karma, I don't have time for your gossip."

"I said it wasn't gossip."

"Girls, do I have to referee you both like you were in ninth grade?"

In unison, we responded, "No ma'am."

"*Cherie,* finish your story. Who did you see?"

"Devi Shankar and her son. Violet, I know you may not know it, but Devi's son is Daddy's son. He's our brother. His name is …"

Momma interrupted, "Not another word about those people."

Ignoring her, I continued, "His name is Ohnedaruth. He wants to meet us."

"Karma, I told you not to mention their names."

"Momma, I'm not going to play along with your games. We need to face the fact that Violet and I have a brother."

"This conversation is over."

"No it's not."

"It's over, Karma. Not another word."

"Violet, I have his phone number. He wants us to call him so we can all meet."

"Young lady, you will do no such thing."

"Are you threatening me?"

"Don't force me."

"Well, Momma, you need to know that I'm going to call my brother. And no matter what you say, I'm going to get to know him. He is family."

"Blasphemer."

"Spare me the drama."

"Belle Violette Francois, if you call that boy and meet him, don't worry about staying here for Thanksgiving."

Storming out of the kitchen, I yelled, "Then don't expect me for dinner."

Violet came trailing behind me, begging me to reconsider. "Karma, don't do it. Momma is all we have."

"Grow up Violet. We have a brother too."

"But she is our mother."

"And?"

"We shouldn't hurt her."

"Well, what about how she hurt you by not telling you about your own brother? Aren't you the least bit curious?"

"I'm sure she had a good reason."

"How stupid can you be? She just wants to control us. That's not going to work on me. I'm a grown woman with my own mind. And so are you. Momma has gotta get over herself."

"Karma, don't call him. Momma is serious about her threat."

"I don't care, Violet. I'm getting ready to make the call."

Turning in the opposite direction, Violet mumbled, "Then I'm not going to stand and watch you make the biggest mistake of your life."

"Violet, you're the one who is making a huge mistake."

As she turned the corner of the long hallway, I heard her whisper, "No you are."

There was no hope in winning them over. I knew that going in. So I walked back to my bedroom and opened my purse to find my cell phone and calendar book. Turning to the page that I scribbled Ohnedaruth's telephone number on, I looked at the ten digits before I dialed them. They were some of the most important numbers I would ever dial in my life. Without hesitating, my fingers started dialing. When Ohnedaruth picked up on the second ring and I heard him say, "Top of the morning," I knew I was making the right decision to act for the truth instead of against it.

CHAPTER 16

▼

"And God shall wipe away all tears from their eyes; and there shall be no more death, neither sorrow, nor crying, neither shall there be any more pain: for the former things are passed away."

—Revelation 21:4

Serendipity is a word with an etymological history I have adored since Daddy explained its origins to me in the second grade. It finds its roots in *Sarandi,* the Arabic name for the island of Sri Lanka. Horace Walpole, an 18th century Englishman, laid claim to it and renamed it Serendip so that it would fit neatly in the title of his Persian fairy tale, *The Three Princes of Serendip.*

Serendipity has always been the force that has caused me to make fortunate discoveries by accident. Accidents, I have learned, are miracles motivated by God's grace. They usher me into the next phase of living and often show up with guardian angels. Ohnedaruth became my guardian angel. He stepped in and demonstrated tremendous strength and compassion. How could a complete stranger manage to wipe away all my tears, inspire life from the ashes of death, and remind me that my sorrow, crying, pain, and the residue of things not working out as I had planned were now passing away? The only answer I have is God.

In a moment of uncertainty, I took a risk, responded with deep honesty, and a whimpering cry that set off a womb wrenching tear session that had me mumbling my words. Exhaustion from Francois female drama created layers of emotional incoherence. Ohnedaruth listened in a way that made me feel he would catch me if I ever found myself falling off another ledge of overwhelming emotion. His spirit calmed the raging storm that ransacked my soul. When he invited me to spend the day with him, I didn't hesitate. Unable to articulate the magnitude of what was happening between us, I intuitively trusted that we were on a journey that would help uncover our family's hidden wholeness.

It was now November 21. I had two days before I could use my ticket to return home. If I wasn't gonna be able to stay at Daffodil Villa, I needed to find another place, fast, quick and in a hurry. Aunt Nina? Nah. She's too close to Momma, but her son Mingus isn't. Yeah, Mingus would be the perfect person to crash with. He could put me up for three nights. Before I could pull out my phone book and dial Mingus' number, Momma tapped on the door, cracked it slightly, and slipped a white dish towel through it. As I watched her manipulate the white dishtowel, I couldn't help but interpret Momma's actions as an insincere cease-fire that would probably develop into more drama. "*Cherie*, can I come in?"

Sarcastically, I responded, "It's your house. Do what you want."

"*Cherie*, can't we put this matter behind us. In two days, we will be celebrating Thanksgiving. Our family needs to come together. We have so much to be thankful for. Your sister's upcoming wedding is just one example."

"And our brother."

I could hear the anger rising in Momma's tone as she tried to pick each word carefully. "Let's not bring that subject up anymore."

Unwilling to surrender or compromise, I pushed the edge of the envelope. "Ohnedaruth is not a subject. He is my brother. Your husband's son. Our family."

"Why must you insist on hurting me and your sister—our family?"

"That's funny that you would say I'm hurting you. What about you hurting Violet and I by denying us the opportunity to know our brother?"

"What's wrong with you?"

"Nothing Momma. I'm just not willing to pretend that Ohnedaruth will go away."

"Karma, you leave me no choice. You cannot stay here."

"Fine."

"Where do you think you'll be staying?"

"Frankly, Momma that's none of your business. Look, I'm not trying to hurt you or Violet. I just want us to get to know Ohnedaruth. He's family."

Waving her hands up in the air in what was a clear moment of frustration, Hyacinth Belle Baptiste Francois turned from me and walked out of my bedroom giving mad Betty Davis drama. The clickaddy-clack sound of her two inch feathery black silk bedroom shoes pounded out a familiar melody called Momma's pissed off and there ain't nothing you can do to change her mind. I wasn't trying. The drama and anger were her choices, not mine. I know Ohnedaruth being Daddy's son is a real stunner for her to accept, but enough is enough. My choice is my brother. And with that, I searched my phone book for Mingus' phone number.

"You've reached the voice mail of Mingus Overture. Presently, I'm unable to answer your call. Please leave me a detailed message and I'll get back to you. Make it a great day!"

"Hey Ming. Guess who this is? Your cousin Karma. I'm in town for a few days. I had a bad run in with my mother and need to crash a few days at your place. I'm headed back to D.C. on Friday morning. So I'll need a ride to the airport too. Talk it over with Ch'ampselysees. Call me back and let me know if you can host a sista."

Fifteen minutes later, my cell phone rang. It was Mingus calling to let me know I could stay with him. He had a few minutes to kill while he was waiting for his editor to give final clearance on his interview with D'Wayne Wiggins, a community activist and guitarist for the nationally known rhythm and blues group Tony! Toni! Tone!. The interview was a follow up to an article he wrote about Wiggins being brutally attacked by Oakland police and later filing a $1 million lawsuit against the Oakland Police Department last year. It was good to hear my cousin making ends meet from his passion. I think it's been two years since he landed the gig as a journalist for the A&E section of the San Francisco Bay Guardian. Sounds like he thoroughly enjoys working for the Guardian.

Ming living life on the straight and narrow wasn't always the case. Before he became a journalist, Ming had a series of odd jobs that included working as a landscaper, service station attendant, bike courier, receptionist, Kinko's customer service representative, cashier at Safeway, a fry turner at Mickey D's, and dog walker. They were all short-lived with low pay. This vagabond employment existence never quite fit his passion for the English language and the finer things in life. It was Ming's desire for the finer things in life that led him to a life of dealing drugs in the mid nineties when crack cocaine was king in Oakland. Nothing has really changed with the crack scene. It still reigns supreme with Ramses' family serving as the royal court, but that's another story for another time. Thankfully Ming is not in that story anymore.

Our conversation reminisced when he got into some trouble after he dropped out of UC Berkeley in his sophomore year. He thought he could live the *bling-bling* life by selling drugs with some of Ramses' *boyz*. That lasted all of about a minute until Uncle Gary put his foot up Mingus' ass and told him he would either live and work respectfully or die by his father's hand. Uncle Gary didn't play. He was old school. That never stopped Mingus from trying to push the envelope, but he dare not try that with his long-term girlfriend, Ch'ampsely-sees. They have been together since high school. She was always about academics and upward mobility. I hate to say it, but I think she probably pussy-whipped Ming into reformation.

I could hear the excitement in his voice when he reported that they were doing well, even thinking about marriage. Ming married? Who would have thought? The timing of the wedding was all on Ch'ampselysees since she was busy climbing the ladder of success at one of those techie firms in Silicon Valley. Not bad for a sista who used to live in the Acorns, a public housing project in West Oakland. Back in the day, a lot of folks questioned Ming for being with her since she appeared to be a hood rat, but that was only a temporary appearance. She obviously had bigger dreams. She has transformed herself into a Stanford graduate and corporate V.P. with a home that she shares with Ming in the highly desirable neighborhood of Crocker Highlands in Oakland Hills. It just goes to show you that you can't judge a book by its cover!

Ming put me on hold for a few seconds. When he clicked back to the call, he told me that his article had been approved, but needed some last minute changes. Not wanting to monopolize his time any longer, I asked for the address. Before ending the conversation, we agreed to meet at his house around seven thirty p.m. That's nine-thirty in Ming's world. He is seriously on *CP* time. After I hung up the phone I wondered whether I should have told Ming to keep quiet about my staying with him and Ch'ampselysees until Friday. Nah. It doesn't matter if he shares it with Aunt Nina and Uncle Gary. It's not like them knowing will change my decision or create any new drama. More than likely, they will stay out of it. And anyway this isn't my problem. It's Momma's. She's the one with drama. I'm the one escaping it. The only thing I need to do now is pack.

Packing was easy. I only had one overnight bag. And it was half packed. I put my pajamas and dirty clothes in a plastic bag before carefully tucking them in my bag. Uneasy quiet filled my room. I chose not to leave my room because another confrontation with Momma would only make matters worse. With nothing left to do, I stared out the window. Fifteen minutes later, I saw a silver Range Rover pull up in front of the house. My cell phone rang. It was Ohnedaruth. Gathering my purse and overnight bag, I walked down the hallway. Momma and Violet were still in the kitchen. They both looked at me with utter disdain as I announced that I was leaving and would not be returning. Neither one of them commented on my departure. They turned away and sat in silence. I kept on walking. My head was held high. I knew that I was right for doing what I had done. As I closed the door behind me, I didn't bother to look back. What good would it do? Why should I even care? They are hell bent on living their lives in a state of denial, absent of truth. If I did look back, I might wind up like Lot's wife. When she did, she was turned into a pillar of salt.

CHAPTER 17

▼

Awake, awake, put on your strength ... Shake yourself from the dust, arise.

—Isaiah 52:1-2.

Is it possible for reconciliation between the living and the dead through the intervention of my father's son? Can a day spent with my father's son transform him into my brother? I sound like a b-movie featuring the conflict of good vs. evil. Internal conflict has me wrestling with my own demons as I search for salvation. Bookmark that thought and consider this one. Perhaps the good in this conflict, the salvation that I have been seeking. is my brother. I am stuck in the middle with no real direction on how to resolve any of it. Perhaps the answers will reveal themselves in their own time. Perhaps they will not. Perhaps they will leave my father's son and I in purgatory with me never able to fully accept him as the brother he wants to become.

I walked with trepidation wondering what have I gotten myself into. Maybe I was making a mistake. Maybe Momma and Violet were right. Maybe I wasn't going to be able to handle this truth. The closer I got to the Range Rover, the more I felt like I was being force fed a tablespoon of castor oil. I knew it was the right thing to do, but I still hesitated in doing it. My fear of the aftertaste stopped me in my tracks. I almost turned back around and banged on Momma's door. My internal turbulence ceased when Ohnedaruth opened his door and walked around to greet me with a smile and kiss on my left cheek. His tender ways urged me to put on my strength, and shake off the dust so that I could fully embrace the richness of our sibling bond.

A man with a striking resemblance to Ma Rainey, the Mother of the Blues, was sitting in the passenger seat. When he opened his car door, he busily wrapped up a phone call on his cell. As he exited, I noticed his tall, lean frame and stylish clothes. He was wearing a black leather jacket, jeans, t-shirt, and a cap. The cap covered what appeared to be a shaved head. How I love molasses-colored men with shaved heads! Who was this mysterious man in black, I wondered as he jumped in the backseat.

As Ohnedaruth and I walked towards the car, he paused before opening the passenger door and explained the man's identity. "My partner, George and I were headed into San Francisco when you called. We were going to attend the final dress rehearsal of his new play at the Lorraine Hansberry Theatre. The rehearsal should last two hours. Afterwards, I thought you and I could have lunch at a Caribbean café that George recommended. Would you terribly mind coming along?"

"Not at all. I haven't been to the Hansberry Theatre in a few years. My parents were early patrons and used to take Violet and me all of the time. I'd love to see the rehearsal. It might take my mind off of things."

"Wonderful."

As I opened the door, Ohnedaruth introduced me. "George, I would like you to meet my sister Karma."

He answered in a baritone voice, "What a pleasure to make your acquaintance. I'm so happy that you are coming along with us today. You'll never know how special this is for O. Right baby?"

Ohnedaruth affectionately replied, "Absolutely, love."

The ride into San Francisco was filled with my questions about George's play entitled, *Ask The Troubadours Who Have Come From Those Who Have Loved.* The title was actually taken from a speech that Lorraine Hansberry made in the mid sixties to a group of young Black writers in Harlem. She told them that if they wanted to understand the meaning of love, they should talk to Black folks because they have consistently chosen to love their way through their struggle for liberation in America. That's why Lorraine proudly referred to Black folks as love's troubadours.

George designed his play using the choropoem style that Ntozake Shange created in her Obie award winning play, *for colored girls who have considered suicide/ when the rainbow is enuf.* His play included a series of sixteen monologues that blended poetry, prose, song, music, and dance into a story about Black people using the power of love to overcome despair, provide emotional and spiritual support, navigate the complexities of relationship, and celebrate life. He hoped that the play would help the audience understand that love can heal all things.

The play was centered on the tragic life of a Brooklyn-born African American artist with family roots in Haiti and Puerto Rico. He was a self-taught artist that started creating art through graffiti and later moved into larger images. Early in his career, the artist became a rising star in the art world, but had challenges managing his fame. He died at the age of twenty-eight of a heroin drug overdose. He left behind an HIV-positive wife and several children who were conceived within and outside of his marriage. His estranged parents and sisters were left to care for his wife and children. Parts of the story resembled aspects of the life of one of my favorite artists, Jean-Michel Basquiat.

Walking into the intimate 300-seat theatre on Sutter Street generated memories of family outings that I tried to block. My efforts were useless. The trip down memory lane continued. 1981 was the year. Momma and Aunt Nina were busy planning the reception for the theatre's grand opening in the Sheehan Hotel. They recruited their husbands and children as staff. In our house that meant Daddy, Violet, and I were at Momma's beckon call. In Aunt Nina's house that meant Uncle Gary, Seneca, Parker, and Mingus. Our role as staff was to do whatever they requested without any backtalk, attitudes or snide remarks.

Gazing at the theatre's modified, proscenium thrust stage made me appreciate the excellent view it gave the audience. Momma always made a big deal about this. I could hear her raving about the fabulous view she and Violet had when they attended the opening of Thulani Davis' play, *Everybody's Ruby* in March. Momma even mailed me a copy of the program detailing Davis' portrayal of Ruby McCollum, a Black woman charged with murdering her white doctor lover in Live Oak, Florida. She knew that the play would interest me because it included one of my favorite authors, Zora Neale Hurston, who happened to be covering Ruby's trial for a Pittsburgh newspaper. Why can't I divorce myself from Momma's voice and the way she intuitively knows what interests me? I hated to hear the answer to this question. Because she's my mother. That's why.

The play began with a dance company performing an Alvin Ailey-like piece. It reminded me of *Revelations.* Donny Hathaway's impressionistic composition, *I Love the Lord; He Heard My Cry (Parts I and II)* played softly in the background. When they were finished, a male actor joined them on stage. He recited the signature poem. Additional selections from Hathaway's final solo album, *Extension of A Man* were seamlessly woven between monologues. The Puerto Rican mother of the deceased artist performed a compelling spoken word piece. Her voice and body language accurately imitated the women I used to see on my way to work at El Museo del Barrio in East Harlem. Elementary school-aged tap dancers resembling Savion Glover and Marc Bamuthi Joseph, blended intense sets of ricocheting rhythms and unfurled movement to compliment the gut wrenching pain pouring out of her heart as she created her own version of the Book of Lamentations. It was a mother's mourning song and a grandmother's testimony of not knowing what to do to prevent her grandchildren from dying before she had a chance to raise them. I wondered how mothers ever made a way out of no way. Love was the only answer.

The entire cast performed the closing monologue. As they recited the last line of the signature poem that George and his mother had written together, Hathaway's classic standard, *Someday We'll All Be Free* began to play. I silently read the words of the poem printed in the program.

Ask The Troubadours Who Have Come From Those Who Have Loved by George and Margaret Lancaster

Paint me a picture of those who managed to shine a glimmer of hope from their weary eyes as they crawled out of slavery's despair with fragmented or nonexistent memories of a cultural richness and legacy that was so far from their grasp in a land that was not their own

Tell me a story of those who had little to nothing, planted it with faith the size of a mustard seed, tended to it with the utmost care, and waited patiently for what they couldn't even begin to imagine or foresee

Sing me a song of those who loved when loving was an impossible reality
Rejoice with me as we watch Creator proclaim that these beloved ones are
Love's Troubadours

Love's Troubadours
Who should have perished in the midst of their Middle Passage hell, but instead made a choice and lived to overcome their fiery trials, emerging from the ashes unscathed like the children of the flame, Shadrach, Meshack, and Abednego

Love's Troubadours
Whose human spirits should have cracked under the weight of legislated Jim Crow, but instead drank from the well of faith constructed by their ancestors for the purpose of restoring their souls

Love's Troubadours
They are the ones that came before us
The ones who left us a legacy of faith, courage, commitment and service born out of love

Love's Troubadours
They are ones who stood in the gap and continue to stand in the gap as our praying, persistent and powerful ancestors

Love's Troubadours
They live in us and their presence has allowed us to become the ones who continue their legacy of faith, courage, commitment and service

Together, we are Love's Troubadours, bound in the beauty and strength of our oneness
As a collective, we intuitively know that each one of us represents a thread in a multicolored tapestry fashioned and made in the likeness of our Creator who strategically spread us across the Diaspora as Africa's daughters and sons

This holy tapestry is our sanctuary
It covers us as a bright and bold quilt, reminding us of our connection, divinity, and power to express and share love as a means of healing all things

Let the Church of Love's Troubadours say,

Amen

Love's Troubadours. Am I one? What about my family? Can love really heal all things between us? Can it make everything right?

After the rehearsal was over, Ohnedaruth excused himself for a few minutes to talk to George. Left with my own thoughts, I fought back tears that aggressively formed in the corners of my eyes. By the time Ohnedaruth returned, my cheeks were sprinkled with wetness. I didn't have the energy to hide my facial expression.

"Why the melancholy face?"

"George's performance got me thinking. That's all."

Touching my cheek and noticing evidence of dampness, Ohnedaruth gently prodded, "Looks like you were doing more than thinking."

Trying to put a pin in what I feared was another emotionally draining conversation, I offered my best joking face. "I'm a sucker for stories about tragedy, tribulations, and triumphs."

"Is that so?"

"Yeah."

"I could be wrong, but it feels like the play may have touched a raw nerve. If you want to talk, I'm here for you."

Sarcasm inserted herself. "So you're a therapist now?"

"Not at all. I'm a brother trying to console his sister."

His comment paralyzed my ability to respond. "Honestly, Karma. I'm not trying to invade your privacy. I just want to help you. That's all. I don't have an ulterior motive. If I have any motive at all, it's to build a relationship with you."

My inner critic chastised me. I guess he put you in your place. What you gonna do now? Pulling myself together, I offered Ohnedaruth an apology. "Please accept my apology. I do appreciate what you're trying to do. Everything is just so overwhelming. I know that's not a reason for me to act out, but it's just been really hard for me."

"I know. And you don't have to apologize. Just know that I'm here for you."

"I'll try to remember that."

Changing the subject, Ohnedaruth suggested, "If you're anything like me, I know you must be hungry. Fancy a spicy Caribbean meal?"

Half-smiling, I answered, "Sounds like a great idea."

Bold shades of vibrant pinks and blues decorated the storefront café on Pine Street. A large copper plaque embedded with cowrie shells was placed next to the entrance. The name Erzulie was engraved in curly script. A heart pierced with a dagger made out of thickly coiled copper wire sat below the plaque. When I saw it, I blurted out, "That's the same symbol as my tattoo."

Ohnedaruth kidded, "So my sister is into exotic body art. Is this a family tradition I need to know about it?"

"It's not exotic body art. I only have one tattoo. Violet and two of my cousins have them too."

"Where is your tattoo?"

"In a secret place."

"Oh I see. A lady never discusses her age, weight, or the location of her tattoo."

We both burst into laughter.

"Now you get it."

"Seriously, Karma. Does your tattoo have the same dagger piercing through the heart?"

"Yeah."

"What does the dagger mean?"

"I'm not exactly sure, but the heart represents Erzulie, the Haitian Voodoo goddess of love."

"I'm not an expert on Haitian Voodoo, but I think the piercing dagger represents the human experience of suffering when we accept fear as our reality and separate ourselves from love. It reminds me that we often cause our own suffering by the choices we make. We either choose love or fear. The piercing dagger is what happens when we choose fear."

"Very insightful. You sure you aren't a Voodoo expert?"

"Absolutely not."

The café décor was simple. Teak-colored whicker chairs and tables dominated the small intimate space. We sat at a table that faced a rosie pink wall with a framed oil painting of a roasted buckwheat-colored woman immersed in a waterfall. Her hands were held up over her head as if she was praising a higher being. Cascades of curly black ringlets gently touched her shoulders. Her white outfit was falling from her body. A red scarf was loosely tied around her neck. Crowds of half-naked coffee bean-colored people surrounded her. They were bathing in the water and letting their clothes float down the waterfall. The caption of the picture read: *Saut d'Eau Pilgrimage—Le 16 Juillet. Phillipe Bonheur.* An artist statement was contained below. The painting illustrated the annual pilgrimage that Haitians make to honor the anniversary of the day in 1884 when the Virgin Mary miraculously appeared in the foliage near the *Saut d'Eau* waterfall. Momma's celebrations of the various holy days dedicated to the Virgin Mary and Erzulie, and *Grandmere's* annual pilgrimage to Marie Laveau's grave in New Orleans came to mind.

The adjacent wall contained five unframed medium-size oil paintings on cheese cloth. They were hung horizontally. The first featured a maple syrup colored woman with an Afro. Her cheeks bore tribal marks. Her hands wielded sharp knives. The title was *Erzulie Dantor, Spirit of Motherly Love.*

An elegantly dressed woman with wheat-colored skin and a thick mane of black hair that fell to her breasts was depicted in the second painting. Her red painted lips contained a smile that appeared to be deceiving. A gold necklace tightly wrapped itself around her neck like a cobra. It complimented the pink and blue floral dress she wore. Her hands rested in her lap. Three gold bands sat comfortably on her wedding finger. I spotted what looked like tiny floating images of candles, flowers, mirrors, white doves, fans, perfume bottles, and champagne painted in a surrealistic style in the upper corners of the painting. The title, *Erzulie Freda, Goddess of love, art, sex, beauty, jewelry, dancing, luxury, and flowers*, perfectly described the artwork.

A toffee-colored mermaid named *La Sirene* with ear-length auburn locs appeared in the third painting. Her facial expression was sensually taunting. She wore a necklace of cowrie shells that decorated her naked breasts.

An elderly grief stricken woman with liver-colored skin was the subject of the fourth painting called *La Grande Erzulie.* Her gray hair was randomly streaked with the wisdom of white as it sat on the back of her head styled in a bun. She sat in a rocking chair in drab, tethered clothing.

A woman suffering similar pain with a youthful dapple brown-colored face shyly looked up as she sat with her knees drawn into her chest and fists clenched in the fifth painting. Coils of tussled straight black hair covered her head. Her name was *Erzulie Ge-Rouge.*

Each painting had a familiar presence. I searched my memory for a connection. *Grandmere's* attic. Right after *Grandmere's* funeral, Momma showed Violet and I similar images that sat on *Grandmere's* altar. She brought them back to our house in Oakland. Momma tried to teach the rituals that her mother had taught her to practice in honor of Erzulie and the Virgin Mary, but we were preoccupied with our lives. This was just another example of how Momma follows me wherever I go. Maybe she put a curse on me.

Caught up in my own thoughts, I failed to notice the presence of a short middle-aged expresso-colored woman wearing a red and blue high-slit linen caftan with embroidered bell sleeves. She handed Ohnedaruth two menus as she joyfully introduced herself. *"Bienvenue mes amis.* I'm Madame Freda, owner of Erzulie, the finest Caribbean café in the Bay area. Our food will make you dream of love. Is that the reason you have come to my café?"

Ohnedaruth remarked, "Our stomachs are dreaming of food. So if your food is love, then we've come to the right place."

"Mais oui. Bien. You came to the right place. Take a few minutes to read the menu."

She turned and walked away with a sassy sway in her womanly hips.

"She's quite a character."

Glancing at the menu, I joked, "Yes she is. I wonder what I will dream of when I eat fried plantains."

In unison, we both answered, "Love!"

"Do you want anything else?" Ohnedaruth asked.

"The dried mushrooms and rice. And you?"

"I'm going to order the crab and eggplant entrée."

"What about a beverage?"

"Ginger beer."

"I am going to get the same."

"Copy cat"

Madame Freda reappeared and took our order. While we were waiting for our food to arrive, I decided to use the time to better acquaint myself with Ohnedaruth. I started with his relationship with George. "George is quite a talented playwright. Is this his first play?"

"By no means. It's actually the fourth in a series about Black family life. Before that, he wrote and directed two plays that examined Black gay life during the Harlem Renaissance, and World War II in Dayton, Ohio."

"Compelling stories, I'm sure. What were his family plays about?"

"They were autobiographical with fascinating titles. *Red Dirt to the Acorns* was his first play. It told the story of how he grew up in Taylor, Arkansas, and the struggles his family encountered after they moved to Oakland, and began living with his grandmother in public housing."

"Have you seen it performed?"

"Only on videotape."

"That's great that he tapes them. Does he sell them also?"

"Indeed he does. George is a quite an entrepreneur. The tapes are sold over the Internet from his company web site."

"What's the web site?"

"www.reddirtproductions.com."

"What does the red dirt represent?"

"Arkansas."

"What was the second play about?"

"That was probably my favorite. It is entitled, *Black Dharma*. The play chronicles George's journey of self-acceptance as a gay Black Buddhist man."

"Spirituality. Race. Sexual Orientation. He seems to cover a wide range of topics in his plays."

"Add the music of blues to the list. His third play, *Blueswoman on 7ᵗʰ Street*, discussed the life of his maternal grandmother who moved from Houston, Texas, to Oakland during World War II, and how the music of blues legends Bessie Smith, Alberta Hunter, Victoria Spivey, and Edith Wilson, helped to shape her life."

"The way you discuss George's portfolio of creative expression lets me know that you are an expert on his work. You really should be George's publicist."

"I already am, but I don't get paid with money. It's all love."

"Speaking of love, how did it happen between you and George?"

"Do you want the long or short version?"

"Whichever one doesn't skip any details."

"Two years ago, when I came to visit *Mum* before starting my studies at Ohio State University, I met George in one of her yoga classes. He volunteered to show me the Bay area. On one of our Sunday outings, we were walking around Union Square when I realized my strong attraction to him, but I hesitated in expressing it. My fears were rooted in my hidden identity as a gay man. I was amazed at how free George was living openly as a gay man. I wanted that same freedom. I know his courage and confidence to live authentically were some of the reasons that I felt attracted to him. They still are. Before George dropped me off at *Mum*'s that evening, he reached over to kiss me. I jerked back and then moved closer to kiss him. That kiss was the beginning of me coming out. During that summer, George encouraged me to come out to *Mum*. With his assistance and support, I succeeded."

"That George is a very special man."

"Yes he is."

"How did your mother accept the news of you coming out?"

"Honestly, she was great. *Mum* was the only member of my family to embrace me. The rest of the family in the U.K. either openly disowned me or backed away. That part has been a bit troubling, but I have *Mum,* George, and now you."

"Enduring your family's rejection must have been hard."

"It was a blessing in disguise because it actually brought *Mum* and I closer together. She admitted that she had her suspicions when she visited the U.K. for my graduation from the university. That's the reason why she insisted that I come to the states for my graduate studies. *Mum* was trying to protect me from an arranged marriage."

"Thank goodness for your mother."

"Yes, I am grateful for *Mum*. She really has a good heart, Karma. She didn't mean to hurt you and your family."

Responding with a tinge of anger in my voice, I replied, "But that's what happened."

Before our conversation could go any further, Madame Freda appeared with our food. We ate in silence. Some of it was due to the delicious food that tickled our palates. And the rest of it, at least for me, was the anger I was still holding against Devi and Daddy. After we finished our meal, Ohnedaruth suggested that we take a walk. I hoped it would help me release my anger. As we approached Union Square, the anger started to leave. Maybe the love in Madame Freda's food worked because I found myself happily giving Ohnedaruth my own personal tour.

Being the daughter of a history and architecture buff, I couldn't resist sharing Daddy's passion for San Francisco. I pointed out how much Daddy marveled at Jasper O'Farrell's design of Union Square as a public plaza. I took pride in showing Ohnedaruth the towering ninety-seven foot Corinthian column with a bronze figure of Victory that survived the 1906 earthquake. He delighted in my trivia. We walked down Maiden Lane. The echo of Momma's voice expressing excitement about the boutiques and art galleries on her favorite street haunted me. Her voice disappeared as our footsteps met Stockton Street. What a hold on my subconscious she has. She definitely put a curse on me for life. Definitely.

While we sat drinking tea and coffee, and eating cookies in the Starbucks at Stockton and Sutter Streets, my thoughts shifted to my growing curiosity about Ohnedaruth's journey in coming out. A tall soy espresso macchiato and chocolate chip cookie sat on Ohnedaruth's side of the table. They faced my venti soy chai latte and oatmeal cookie. Our bodies tattooed the bottoms of two large comfortable burgundy chairs. As we relaxed into the moment, I launched a litany of questions that I hoped might help me better understand Branford.

"Do you mind me asking when you first discovered that you were gay?"

"Not at all. I always knew that I was different from my male cousins. One telltale sign was the way my uncle treated me like a burden he had to endure for the sake of his family. I never felt like I belonged. When Mum confided in me that I was her son in my late teens I was able to make sense of some of my uncle's cruel treatment. You know I could see why he might feel burdened for having to financially support his sister's illegitimate child."

"When did you realize that you were attracted to boys?"

"I was twelve. My schoolmates and I were horsing around after a football match. We were getting pretty physical. I found myself aroused by all of the close contact and touching. One of my mates, Andy, a Protestant blue-blood chap, seemed to enjoy touching me. Weeks later we started meeting at his parents' flat when they weren't home. It started with innocent petting and gradually led to sex. We were together until we went to university."

"So how did you manage life during college?"

"That part of my life was challenging because my older cousins were around and always trying to set me up on dates with Hindu Indian and Pakistani girls. I went along for the ride."

"Did you ever consider marrying one?"

"The closest I got was in my last year. My uncle issued a mandate that I select a Hindu girl from a respectful family to marry after graduation. Feeling like I had no way out, I got desperate and found a web site that helps gay and lesbian Hindus avoid family humiliation and explore the possibility of a marriage of convenience."

"Damn. The Internet has everything. So did you post an ad?"

"Indeed I did."

"Did you get any hits on your ad?"

"Several lesbian and bi-sexual women answered my ad. I met four women and was able to establish a rapport with one young woman."

"What happened?"

"We talked by phone and met a few times, but I couldn't stomach the possibility of living a lie for the rest of my life. So I ceased all communication with her."

"What did your uncle say?"

"Naturally he was furious that I was without a suitable fiancé, but luckily *Mum* arrived for my graduation and insisted that I come to the states. Her actions thwarted my uncle's attempts to arrange a marriage."

"You've had quite a journey."

"Haven't we all?"

"I guess so."

"Karma, you seem to be very interested in my coming out story. I'd like to think it was because I'm your brother and you are interested in getting to know me better, but I sense that there's something else provoking your interest."

"I'm interested in getting to know you, but I also wanted to get your perspective on living life as a gay man because of a situation I am currently dealing with."

"I might be able to help you more if you described your situation. That's only if you feel comfortable"

"I need all of the help I can get on this one. Here's the deal. Earlier this year, I discovered that I was falling in love with my best friend, Branford. We've known each other since undergrad. He was married for ten years. Branford's wife divorced him when she discovered his relationship with his male lover."

"Prickly situation. Is Branford living openly as a gay man now?"

"That's the confusing part. He claims that he is bisexual and has preferred male partners in the past few years."

"How is that confusing?"

"I haven't seen him with a woman since he was married. So he must be gay."

"Not necessarily so. Just because he has chosen male lovers doesn't mean that he identifies with being gay. You did say that he considers himself bisexual right?"

"That's what he claims."

"It sounds like you don't accept Branford as he is. Do you have a problem with his sexual orientation?"

"Not really. I just think it is a barrier for me in expressing my feelings."

"How is it a barrier?"

"He prefers men."

"And women."

"That's what bothers me."

"Karma, it sounds like you have a problem with Branford's bisexuality."

Getting angry, I emphasized my point, "No, I don't have a problem. I just know that it's the reason that I wouldn't pursue a relationship with him."

"Okay, so let's say Branford was a straight guy. Would you be able to tell him how you feel?"

"It would be hard, but I think I could do it because there might be a possibility of us having a relationship."

"Is that because he is straight?"

"Of course. I wouldn't have to worry."

"Worry about what?"

"Him being attracted to men and pursuing the attraction behind my back."

"If he was committed and decided to have an exclusive relationship with you, would you worry about him cheating on you? Couldn't a straight man do the same thing with another woman?"

"Yeah, but what's your point?"

"My point is that you have assumed that Branford could never make a full commitment and be faithful to you because he is bisexual."

"I haven't assumed anything. It's just my personal preference to be involved with straight men."

"I can accept your preference, but what would you do if Branford returned your feelings and wanted to pursue a committed relationship with you?"

"Nothing could come of it."

"You would throw away a chance to love and be loved just like that?"

"I don't see it as a chance at love. It's more like a recipe for disaster."

"Based on everything that you have shared with me, why are you even friends with a man that you obviously don't accept?"

"Wait a minute. You are twisting my words. I accept Branford as a friend ... as a man who is attracted to both men and women. I just can't see myself in a committed relationship with him because of his lifestyle."

"I'm sorry Karma it still sounds like you don't accept him."

"This is getting us nowhere. The bottom line is that it all just makes me so mad."

"Mad that he is choosing to live life the way he wants to?"

"No no no ... you keep getting it all wrong. I want him to live freely, but I can't help the way I feel. That's the source of my struggle."

"Have you ever discussed the possibility of a relationship with him?"

"What for? It wouldn't change anything. I could never have the kind of commitment that I want with Branford. Telling him would be a huge mistake. I'm already humiliated by the way I feel. It would further humiliate me."

"I can certainly sympathize with your fear, but it might help to get the issue out in the open. You never know what can happen once you put all of your cards on the table."

"I don't think I can do that."

"So what have you been doing to cope with this matter?"

"I avoid him."

"That cannot help the friendship."

"I don't know what else to do."

"You probably don't want to hear me say this again, but talking is a solution. If you value the friendship, then try talking to Branford about your feelings. What is the worse thing that can happen?"

"I could further humiliate myself and cause him to back away from my friendship."

"I really don't think you are giving Branford enough credit. Given your years of friendship, I think there is a strong likelihood that he would sincerely listen to you.

"I don't want to take a risk like that."

"That's a shame because I think you at least owe it to the friendship to be honest. You aren't giving Branford an opportunity to respond."

"I just can't do it. I feel like I don't have any choices."

"Karma, you most certainly have a choice."

His statement ended our conversation. Ohnedaruth rose from his seat and headed to the men's bathroom. What he shared rang true in my heart, but the thought of actually making it happen was overwhelming.

We picked George up at the theatre and enjoyed an evening dinner of sushi takeout at his bungalow in Oakland. When we pulled in front of the house, I immediately recognized the architectural style. It was one of Daddy's favorites. George confirmed that it was a bungalow designed by Sidney Newsom, a partner in Newsom and Newsom, one of Northern California's famous architectural firms. They were responsible for designing livable homes with whimsical, quasi-historical detailing, large rooms, broad hallways and staircases, French doors, and door-sized casement windows flooding light into the entire space.

George took a minimalist approach in his Mission style home décor. The walls were painted in earth tones: sage, sienna, and burnt orange. The colors added a richness to the walnut hardwood floors. Black and white Ansel Adams-like photos decorated the walls.

Our dinner conversation revealed six degrees of separation between George and me. His mother had been romantically involved with Bishop, Ramses' father. Bishop was the reason George's mother was in prison. In the early nineties, she was caught with a large possession of crack. She refused to cooperate with the federal investigation that was trying to shut down Bishop's stronghold on the crack cocaine business in Oakland. Her failure to cooperate cost her a lengthy prison sentence that she continues to serve out. When I disclosed that Violet was engaged to Ramses, I expected him to curse the Arquette family name. Lord knows I would have, but instead he expressed his gratitude for what happened because it gave him an opportunity to establish a healthy relationship with his mother. Once again, I was reminded of how tragedy offers us opportunities to harmonize our relationships with our parents. Unfortunately, I still didn't know how to make it happen with Momma. I wasn't even sure if I wanted to.

After dinner, we watched *Earth*, a film by Deepa Mehta, which explored the lives of a small community of Hindu, Muslim, and Sikh friends during the harsh times of Indian independence in Lahore, India, in 1947. Watching the film made me wonder about the challenges Ohnedaruth faced as a child when he spent summers with his grandparents in Muslim-dominated Lahore.

When the film credits were rolling, my cell phone rang. It was Ming calling to find out when I would arrive. I glanced down at my watch and realized that it was ten forty-five. I was seriously on colored people time. So we wouldn't get lost, George drove me to Ming's house. On the ride over, they invited me to spend Thanksgiving dinner with them. I declined because I wasn't ready to face Devi. My anger might get the best of me.

Before I knew it, we were pulling up in front of Ming's house. Trying to be polite, I invited George and Ohnedaruth in to meet Ming and Ch'ampselysees. They declined due to the late hour and asked for a rain check. Secretly, I was happy to avoid introductions. I didn't want to have to endure any more questions tonight. Ohnedaruth's presence would have easily provoked an all nighter with Ming.

In a voice as smooth as butterscotch, Ch'ampselysees greeted me at the door wearing a lime green and fire engine red polka dotted bandana and coordinated workout ensemble. I felt like I needed a pair of dark shades to be received by her.

The bandana was covering what appeared to be shoulder length brunette straightened hair. A pair of Manolo Blahnik shoes were dangling in her hands. She and Momma have the same shoe tastes!

"Come on in. Girl, it's been a minute since we last saw you."

"Thanks for hosting me."

"No need to thank me. You're family. Always have been. Always will be. We're happy to have you."

"It's good to be wanted."

"So are you hungry?

"No, I ate already."

"Can I get you some tea, juice or water?"

"Tea would be fine."

"We have chamomile, peppermint, earl grey, and lemongrass."

"Lemongrass sounds good."

Music was playing in the background. It sounded like a Miles Davis' cut, but I couldn't identify the exact title. He was never one of my favorites especially after I read Pearl Cleage's book, *Mad About Miles,* in which she discussed how he violently abused Cicely Tyson.

"So where's Ming?"

"Girl, he's in his cave or let me rephrase his shrine dedicated to Miles Davis. That's his music playing so loud. He can't even hear the doorbell when it rings."

Ch'ampselysees walked around the corner and knocked on the door while yelling, "Mingus, come on out. Karma is here."

Minutes later, they entered the champagne-colored foyer together where I sat comfortably waiting on a rot iron bench. Ming was sportin' a head full of sandy brown baby two-stranded twists. His full beard shaped his pumpkin pie-colored face.

"Look what the eastern winds blew into Oaktown."

"Yeah, look what it brought back to you, Ming."

"That's Mr. Mingus to you."

"Stop frontin' Negro."

"Get over here and give me a hug, girl."

As we hugged, Ming asked, "So what's the word?"

"Family drama, but we can talk about that later."

"I wanna hear all about it."

"So is that Miles Davis playing so loudly?"

"You got it."

Turning to Ch'ampselysees he smiled and confidently said, "Baby, I think I have a fellow Miles fan on my hands."

Rolling her eyes, she responded, "Damn not two of you."

Happy to bust Ming's bubble, I gladly exclaimed, "Actually he's the only fan."

"Karma, I'm shocked. You grew up on a steady diet of Coltrane and Miles. What happened?"

"Miles just lived his life too confusing for me. I have a hard time understanding how he can beat women up. He's a demonic Black male genius."

"Hold up there. Those are pretty strong words you are using bout' my man. What does that mean?"

"It means that I don't support the music of men who commit violence against women."

Ch'ampselysees added, "Preach sista, preach!" .

"Awright. I'm familiar with it, but you gotta give him mad dap for his genius. I can separate the man from the music."

"Typical man answer."

"Why you gotta go there? You sound like Ch'amps."

Ch'ampselysees and I high-fived each other.

"Oh so now I'm outnumbered."

Ch'ampselysees quipped, "You damn skippy. Karma speaks the truth. So go on back in your Miles Davis shrine and turn that stuff down."

"Woman, what did I tell you about calling Miles' music stuff?"

Playfully gritting her teeth, Ch'ampselysees cautioned, "Just cuz' we have company, don't mean you should get cute, Mingus. You might miss something you really need."

Ming muttered, "It ain't no shrine."

In an effort to pacify him, I asked, "Did you say shrine? I gotta see this for myself."

"For the last time, it's not a shrine. It's a home office decorated with Miles memorabilia."

Teasing, Ch'ampselysees interjected, "Don't believe him. It's a shrine. Jeanette, our interior designer, gave him that fancy phrase to describe his shrine."

Excited, I replied, "Wow. She decorated your house!"

"Mingus' mother turned us onto her when we moved in. She was the only person who helped us blend our personal styles. I love her PsHome showroom. Have you ever been?"

"No I haven't."

"If you want to, we'll have to make sure you get to see the store while you are here."

"That would be great."

Looking like a neglected child, Ming stood with his hands crossed against his chest. "So you wanna see my office or not?"

"That's my cue to leave you two alone to catch up. Karma, I'll bring your tea right down."

As I walked into Ming's kangaroo red office, I noticed a large color photo print of Miles Davis and a woman with an Afro. The woman's hand caressed Miles' face as she blissfully gazed at him. Miles stared straight ahead with his bulging eyes and serious demeanor. The woman bore a striking resemblance to Ch'ampselysees. Black and white photos of Miles were sporadically placed on different walls. Right above Ming's computer was a series of framed LP album covers of the woman with the Afro. I read the three album titles: *Betty Davis, They Say I'm Different,* and *Nasty Girl.* A CD case with a picture featuring the same woman lay on Ming's antique oak desk. Picking up the CD, I asked, "So is this what's playing?"

"Sure is. It's *Filles de Kilimanjaro,* a Miles 1968 classic. The track that we are listening to now is called *Mademoiselle Mabry.* He composed it in honor of his wife, Betty, a flamboyantly, wild funky diva and former model. When she married Miles, he was twice her age. Although their marriage only lasted a year, Betty influenced his music tremendously by introducing him to Jimi Hendrix, Sly Stone, and psychedelic rock. She helped him give birth to the jazz fusion that first appeared on his 1970 classic *Bitches Brew* CD."

"You sound like a Miles historian. Is Betty plastered all over your wall?"

"Uh huh. I love me some Betty."

"No kidding. You even have your own Betty living with you."

"She and Ch'amps do favor each other in many ways."

"Besides physical features, what do you mean?"

"Well, they both have this crazy sensual energy that moves me. It's just the right mix of home girl and nasty woman for me. Betty's music is all about a wild woman with a Jimi Hendrix rock, gut-bucket blues, soulful funk vibe. I think she was definitely ahead of her time. Her music was about the things that make love an addiction. I remember reading that some of her lyrics were considered too sexual for the radio in the seventies. A good number of her performances were even cancelled. I can't imagine that happening today. I think folks would totally embrace her raw sexual energy as she screams, growls, and roars her lyrics. You gotta give it up to a woman who flaunts her sexuality, speaks her mind, and does her thing. Ch'amps is my wild woman roaring, flaunting all of herself … the mental, physical, emotional, and spiritual. She stops me in my tracks damn near every day."

Ch'ampselysees' presence paused our conversation as she entered the room with my tea. "Were you talking about me?"

"Sure was. I was telling Karma about your Betty Davis flava and why I love the Betty in you."

"Karma, this man has it bad for Betty. He even made me dress up like her one Halloween and on some other occasions."

"Why you tellin' my bizness? You make me sound like some kinda freak."

"Cuz you are, but you're my freak."

"That's what I like to hear."

Kissing Ming on the cheek, Ch'ampselysees reminded him, "Baby, don't forget to put Karma in my room. I changed the linen and have laid out her towel and wash cloth."

Fondling her buttocks, he smiled and pecked her on the lips, "Will do, sugar."

I commented, "Now y'all are something."

"That woman is the only one who can keep my attention."

"Looks like y'all are still the same. Fire and Fire."

"That's what happens when a peanut butter-colored Aries woman and I come together."

"Oh is that what it is?"

"Fire passion, love, and God. That what keeps us together."

"Then it is a good thing that she has you hooked."

"Enuf about me. Let's get back to you. What's really goin' on with you and your moms?"

"Same ole' story with a twist. She wants to control my life and I ain't having it."

"What's the twist?"

"Daddy's affair with Devi Shankar and their son."

"I kinda figured."

"Who told you?"

"My moms, of course."

"News travels fast."

"So what's with this brother?"

"We actually spent the day together."

"That sounds like a start."

"Ma said he was named after Coltrane. What's his name?"

"Ohnedaruth. It's a Hindu Sanskrit name that Coltrane adopted."

"Your pops was always a pretty progressive brotha. He took that jazz thing seriously just like my pops. So what was it like talking to your brother?"

"A little weird. He looks like Daddy. He's a deep guy. And his heart seems to be filled with genuine concern. He has a very tender soul. I feel good about most of the things we shared, but a lot still weighs on my conscience."

"Like what?"

"The way Momma is trying to stop me from getting to know him."

"Come on Karma. Be real. How did you think she was gonna act?"

"I was hoping that she would be open to getting to know him, but that was a mistake. She is too damn controlling. She has always been that way. It is her way or the highway."

"Karma, we both know that your moms and my pops are cut from the same cloth. Hell, they could be identical twins when it comes to their style of parenting. They are both control freaks. One thing that I had to learn the hard way is to accept my pops as he is. Gary Alvin Overture is a hardworking man with some buried insecurities that can wreak havoc on those closest to him. Over the years, Ma has assured me that he has gotten better with her constant prodding, but remnants of his old self emerge from time to time. Pops has an old school attitude about most things when it comes to Parker, Seneca, and me. Ma says he got that from his moms."

"So how did you get to the point of acceptance?"

"I can't take any credit for that. My acceptance started with Ma, Ch'amps, and of course, God. Ma and Ch'amps got together and convinced me to see a counselor about the growing rift between Pops and me. I resisted at first, complaining that it wasn't my job to fix the relationship. Ch'amps kept prodding and telling me that she wouldn't be able to marry me and have children if I didn't heal my relationship with Pops. She said she didn't want any conflict in our lives. Family confusion wasn't a legacy she planned on passing down to her children. You know she is real sensitive about keeping family peace since her family is fragmented and filled with crazy drama."

"That's great that she and your mother were so proactive. Did Parker and Seneca get involved?"

"Nah. Parker has always dealt with Pops from a distance. That Negro had to go to Australia and study the lives of Aborigines to get some peace. Seneca is busy with her own life issues being married to Ashanti and raising a brood of sons in Portland."

"So what did you learn in counseling?"

"The counselor helped me see that Pops is just a person, not the superpower he presents himself to be. I had to recognize that Pops is like everyone else, a human being with flaws as well as virtues. This was the link I had to make in order to accept him."

"How long did it take?"

"The question is probably better rephrased as how long is it taking."

"You're still dealing with it?"

"It ain't no joke. It's a work in progress. It's so important to my future with Ch'amps that I will do what I have to do to manage my relationship with Pops so that it creates peace in the family."

"How does your dad relate to you now?"

"Since I got out on my own two feet and have what he thinks is a respectable job, things have eased up a bit. I try to focus on the good things. The things we have in common. We can hang out and enjoy each other's company at sporting events like we did when I was younger. I enjoy helping him take care of some of his properties. Since we both dig jazz, we try to take in sets at Yoshi's and other spots. Pops is Pops. I'm me. That's just how I look at it. I'll always love him. I may not like everything he does or says, but he is still my pops. You feel where I am coming from?"

"Sorta, but I'm still left in a quandary as to how to approach Momma."

"The only thing you can do is change yourself. You can't change her."

"I just don't …"

Ming abruptly interrupted me. "See that's where you gotta stop. Stop saying what you don't want to do. Be open to whatever way the universe helps you heal the relationship. You gotta forget about the mistakes your moms has made when you were growing up … and even the ones she makes now. You gotta forgive her, Karma. That's the real starting point. Forgiveness."

"When did you become this wise sage?"

"I'm just an ordinary brotha doing his best to remember the message that was preached last week at our church."

"Hold up. You're going to church now?"

"Ch'amps got me going to this progressively hip place called the First Church of Religious Science. Are you familiar with it?"

"Isn't it on Clarewood Drive?"

"Exactly! You ever been?"

"No, but I remember that one of Daddy's friends went there."

"The reason I dig the church so much is because of its vision and mission. It is all about God's love and oneness. They are dedicated to individual transformation and collective growth."

"Sounds like you have found a spiritual home."

"I never really realized how important it was to have one until I rolled up on this place. Reading the teachings of Ernest Holmes has really helped me expand my consciousness. I can't tell you how much it has helped me manage my anger and impatience. I really dig reading the daily devotions in the Science of Mind. Ever read it?"

"Once or twice. Daddy used to get it."

"Your pops was always on the progressive tip. I still can't believe he's gone."

"But look at what he left … a confusing mess for us all to deal with."

"Karma, I got one word for you about that stuff with your pops. Forgiveness."

"Thanks Ming, but I think I've had all I can take about my parents for one night."

"I hear that. You know I ain't trying to sound like a preacher or therapist."

"I know you mean well."

"That's all I can do is share. You gotta let your soul be the pilot and do the rest."

"Well, it's getting late."

"Let me show you where you'll be sleeping."

We walked out into the foyer where my overnight bag and tote bag were sitting. Ming grabbed the overnight bag and guided me upstairs to what he warned was Ch'ampselysees' polka dot palace. As I entered the room, my eyes were bombarded by a wall filled with kidney bean red, spinach green, and mustard yellow polka dots. The same pattern replicated itself on the comforter and cluster of pillows lying on the Edo-style bed. It faced a mustard yellow wall. The other two walls were painted in kidney bean red and spinach green. Dizziness set in. The solid colored walls contained several black and white photos of artwork and images of an Asian woman.

"Now this is Ch'amps' polka dot shrine. With the help of our interior designer, she was able to find some prints by a Japanese artist that complimented her polka dot fetish."

When I got a close up of the photos, I recognized the artist. It was Yayoi Kusama, the sculptor, writer and painter that I wrote my modern art paper on at Morgan. Her trademark polka dot pattern and theme of repetition were the main reasons that I enjoyed her work. However, sleeping in a room dedicated to her art might change my opinion.

Looking at one photograph entitled *Collage* (c. 1966) where Yayoi was reclining on *Accumulation No. 2* made me think back to the last time I saw her work. It was two years ago in July. The Museum of Modern Art was showcasing her work. I think Laurence and I saw it together. What a disaster that was!

"Now I see the connection to the polka dots. It's Yayoi Kusama's work. I have always loved her art."

"She's one of Ch'amps favorite artists. Wait until she hears that you both love Yayoi. Two years ago, she pissed a hissy fit and forced me to fly with her to L.A. to see the woman's exhibit. Personally, I'm not moved by any of it, but I've learned that whatever moves Ch'amps better move me if you know what I mean."

"Sounds like she got a brotha in check."

"Yeah she does. I told you I'll do whatever it takes to keep the peace. Awright Karma, I know you have had a long day so I'm gonna let you get some rest. Think about what I said tonight. Forgiveness really works."

"Stop the preaching!"

With that last comment, we hugged and said goodnight.

As I unpacked and changed into my pajamas, thoughts of forgiving Momma, Daddy, and Devi invaded my mind. Bearing my soul to Branford was tossed in like a buy three and get one free sales gimmick. When I laid down in the bed and turned the lights off, images of the five different faces of Erzulie danced across the horizon of my mind in kaleidoscope fashion. The next vision featured *Grandmere* holding a heart with a pierced dagger. Seconds later, I saw an image of myself standing half-naked in a waterfall with a dagger piercing my heart. *Grandmere* appeared with a Black Virgin Mary. Mary sprinkled holy water on my face as *Grandmere* tried to remove the dagger. A mermaid emerged from the water and began preaching to me about forgiveness and the need to heal. She repeated comments that Ohnedaruth and Ming shared earlier. When she finished, she disappeared along with the images of *Grandmere* and Mary. The next thing I heard were the voices of actors from George's play chanting Love's Troubadours. It went on for what I think was an hour until I sat up in the bed and prayed for a quiet mind and restful sleep. Moments later, my prayer was answered.

CHAPTER 18

▼

"Be not wise in your own eyes ... It will be healing to your flesh and refreshment to your bones."

—Proverbs 3:7-8

Sounds of a woman howling to the beat of funkadelic rock awakened me at an ungodly hour. My eyelids flickered open, catching a glimpse of the clock. It flashed three fifty-two a.m. in day glow green. My eyelids quickly shut. That was the first sign of resistance from my body. It refused to acknowledge the noise and preferred to lie still in a bed of denial. My mind wished it would move and tried to strong arm my body, but she wasn't having it. So I lay quietly wondering who the perpetrator of this early morning crime was. It could only be one person. Ming. Why is he up so early playing what appears to be a Thanksgiving tribute to Betty Davis? The answer came as the last track of the CD ended. Without the music playing, it was easy to hear the sounds of lovers' ecstasy amplified in surround sound. That's when I knew Ch'ampselysees was an accomplice to Ming's early morning crime.

Desperately trying to return to sleep, I buried my head in between pillows, hoping that I wouldn't be able to hear the echo of their sexescapades. It seemed to work until soundbytes of previous conversations raced through my mind at warp speed. Forgiveness and emotional disclosure were the themes that linked each thought. I tried my best to escape them by focusing my energy on doing yoga in the bed. Centering myself, I did several breathing exercises followed by a series of

Om Shanti chants. Almost an hour passed as I lay in *Balasana*. My mind remained stuck in a flurry of thoughts. The only thing that changed was the pace, from roadrunner fast to tortoise slow. The themes etched themselves on the right and left hemispheres of my brain. Frustration from this ying and yang chaos got the best of me. Teardrops began to form in my eyes. I opened them and stared at the clock. Four forty-four a.m. It was seven forty-four a.m. in D.C. I decided to call Francis for some relief. So I reached into my Annie Lee *Maxed Out* cotton tote bag and pulled out my cell phone. The probability of her answering was next to nil, but at least she would have my message early enough to call me back by the end of the day. No answer. I tried not to sound so desperate in my voicemail message, but the truth was that I was hanging on to loose ends. I needed wise counsel. My need was so great that I could easily pass for a woman searching for water and food in a barren desert … a woman in need of healing for my flesh and refreshment for my bones.

The urge to relieve my bladder summoned me to my feet. The bathroom was another adventure in Asian culture. I was immediately attracted to the comforting lilac walls. Small statues of the Amitabha Buddha, the Buddha of infinite light and love, and Kuan Yin, the Buddhist goddess of compassion, patience and forgiveness, sat in a white curial wall cabinet above the toilet. A poem written on lilac parchment paper and in black ink from a calligraphy pen made its home in a white wooden frame next to the cabinet. The title caught my attention. *Kuan Yin's Faces.* There were exactly eleven lines in the poem. Each line was dedicated to one of Kuan Yin's eleven faces: generosity, Buddha action and behavior, renunciation, wisdom, courage to achieve, patience, truth, resolution, loving kindness, equality, and supreme enlightenment. I was reminded of my struggle to offer loving kindness and impartiality towards Momma, Daddy, Devi, Branford, and myself.

Staring into the bathroom mirror, I quietly wished I could evaporate into the emptiness of the universe. I wanted to leave all of this emotional upheaval behind. Unfortunately, my superwoman powers didn't kick in. So I was stuck in reality with dark puffy circles underneath my eyes.

Climbing back into bed, I asked God, "Why haven't you responded to my plea?" It was simple enough. All I wanted was a peaceful sleep. Why won't God let me sleep? A second passed before I buried myself in the polka dot comforter. Underneath the covers, I hoped that sleep would accept my invitation, but she declined. Restlessness set in. Cranky became the best word to describe my disposition.

Unable to sleep, I decided to explore the house. Silence met me as I opened my bedroom door. It kept me company as I traveled down the staircase. Once I reached the milky white kitchen, I heard the soothing sounds of a rock fountain. Ch'ampselysees was sitting at the kitchen table reading a book. Several vanilla scented candles burned in the middle of the table. Inhaling the scent, I thought about how much I hungered for a perfect sanctuary. A coral tea cup sat near her. She looked like she was enjoying her morning ritual. I hated to disturb her. By the time I turned around and took two steps in the opposite direction, she discovered my presence.

"Hey Karma. Come on back."

Half smiling, I greeted her. "Good Morning."

"You're up early."

"I couldn't sleep."

"Is your room okay?"

"Oh yeah. It's me. I'm wrestling with some things. My mind wouldn't let up. That's all."

"Come on in and take a load off. Can I get you some tea?"

"That's okay. I don't want to intrude on your quiet time."

"Girl, stop tripping. Get yourself in here."

"If you say so."

"Now what kind of tea do you want?"

"Lemongrass."

"Same from last night."

"Yes."

"So what's got you up?"

"Stuff with my mother."

"Ming told me about some of the stuff. It sounds like a lot of drama."

"It is. Believe me."

"Feel like talking about it?"

"Not really."

"Well, let me get you some tea."

As Ch'ampselysees fixed my cup of tea, I noticed she was reading a book about Kara Walker. We highlighted her work at the Walden during my last year. I remember how angry artist Bettye Saar was with Kara's cutout silhouettes of antebellum racial stereotypes. Those were hot days. When Ch'ampselysees returned to the table and handed me the cup of tea, I couldn't help but ask, "So what has you so interested in Kara Walker?"

"Girl, her work bugs me out."

"How so?"

"She pushes more than the envelope as she shows the real deal about what happened to our people. I dig her because she says what a lot of folks resist saying in America. She wakes America the fuck up from its precious dream. She dances with dualities, and challenges everybody with their notions of good and bad, right and wrong."

"I know what you mean. She became one of my personal favorites from the day I discovered her work at the Drawing Center in New York. That was the first time I saw her provocative black paper cutouts pasted across a white wall depicting a southern plantation scene."

"That's one of my favorites. I was blown away at the images of the children engaged in sex play, while the woman lifting her leg dances a jig and births babies."

"You sound like a Kara Walker disciple."

"Not really. I just got into her recently when one of my book club members showed me some of her work."

"I never knew you were into art this deeply."

"I got into when I joined this book club a few years back. A couple of sistas are into contemporary artists of color. They are responsible for my exposure."

"I gotta tell you that your polka dot room with Yayoi Kusama's photo and prints took me back to my undergrad days at Morgan."

"Not many people know her work."

"I know. She was someone I truly admired. Her style was creatively raw and cutting edge. So much so that I wrote a major paper about her."

"Did you get an A?"

"You know I did."

"So since you have been in D.C., have you been able to do any work as a curator?"

"Here and there at Howard University's Gallery of Art."

"Anybody significant?"

"Chris Ofili, a phenomenal British brotha of Nigerian descent. Have you heard of him?"

"Nah, but I'm interested. What's so fascinating about his work?"

"He takes the technique of collage to an entirely new level with glitter, vibrant colors, magazine cutouts, glow-in-the-dark pieces of plastic, and elephant dung."

"Elephant dung. You're kidding?"

"Absolutely not. It's actually his trademark."

"So what does he create with the elephant dung?"

"His work is filled with a complex matrix of images from the worlds of blaxploitation films, hip hop music, comic book superheroes, decorative art, kitsch, religious themes, sexuality, and the Zimbabwe plains. He uses a lot of parodies and explores the Black urban experience. You may have heard about his controversial work, *The Holy Virgin Mary*. It was on exhibit at the Brooklyn Museum of Art last year."

"I must have missed that one."

"Things really got out of hand. Ofili painted the Virgin as a Black Madonna with a clump of elephant dung on one breast. He also used cut-outs of genitalia from pornographic magazines in the background. Outraged by Ofili's creative expression and other work in the collection of young British artists, Mayor Giuliani threatened to eliminate the city subsidy the Museum receives. He eventually followed through on his threat only to have a judge overturn it. In the midst of all of this drama, a man smeared white paint on Ofili's work. It was later removed."

"How can one person determine interpretation?"

"I feel you. What may be offensive to one person may not be to another."

"Giuliani forgot that we do live in the land of free speech."

"That's exactly what happened."

"Sounds like Ofili challenges Black stereotypes like Kara Walker. Are samples of his work on the Internet?"

"Howard has a web site with photos for his upcoming spring show. We can take a look at it right now if you like."

"That would be great. Let's use Ming's office."

After I showed Ch'ampselysees the web site, I asked if I could check my e-mail. She went back to the kitchen to give me some privacy. When I logged on to my account, I noted that I had four messages worth reading. The first one was from Yamuna. She wrote to tell me that things between she and Grant were hot and heavy. Talk of engagement was in the air. So soon, I thought, but who am I to judge. Love comes when it comes. When it's right, you are supposed to know it. That sure hasn't happened for me yet. Yamuna hinted that Grant had a frat brother that they both thought would be perfect for me to meet. Something about him being an investment banker living in my neighborhood. I wrote Yamuna a quick note to express my happiness about her relationship going so well. At the end of the message, I thanked her for her matchmaking and reminded her that men were off limits.

The second message was from Serengeti. The subject line read "Urgent Center News—Please Read." I wonder what the drama queen has cooked up now? I couldn't believe my eyes as I read her exciting news. The Center received a generous donation of five million dollars from Oprah Winfrey's Angel Network to support the work it does for women of color. To top it off, the Center's staff will be featured in a segment on Oprah's show celebrating Women's History Month and in the March issue of O Magazine. Serengeti and Kalahari will fly to Chicago to appear on the show. The last sentence of the e-mail made me clutch my heart. She wanted to know if I was available to work as a consultant for the new art gallery.

Odessa, a colleague from my Walden days sent the third message. She wrote to tell me about her new position as curator of Spelman College's Museum of Fine Art. I was happy to hear her good news. The past decade hadn't been easy for her. I remember her gypsy-like rotation on the African American museum circuit. Hampton University Museum was the place we first met. The rest of Odessa's e-mail discussed Spelman's collaborative partnership with the National

Museum of Women in the Arts on an exhibition featuring Lois Mailou Jones, Amalia Amaki, Renee Stout, Joyce Scott, Lorna Simpson, Adrian Piper, Faith Ringold, and Alyson Saar. The title of the exhibition is *Three Cheers for the Red, White and Blue*. It was inspired by one of Amalia Amaki's works, *Three Cheers for the Red, White and Blue #7 (I Guess That's Why They Call the Blues)*. I remembered seeing it in 1997 when I visited Spelman. Photos of some of America's treasured blues artists like Billie Holiday and Bessie Smith decorated the collage-like cotton cyanotype. Buttons and beads also covered the blue fabric.

Odessa had access to the work of most of the artists, but getting her hands on one of Lois Mailou Jones' earlier works was proving to be difficult. The one that Odessa wanted to showcase was called *Jennie*, a 1943 painting of a Godiva dark chocolate girl standing in a kitchen busily cleaning fish in a yellow dress. It was housed in Howard's gallery. Odessa thought I could put in a good word for her request.

The final message was from Branford. Not wanting to lose my emotional high, I deleted it and logged off. Immediately my conscience got the best of me. Maybe I should have read it. What if it was something important? Maybe I better call him. No that will just force me to explain why I have been avoiding him. He'll get me to talk. I know he will. I hate this place I'm in. There seems to be no way out. If I communicate with him, I'll probably hurt myself even more. If I don't, I'll lose my best friend. Ch'ampselysees entered Ming's office.

"Excuse me Karma. I don't mean to interrupt."

"That's okay. I just logged off."

"Ming just yelled downstairs to tell me he heard your cell phone ringing."

"Thanks."

As I walked back up the stairs, I ran into Ming. Doesn't anyone is this house sleep?

"Hey baby girl. Your phone has been ringing off the hook. Whoever he is, he sure misses you."

"That ain't even the case."

"Whatever you say sistagirl! "Why don't you come on back downstairs and join us for an early breakfast? Ch'amps makes some mean fried chicken and waffles. Almost like Roscoe's in LA."

"No thanks."

"Oh, so you expect to be on the phone for a long time? That cat must be something if you're gonna pass up some good food."

"Look, I told you it isn't a man."

"Whatever. Go on and call the brotha."

As I opened my bedroom door, I heard my cell phone ringing. Hoping it was Francis, I quickly grabbed my cell phone. "Good Morning."

"Karma, this is your mother."

I remained silent.

"Karma, are you there?"

I maintained my silence.

"Belle Violette Francois, this is your mother."

Something about hearing my full name provoked a response. Parental respect was always something I had difficulty denying even with the drama queen. "I know who you are. Momma, what on earth do you want this early in the morning?"

"Today is Thanksgiving."

Interrupting her with sarcasm, "So you are feeling sentimental?"

"If that's what you want to call a mother trying her best to mend fences with her daughter."

"I'm not in the mood for any more drama."

"And I'm not calling to create any, *Cherie*. Just hear me out."

"Okay, but the minute I …"

"Karma, you don't have to worry about that. Your Aunt Nina sat me down last night. She gave me a piece of her mind about how I've been acting and the trouble I've been causing you."

"Well, good for her, but did you listen?"

"Matter of fact I did. Nina got me to see that I've been acting like a selfish diva towards you."

"Selfish diva. Those are words I never thought I would hear you use to describe yourself."

"I can be that way sometimes. I know this. Your father constantly reminded me of my nature."

"Good for Aunt Nina and Daddy, but what does all of that mean?"

"I'm trying to apologize to you for not listening to you about your brother. I know now that you and Violet have a right to establish a relationship with him."

"Momma, I find it difficult to imagine."

"Well, I have. And just to prove I have, I want you to come to Thanksgiving. Please bring Ohnedaruth."

"You got to be trippin'."

"No *Cherie*, I'm serious. I have spoken to your sister and told her that we were wrong not to support you in your effort to bring our family together. Ohnedaruth is a Francois. He should be with his sisters on Thanksgiving. And you are my daughters so you should be with me."

"Momma, this is too much for me to believe."

"Look Karma, all I can do is speak from my heart and open my home to you and your brother. It's time we all put the past behind us. There's been too much anger, suffering, and living in the past."

"So you are gonna just drop everything that Daddy did with Devi like that?"

"I didn't say it was that easy. I am still working through my feelings about your father and Devi, but what they did happened more than twenty years ago. What sense does it make to punish three children for things that were beyond their control? What I feel about your father and Devi is not your issue. That's what Nina helped me see."

"Well Momma, I'm still shocked, but if you are serious about your dinner invitation, I will call Ohnedaruth now and see if he and George will consider coming over to the house. They might decline because they are supposed to have dinner with Devi."

"If they can't come, please invite them over for dessert."

"Okay Momma, but you better not be bluffing or planning to start some drama."

"*Cherie*, I assure you that I'm not. I just want us to be a family again. That's my intent."

"What time is dinner by the way?"

"Five o'clock. So can I expect to see you with Mingus and Ch'ampselysees?"

"Yes, you will see me Momma."

"*Bien Cherie. Je t'aime.*"

"*Moi aussi.*"

Whenever Momma and I speak in French, I know things are sailing along smoothly. It always amazes me to see how the universe clears up situations so easily. Perhaps if I continue my hands off approach, the universe will clear up my situation with Branford.

Ohnedaruth and George were unable to make Thanksgiving dinner, but they dropped by later for dessert. Most of the guests … Aunt Nina, Uncle Gary, Ming, Ch'ampselysees, Ramses' father and his brothers departed earlier leaving me, Momma, Violet, and Ramses to entertain them. Violet was cold as a fish when Ohnedaruth introduced himself. Fifteen minutes after Momma served George and him dessert and coffee, Violet announced that she and Ramses were leaving because they needed to discuss wedding plans. We all knew it was bullshit because Ramses didn't know anything about her plan and couldn't even catch on to play along. Instead of busting Violet out, Momma rolled her eyes and let her go in silence. That's when I locked eyes with Momma. It was strange because it seemed like we could read each other's mind. We both knew that Violet was making a huge mistake by choosing to leave.

For the remainder of the evening, I sat quietly watching my mother fawn over her husband's son with a graciousness I had never seen. He fawned back. Momma had single handedly gained a new president of her personal fan club. When would her house of cards fall? They never did because Hyacinth Belle Baptiste Francois was genuinely happy to spend time with Ohnedaruth Eugene Shankar. In a strange way, he seemed to offer her a sense of peace. Momma was back in her element, telling jokes about folks who couldn't believe she was fifty something with two grown daughters and no plastic surgery. She went on and on about how she was unwilling to worship at the fountain of youth. Why should she when she earned every decade? It helped that she inherited youthful looking skin from *Grandmere*. Watching Momma I started to see a feisty spirited woman. She was fierce. Courageous. Poised. Sophisticated. No longer a black widow spider, but a butterfly full of vitality.

Ohnedaruth's jovial rapport with Momma extinguished my anger. What Francois alchemy! Together they made me believe that in time I might be able to completely forgive her, Daddy, and Devi. Perhaps our family could one day be Love's Troubadours. Maybe we already were and I just didn't know it.

CHAPTER 19

▼

"The Lord will keep your going out and your coming in from this time forevermore"

—Psalm 121:8

Twelve forty-six in the morning marked the time that Ohnedaruth and George departed from Daffodil Villa. It was too late for me to return to Ming's house. I resigned myself to spending the night and silently prayed away any trace of the Francois female drama. My prayer seemed to work because while I was helping Momma clean up, something magical happened. We were able to keep the peace for almost three full hours. Miracles do in fact come in mysterious ways! And this was one of them! I wondered what prompted it. Perhaps it was more of that Francois alchemy that did the trick. Whatever it was, I was grateful.

As I wrapped up the leftovers and placed them in the refrigerator, I turned and saw Momma selecting a CD from the rack on the kitchen counter. It was Vinx's *Rooms In My Fatha's House*. I had given her an audiocassette copy for a birthday present in 1990. Who knew she liked it enough to purchase it in a CD? Track one played loudly as I watched Momma sing *Tell My Feet* off key as she moved around the kitchen swaying her Baptiste womanly hips that women on her father's side were famous for. Unable to resist the energy of Vinx's voice and drumbeats, I joined her swaying my inherited Baptiste womanly hips and singing the lyrics off key. We were two crazed kitchen dancers throwing our bodies all over the place. At one point, I looked at Momma and thought that we should consider auditioning for Soul Train. Our moves were incredibly sensual and unique. Surely we could do our thang and give those Soul Train dancers a run for their money. The only thing we would need is Vinx's music playing nonstop. It's the only way to guarantee our dance moves.

After we cleaned the kitchen, we started listening to Marvin Gaye's classic 1971 *What's Going On*. It made me think of Daddy and the way he loved to refer to Marvin as Black folks' philosopher and social critic. I didn't mention my sentimental thoughts to Momma. After having such a great evening with Ohnedaruth and George, I didn't want to open up Pandora's box of wounds about Daddy. In between *Save The Children* ending and *God Is Love* beginning, Momma invited me to partake in a Francois female ritual: lemon ginger tea before bedtime. She started it the year that Violet and I began menstruating. The only thing missing from the ritual was Violet, but to be honest, I wasn't really missing her. It was good to have this time with Momma. We took our tea into the sun room and settled into our conversation.

Momma had the sun room built onto the house the year after Violet left for college to Spelman and me to Morgan. The walls remained their traditional antique white color. Over the years, the international theme of the room changed with each trip Momma and Daddy took abroad. The current theme was Turkish. Turkey was the last trip they took together before Daddy died. While they were in Istanbul in 1997, Momma developed a craving for the country's prized tapestry and tile work. As usual she transformed her craving into a living memory. Carefully selected floor rugs in earth tone colors with Mediterranean blue patterns and matching pillow throws sat comfortably on the maple hardwood floors. Circular tile with Islamic inspired Mediterranean blue and Sunkist orange floral designs were placed in between black and white photos of some of her favorite sites: Domabachi Palace, Hagia Sofia, and the Blue Mosque. Rattan wicker furniture with earth tone cushions kept company with a collection of aloe vera and cactus plants. Momma's herb garden was in the area with the most sunlight. It was one of her pride and joys.

Our conversation shifted back and forth like the first time I learned how to drive a stick on Daddy's vintage 1972 candy apple red VW. It stayed stuck in some places longer than it should. We started with polite conversation about Uncle Charles and Aunt Jo, the Baptiste cousins, cultural events we attended, new musical discoveries, and recent museum visits. After we covered these topics, the feminine girly talks that I always loved having with Momma began. I learned that Momma was on a quest to identify the perfect summertime scent. She was looking for something to replace Daddy's favorite, Vent Vert by Balmain. She's worn that forever. It was hard to believe that she wanted to change it. Not wanting to speculate on the rationale, I seized the moment and asked what type of fragrance she was looking for.

She answered, "Something fresh, crisp yet warm and sweet. Something bright and refreshing with hints of citrus."

Momma sounded like a teenager let loose in Saks Fifth Avenue with a sky's the limit on her mother's credit card. Because Kiehl's was one of my personal favorites from my days at the Walden, I recommended she try one of the toilette sprays that meshed together an array of oils: bergamont, nectar, orange blossom, rose, lily, ylang ylang, and neroli. She graciously thanked me and asked if I was going to use one of the sprays as my summer scent. For a few seconds, I resisted confessing my financial reality. When I shared my situation, Momma didn't pounce on me with any disparaging remarks. Instead, she moved the conversation forward by asking what I was planning to use. I shared that I discovered my summer fragrance last month while helping to put together self-care bags for the World AIDS Day Self-Care Fair, co-sponsored by the Center, The Women's Collective, Us Helping Us, All Souls Unitarian Church, and several local chapters of African American fraternity and sororities. "A caseworker that Colette works with at The Women's Collective hooked me up with sample fragrances when she discovered that Lisa Price, the founder of Carol's Daughter, sent extra samples to stuff in the bags. I was immediately drawn to the Ecstasy Fragrance Oil."

"I would love to purchase some of Carol's Daughter's products as gifts for my bridge club members. Where can I get them?"

"You can visit the web site and make purchases online."

"What about smelling the fragrances?"

"If I tell Colette that her godmother wants a free sample, I'm sure she can have the caseworker hook you up."

"*Merci Cherie.*"

The subject of the conversation switched to holiday plans. "So *Cherie*, what are your plans for New Year's?"

I felt like I was getting ready to be set up on a blind date. So I hesitated in answering. "As of now, I haven't made any plans."

"Since I am going to be on the East Coast celebrating Christmas with you and the Baptiste clan, I thought I might fly up to Boston and spend some time with my high school classmates, Lisette and Benedict Flambeaux. You remember them, don't you?"

"Of course, their daughter Avery went to Spelman with Violet and Colette."

"Did you know that Avery is living in Atlanta now with her husband and son?"

Shaking my head no, I couldn't let go of the words husband and son. They set off a red alarm. I expected Momma to chastise me about not being married, but she didn't. "Well, I thought you might like to join me in Boston for this New Year Eve's gala that Divas Uncorked is sponsoring. Lisette and eleven other women started this wine tasting group two years ago. They are a powerful group of women who got fed up with being underserved in wine shops. So they took matters into their own hands by organizing monthly tastings. Their gala is a fundraiser to help expand their efforts to teach women and people of color about the wine industry. I thought we could make a weekend of it. Stay in a five star hotel, get some spa treatments, and have a ball celebrating the beginning of 2001."

"Is Violet coming?"

"I didn't extend an invitation to her. She already made plans to spend the holiday with Ramses."

"It sounds like a great idea, but I can't afford that right now."

Momma didn't try to guilt me into going. She accepted my decision. "If you change your mind, the invitation stands."

That was the end of that conversation and the beginning of me starting to trust that Momma is capable of changing.

Somehow Momma managed to link her trip to Boston with her last Bridge Club meeting. I found myself drifting in and out of her play-by-play reports. I don't think she even noticed my sleepiness. There were three card games that Violet and I had to learn: Bridge, bid whist, and tonk. Out of the three, my parents were avid Bridge players. How they became so passionate about this, I'll never understand. I suspect it was Momma's doing. Southern belle socialite is written all over the game. Daddy was obviously blinded by her feminine whiles and went along with her wishes.

"Last week, Yvelette hosted the club at her house in Richmond. Your Aunt Nina and I were playing against Yvelette and her sister-in-law, Ms. Poinsette. By the way, she sends her love."

"How is Ms. Poinsette?"

"She is doing better now. Her sugar has been running wild lately. She had to stop working with the chemicals and dyes in her salon."

"I'm sorry to hear that. I know how much she loved doing hair. I can't believe she did our hair from the age of four until we left for college."

"That's a long time. She loves you girls like her own."

"She was our second mother. On many occasions, she was able to correct my behavior and help me stay on track."

"Your father and I were grateful for her influence over you girls. You should call her before you leave."

"Yeah that sounds like a great idea. Does she still work in the salon?"

"Right now she does, but she is looking to retire as soon as her niece learns the business."

"What is her daughter doing?"

"Lynette is living in Oakland Hills with her husband. They are working at the same law firm. Municipal bond financings are their area of expertise."

"Does Violet work with them on any deals?"

"Your sister considers them competition."

"I'm sure Lynette and her husband give Violet a run for her money."

"They do. Your sister can't stand them. This year alone they have beaten her firm out of six major deals."

"Knowing Violet, she is probably waging World War III."

"Indeed she is, but I can't blame her. She's just like me when it comes to losing. We hate it. That's the only attitude that we bring to life. We must win. And this is the precise attitude that I brought to the bridge game Nina and I were playing."

"So how did execute your take no prisoner playing strategy?"

"I wouldn't call it no prisoner. Let's simply say a winner's attitude. Karma, you should have seen our strategy when Yvelette opened with a weak two bid, promising a six card suit, and eight to ten points. She was playing west. Ms. Poinsette was east. Nina was north. I was south. After Yvelette opened, I ducked the queen and jack of spades, winning the third game with diamonds, pitching two hearts and a club. Ms. Poinsette dished out the eight and ten of clubs. Yvelette released all of her hearts. I was so caught up when I cashed in the ..."

I started snoring and didn't even realize it.

"Karma, wake up and get in the bed. You're falling asleep."

Apologetically, I responded, "I'm sorry, Momma."

Smiling, Momma comforted me with her words, "No need to apologize *Cherie*. We've had a long day. Let's get you tucked into bed."

As I gathered myself up, I could feel huge chunks of forgiveness passing from my spirit to Momma's. I heard Francis' voice reminding me that healing is not how fast you let go of baggage and find peace. It's what you learn along the way. Healing happens one day and one step at a time. I learned that I have a mother who is working on herself in her own way, struggling with the choices she has made, the ones Daddy made, and their impact on how she has interacted with me and Violet. I always thought we were so different from each other, but I realized we really do share a lot of things in common. I always felt like Momma never understood me. Our conversation opened a door to a richer relationship between a mother and her adult daughter. The one thing I'm certain of is that all of this is possible because of the presence and power of the Divine Spirit. It's the one force that has watched over our family. It has kept us centered throughout all of our goings out and comings in. What a blessing to lay down my head with!

CHAPTER 20

▼

"Agree with God and be at peace; in this way good will come to you."

—Job 22:21-22

When I woke up the next morning in Momma's bedroom, she was nowhere to be found. I was covered in a quilt that *Grandmere* made for Momma after she made peace with Momma's marriage to Daddy. It made me remember the feeling I had last night as Momma invited me to sleep with her as a part of our impromptu sleepover party. It's been ages since I rested my body in between my parents' sheets. Violet and I used to do it a lot when we were smaller.

Feeling the urge for morning tea, I got up and walked down the hallway past Daddy's office. Noticing that the door was half-cracked, I peaked in. Most of the original décor of the office had been transformed into what appeared to be Momma's private sanctuary. Gone were the bright colors that Daddy adored. She replaced them with lighter hues. Walls went from royal blue to light blue. Floorboards that used to be violet were now lavender. The rainbow color speckled carpet that we use to roll around on was removed. Hard wood maple floors were now the foundation for a room with much less stuff. It was airy, spacious even. I hated to admit it, but the absence of Daddy's things gave the room new life.

Now the room had a built in lavender bookshelf that spanned one wall. A lot of space was left in between the six shelves. The contents on each shelf were radically different from what I was used to seeing in the room. Books were absent from the scene. Found objects such as ocean shells, rocks, dried flowers, and gemstones sat in small glass jars on the top shelf. Statues of Mary, Jesus, and some saints I couldn't readily identify were spread out on the fifth shelf. The fourth shelf offered a home to Momma's favorite cactus and aloe vera plants. Sitting at one end of the third shelf was a nineteen-inch TV/VCR and several VHS tapes neatly stacked on top of each other. At the other end sat a small portable CD player along with several racks of CDs. Pictures of family members and folks I couldn't recall decorated the second shelf. The first shelf contained several wooden statues of women in the marketplace that Momma purchased while she and Daddy were celebrating their tenth wedding anniversary in Kingston, Jamaica. I hadn't seen them in years. Violet and I use to pretend that they were Sun Tan Barbie's Jamaican cousins.

Large pillows in shades of light blue, lavender, and rose decorated a corner of the wall facing the bookshelf. A pewter candle stand with candles in every shade of the rainbow sat next to the pillows. The only picture in the room hung in the middle of that wall. I was shocked to see that it was a collage that I made in a high school. It was an abstract interpretation of the knowledge contained in the Vedas, one of the oldest spiritual resources on Earth. I never thought Momma really liked this piece. She wasn't really big on Eastern spiritual practices like Daddy and me. That seemed to have changed from the looks of the room and the thing that I witnessing Momma doing.

Momma stood with her eyes closed against the wall opposite the bookshelf. She was perfectly coordinated. Light blue tunic with white stretch pants. Perfectly polished and French manicured toes. The back of her head, shoulders, buttocks, and heels lay against the wall. She looked like she was doing one of my favorite poses, *Tadasana*. Momma doing yoga? Since when? She never seemed to support Daddy's practice and ignored mine; always emphasizing that it was a hobby, not a career choice that she expected her daughter to pursue. Maybe it reminded her too much of Devi. So what changed her mind?

Before I could answer my own question, my body leaned a little too hard against the door and caused it to open widely. Momma's eyes opened. "*Cherie*, you can come on in."

"I don't wanna disturb you."

"Nonsense, come in."

"You sure. You look like you were in the middle of ..."

"My morning meditation and yoga routine."

"When did you start practicing yoga?"

"Ever since your father died. Nina took me to a class for women our age that meets at Mingus' church."

"I thought you didn't like it"

"What gave you that impression?"

"Come on Momma. You always moaned and groaned about Daddy's practice. Whenever I would call you from Morgan and tell you about the on-campus yoga class that I taught, you would immediately change the subject."

"You're right."

Hearing Momma admit that I was right about something paused the conversation. The world as I knew it had definitely changed. Hyacinth Belle Baptiste Francois never, and I underscore for emphasis the word never, admitted that I was right about anything.

"Yoga always represented a threat to my relationship with your father. After his affair with Devi, I never felt comfortable with him taking classes. As for you, I just didn't want you to forgo college to become a yoga teacher. My goal was to raise two intelligent professional educated daughters. I wanted you and Violet to have your education completed early in life so you would not have to endure the struggles I faced when I returned to school with a husband and small children."

The only response I could offer was, "Oh."

Momma's candor and the way she shared herself with me so easily was overwhelming. "All you can muster is an oh." No follow up piercing third degree questions from my curious daughter?"

"I just wanted to know."

"Karma you are something else. Your curiosity, courage to ask questions, and speak your mind are things I have always admired about you."

Momma walked over to the shelf where the stack of videos was located. She picked up one and brought it over to me. As she handed it to me, Momma commented, "I really like Lilias Folan. What do you think about the way she teaches?"

"What's not to like? She is probably the grandmother of American yoga."

"When I started my yoga practice, she was the only teacher that I knew. Remember how your father used to faithfully watch her on public television."

"Yeah. Daddy was a Lilias disciple, of sorts."

"That man swore by her. When he was watching her show, you couldn't interrupt him with anything."

"Whatever he got into, he was into it deeply. From Coltrane to Swami Satchidananda's teachings."

"I can hear him now giving his blessing before we ate a meal. He always closed with truth is one, paths are many."

"Eugene was something alright. He was big on exposing our family to sacred truths."

"I miss that about him. We would spend hours talking about Hindu teachers like Vivekananda and Parmahansa Yogananda."

"Yes, I do recall those Karma and her father moments. Two peas in a pod. You were his unspoken favorite."

Feeling like I was in the hot seat, I quickly responded, "No I wasn't."

"*Au contraire, Cherie* you were. Your father never quite connected with Violet. I used to get on him all of the time."

"She had your attention all of the time."

"Not true. I paid both of you attention, but I did have to make up for the time your father spent devoted to your interests. So if my trying to balance things out with your sister made me it look like she had my full attention, then too bad for you."

All I seemed to hear were Momma's last words 'too bad for you.' I tried not to get caught up in them, but I wouldn't let them go. "What do you mean too bad for me?"

"*Cherie*, I was just teasing."

Tears started rolling down my face as I uttered, "It didn't sound like it."

Momma walked over to me and gave me one of her famous bear hugs. "What's really going on?"

I cried a waterfall of tears that wet the top of her tunic before I responded to her question. "I just …"

"You just what?"

"I never understood why you loved Violet more than me."

"My silly daughter. I have loved you both equally in the ways you needed to be loved."

"Not so."

"Karma, look at me. You have got to stop this craziness. I want you to hear me loud and clear. *Je t'aime, ma fille.* I will always love you. Do you understand?"

In the middle of what was another scene in the ongoing Francois female drama, I looked directly into my mother's eyes and saw God's truth. In that moment, I knew that the only way we could have a healthy relationship was to surrender my ego and let my soul be my pilot. So I surrendered and chose to be at peace, knowing that in this way the goodness of our relationship would reveal itself in due time.

PART III

▼

"Accustom yourself continually to make many acts of love for they enkindle and melt the soul."

—Saint Teresa of Avila

CHAPTER 21

▼

"Above all, clothe yourselves with love, which binds everything together in perfect harmony."

—Colossians 3:14

After we completed the last scene in the Francois female drama for the Thanksgiving holiday season, Momma and I went into to the kitchen and began to prepare a tropical fruit breakfast fit for two queens. In the middle of slicing fresh fruit, the telephone rang. It was Mingus calling to remind me that my things were still at his house. That's when I remembered that I had an early afternoon flight to catch. He agreed to bring my things over to Momma's house and offered to drive me to the airport. When Momma heard me say it was okay that he drive me, she signaled that she wanted to. So I declined his offer and accepted Momma's. It was one of the best decisions I could have made.

On the way to the airport, Momma and I planned how we would spend the Christmas holiday going to several concerts at the Kennedy Center. I invited her to stay with me. She was excited to be invited and was looking forward to another sleepover. That would be a first for us. It marked a new beginning in our mother-daughter relationship. By the time, we said our final goodbyes, we were both clothed in a love that allowed for a harmonious acceptance that neither of us had known before.

Thankfully the flight was nonstop. The only delay was waiting for a cab outside of Reagan National Airport. The line had to be seventy-five people deep. Eavesdropping was not something I normally enjoyed, but the conversations that I overheard about the recent Presidential election begged my attention. Looking like the twin of Texas Republican Senator Kay Bailey Hutchinson, a wide-hipped middle-aged white woman with blond hair dressed in a grey herringbone pantsuit from Talbot's winter catalogue stood next to her husband. He was a very tall, thin, clean-shaven white man dressed in what looked like his own interpretation of J.R. Ewing. His cowboy hat was a dead give away. She was doing all of the talking as he listened, an obvious trait he was either born with or mastered being her mate. In a thick Texas drawl, she whined about the direction this country would take if Gore were elected. The gospel according to her predicted that we would all be going to h-e-double hockey sticks (her words not mine) if the election results favored Gore. There was no mystery in the party she supported.

A group of African American women, some of who were wearing black jackets with the words Black Women Playwrights' Group embroidered in yellow on their backs, stood behind me discussing a play they had recently put on in New York. Before the last scene was completed, the actors were rudely interrupted by a loud antagonistic discussion between two audience members. One man vehemently argued that a win for Gore was a win for the Black community. The other man argued that a Bush victory would teach Black folks not to rely solely on the crumbs of the Democratic Party. Before I could catch the end of the story, my phone rang. It was Momma calling with bad news. Colette was in intensive care at Howard University Hospital. Her boyfriend, Julian discovered her sitting in a chair unconscious. Rushing to the front of the line, I asked two Asian male college students who were waiting for the next available cab if I could jump ahead of them because I had a family emergency. Their half smiles answered in kindness.

When I arrived at the hospital, I saw Cane pacing in circles in the first floor lobby. He was dressed in a green sweat suit. The hood of his sweatshirt covered his head. His black peppercorn face was stained with evidence of a sleepless night.

"Hey cuz."

"What you doing here? I thought you were still in Oakland with Aunt Hy."

"My plane just got in. Momma called me while I was waiting for a cab."

"Karma, I'm glad you're here."

"What happened to Colette?"

"Julian found her unconscious this afternoon. He wasn't sure how long she had been in this state. He hadn't talked to her since Thanksgiving morning. They had been arguing about Colette not telling us that she had sarcoidosis."

"What the hell is sarcoidosis?"

"From what her doctor told us, it is an inflammatory disease that can affect every organ in the human body. The lungs are most often affected. Oddly enough, African Americans between the ages of 20 and 40 along with Danes and Swedes have the highest rates in the world."

"How come we didn't know she had it?"

"You know my sister. If she wanted us to know something, she would control what we knew."

"Was she displaying any signs of the disease?"

"See that's the thing. We just thought she was overworked. Julian told us that he badgered her into going to see her doctor late last year. Like us, he thought that she was just overworked from her job and volunteering at St. Augustine. When she did get checked, her internist attributed her fatigue to a stressful work-load. So she took it easy and resigned from St. Augustine's Youth Club and Social Action Committee. Her hours at the Women's Collective were reduced to a thirty hour work week."

"Did you all know anything about her doctor's visit?"

"Not a thing. We just thought she was finally getting some balance in her life until she started having fevers a few months before Charlie and Millicent were married. Mom had a heart to heart with her about her health, but she insisted that it was some virus. She even had Julian fooled until he noticed at the end of the summer that she was experiencing a persistent cough, shortness of breath, night sweats, and arthritis in her ankles, elbows, wrists and hands. That's when he arranged for her to see a thoracic expert at the hospital. The thoracic expert ordered a chest x-ray that showed a dramatic inflammation in both her lungs and diagnosed Colette with sarcoidosis in August. She persuaded Julian to keep it a secret until she was ready to tell the family. Apparently, he got tired of waiting and threatened to tell us at Thanksgiving dinner. On Thanksgiving morning, he issued an ultimatum that she tell us about her illness."

"We know what Ms. Control Freak chose."

"She called Mom and told her that she would not be able to attend Thanksgiving dinner because she was tired and needed to rest. We all bought her lie."

"So what caused her to fall out?"

"We still don't know. When she arrived at the hospital, the doctors determined that she had a stroke and internal bleeding in her brain. They had to operate on her immediately. We've been told that she might have some brain damage."

"Damn it. Why didn't she tell somebody?"

"I know how you feel. All of us are angry at her for not telling. Mom, Dad, and Millicent have been trying to get us to move beyond our anger. Mom keeps telling us that she didn't want to worry us. That might be the case, but if she hadn't been so hell bent on having things her way, we might have been able to help her. Colin and Chase had to hold Charlie and me back from hitting Julian. When we saw him, we both bum rushed his punk ass for not telling us what was going on with our sister."

"That wasn't right. He was probably just trying to honor your sister's wishes."

"Yeah, I know that, but she was sick. We should have been told. What kind of man is he? Forget about us. He should have at least pulled Mom and Dad's coattails about this illness especially since he knew they worried about her constant fevers and fatigue."

"Look Cane, he was doing the best he could."

"Maybe you're right."

"Why don't you come upstairs with me?"

"Nah, that's okay. I came down here to get away from Julian. His mere presence angers me."

Hugging him, I whispered in his ear, "This isn't the time to be mad. What Colette needs most now are positive vibes from her loved ones."

He backed away with what looked like the beginning of a face full of tears and started walking in the direction of the front door. When I asked where he was going, he neither responded nor looked back. As I turned towards the elevator and pressed the button marked up, I said a silent prayer affirming that my family remain clothed in love and centered in harmony as we help Colette heal.

CHAPTER 22

▼

"Let us then pursue what makes for peace and for mutual upbuilding."

—Romans 14:19

Two days after receiving the news about Colette, I found myself living between my apartment, Aunt Jo's house, and the intensive care unit at Howard University Hospital. The only good news we had received was that she was awake. She didn't look like herself. This morning when I entered Colette's room, Julian sat holding her cumin colored hand. As I touched it, I noticed her skin was very dry and ashy. My eyes scanned her body from head to toe. Surgery butchered her sixties sculptured bob hairdo. Colette's body was fragile. Her ability to speak hadn't returned. Colin and Chase stood like clean-shaven soldiers against the wall. They were both five foot seven and the spitting image of Uncle Charles except for his five foot five short stature, balding hair, and curly sideburns. Colin was stockier than Chase and had burnt almond skin. Chase was lean like a runner with pecan-colored skin.

An hour later, Momma arrived. Her upbeat attitude and high energy helped chase some of my cousins' anger away. Cane still hadn't returned to the hospital. He was, however, checking in with his mother every few hours to get a status update on Colette. Nobody questioned his absence. Everyone seemed to be in his or her own world wrestling with Colette's illness the best way they knew how. Aunt Jo and Uncle Charles presented a united front of peace and serenity. Uncle

Charles greeted everyone who entered Colette's room with a kind smile. To me, he looked like a teak-colored version of a jolly Santa Claus. They spent their time making sure Colette had the best of care and consoling their sons, Julian, and his parents.

After leaving the hospital late Sunday night, I headed home. Unable to sleep, I played catch up on the mail that had piled up in my mailbox. ABC Overnight News kept me company. My attention was drawn to a report about Shen Wei, the Chinese-born, New York-based modern dance choreographer that I saw perform at The American Dance Festival in Durham, North Carolina in 1995. Branford and I had gone down to see him perform. Memories of the good time that we shared came back. I started thinking about how much I wished we could return to the way things were before I fell in love with him. I wondered if it was possible. Sinclaire, Branford's ex-wife delivered the next news report. She reported on a fiery anti-gay sermon that an influential African American Baptist minister in Madison, Wisconsin gave earlier in the day. In his remarks, the minister charged that homosexuals and bisexuals were taking over the Black community and the reason for high HIV/AIDS rate in the Black community. What made the sermon most newsworthy were his graphic descriptions of sexual acts performed by same gender loving men and women. Claiming that he was not homophobic, he went on to use the Bible as the moral compass for passing judgment. Clips of the congregation cheering on the minister were included. I was shocked by the minister's comments: "Men falling upon men. Women falling upon women. When they stick their genitals or toys in each other's buttocks, that ain't natural. Our buttocks were not made for that. And they wonder why they bleed." I wondered how Sinclaire felt about reporting on a subject so close to home. She didn't seem to be affected as she moved to the next story.

Unlike Sinclaire, I wasn't able to move forward. I was stuck and unable to respond to Branford. There was no reason to continue mistreating one of my best friends. If I could begin to forgive Daddy and Momma, and accept Ohnedaruth as my brother, then it was time I let the feelings that I had for Branford go. Our friendship was a gift too precious to continue to mistreat. Watching Colette struggle for her life over the past few days has taught me that it is better to live with our loved ones in love, truth, and peace. I dialed Branford's phone number and woke him from a deep sleep. "Hi Branford. I'm so sorry to wake you."

"Karma, is that you?"

"Yeah it's me."

"Is everything alright?"

"It will be in a few minutes. I need you to listen to me without commenting, okay?"

"Okay shoot."

"I'm so sorry for not returning your e-mails and phone calls. That was not right. You're one of my best friends. You deserve to be treated as such. I chose not to contact you because of my feelings for you. A few months ago, I realized that I was falling in love with you. That's why I have been acting so strange. I knew you didn't feel that way towards me. So I never said anything. I wanted you to know the truth."

"Your apology is accepted. I kinda felt that something was going on with you, but I figured you would tell me when you were ready."

"Thanks for giving me the space."

"That's what friends do. Now about your feelings for me. You should have told me about them earlier. Then I could tell how I used to feel the same way about you when we were in undergrad. I had the hardest time watching you with other guys. It hurt my heart so much, but I valued your friendship more."

"Why didn't you tell me back then?"

"There was never a right time."

"You could have made the time."

"And what would you have done?"

"I'm not sure."

"I am. You would have eventually worn the same shoes as Sinclaire. I regret messing her life up with my internal struggle to define who I was."

"Since I'm being totally honest, I need you to know that your preference to date and be intimate with men is something that made me really angry. It's the real reason that I didn't tell you about my feelings. I felt like you cheated me out of an opportunity to love. I know that sounds crazy, but that's how I felt."

"Your feelings aren't crazy. I'm glad that you feel comfortable sharing them. What I am about to say may not sound like much right now, but Karma, you still have an opportunity to love me as your friend. I still think of you as one of my best friends. I hope we can move through this. Just let me know how I can help."

"Just letting me speak my mind is good enough for me."

"You know I love you deep, right?"

"Yeah, I know."

"Okay, I gotta an early appointment in the morning that I can't miss. So if you don't have anything else to share, I am gonna ask for a reprieve until tomorrow afternoon when I get a break at work."

"Your reprieve is so granted."

"Good night Belle Violette Francois."

"Good night Branford Douglas Gillespie."

I went to sleep with a clear conscious. My life was on track. It will stay that way provided I pursue experiences and relationships that create peace and mutual upbuilding.

CHAPTER 23

▼

"God is our refuge and strength, a very present help in trouble. Therefore we will not fear, though the earth should change, though the mountains shake in the heart of the sea."

—Psalm 46:1-2

This year's theme for World AIDS Day was "AIDS: Men Make A Difference." The Center decided to host a Self-Care Fair. In an effort to engage men and encourage them to contribute to the fight against the spread of HIV/AIDS, the Center invited local men's groups including the 100 Black Men of America, Inc., African American fraternities, Us Helping Us, National Dental Association, National Bar Association, and National Medical Association. They participated in a health series of roundtable discussions about the compelling reasons to focus on men and HIV/AIDS, the contributions men should be encouraged to make in fighting HIV/AIDS, gender awareness, sexual communication and negotiations, violence and sexual violence, and support and care. In preparation for the Fair, they distributed information about the roundtable discussions, HIV/AIDS awareness fact sheets, and resource lists of local service providers to their membership and client base. I was surprised to learn that Yamuna's boyfriend, Grant agreed to serve as a facilitator for the sexual communication and negotiation session. Grant recruited several of his Kappa brothers to lead segments of the discussion. Yamuna tried to persuade me to attend the evening discussions to meet the guy that she thought I would be interested in. Despite her insistence, I knew it wasn't an option for me. Fortunately for me, I had two legitimate excuses to get out of meeting him: my work schedule at Howard and need to spend time with Colette.

A few days after the Fair, I walked into Kalahari's office at the Center to drop off my monthly invoice. She was in the middle of a telephone conversation. As I waved hello to her, she placed her hand over the phone receiver and whispered that she needed to speak to me about something important. I smiled and told her I would stay and wait.

Colorful photos taken of the Machu Picchu Cital, Qhapag Nan, and the Great Inca Trail decorated the exposed brick wall in back of Kalahari's desk. They were carefully placed in two rows of six. Their placement clearly reflected Greer's touch. As I put my invoice in the in-box sitting on the console, I looked up and admired the framed black and white print of Ursula de Jesus, the 17th century Afro-Peruvian mystic and religious servant. I remembered the story that Kalahari told about how she came to own the print.

The print was a replica of an original portrait that hung in the vestibule of the convent of Santa Clara in Lima, Peru. Kalahari's grandmother worked there as a domestic servant. Her mother spent many days of her childhood admiring the portrait and the story behind the woman in it. For twenty-eight years, Ursula de Jesus worked as one of the hundreds of slaves who prepared food, washed clothing, and performed communal labor for the nuns. What made her so different was the way in which she dedicated any spare moment to prayer and her willingness to accept additional tasks.

Eventually, Ursula took the vows of poverty, chastity, obedience, enclosure, and to obey the Rule of the Order of Saint Claire. She began to experience visions in which dead souls eager to leave purgatory approached her to serve as an intercessor for their sins. Through her lifelong devotion to Our Lady of Carmen, a Virgin who specialized in aiding souls in purgatory, Ursula said prayers and requested masses on behalf of souls in purgatory. Kalahari's mother's devotion to Ursula reminded me of *Grandmere*'s devotion to the Virgin Mary, Marie Laveau, and Erzulie.

"Karma, I wanted to talk to you about the Center's newest endeavor. I'm sure you heard about the recent anti-gay remarks made by that minister in Wisconsin."

"I saw the news report. It's hard to believe someone could make those statements and profess them with such certainty to his congregation in the year 2000."

"We're all finding it hard to believe. Since the minister made those remarks, a dear friend of Serengeti's, Ayo and her partner were violently attacked. Ayo is a LGBT activist and Unitarian minister in Madison. She responded to the minister's attacks in her newspaper column and on several local radio shows."

"What happened?"

"Immediately after Ayo's column was published, she started receiving threatening e-mails and phone calls warning her to stop speaking out against the Baptist minister. When she shared that she had been threatened publicly, bricks were thrown through the windows of her car and home. Shortly thereafter, Ayo and her partner were physically attacked one evening as they were leaving their church. Two men dressed in black clothing with black ski masks covering their faces, screamed obscenities about gays and lesbians as they punched and kicked them. Ayo suffered a broken arm and bruises on her face. Her partner was knocked unconscious and received several blows to her face. She regained consciousness, but her eye sight is permanently damaged."

"What are the authorities doing about this violence?"

"The local police declared the violence a hate crime. Right now, they are tracking the e-mails and phone calls that Ayo received."

"Have they been able to identify any suspects?"

"Ayo saw the skin color of both men's arms. They were African American. This morning, she called let us know that the U.S. Department of Justice is involved in the case."

"That's reassuring. So what can I do to help?"

"Serengeti said that would be your first response."

"And she was right on point."

"Ayo asked Serengeti if she could partner with the Center to create a national initiative to heal and transform sexist and homophobic attitudes, beliefs, and violence in the African American community. We would use prayer, meditation, anger management training, gender awareness and male privilege discussion groups, expressive arts therapies, and information campaigns. They will challenge the physical, rhetorical, and emotional violence inflicted on youth, women, feminists/womanists, gay, lesbian, bi-sexual, and transgender members of our community. Naturally, Serengeti agreed and delegated the responsibility of organizing the coalition to me. I happily accepted."

"Healing and transformation in our community are so needed."

"I couldn't agree with you more. It's something that I've been doing on a daily basis for the past fifteen years. It started when my mother asked me to join her in praying to Our Lady of Carmen and Ursula de Jesus for my grandparents' souls whom she believed were stuck in purgatory because they failed to accept my sexual orientation. As time went on, I began to include individuals, named and unnamed, who perpetrated hate crimes."

"The devotion that you and your mother share in praying to these holy women reminds me of my mother and grandmother. They called upon the Virgin Mary, Erzulie, and Marie Laveau for intercession."

"Did you adopt the practice?"

"Not really, but I am starting to understand some of the reasons they cultivated a prayer connection to these holy women."

"Well, I encourage you to explore the connection. It has helped me tremendously."

Thinking back to my recent dreams, I wondered if Kalahari's words were the universe's way of encouraging me to seek out Erzulie for spiritual advice and wisdom. "Thanks for sharing."

"You're welcome. I've called Sista7 members to ask for their support as steering committee members."

"Count me in."

"Girl, I'm so grateful for Sista7."

"So what's our next step?"

"Serengeti, Ayo, and I are scheduled to have a conference call tomorrow to discuss the coalition's priorities. Funding will be a major topic. I will e-mail the steering committee members a summary of our call and a project plan by Friday. I'll also schedule a dinner meeting for the following Friday."

"I'll look out for your e-mail."

Serengeti walked into the office and announced, "Excuse me Kalahari and Karma. Mr. Allure just arrived. He is waiting in my office to discuss the Center's investment strategies."

Kalahari looked over at the clock. "Sorry, honey. I lost all track of time. I'll be in a minute. I was just finishing up with Karma about the steering committee. She has agreed to participate."

Serengeti responded, "Karma, I can't begin to tell you how much your participation means to us."

Standing up to leave, I said, "It's just my way of giving back."

Serengeti walked over to me and gave me a hug as she thanked me. "And we love that about you."

I hugged her back and gathered my things to leave. Kalahari walked around her desk to give me a hug. We embraced and then joined hands, making a small circle as Kalahari offered an impromptu prayer. "Father, Mother, God, we want to thank you for blessing us with the resources and support to help Ayo's dream become a reality. We give thanks that you are our refuge and strength, a very present help in trouble. We ask that you remind Ayo, her partner and congregation, the residents of Madison, and everyone in the universe that you are also their refuge and strength, a very present help in trouble. Help us all know that we have nothing to fear, though the earth should change, though the mountains shake in the heart of the sea. We give thanks that the African American community is healed and transformed. We trust and have faith that everything is being worked out for everyone's highest and greatest good. May it be so. Ase. Amen."

CHAPTER 24

▼

"To appoint unto them that mourn in Zion, to give unto them beauty for ashes, the oil of joy for mourning, the garment of praise for the spirit of heaviness; that they might be called trees of righteousness, the planting of the Lord, that he might be glorified."

—Isaiah 61:3

December is typically a happy month in my life, but Y2K offered a different scenario. It started with December 3, the day Illinois' poet laureate, Gwendolyn Brooks died at the age of 83. My heart was heavy as I thought about the first time Uncle Wilson read Violet and I poems from Ms. Brooks' *A Street in Bronzeville*. My eyes filled with tears as I revisited one of my favorite childhood memories, the afternoon I heard Ms. Brooks recite *We Real Cool* at Uncle Wilson's house. I think that's when my love of poetry began.

My tears became a waterfall on December 9 when I learned that in a 5-4 ruling, the U.S. Supreme Court halted the manual recount of Florida's ballots. Al Gore relinquished any claim to the presidency on December 13. George W. Bush and his crew legalized the obvious hijacking by seizing the throne on the very same day.

On December 14, the Baptiste family's jovial Christmas spirit took a nosedive as we struggled to make sense of Colette's deteriorating health condition. Her memory and ability to walk were steadily deteriorating. Doctors couldn't answer most of the questions that we asked. The only thing they could do was try to convince us that Colette's recovery may never end. No one wanted to accept their prognosis. Fortunately for us, Aunt Jo became our family's official prayer warrior. Ever on guard, she insisted that we affirm Colette's wholeness and full recovery at all times.

December 15 marked my birthday. Momma arrived the day before. She did her best to brighten everyone's spirits with a small birthday celebration for me at the hospital. She decorated the waiting room with purple and pink balloons. A purple tie-dyed birthday banner that I hadn't seen since sixth grade was hanging against the wall. Momma's ability to resurrect precious childhood memories is priceless. Seeing the banner made me smile and think about the first co-ed party Violet and I had. Eric Richmond, a Michael Jackson look-a-like and the dream date of every sixth grader, asked me to dance and became my steady boyfriend for the next seven weeks. We danced to Stevie Wonder's *Love's In Need of Love Today.* Momma and Daddy stood in the background hugging each other and mouthing the words to the song. Thanks to our new neighbor, Devon Connelly, Violet was absorbed in conversation and unable to bother me for once. Everything was everything. And then it happened. My first kiss. As Stevie spelled out the words l-o-v-e, Eric's lips touched mine.

Watching Cane, Charlie, Colin, and Chase muster the energy to sing happy birthday to me with fake smiles plastered on their faces reminded me that I was a long way from heaven. Their eyes were windows to their souls. When I stared into them, all I could see was fear and sorrow. They sat quietly eating slices of the New German Chocolate Cake that Momma bought from CakeLove. It was a delicious, scratch-made, densely chocolaty cake paired with a coconut and vanilla infused butter cream. Aunt Jo's neighbor hosted a tasting party for CakeLove. She dropped off one of their cakes for Uncle Charles. After one bite, Momma fell in love and became a fan. She ordered New German Chocolate cakes, one for me and one for Violet.

This morning Momma called Violet to wish her a happy birthday and to confirm the delivery of the cake. That's when Violet dropped her atom bomb. She married Ramses in one of those tacky all night Las Vegas wedding chapels. As Momma was cleaning up, she casually announced to the family that Violet was married. When Cane tried to find out the details, Momma headed him off with polite humor. "You know your cousin. She's always trying to save money. I guess she saved me thousands of dollars."

Momma's quick wit hid the fact that Violet's nuptials killed her dream to marry off one of her daughters in grand style. The style I imagine she wanted with Daddy, but couldn't have because her mother disapproved of him.

To make matters worse, Aunt Willie, Daddy's eldest sister in Chicago, left a long message later that day about her twin brother, Uncle Wilson, dying from a sudden heart attack. The news hurt Momma because Uncle Wilson was the only Francois sibling that liked her and visited us in Oakland. Aunt Willie and the other four Francois sisters didn't share his affections. She also revealed that they knew about Ohnedaruth and wanted him to join us at the funeral in Chicago so he could meet the relatives. As Momma told me her decision, I wondered whether her old wounds surrounding Daddy's affair with Devi would resurface. "Karma, I don't feel comfortable leaving Colette and the family right now. So I'm not going to fly out to Chicago for the funeral. I want to make sure that you, Violet, and Ohnedaruth go. I think it would be good for you all to go together. It might give your sister just the push she needs to get to know Ohnedaruth. He would have a chance to meet his other family members."

"Momma, I'm not sure if I can even go. My budget is pretty tight."

"If you don't mind, I would like to cover everyone's expenses."

"Thanks Momma. I'm not optimistic about Violet going. Remember how she acted at Thanksgiving."

"I know, but maybe your sister has had a change of heart."

"I doubt it."

"You may be right, but I want you to call her and Ohnedaruth to see if they will go."

"Okay, Momma I'll try, but I can't promise anything."

"Let me know as soon as you hear back from your sister and brother."

I couldn't help but wonder if Momma was using Colette's illness to escape facing the Francois sisters. So I asked her. "If Colette wasn't sick, would you go to Uncle Wilson's funeral?"

"Honestly, I don't think I would."

"Why not?"

"Karma, you know that I never really connected with your aunts."

"Yeah, I think I got the message while we were growing up, but I never understood what happened."

"That was such a long time ago. We don't need to bring up the past now."

"Come on Momma. Don't you think we have suffered enough behind the Francois family secrets?"

"You're right, *Cherie*. I didn't want to say anything that would damage your relationship with your aunts. My mother did that with your Uncle Charles and me whenever she spoke about Papa. We grew up not really wanting to be connected to him or his family. I didn't want you girls to miss out on knowing your Francois family. They've always loved you and your sister."

"Momma, I'm a grown woman. I think I can handle the truth. Besides how bad can it be?"

"It's pretty bad. I told your father that I would never tell you girls what happened."

"Daddy's not here. I wanna know what happened."

"Okay, I'll tell you, but you have to promise me that you aren't going to go off and say something to your aunts."

"You have my word. This stays between us."

"Your father loved his sisters, but they never accepted me as his wife. When I was pregnant with you and your sister, I was diagnosed with toxemia. As soon as I went into labor, the doctor informed me that he couldn't find your heartbeats. That's when I became hysterical and screamed for your father. They let him in because of my hysteria and continuous screams that I was giving birth to stillborn twins. They thought that he would calm me down. Instead, I freaked him out so much that he ran and called your Aunt Willie. Eugene begged her and his other sisters to come to Oakland, but they refused. Your Aunt Willie told him that I deserved to give birth to dead babies since I trapped your father into marrying him. Her words numbed your father. Fortunately, a great team of doctors discovered that you were both lying sideways. So they massaged my stomach until you girls turned around. After you and Violet were born, Eugene refused to contact his sisters. Uncle Wilson was the only person he communicated with. Throughout our marriage, I tried to get Eugene to forgive his sisters, but he wouldn't let it go. Every time Wilson and Ophelia came to visit, they would try to get your father to forgive your aunts, but he never yielded. That man could be so stubborn."

"If Daddy didn't want to forgive them, why did we spend time with them in Chicago when we were growing up?"

"When you all were seven, Uncle Wilson begged Eugene to bring you and Violet to a family reunion in Chicago. I put my foot down and told him that you both needed to know your Francois family. So he agreed to let you both fly to Chicago provided Uncle Wilson took care of you. That's how you both started spending every other summer in Chicago. I didn't think it was right to keep you from knowing your aunts."

"Did you forgive them?"

"*Cherie*, I had no other choice. I couldn't be bitter about them not liking me. I had to do the same thing I did with my own parents."

"What was that?"

"Accept them for who they were and love them from afar."

"Just like that?"

"No *Cherie*. It was not instant magic. Forgiving them was a process."

"Is it the same process you're using to forgive Daddy?"

The room got silent. One minute multiplied into five. Before I knew it ten minutes had passed. Feeling like I had overstepped my boundaries, I withdrew my question. "Momma, I think I may have asked too many questions. Don't worry about answering that one."

"Nonsense. I just needed to gather myself. My feelings about your father and his choices remain a struggle for me. My forgiveness work is probably the hardest thing I've ever done. I'm trying to forgive myself for accepting Eugene's behavior without directly addressing it. I never told him how I really felt. I just made demands of him. He felt so guilty that he worked himself like a mad man to fulfill them. That was my revenge."

"When did you realize that you needed to let go of your resentment and unforgiveness?"

"Two months ago. I called Wilson to tell him about Ohnedaruth. After I vented and cried about how betrayed I felt, he reminded me that I had a choice in how I responded to the pain. Then he read me a letter that Eugene wrote to him about how much he has learned through loving us. Your father talked about how we were helping him to understand and manifest what Stevie Wonder refers to as love +love-hate=love energy in the liner notes of *Songs In The Key of Life*. You know how your father was about love mentalism. He enjoyed analyzing the messages in Stevie's music."

"You don't have to remind me. Daddy was always preaching about our duty to spread love mentalism on the planet. I remember when I asked him to explain the concept to me. He said t began and ended with three sentences: Be Love. Love Light. Live as the Spirit of life. Then he had Violet and I memorize it."

"That was your father. A true son of the sixties."

"He was all about love, light, peace, equality, economic justice, humanity, Black power, Swami Satchidananda, yoga, John and Alice Coltrane, Santana, and Stevie Wonder."

Momma smiled as she joked, "There was never a dull moment with Eugene. He was always exploring. Every month, he seemed to be on a new journey of enlightenment. I learned early on that his spirit needed to explore all sources of illumination. Sometimes I explored with him. Other times, I opted out. The beautiful thing about your father was that he never made me feel guilty about not following his interests. He gave me space to find my own way. That was his way of spreading love mentalism."

"Daddy was good at that, but I have to admit that I'm still wrestling with making love mentalism a reality in my life, especially with Violet."

"*Cherie*, so am I."

"Are you really okay with her elopement?"

"No, but what choice do I have? I have to accept your sister's decision."

"How can you just accept it?"

"I didn't say I've done that yet. I'm working on it in the same way that I'm working on forgiving your father and Devi."

"How?"

"When I talked with Wilson, he encouraged me to work on changing my perceptions about what happened by looking at your father's affair as an opportunity to learn and grow. You know how your uncle weaved in his metaphysical wisdom and new thought teachings that he acquired while attending Reverend Johnnie Coleman's church. By the end of the conversation, Wilson persuaded me to look at the pain I was carrying as beauty for ashes. He compared my suffering to the ashes and reminded me that new beginnings were born out of brokenness. Transformed consciousness, stronger minds, kinder and gentler hearts, and commitments to live in love and with peace would naturally be a part of the new beginnings. So I decided to start thinking that everything that happened between

Eugene and Devi was beauty for ashes. That's what I'm going to have to do with your sister's elopement."

"Uncle Wilson was a wise man."

With tears in her eyes, Momma replied, "Yes, he was."

CHAPTER 25

▼

"Hope does not disappoint us, because God's love has been poured into our hearts."

—Romans 5:5

The last time I was in Chicago was the summer after my freshmen year at Morgan. Uncle Wilson's colleagues at Johnson Publishing Company had arranged an internship at the DuSable Museum of African American History. That was an experience of a lifetime. I still get goose bumps about working in the museum founded by Dr. Margaret Burroughs, one of my cultural heroines. Her commitment to preserving African American culture was one of the greatest influences on my museum career.

Chicago in July is radically different than Chicago in December. Before I called Ohnedaruth to extend Momma's invitation, I made certain to check the weather report. Bad news. A few days before Uncle Wilson's death, the city braced itself for blizzard conditions as a major winter storm made its way out of the northern Plains and across the Great Lakes region. From the reports, it sounded like the Windy City was in the middle of its snowiest December. The city's full compliment of two hundred and fifty snowplows were on the scene. An additional one hundred and ten trucks were rustled up to push snow. City traffic was snarled. Public schools were closed early. Seventy-five to eighty percent of air traffic into O'Hare International and Midway airports was cancelled. To make matters worse, I had never been forced to face Chicago's winter wonderland.

Uncle Wilson always tried to get me to visit in the winter, but there was no way my Northern California blood could endure below zero weather. He always cautioned me to never say never. I guess he was right.

United Airlines confirmed three available flights into Chi-town from D.C., Columbus, and Oakland. Look at me, I sound like Uncle Wilson talking about his adopted city. Chi-town was one of Uncle Wilson's pet names for his adopted city. Despite his Lake Charles, Louisiana roots, that man loved him some Chicago. His love ran so deep that it was hard to believe he wasn't a native son. Daddy didn't carry the same love for the place. They were day and night when it came to appreciating the Windy City. Maybe Daddy's love faded when his sisters refused to accept Momma as his wife.

Uncle Wilson and Miss Ophelia made sure Violet and I saw every inch of Chicago during our summer visits. The first few days of our trip were spent touring his culturally rich neighborhood of Bronzeville. Our history lesson started with Uncle Wilson's home. 3624 S. Martin Luther King, Jr. Drive was a three-story greystone home that crusading journalist and anti-lynching activist, Ida B. Wells-Barnett lived in with her husband and their four children. When the house became a National Historical Landmark in 1973, Miss Ophelia and Mrs. Barnett, one of her Alpha Kappa Alpha Sorority sisters and Uncle Wilson's neighbor, organized a summer garden party to celebrate the occasion. That was a party I will never forget. Miss Ophelia had Violet and I dolled up with Shirley Temple curls courtesy of Aunt Willie, black patent leather Mary Jane's, pearl stud earrings and matching necklaces, and pink and green linen dresses. Our photo with Uncle Wilson even made Jet Magazine. When Momma saw the photo, she called and teased Miss Ophelia about trying to brainwash the daughters and granddaughters of Sigma Gamma Rho Sorority members. They always joked with each other about their sororities.

Mrs. Barnett was the mistress of ceremonies. That afternoon, I learned that she was a diva just like Momma and *Grandmere*. Etta Moten Barnett was multifarious. Her resume included women's rights activist, patron of the arts, civic leader, historian, concert artist, movie star, Broadway actress, and entrepreneur. Early in her career, she became the first African American invited to sing at the White House. Maybe it was the movie star drama that enhanced her stage presence. Whatever it was, I listened to her every word as she introduced Gwendolyn

Brooks, Uncle Wilson's favorite poet, who recited several poems including *We Real Cool.*

When Violet and I returned to Oakland that September, that poem became my show and tell report on the first day of school. My fondness for the poem turned into an obsession. Things got so bad that the nuns sent a note home asking Momma and Daddy to please get me to learn some other poems. Daddy got pissed and started helping me to read and understand the poetry of Nikki Giovanni and Amiri Baraka. Daddy had me pinky swear not to tell Momma. She found out anyway when Violet blabbed. Instead of chastising me or picking a fight with Daddy, Momma calmly explained that the nuns might not appreciate the creative expression of the Black nationalists, so it would be better to share it with family. Daddy never found out. How could he when Momma was so smooth?

Uncle Wilson shared the same smoothness as Momma. They were cut from the same cloth. Meticulous, well-dressed, proper folks who insisted on vicuna cashmere, white linen napkins and table cloths, exotic floral bouquets on a weekly basis, expensive Italian wines, nine course meals with the appropriate silverware, and French desserts with Turkish black coffee. He was the gentleman's man in much the same way that Momma was a grand dame. They even had nicknames for each other. He was the Duke of Bronzeville. She was the Crescent City Queen.

I loved watching Uncle Wilson on Sunday afternoons reclining in his burgundy leather chair with a glass of pink lemonade and a slice of Miss Ophelia's seven up cake. They kept him company as he read the Chicago Defender and Tribune. You could always tell when he was reading something intensely. He would pull at his sterling silver cufflinks and scratch the sleeves of his starched white shirt as he rested his large red brick brown hands on his clean-shaven face. Periodically, he would look up and check to see if Violet and were okay. Those steel grey eyes would meet mine and smile a grin that I'll never see again.

I decided to call Ohnedaruth first. Convincing him to come would be easy, painless, and free of any drama. "Hi Ohnedaruth! This is …"

"My sister."

Surprisingly, it didn't sound strange for him to refer to me as his sister. I guess I'm growing. "You know my voice already?"

"You're my sister. Don't you think I should?"

"If you say so."

"How are you doing?"

"Well, I'm doing ..."

"Your voice sounds a little tired. What's been going on with you?"

"Family."

"What happened?"

"A few things. My cousin Colette is in intensive care. She's been diagnosed with sarcoidosis."

"When did this happen?"

"Thanksgiving weekend."

"How bad is it?"

"I'd rather not say. The family is trying to focus energy on her wholeness and health."

"Can I do anything to help?"

"Keep her in your prayers."

"I'll tell George and *Mum* too."

"Thanks."

"So what else is going on?"

"Uncle Wilson, Daddy's eldest brother, made his transition last night in Chicago."

"How old was he?"

"85. Uncle Wilson died of a sudden heart attack. The funeral is next week. Daddy's sisters want us to come. You, me, and Violet. Momma is willing to pay for everyone's travel expenses."

"That was generous of her. Is she coming?"

"No. Momma needs to stay in D.C. with my Aunt and Uncle right now."

"So when did our aunts find out about me?"

"Apparently, they've known for awhile."

"How long is awhile?"

"I'm not sure."

"Do you think that a funeral is the best place for me to meet everyone?"

"From what Momma told me, they really want you to come. So I don't think it will be uncomfortable for them."

"Okay, then I'll go."

"One sibling down. Another to go."

"You said that like you don't expect Violet to come. Is she still having a problem with me being her brother?"

"To be honest, I don't really know or care. I haven't talked to her since Thanksgiving evening. Momma talked to her this morning and learned that she and Ramses eloped in Las Vegas."

"Stop teasing me. I thought your *mum* was organizing their wedding as the event of the decade."

"Unfortunately I'm not."

"What made her do it?"

"I don't have a clue. She's an adult. Adults do what they want."

"You sound so detached."

"Violet made a choice and married the man she wanted to be with despite his thuggish ways, illegal activities, domineering attitude, and verbal abuse. There's nothing Momma or I can say."

"You have a point, but don't you think you should try and keep the lines of communication open?"

"There was never a line to keep open."

"That's strange. I thought twins were supposed to be close."

"Not for Violet and me. We're night and day, and have always been that way. Maybe we'll always be that way."

"Well, is your *mum* going to stay in touch with her?"

"She probably will."

"I hope so."

Tired of talking about Violet, I changed the subject back to our trip to Chicago. "After I talk to Violet, I'll call you back. I think we should try and leave the evening before the funeral and return a day later. What do you think?"

"Please make my return flight to Oakland because I am spending the holiday with *Mum* and George."

"Not a problem."

"Good luck with convincing Violet."

"I won't be convincing her to do anything. I'm just calling to provide information. If she accepts, cool. If not, cool."

"I'll chat with you later."

As I dialed Violet's cell phone, I realized that having Ohnedaruth as a brother was starting to feel like a gift. The thing I always wished I had with Violet, but knew it was damn near impossible, a sibling who gets along with me. His presence inspired a hope I believed would not disappoint me in the way I have allowed myself to be disappointed by Violet. Through our connection, God was pouring love into my heart and healing the wounds created by Daddy's indiscretion. Perhaps it might also heal the disappointment I have towards Violet.

Unable to speak to Violet directly, I left a voicemail. Violet declined the invitation by having Ramses deliver the return message on my cell phone's voicemail. After hearing him explain as the household "spokesperson" that Violet couldn't support a family event that included a bastard child and enemy, I knew she was light years away from accepting Ohnedaruth. The sad thing about all of this is Violet can't see that she has become her own enemy. My prayer is that she wakes up before it's too late.

CHAPTER 26

▼

"Everything old has passed away; see everything has become new!"
—2 Corinthians 5:17

Ohnedaruth suggested that we fly into Chicago two days ahead of our original schedule so we could hang out and see the places that shaped Daddy's adolescence: Jean Baptiste Point DuSable High School, Amy & Lou's, Union Park, Glady's Luncheonette, the South Side Community Art Center, Wabash Avenue YMCA, and the Field Museum. Momma made arrangements for us to stay at Dusk to Dawn, a bed and breakfast located a few blocks from Uncle Wilson's home in the historic Calumet, Giles Prairie District. Uncle Charles recommended it to Momma after he and Aunt Jo stayed there during the Fourth of July weekend.

It was a little after two in the afternoon when I arrived. The owners, Dawn and Jim, greeted me with a welcome basket filled with goodies. I was charmed by the nineteenth century original woodwork, high ceilings, fireplaces, and stained glass windows. We sat in the main parlor sipping vanilla almond tea, listening to Bobby McFerrin's *Bang! Boom* CD, and talking about Dawn's family history. As Bobby belted out his song, *Friends*, I couldn't help but feel a kindred spirit bond of friendship forming. You know how it is when you naturally click with someone. It's like you've known them forever and a day. That's how it was with them.

It was fascinating to learn about Dawn's family business, Griffin Funeral Home. It was located on the former site of Camp Douglas Civil War Training and Induction Center. During the Civil War, the Center served as a Confederate prisoner of war camp. Sam Houston, Jr., former governor of Texas, was one of Camp Douglas' most famous prisoners. Forty-five minutes into the conversation, I felt my eyes closing. So I excused myself and settled into the Emerald Room. The large queen bed became my afternoon nesting spot until I heard Ohnedaruth's voice calling me on the other side of the door. Pounding hard on the door, Ohnedaruth called out, "Karma, bloody wake up."

"Is that my brother trying to knock the door down?"

"Indeed it is, fair lady."

"The door is open. Come on in."

Carrying a large box wrapped in red paper, Ohnedaruth entered the room. "I come bearing gifts."

"You shouldn't have."

"But I should and you know it."

"Somebody's been reading Miss Manners on how to be a good brother."

"I'm more than that. I'd say your dear, superb brother."

"You're so right."

Handing me the gift box, Ohnedaruth began to sing. "Happy Birthday to you. Happy Birthday to you. Happy Birthday to my dear sweet Karma. Happy Birthday to you."

Standing to hug him, I replied, "Thank you, sweetie. I really appreciate your kindness."

"It's just a small token from George and me."

As I opened the box and read the label, I noticed a Sanskrit word that I was familiar with. *Chaturanga*. It means divided into four parts. It is one of my favorite yoga poses because it challenges me, helps strengthens my wrist and arms, and tones my stomach. Before breaking the plastic wrap on the box, I asked, "Is this a yoga-inspired gift?"

"You'll have to open it and see."

"No clues."

"None. Open the box."

"Alright. Alright. Let's see what this *Chaturanga* is all about."

It was a game set with an uncheckered playing mat, velvet storage bags, and intricately carved pieces including kings, elephants, knights, and chariots.

"Do you like it?"

"I'm not sure what it is."

"It's a *Chaturanga* game."

"How do you play it?"

"Before you play, you have to understand the game's origins."

"I guess I'm gonna get a history lesson."

"You sure are."

"You're definitely our father's son."

Smiling Ohnedaruth began to explain, "*Chaturanga* was played in India before the seventh century. It's the oldest known form of chess. The word itself was used to describe the Indian army of Vedic times. There was a four-part platoon consisting of an elephant, chariot, three soldiers on horseback, and five foot-soldiers. The game's pieces include the elephant or *gaja,* chariot or *ratha,* king or *rantra,* counselor or *mantra,* horse or *asva,* and the infantry or *pedati.*"

"Why is the board uncheckered?"

"That I don't know, but it shares the same number of squares as a chess board. 64."

"I take it you are an avid player."

"Yes. I grew up playing it and chess."

"Daddy loved chess."

"Do you play?"

"He taught Violet and I, but I never developed an interest."

"That will change with *Chaturanga.*"

"How sure are you?"

"Very. I'll teach you."

As Ohnedaruth began to set up the board, I realized that I really do enjoy having a brother. All of the old feelings that I've been lugging around seemed to be gone. Even though we're here to say goodbye to Uncle Wilson, I can't help but think that life is getting better. Everything feels new filled with possibilities.

CHAPTER 27

▼

"Let love be genuine."

—Romans 12:9

Ohnedaruth's hunger pains ended our first *Chaturanga* game. Although he won, I was determined not to let my loss extinguish my newfound desire to master the game. Since he won, Ohnedaruth insisted that we go to Gandi's Indian Restaurant for dinner. One of his Ohio State classmates recommended it. I had no objections. I could never resist Indian cuisine.

We bundled ourselves up and drove to Devon Avenue in Ohnedaruth's Ford Taurus rental car. The car radio was tuned to WBBM-FM. It was a station known for playing some of Chicago's best house music. We were both so caught up in the groove that when the DJ announced that the Funky Buddha Lounge was featuring some of Chicago's best house music DJs, we both smiled and nodded in agreement. We knew we would be there dancing until the lights came on and the proprietors asked us to leave.

The restaurant was nearly packed when we arrived. There was a large altar in the front dedicated to the Hindu goddess Lakshimi and Lord *Rama*. An assortment of fruit lay at the feet of each bronze sculpture. Red dominated the restaurant's décor. An array of small clay plots containing oil and cotton wicks were set in each window. Our server, Anand looked like a professor with his gold wired framed glasses. He and Ohnedaruth struck up a conversation about Lahore. It turns out that Anand's family was also from Lahore. They left India right before independence and settled in the same part of London where Ohnedaruth's family lives. What a small world. When I asked why the altar was dedicated to *Lakshimi* and Lord *Rama*, Anand explained that his mother felt that their family business would be prosperous at all times if it reflected and celebrated *Divali*, the Hindu New Year known as the Festival of Lights. Because the celebration occurs at the end of the harvest season, *Lakshimi*, the goddess of wealth and prosperity, is worshipped. Anand also shared that *Divali* celebrates the triumph of good over evil which is based on three legendary Indian epics featuring Lord *Rama*'s return to *Ayodha*, after his self-imposed exile of fourteen years; King Bali's descent into hell after he extended his evil kingdom over the earth; and Lord *Krishna*'s destruction of the demon king *Narakaaura*.

Anand recommended that we try the *Dahi Vada*, mouth-watering lentil fritters in yogurt spice, and *Pakoras*, assorted vegetable fritters with chickpea flour, for appetizers. I ordered *Bhindi Masala*, okra cooked with homemade spices as my entree. Ohnedaruth selected *Alu Bangen*, eggplant and potatoes. *Masala* tea warmed us as we waited for our appetizers. While we feasted, we mapped out our evening plans. A couple seated next to us discussed their plans to see Frank "Little Sonny" Scott, Jr., a Maxwell Street bluesman, play a homemade instrument made of hundreds of door keys at Blue Chicago. I nudged Ohnedaruth and told him that we should check out the first show since it was still too early to head over to the Funky Buddha Lounge. As soon as Ohnedaruth began asking the couple for directions to Blue Chicago, my cell phone rang. "Hello"

"Good evening, *Cherie*."

"Hi Momma."

"Did you and your brother make it to Chicago okay?"

"Yes, we did. We're actually eating dinner right now."

"I won't keep you long then. I'm calling to let you know that your Uncle Wilson's lawyer, Antoine Lafayette, left a message with me requesting that you and Ohnedaruth attend the reading of the will the day after the funeral."

"Do you think Uncle Wilson left us something?"

"Karma, I really don't know, but if you are both invited to attend the reading of the will, then it's my guess that Wilson intended you both to have something from his estate."

"It's probably a small token of affection."

"Whatever it is, I want you both to be careful. If you've been given something that your aunts want, I know they'll try to manipulate you."

"Come on, Momma. They wouldn't fight over Uncle Wilson's property."

"Karma, you don't know your aunts like I know them."

"Momma, they wouldn't create any drama. They're looking forward to meeting Ohnedaruth."

"Belle Violette, take my word on this one. Watch out for those Francois sisters. Willie, Mabilene, Lucille, and Elizabeth will smile right in your face and stab you in your back. You be careful. Whatever you and your brother do, remember not to sign anything over to them until you have talked to me."

"Momma, I'm sorry, but I just can't believe that they would do anything to hurt us."

"Play Pollyanna if you want to."

Whenever Momma cautions me with that Pollyanna stuff, I know she ain't playing with me. So to avoid any drama, I promised, "Okay Momma, we'll be careful."

"Call me *Cherie* if you need anything."

"I will."

"Tell Ohnedaruth hello. You both have a good night."

"Bye Momma."

When we walked into Blue Chicago, "Little Sonny" was giving the audience an oral history lesson about how he got his start on Maxwell Street. Born and bred in Texas, he came to Maxwell Street in the 1950s. I imagined that Daddy probably knew about him and enjoyed his music. "Little Sonny" started playing the keys when blues bands that he booked didn't show up to perform. Over time he collected over three hundred and fifty keys from musicians, friends, and the historic buildings that were later demolished on Maxwell Street. His story and talent amazed us.

After Little Sonny completed his first set, we left for the Funky Buddha Lounge. The directions that the bouncer at Blue Chicago gave us got us lost. What was probably a fifteen-minute drive turned into an hour sojourn. By the grace of the Buddha himself, we found our way to a parking spot a block from the club. Waiting in line to get in, we noticed the diversity of the crowd. It was a United Nations gathering that looked like one of those Benetton ads. Inside of the club, we found even more diversity. Some women were dancing with men. Others were dancing with women. Several men were dancing with each other. And then there were folks who were dancing alone. I was amazed that there was no drama on the dance floor. Everybody was there to have a good time.

Ohnedaruth and I flowed in and found a space in the center of the floor of the first room. Our bodies naturally moved to the beat. That night, I learned that we both were dance maniacs. We can rock a dance floor like you would not believe. Our moves were fluid. They were an eclectic blend of free-style expression, meringue, salsa, seventies disco moves, and stepping. We took the appropriate beverage and bathroom breaks in the three hours that we rocked the floor. Just when we were getting our groove on, my watch registered three a.m. The lights came on and the proprietors announced that our evening of dancing was over. We had no choice but to head back to the bed and breakfast.

Dawn and Jim left us a note about a surprise dessert and apple cider in the kitchen. A white box with a purple bow and gold label sat on the table. It was from Isn't That Special Outrageous Cakes in New Jersey. When I opened the box, I knew Momma had requested the heart-shaped German Chocolate cake with purple icing and a gold Egyptian ankh in the middle. The message on the cake made me smile: Be Love. Love Light. Live as the Spirit of Life! It was Momma's way of reminding me to let love be genuine. I shared the meaning of the message with Ohnedaruth as we savored two huge slices of cake. We both promised to make it a reality in our lives and family.

CHAPTER 28

▼

"It is for this that you were called—that you might inherit a bless-ing."

—1 Peter 3:9

Lately, my morning meditations have included visions of colorful mandalas. They appeared as highly decorative, symmetrical diagrams. The mandalas have been taking me on a wordless journey into my mind's deepest mysteries in the same way that Alice Coltrane and Carlos Santana's music used to when I listened to their 1974 classic, *Illuminations* during my Morgan years. This morning, all kinds of visions entered my third eye. Angels of air, water, and sunlight invited me to travel deep into my heart where I touched the bliss of the eternal now. I was exactly where I wanted to be. Questions arose. What happens when I end my meditation and go into the world? How do I maintain my focus? Inner wisdom advised me to focus on the circular shapes of the mandalas. They had no begin-ning or end. They allowed me to connect with the stillness of their center, the symbol of ultimate perfection and eternity. It brought me to the sacred space within myself where tranquility and peace reside.

I saw two images of mandalas in my meditation. The first mandala was an image of yellow sunflowers. For me, they represented a flowering of self-aware-ness, the eternal self in full bloom, my unchanging essence. The second image was filled with white doves surrounding Daddy and Uncle Wilson's smiling faces on a chalice overflowing with happiness. It felt like the greatest blessing I could inherit. A blessing I could share with Ohnedaruth and the Francois family. A blessing that could cancel out any drama that Momma thought Aunt Willie and her sisters were capable of causing.

Before Ohnedaurth and I could begin our day with breakfast at Gladys' Luncheonette, I realized that I'd spoken too soon about the power of the blessing. Marvin Gaye's *What's Going On* CD was blasting from the speakers as the smell of southern home cookin' tickled our noses. Fresh biscuits, pastries, and corn muffins seduced my tummy as I noticed that the turquoise walls were lined with the same colorful paintings and black and white photos of famous patrons that I remembered seeing during my summer visits. Mayor Harold Washington's picture made me smile and remember the pride and possibilities he offered Chicago. His presence is definitely missed.

The restaurant was separated into non-smoking and smoking sections by a latticed room divider. We chose the non-smoking section. A candelabra chandelier caught my eye as I looked up at the ceiling. Our waitress, Anita, was dressed in a crisp white uniform. After she politely introduced herself, Ohnedaruth asked her for a brief history of the restaurant. Anita was happy to share. I pretended to be interested even though I new the story by heart. Gladys Joyner Holcombe started serving plate lunches to Black folks in the waiting room of a Greyhound Bus Station in Memphis in 1935. Ten years later, her family persuaded her to move to Chicago with her husband. Shortly thereafter, she opened up Gladys' Luncheonette in a basement to make ends meet for her family. Her husband waited tables while she cooked. In 1963, they moved into the current location.

Daddy told me so many stories about the people he met here like the Negro League baseball player Double Duty Ratcliffe. Daddy's descriptions of the lunches he fondly treasured used to haunt me in my sleep. My biggest fear during my summer visits was that I wouldn't be able to eat it all: fried chicken, baked turkey neck, deliciously crisp cornmeal fried catfish smothered in hot sauce, chicken smothered in rich brown gravy, spicy barbequed rib tips, fried corn, chitterlings, black-eyed peas, pickled beets, smoky and tender collard greens, macaroni and cheese, mashed potatoes with gravy, fried cabbage, peach cobbler, and sweet potato pie.

After Anita took our order of scrambled eggs, grits, biscuits, and hash browns, the first phase of Francois family drama Chicago-style began. Aunt Willie called with news about an evening memorial service planned by Uncle Wilson's church, Christ Universal Temple. She wanted family members to boycott it. Because I was confused by her request, I asked for an explanation. My question set off World War III. "Karma, you got the same kind of sass your mother has. You girls ain't never had no respect for this family. Don't ask me shit about why. Just do what I say. I'm head of the Francois family now. What I say goes."

Ignoring her comments, I tried to bring some calmness to the conversation. "Aunt Willie, there's no need to get upset."

"Don' talk back to me. I'm your elder."

"I'm not trying to disrespect you. I just want to know why."

"That's the problem with you girls."

"Aunt Willie, you're obviously upset. I'm not trying to make things worse, but I really don't understand why we can't attend the service. If you can explain then I'm sure I'll understand."

"Look, I don't know what kind of way you're used to dealing with your elders, but I'm not your father with his free love, free thinking bullshit."

"Aunt Willie, as long as you're upset, we won't be able to talk so I'm going to end the conversation before we say some things we'll both regret."

"Who do you think you're talking to?"

"Like I said, Aunt Willie, I'm ending the conversation now. If you calm down and find that you can talk to me without disrespecting my parents and I, then call me back. Otherwise, I'll see you at the wake tomorrow evening."

"You're just like that high *yella* bitch Eugene married."

The only response I had for Aunt Willie was an old fashioned hang up. So much for the blessing of happiness that I thought I could share with family members. My phone rang immediately. Instead of answering it, I turned off the ringer and smiled at my brother.

"Karma, what was that all about?"

"I really don't want to spoil our day with Aunt Willie's drama."

"Okay, but if you want to talk about it, let me know."

"It's not worth it."

"Well, then let's talk about something that is."

"Uncle Wilson's church is having his memorial service tonight at seven o'clock. I really think we should go. I know he would have wanted us to be there to celebrate his life with people he loved."

"Then we'll go. Do you know where the church is?"

"I vaguely remember, but I can call and get the address."

"Sounds like a plan."

When I turned my phone back on, I had three new messages. They were all from Aunt Willie. Message number one was filled with a chorus of fuck you's. So I deleted it. Messages two and three followed suit. As I deleted the messages, I could hear Momma's voice warning me about Aunt Willie and her sisters. Once again, I hated to admit that she was right.

After breakfast, we decided to check out an exhibit of female artists at the Mexican Fine Arts Center Museum. It was the perfect distraction for family drama. I was excited to see the vibrant paintings of María Izquierdo, a key figure in twentieth century Mexican art. Her still life portraits were engaging and sensual. As I read her bio, I was intrigued to learn that Diego Rivera praised her student work at the National Fine Arts School. Her watercolors of circuses were both melancholy and joyfully innocent. Ohnedaruth and I were moved by Maria's painted scenes of mankind pitted against natural forces beyond human control. He commented that they appeared to be strange allegories. Like Frida Kahlo, she painted several self-portraits and surreal compositions.

After viewing the exhibition, we spent time in the museum gift shop. I purchased an English translation of *Las trampas de la fe* [*The Traps of the Faith*] by Octavio Paz. It was a book about Sor Juana Ines de La Cruz, a seventeenth century Mexican feminist, nun, poet, song writer, and scientist who chose to be a nun because it was the only possibility she had to study and be independent. She was my kind of woman ... feisty and fierce!

Ohnedaruth struck up a conversation with the gift shop manager about Pilsen/Little Village, the neighborhood surrounding the museum. Located in Chicago's lower West Side, Pilsen's borders extend north to south from 16th Street to the Stevenson Expressway. Since the nineteenth century, countless immigrants including Germans, Czechs, Poles, Croatians, Lithuanians, Italians, and Mexicans settled in this area, and left their imprint on the landscape with struggles for political representation, educational reform, social justice, and worker's rights. Ohnedaruth's curiosity increased as the gift manager shared information about the Museum's 1997 exhibition, *Our Home, Our Struggle,* that depicted the neighborhood's history of struggle in a series of portable murals.

Throughout their conversation, the gift shop manager flirted. Caught up in the rapture of the neighborhood's history, Ohnedaruth missed them all. Somewhere in between my exit to and return from the ladies room, Ohnedaurth accepted an invitation for a midmorning cup of coffee from his smitten young female admirer. Her name was Guadelupe. She looked to be in her twenties, but appearances are always deceiving when it comes to women of color. A driver's license is more accurate!

Vibrant red lipstick decorated Guadelupe's full lips. They matched the color of her skirt. It emphasized her wide African-like hips and buttocks. As Guadelupe shared details about her family tree, I was able to see the connection between her African-inspired figure and Afro-Mexican roots that originated in Veracruz, Mexico, later transported to Cuba before arriving in Chicago. Her conversation was infused with the words of Jose Marti, Cuba's victorious revolutionary: "There is no tolerance when dealing with acts of hate." Guadelupe's words created a fiercely passionate rhythm that immediately reminded me of Sor Juana.

As we walked up the street to Café Jumping Bean on W. 18th Street, it was clear that Guadelupe had reluctantly cast me in the supporting role of the invisible tolerated sister. Had she been gifted with magical powers, I'm certain that she would have blinked me out of existence. Little did she know that her conversation and attention were being wasted on my gay brother. Not wanting to bust her bubble, I sat quietly at the table as she ordered her coffee black and insisted that Ohnedaruth try a cup of Mexican cinnamon hot chocolate. Thankfully, Ohnedaruth insisted that I also try a cup. When I took my first sip of this unassuming winter treat, a rich rush of pleasure seduced my palate. I dare not admit that it was the closest I had come to having an orgasm in months. Can food really do that?

When I returned from my semi-orgasmic, chocolate high, Guadelupe was knee deep into her historical monologue about the African presence in Mexico. Ohnedaruth was all ears until Guadelupe casually placed her right hand on top of his left hand. Before she could make another move, Ohnedaruth took his hand from hers and turned in my direction. "Would you look at the time? It's getting late. Karma, I think we better leave."

"Okay."

Guadelupe placed her hand back on Ohnedaruth's hand and interjected, "How much longer are you planning to be in town?"

"A day or two."

"If you have some free time, I'd like to show you around Chicago. Perhaps we could have dinner at Nacional 27, a restaurant and dance club that would give you the flavor of twenty-seven Latino countries in their cuisine, drinks, and music."

"Thank you for the offer, but I'm afraid that we won't have time."

"Oh, I wasn't referring to your sister. I meant you and me. One-on-one."

"Oh."

"I hope that you don't mind me being so aggressive, but I rarely meet men that I connect with so easily. I thought we could spend some time getting to know each other. If the dancing is too much, we could have dinner at Las Palmas where the waiters make the guacamole right in front of you or I could treat you to a home-cooked meal at my apartment."

I sat on the edge of my chair wondering what my brother's response would be. As he opened his mouth and carefully formed his words, I knew that Guadelupe was about to be disappointed. "Guadelupe, while I am flattered by your attention, I have to tell you that I'm seeing someone."

"Is it serious?"

"Very."

"That does not bother me. Let's live in the moment."

Their dialogue was beginning to sound like an afternoon soap opera until Ohnedaruth stood up and extended his hand. "It was a pleasure meeting you. My sister and I really enjoyed spending time with you."

Guadelupe stood up and pressed herself into Ohnedaruth's body and whispered something. He immediately stepped back and signaled me to follow him to the car. As we walked towards the door, Guadelupe stood at the table with her hands on her hips loudly shouting, "No man has ever turned down Guadelupe Rosita Magdalena Consuela Rodriguez. What's wrong? You must be gay."

Ohnedaruth proudly turned back around and replied, "As a matter of fact, I am."

Guadelupe stood speechless as we walked out of the café. Our midmorning soap opera with Aunt Willie's phone drama and Guadelupe's full court press on Ohnedaruth appeared to be over. The third was waiting for me in the foyer of the DuSable Museum.

Mosaic-tile portraits of Margaret Burroughs, Wilberforce Jones, and Hammurabi Robb greeted us as we entered the museum. I became nostalgic as I fondly remembered my college internship days. I laughed to myself about being called the museum staff's personal pest for information about the exhibits and African Diaspora art. I clearly remember Dr. Burroughs telling me to pursue my passion with patience and openness. Her words proved to be timeless wisdom. My trip down memory lane was interrupted when I heard a vaguely familiar deep and burly voice call my name. "Karma, what you doin' here? Ma told me you were in town causing trouble."

The voice belonged to Vivian Francois, Aunt Willie's daughter. She was the spitting image of her mother except in skin tone. Vivian's skin was the color of dried tobacco that made for an interesting contrast against the cinnabar color of her mother and half-brother's skin. The best way to describe her features is Fulani. Tall, lean body with fine, aqualine facial features. She had those Francois funny colored-eyes. One minute they were grey, the next minute they were hazel. Her lips were exactly as I remembered growing up: perpetually stuck out to advertise her identity as an angry bully. As a child, I used to be intimidated by Vivian and her angry bully stares, but now they looked like wasted energy emanating from an unhappy soul with a troubled past.

The last time I heard about Vivian, she was having a real hard time serving out her drug possession sentence at Dixon Correctional Center, a co-ed prison located in rural Illinois. She was the black sheep of her family and was mildly tolerated by her stepfather, Uncle Junius and half-brother, Ellis. Aunt Willie had no idea that Vivian was raped. When she reported the rape to prison officials, she was punished with one year in segregation for sexual misconduct. During that year, the same corrections officer continued to rape Vivian who later became pregnant. That's when Aunt Willie got involved.

As soon as Vivian told Aunt Willie about the rape and pregnancy, she turned to Uncle Wilson for support. She couldn't rely on Uncle Junius and Ellis because Vivian had previously stolen large sums of money from them to pay for her heroin habit. Uncle Wilson pulled some strings and arranged for several lawyer friends from the ACLU's Prison Project to help Vivian. Because Illinois law required prisoners to try and resolve grievances informally before filing a formal grievance, the lawyers advised Vivian to request an institutional counselor to resolve her grievance. The counselor ignored Vivian's request. She remained in segregation for her entire pregnancy and gave birth to a son.

Aunt Willie convinced Vivian to name the baby after Uncle Junius. She hoped that he would accept the child as his grandson and help raise it. Uncle Junius rejected the idea. Aunt Willie sent little Junius to live with relatives in Lake Charles. The officer continued to rape Vivian throughout the duration of her incarceration. Each time she became pregnant, she was forced to have an abortion. Mindful of her prison experience, I approached her cautiously. "Hello, Vivian."

"Hello my ass. Ma told me you were in town."

Surprised by her tone, I quipped back, "It's good to see you, too."

"I know you not trying to pick a fight at my job!"

"Calm down Vivian. I'm just trying to say hello."

"Don't try to talk to me like I'm crazy. You always thought you were better than me."

Trying to steer clear of a Francois family drama scene, I quickly shifted the subject. "I don't believe that you have met my brother, Ohnedaruth."

"I know all about your daddy's bastard."

Despite my attempt to avoid drama, it found me anyway. Smiling politely, I replied, "I think you mean my father's son and my brother."

"No. I know what I said, you high fallutin' debutante. Your daddy's bastard."

Losing patience, the tone in my voice increased. "Look, Vivian there's no need to …"

Ohnedaruth intervened and tried to pretend that Vivian hadn't called him a bastard to his face. "Vivian, it's a pleasure to meet you."

Ohnedaruth's polite gesture brought out Vivian's inner beast. Her eyes started rolling as her blonde and brown ghetto girl extension braids shook from side to side. "Well, it ain't a pleasure to meet some half-breed. I hope y'all don't think you can come in town for a few days and take over Uncle Wilson's estate without Ma and the rest of the family fighting you for it."

Ohnedaruth calmly answered, "Vivian, I'm not sure what you are talking about. Karma and I are only here to attend Uncle Wilson's funeral and reading of the will. I'm also here to meet my family which includes you."

"Bastard foreigner, you ain't family. So don't even think about trying to take what Uncle Wilson left Ma and her sisters."

Vivian's supervisor came over and asked her to lower her voice. That's when I pulled Ohnedaruth aside and whispered, "Don't mind her. She's had a very rough life. I'll tell you about it later. I think we should just leave her alone and take our tour of the museum."

"I sensed that."

"You're very perceptive."

"It's not hard to miss. I just listened to her words. That's why I wanted to show her love and compassion."

"I think that's commendable, but it may be a wasted effort. My uncle never accepted Vivian. She grew up in his house and was never given his last name. To make matters worse, Vivian never knew her biological father. She has also been in and out of drug recovery programs, and spent time in prison. To make matters even worse, Vivian was raped in prison several times and gave birth to a son that she barely knows. Trust me when I say that she has led a very hard life."

"Karma, making an effort to give someone love and compassion is never a wasted effort, especially a family member. Now that I know Vivian and I didn't know our fathers, I am more committed to extending myself."

"I hear what you're saying, but I just think she needs therapy. You may be getting way over your head."

"I disagree. Somebody has to make the first move to stop the family drama. Why should we wait for someone else to do what we can do now? Isn't that what our father wanted us to do: Be love. Love light. Live as the Spirit of life?"

"When you put it like that, I'd have to agree."

"I think we owe it to Vivian, ourselves, and the Francois family to let her know that we love her."

"That sounds good in theory, but where do we begin?"

"We can start by telling her that we love her."

"I have to admit that I still don't think she will receive our words."

"It doesn't matter what she does. What matters is that we answer God's call to help heal and restore our family. If we take one step forward, God will do the rest and our entire family will inherit a blessing of love and healing."

"This is dangerous, but I'm willing to step out on faith."

"That's all God wants us to do."

CHAPTER 29

▼

"Bear with one another and if anyone has a complaint against another, forgive each other, just as the Lord has forgiven you, so you must also forgive."

—Colossians 3:13

Echoes of Vivian's voice uttering the word "bastard" followed me into the room where the DuSable Museum housed its permanent collection. The tone of her voice made the word sound like a cussing sailor's soundbyte. Bastard. It's an old French word with Germanic origin. When used as a noun, it refers to a child born out of wedlock or something that is of irregular, inferior, or dubious origin. If it is used as slang, Webster's Dictionary describes it as a person, especially one who is held to be mean or disagreeable. Why did Vivian choose this word to attack Ohnedaruth? Perhaps, her own pain provoked her. Maybe just maybe, she was fighting the fact that she personified Webster's definition: one who is held to be mean. A wise sage once said that we attack others based on what we hate in ourselves.

Ohnedaruth coaxed me out of my mental preoccupation as he stood in front of three sculptures by Marion Perkins: *Jean Baptiste Point DuSable* (Bronze, 1959), *Don Quixote* (Lime Stone, 1958), and *Sancho Panza* (Lime Stone, 1958). "So what do you think about this work?"

"I've always admired the enduring power of Perkins' figurative sculptures and his technique of directly carving into stone and wood. In 1990, Uncle Wilson and I attended an exhibition at this museum featuring his work. It was called *Two Black Artists of the FDR Era—Marion Perkins and Frederick D. Jones.* One of Perkins' sons was present and personally explained that his father began sculpting stone and wood while working at a newspaper stand on Chicago's South Side during the Depression. When he took breaks from his work, he could be found whittling bars of soap. Perkins was discovered by the Illinois Works Progress Administration and encouraged to attend classes at the South Side Community Art Center where he learned how to chisel in stone. His responsibilities as head of a family limited the time he could spend pursuing his passion for sculpture. Despite this limitation, his work was recognized and exhibited by the Art Institute of Chicago in the forties and fifties."

"His work reminds me of European modernists Constantin Brancusi, Andre Derain, and Amedeo Modigliani."

"You sound like an art scholar."

"I'm an amateur at best. I'll leave the scholarly work to you."

Across from Perkins' sculpture were several pieces of visual art by Chicago Black Renaissance artists, William Eduard Scott, Charles White, Eldzier Cortor, and Archibald J. Motley, Jr. Seeing Motley's work brought back memories of his exhibit at the Corcoran Gallery of Art in D.C. Uncle Wilson and Miss. Ophelia were in D.C. for the weekend. Uncle Wilson flew me down from New York to see the exhibit. We were all mesmerized by Motley's depictions of life in Bronzeville and jazz culture. His bold paintings made me feel like I could step back in time and experience the joyous celebration of Chicago's Black life.

Ohnedaruth walked off into a far corner of the room to examine photographs of prominent authors, musicians, dancers, and artists from the Chicago Black Renaissance. They included authors Margaret Walker, Gwendolyn Brooks, Arna Bontemps, and Richard Wright; musicians King Oliver, Louis Armstrong, and Thomas Dorsey; dancers, Katherine Dunham and Talley Beatty; and artists Hughie Lee Smith and Elizabeth Catlett. "Karma, is Elizabeth Catlett a Mexican artist?"

"No. She's African American. She was born in D.C. Why do you ask?"

"I thought that I saw a book about her work in the Mexican Fine Arts Center Museum."

"You probably did. She has been living in Mexico since the late forties. Catlett married a Mexican muralist, Francisco Mora and taught at the National University in Mexico City for many years. Her work has been exhibited widely in Mexico."

"Does the DuSable have any of her work?"

"I think there are several sculptures and lithographs in the adjoining room."

Catlett's *Mother and Child* (1939) greeted us as we entered the room. Her lithograph, *Singing Their Songs* (1992) caught my eye. I had never seen it before. The text describing the work indicated that it was a part of a series of prints created to visually illustrate a poem by Margaret Walker. The title of the print was inspired by the first stanza of the poem that referred to the power that African Americans derived from singing their slave songs. "Ohnedaruth, come check out the detail of the four figures in this print."

"Their eyes reflect an intense perseverance that can't be touched by human beings."

"It's a fierceness that belongs to quiet warriors who move with grace and overcome insurmountable odds."

"This print reminds me of George's play."

"I can see the connection."

I stepped back and watched Ohnedaruth as he continued to drink in the richness of the artwork. Thoughts about Vivian calling him a bastard rented space in my head. I tried to erase them, but this nagging feeling wouldn't let go of me. The question that repeated itself the most was, why didn't Ohnedaruth defend himself?

"Karma, you're so quiet. Are you okay?"

Lost in thought, I stood silent.

"Earth to Karma."

"Sorry, what did you say?"

"What are you thinking about?"

I hesitated before opening my mouth. Should I pose the question or bury it deep in my psyche? My mouth was on automatic pilot and answered for me. "Why didn't you respond to Vivian calling you a bastard?"

"I didn't think I needed to respond."

"You should have stood up to her bullying."

"Her bullying was nothing more than a lifetime of pain locked inside."

"That may be so, but you shouldn't let anyone call you out of your name."

"Karma, I spent many years being called bastard by my uncle and cousins. Those years were made even more difficult by not knowing my father and mother. I felt very lost in life. My self-worth was at an all-time low. Rejection and abandonment were my first and last names. It wasn't until *Mum* told me that she was my mother that I started to let go of the pain. When I came to live with her, she helped me see that the painful experiences that I was forced to endure were things I could choose to grow beyond. *Mum* described it as a divine invitation to become the phoenix rising from the ashes into my God-given potential as divine love. I accepted the invitation. That's why I didn't respond to Vivian. I couldn't mistreat her because she mistreated me. The only thing I could do was empathize."

"I just can't see how you can do this so easily."

"I didn't say it was easy. It was hard to have a family member that I don't know call me a name that used to cause me so much pain, but I couldn't dwell on my past. For me, it's about making choices in the present moment that heal instead of harm. We always have a choice to look within to the love that we have been given by Spirit. We can open our hearts so that this love can pour forth. We can allow it to flow freely in our thoughts, words, and actions. We can open our eyes and see that this love is the balm in humanity's Gilead … the unifying force that transcends all separation and duality. We can choose to be love, do love, see love, sing love, hear love, walk love, talk love, make love, and celebrate love if we just remember that love is all we are, have and need at all times."

"How do you remember to make the choice to love when people push your buttons?"

"I try to come back to myself and ask Spirit what I need to be or give to harmonize the imbalance. The answer is always related to some aspect of love. For example, with Vivian I was called to bear with her and forgive her as Spirit has forgiven me."

"What if you can't gather yourself and calm down long enough to ask this question?"

"In those times, I silently chant *Aham Prema*. It's a Sanskrit mantra that means I am divine love. I say it until I calm myself."

"*Aham Prema*. I can't feel anything."

"Close your eyes and touch your heart with both hands. Repeat the chant forty times."

As I touched my heart and repeated the sacred Sanskrit words to myself, I could feel my anger at Vivian melting. When I opened my eyes, I realized that I was standing before one of Love's Troubadours.

CHAPTER 30

▼

"For the sake of my relatives and friends, I will say peace be within you."

—Psalm 122:8-9

The Hopi Indians teach that we are the ones we have been waiting for. I interpret that teaching to mean that if I want healing in my life and family, I have to be an active force in bringing it about. I can't wait for someone else to do the work. It's my responsibility. I'm the one that I've been waiting for to bring healing into my life and family.

As Ohnedaruth and I approached the entrance of the museum, Vivian stood stone-faced. Her grimace was purposely uninviting. The closer we came to her, the more I realized that the universe was inviting me to choose to end the suffering that has plagued the Francois family. For the sake of my relatives, I opened my mouth and greeted her. "Vivian, may peace be with you."

Her facial expression spelled out the word stunned in capital letters.

"Vivian, I want you to know that I love you and wish you well."

She mumbled, "Huh?"

Reaching in my purse, I pulled out one of my business cards and handed it to her. "We're family. Call me if you're ever in D.C. or want to talk. God bless you, cousin."

Vivian's silence lingered in the aftermath of my gesture. It felt uncomfortable. I didn't know what to expect. Thankfully, Ohnedaruth broke the silence. "Vivian, Karma and I are here for a few more days. We'd love to spend time with you. Here's my cell number. Give us a call."

When Ohnedaruth handed Vivian his phone number, she refused to take it. So he placed it on the information desk as we exited the museum.

Uncle Wilson's memorial service was an evening of six degrees of separation. The first person we saw in the foyer of Christ Universal Temple Chapel was Guadalupe. Standing in an elegant ruby red two-piece silk skirt suit, she greeted us with a half-smile. "What a small world it is."

Ohnedaruth politely laughed, "So we meet again."

Since her last encounter with us didn't end on a pleasant note, I wondered if she was the type of woman who would make a scene in a church. She proved to be a woman of quick wit and humor. "At a funeral of all places. I didn't know that Chicago tours included stops to memorial services."

"It's the latest thing."

"So where are you and your sister headed next?"

"Tomorrow, we're scheduled to attend a wake. The next morning we'll be at a funeral and family repast. The following day is the reading of the will."

"Sounds deathly exciting!"

"The whole trip has been to die for."

"Seriously though, what brings you to the service?"

"Wilson Francois is my father's brother."

"*Dios Mio!*"

"Did you know him?"

"Did I know him? Yes indeed I knew him. Mr. Wilson was one of my mother's favorite dry cleaning clients for many years. He is the reason we started attending service at this church. He also helped me get through Chicago State University."

I interjected, "That sounds like Uncle Wilson. He was always exposing others to his church's teachings and helping young people get an education."

Guadalupe chimed in, "My mother often said he was *un hombre con un grand corazon.*"

Guadalupe escorted us into the sanctuary, which was filled with several luxurious sprays of red gerberas, stargazer lilies, and lavender. A jazz orchestra filled with men dressed in tails took us on a musical journey that traveled through one of Uncle Wilson's favorite Duke Ellington's suites, *Black, Brown and Beige.* It culminated when a petite woman with short chestnut hair, pecan skin, and green eyes appeared on the altar in a lavender silk floor-length gown embellished with fuchsia beaded flowers. She began singing *Come Sunday* in the soulful style of Mahalia Jackson. The woman turned out to be Guadalupe's mother, Isabella.

Reverend Dr. Johnnie Coleman stood in the chapel's pulpit dressed in an array of purple hues. She welcomed everyone to Uncle Wilson's celebration and remarked on the fact that the four hundred-seated chapel was completely filled with people who loved him. Her message focused on how Uncle Wilson lived as a spiritual man, made in the likeness and image of God. She encouraged us all to accept and reflect our own divinity. The service closed with a slide show of photographic memories from Uncle Wilson's life. A recording of Ellington's first Sacred Concert opening number, *In the Beginning God* played in the background. The music filled the church with an abundance of love and light. It reached deep inside of my heart and reminded me how important it is to be love, love light, and live as the spirit of life.

After the service, Guadalupe introduced Ohnedaruth and me to her mother, Isabella. Holding both of our hands, she asked her mother, "*Mami*, guess who this is?"

Looking at me very closely, Isabella responded, "*Dios Mio*, you must be one of the twins."

I answered, "Yes ma'am. My name is Karma."

"*Senor* Wilson had your pictures with him all of the time. Where is your sister?"

"She wasn't able to make it. I'd like you to meet my brother, Ohnedaruth."

Shaking Ohnedaruth's hand, Isabella exclaimed, "Yes, yes. *Senor* Wilson told me about you a few weeks ago."

Ohnedaruth replied, "What did he tell you?"

"That he was happy that everyone finally knew who you were."

Isabella turned to Guadalupe, "*M'ija*, how did you meet them?"

"It was the universe."

"Yes *m'ija*, I know this, but how did it happen?"

"We met earlier today at the museum."

"Did you tell them about the service then?"

"No. I had no idea that they were related to Mr. Wilson. I found out a few minutes before the service started."

"What else happened?"

"That's it, *Mami. No mas.*"

Guadalupe apologized, "I'm sorry about my mother's curiosity. She likes details."

Isabella countered, "My daughter doesn't like me to ask questions. She thinks I embarrass her."

"*Mami*, let's just drop it. Karma and Ohnedaruth don't need to see our mother daughter drama."

Trying to ease the tension, I playfully added, "It would be no different from the moments that I have with my own mother and sister."

Isabella retorted, "See Guadalupe, your mother isn't the only one with questions."

"*Mami*, let's just drop it."

"Okay, *m'ija*. Karma and Ohnedaurth, the church is having a reception with refreshments. You are both welcome to come. I know your Uncle's church family would love to talk to you both."

Trying to shield us from her mother's invitation, Guadalupe asked, "Don't you all have to get up early tomorrow morning for the wake and funeral?"

Ohnedaruth politely agreed by nodding his head. "*Mami*, they probably want to go back to their hotel and rest up."

Grabbing our arms, Isabella directed us to the reception. "Nonsense, *m'ija*. They came all this way to celebrate *Senor* Wilson's life."

Finding it difficult to resist Isabella's forceful nature, we went along. Guadalupe walked behind us mumbling something in Spanish that was probably similar to the things I used to say about Momma when she got too pushy for my liking. One thing is for certain, the emotional drama that plays out between mothers and daughters transcends race, culture, and class. It's just human nature. Mothers are going to be mothers, just like daughters will be daughters. In the end, they both have to learn to accept each other as they are. That's the hard part, but at least Momma and I are on the right track.

CHAPTER 31

▼

"'Lord, if you choose, you can make me clean. He stretched out his hand and touched him, saying, I do choose. Be made clean!"

—Matthew 8:2-3

When I got home from the memorial service, I wrote in my journal. The words surprised me.

Watching Guadelupe and Isabella made me think about the emotional patterns that exist between mothers and daughters. There are so many places and spaces in these relationships that call for healing and acceptance. Sometimes the emotional patterns are deeply imbedded in the genetic makeup of each woman. They can be so deep that the woman herself may not even see them. She may feel them or experience their impact in her life, but have no working vocabulary to name and understand the cause of her feelings and experiences. Without the vocabulary and understanding, the woman remains unaware of the fact that generations of women in her family have passed on a pattern of emotional pain. This pattern represents an inheritance of woundedness. It has the ability to spread like a malignant cancer cell to other parts of her life. When it spreads, it often opens old wounds and creates new ones. Its scar tissue is invisible to the human eye, but emotionally visible to the woman's heart. It weighs enormously and has the power to create unwanted disease in the human body. I'm starting to see that *Grandmere*, Momma, Violet, and I have inherited this wounded trait. So have Aunt Willie and Vivian. I suspect the rest of the Francois women have too. We're all members of the same club, paying the same fee for the privilege of suffering. When will we reject our membership benefits? How can we as daughters and mothers open our eyes, hearts, and spirits to the work of healing and accepting each other? It's a process that begins with each woman surrendering her ability to fix herself and the emotional patterns she has inherited in her mother-daughter relationship. As she surrenders, she must go within to the secret place of the Most High. Here, she must ask God to make her clean. This request to be made clean is a prayer to allow divine love to do the healing work. In saying this prayer, the woman finds courage to trust and remember that it will lead to wholeness. If she ever doubts her prayer, she can come back to the place of inner knowing where she understands and accepts that God's will for her is health and wholeness, not suffering and pain. Her healing will begin to take place when she sees herself as a daughter of the Most High. With this vision of truth, she will be able to approach her life with grace and peace. She will also come to understand that her journey will always be filled with learning opportunities. They will teach her how to love and accept herself better. She will in turn make better choices in selecting who sits in the front row of her life. She will release those who are careless with her heart and set healthy emotional boundaries when appropriate. She will take better care of her spirit, heart, mind, and body. These actions will allow the woman to be open, receptive, and grateful for all of God's blessings in her life. In the end, she will know without a shadow of doubt that God has made her clean. I need this to happen to me. God make me clean.

The next morning, my yoga practice focused on strengthening the core region of my body. Coming onto my hands and knees, I placed my elbows under my shoulders and pressed my palms firmly together. Lifting my hips into the air, I began to feel my abdominal area hollowing out and perineum lifting. I stayed in Dolphin pose for ten breaths. What an intense pose! Before moving into the next pose, I collapsed onto my belly and rested in *Savasana*. After a few moments, I came back into Dolphin and walked my feet back until my body was parallel to the floor. As I pressed my hands together and hugged my inner thighs towards my midline, I tried not to break my concentration. A few breaths later, I lowered myself back down to the floor. I surprised myself by chanting the divine love mantra, *Aham Prema*.

The vibrational sound of the mantra traveled through my body. Devi used to regularly remind me throughout my yoga teacher training that chanting mantras draws you into your core. It calms the mind and heart, releases the effects of any emotional discomfort in your life, and clears space for you to experience peace, clarity, and joy. To honor her teaching, I closed my morning practice with one final chant that she taught me: *Lokah Samastah Sukhino Bhavantu.*

For the first time in a long time my thoughts of Devi were absent anger, blame, or disappointment. They were pure reflection. Uncluttered. Uncomplicated. Perhaps I'm starting to let go of the hurt. Perhaps this is the first sign that God is making me clean. Miracles do happen, you know.

CHAPTER 32

▼

"I have set before you life and death, blessing and cursing, therefore choose life that both thou and thy seed live."

—Deuteronomy 30:19

As I showered and dressed for our breakfast with Isabella, my thoughts returned to the conversation that Ohnedaruth and I had with her last night. I wondered why Uncle Wilson never disclosed the work he was helping Guadelupe do to document the connection between Afro-Mexicans and Black Seminole Indians. Why did Isabella think our family needed to know about the details of this project?

Isabella's house was located across the street from the Mexican Fine Arts Museum Center on W. 19th Street. A small Mexican flag proudly hung on the side of the mailbox. The welcome mat on her porch read *Bienvenidos a la casa de Mexico.* Isabella's front door contained a sticker with a colorful Mexican sombrero and the date of Mexican independence printed in bold green letters. She opened the front door of her home before we could ring the doorbell. She must have ESP. She was dressed in a mustard caftan with burnt orange batik designs and mocha leather wedge slides. Oval-shaped gold wire reading glasses were comfortably perched on her nose. Bronze lipstick was the only trace of make-up on her face. Her ears subtly sparkled with forever diamond studs. A striking sapphire empowered her left ring finger. A tank watch and 14K gold charm bracelet kept company with her wrists. A gold necklace with a Mother Mary pendant glistened against her pecan-colored neck. Isabella gave the image of morning hostess new meaning. Greeting us with exuberant flair, she said, *"Buenas Dias! Bienvenidos a mi casa."*

In unison, Ohnedaruth and I replied, *"Buenas Dias."*

"Hablan espanol?"

I quickly answered, "Just a few social phrases."

Ohnedaruth chuckled, "Hello and goodbye are my forte."

Smiling cleverly, Isabella teased, "Well we will have to change that. Come in and have some breakfast."

Before I followed Isabella and Ohnedaruth up the stairs, I stared at the silver framed photos that lined the walls of the burgundy foyer. They were filled with Isabella's pride and joy, Guadelupe. Photos from her birthday celebrations, school performances, high school prom, and family events were prominently displayed. My favorite photo included Guadelupe, Isabella, Uncle Wilson, and Miss Ophelia. Guadelupe's hair was pinned in a classic upsweep held in place by a small tiara. Her face was slightly decorated with pink lipstick and a hint of eyeliner. Pearl earrings and a matching necklace perfectly accented her white lace strapless floor-length gown. Standing with a bouquet of pink roses, she offered the camera a shy smile that most fifteen-year old girls displayed during their *Quinceanera* celebration.

Isabella's ivory living and dining rooms were tiny in size and modestly decorated with a few pieces of mahogany Victorian furniture covered in gold silk. Gold silk curtains that barely grazed the oak hardwood floors hung from her front and back windows. Black and white photos of what appeared to be family members were scattered throughout each room. The dining room table was formally set: silverware, china, glassware, and linen. A gold rim glass pitcher of orange juice sat on the right side of a matching oval-shaped vase with red roses tied together with gold thread. For a minute, I thought I was sitting in Momma's Daffodil Villa.

Next to the vase of roses was a small gold plaque with a quote by St. Teresa of Avila: Accustom yourself continually to make many acts of love for they enkindle and melt the soul. After reading it, I smiled and looked up at Ohnedaruth. "What has you displaying such a fantastic smile?

Pointing to the plaque, I said, "This quote is a perfect description of how you are to me."

He read it out loud, "Accustom yourself continually to make many acts of love for they enkindle and melt the soul. I think that it describes how we should all seek to live."

Touching Ohnedaruth's shoulder, Isabella commented, "I couldn't agree with you more."

Isabella escorted Ohnedaruth to the head chair and placed me at his right side. Then she disappeared into the kitchen and returned with a tray of scrambled eggs, hash browns, cantaloupe, toast, and freshly brewed coffee. Neither Ohnedaruth nor I reached for the food until she sat down and joined us in prayer. We held hands as she recited a simple blessing. "Bless O Lord for this food we are about to eat. Keep us warm, protected and surrounded by your love and light. Amen"

We responded, "Amen."

"Now don't be shy."

As we feasted on Isabella's breakfast, she gave us a brief history of the African presence in Mexico. She started with the story of Yanga, an African who ran away from his master in 1609 and founded the first free African township near Veracruz, the home of her birthplace. Isabella shared how Yanga and other Africans used guerilla tactics to attack the Spanish and force them into signing a peace treaty. "Two months ago, your uncle became interested in the history of American born African slaves who fled to Mexico in the mid 1800s. His interest was sparked after examining copies of family photos and a family tree that his mother's cousin sent to him. They revealed that his mother descended from Juan Caballo, Chief of the Black Seminole Indians."

"The only thing I know about Grandmother Sadie is that her mother was from Brackettville, Texas. Daddy really didn't have any other memories of his mother since she died when he was a little boy."

"Brackettville borders a Mexican town called Nacimiento. Both places were home to Black Seminoles. In Mexico, we call them Mascogos. When your uncle told me the news, I recalled that my mother's father was born and raised in Nacimiento. Guadelupe did some research and learned that our families share a common ancestor, Juan Caballo."

After hearing the news, Ohnedaruth exclaimed, "Karma, can you believe how diverse our family is?"

I mumbled, "More secrets. What else is there to learn?"

"The saddest part of the news is that we were all planning to visit Nacimiento in April, but now that won't happen."

Ohnedaruth suggested, "We should tell the family at the wake tonight."

"I'm not so sure that would be a good idea."

Isabella cautioned us in a toneless voice, "If I were you, I'd wait until the will was read."

Probing her, I inquired, "Why should we wait until then? Is there some other deep dark secret that will be revealed?"

"I just think it would be best to let your uncle's words do the talking."

Isabella's vague answer prompted Ohnedaruth to follow up. "So what are you saying? Is there something you know that we need to be made aware of?"

"For your own sake, trust me when I say that you should wait until the will is read."

Her warning piqued my interest. "Isabella, it's obvious that you know something. Please tell us so we aren't blindsided."

She remained committed to her vagueness. "Karma, I'm not able to disclose those facts. Your uncle's will should tell it all."

"Okay I understand that you aren't going to tell us, but at least let us know if the news is going to hurt us."

"It's nothing bad. You won't be hurt by the news."

Ohnedaruth added, "But will Aunt Willie and the rest of the family be hurt?"

Isabella responded with a sly look and a gentle wink of her eye before excusing herself to answer her phone. When she returned we asked her if she was planning to attend Uncle Wilson's wake and funeral. Her reply was our caveat emptor. "Not if my life depended on it. Your Aunt Willie and her sisters are too much for me. I'm allergic to their negativity."

Feeling like we were about to walk into a hot mess, I pleaded, "Come on Isabella, tell us what you think might happen."

"I don't have ESP."

"Can't you speculate?"

"No, but I can do a Tarot card reading."

Thinking that she might reveal a few more details, I agreed to a reading. Ohnedaruth tried to convince me to leave the subject alone. "Karma, let's not trouble Isabella for a reading. I'm certain that we have already overstayed our welcome."

Isabella interrupted, "It's not a problem. I would be honored to give you both a reading."

Smiling at Ohnedaruth, I answered, "See it's not a problem."

Isabella motioned to Ohnedaruth, "Look behind you and hand me that black velvet box sitting on the buffet."

He remarked, "What a lovely box."

"Your uncle gave it to me one year for Christmas."

"Who will go first?"

Ohnedaruth suggested, "Ladies first."

Isabella opened the box and pulled out a beautiful deck of Tarot cards. It resembled *Grandmere's* Rider-Waite tarot deck. "Is that a Rider-Waite deck?"

"Yes it is. What do you know about Tarot?"

"My grandmother owned a deck."

"Did she teach you how to use it?"

"No. She never shared it with me, but she taught my mother."

"So does your mother use Tarot cards?"

"I'm not really sure how deep she is into it."

"Have you ever received any readings?"

"Once in college, but I never trusted the lady reading the cards. She seemed shady."

"Well, I can't tell you to trust me. I can only encourage you to keep an open mind. So before we begin, I want to explain the type of reading I'm going to do. You will choose five cards, one at a time. Each of these cards has a meaning for the position it is drawn in. Position 1 gives you the background of your reading and explains what the main focus is. Position 2 tells what your motivations are and why you are driven to do certain things. Position 3 highlights the problems and fears you need to handle. Position 4 helps you gain perspective on areas that you need to focus on, but aren't currently aware of. Position 5 lays out your action plan on how to use the advice given in the previous positions to your benefit."

"That's a lot of information to take in."

"No worries *mi amor*, I'll remind you what the positions are. Karma, I like to do readings in my sitting room. It's my tranquil space. Ohnedaruth, I will need you to stay here while I do your sister's reading."

"I understand Isabella."

Following Isabella, I walked down her hallway to a small room. When she flipped the light switch on, I noticed that there was very little furniture. Two Queen Anne style arm chairs and a small reading table were placed in the center of the room. I smiled at the Oak framed print of Lois Mailou Jones' oil painting, *Les Fetiches*. It was one of my many favorites. The orange colored figure on the far right of the print perfectly complimented the room's curry colored walls. Closing the door behind me, Isabella invited me to have a seat. "*Mi amor*, make yourself comfortable."

"What a beautiful room! I love the art on your wall."

"Guadelupe gave it to me."

"She has great taste in artists."

"Yes she does. Before we begin, I want you to take a few moments to clear your mind of any extraneous thoughts. Close your eyes and take several deep breaths. When you're ready, open your eyes, and tell me what is your major concern."

As I inhaled and closed my eyes, I giggled to myself. Isabella's instructions felt like the beginning of my yoga class. After breathing in and out a few times, I opened my eyes and proudly stated my concern with the hope that it might get Isabella to share more details about Uncle Wilson's will. Isabella handed me the deck of cards. "Before you state your concern, the cards need to feel your energy. Shuffle them one at a time. Then state your concern as you shuffle them a few more times. When you finish, hand them back to me."

"My concern is learning how to navigate drama in my life, specifically my family drama surrounding Uncle Wilson's death."

After I handed the cards back to Isabella, she turned five cards over from left to right. "The first position is the XX Judgment card. It's a card of transformation and represents a time of forgiveness and soul-searching. This is the focus of your reading. The second position is a reversed X Cups card. It shows that family is squabbling over petty issues. The message is don't fret over these issues. The energy motivating your focus is moving you past the petty issues that your family is fighting about. The third position is IX Rods. It depicts a wounded and worried man who is braced for the next attack or wound. This card is about being in the eye of the storm. It's telling you to be prepared because your situation will worsen before it improves. Based on this card's position, it represents what you are fearing or anxious about. The fourth position is X Pentacles and it features an old man surrounded by family and possession. His face expresses contentment as he holds a child and pets a dog. This card is telling you that life is full and wealth will be passed down through generations. Because this card is in the fourth position, it will help you gain perspective about an aspect of wealth in your life that you are not currently aware of. The fifth position is II Rods. The card shows a man grasping the whole world in his hands. He is letting you know that you are strong enough to change your dreams into reality. As the fifth position, this card outlines your action plan for achieving forgiveness and soul-searching in your life. Know that everything is within your reach. So be bold. Do you have any questions?"

I sat speechless. I hadn't expected the reading to speak directly to my concerns.

"Karma, are you okay?"

Stuttering, I replied, "Ih … ih…. ih … it sp…. sp … sp … spoke to me."

"How?"

"All of it."

"That's a good thing. I hope you can use this information to help you handle your family concerns."

Looking at the painting on the wall, I realized that Isabella's reading had removed the mask of my life's challenges. How did she know what I was going through? How did she know the advice I needed? What did she do to the cards? My thoughts continued to run wild. So I created an excuse and announced, "I think it's time for Ohnedaruth and I to go. We have a lot of things we need to ..."

"*Mi amor*, that's okay. I understand."

Isabella hugged me before walking me down the hallway to the living room. Ohnedaruth was seated on a couch with his eyes closed. Isabella walked over to him and gently touched his shoulder. "Ohnedaruth, I'll have to give you a rain check on your reading."

"Karma, how was it?"

"Let's talk about it later. I told Isabella that we better get going since we have a lot of things to do before the wake."

"Things like ..."

"I'll tell you later."

Becoming frustrated, Ohnedaruth shrugged his shoulders as he rose from his seat to hug Isabella goodbye. "Thank you for your hospitality."

Patting his locs, Isabella exclaimed, "*Mi amor*, you are family. There is no need to thank me."

I interjected, "We really do need to get on the road."

"Karma, do not be so rude."

"Sorry, but we ..."

Isabella walked over to me and reached for my hand. "Your sister is right. You both need to get going."

She came closer to give me a hug and whispered, "Follow the wisdom from your reading. It won't steer you wrong."

Lois Mailou Jones' painting, *Les Fetiches* came to mind when I walked into Leak and Sons Funeral Home and saw Aunt Willie and her three sisters. They were greeting visitors in the waiting area. Like the oval-shaped mask in the center of the painting, Aunt Willie was the focal point. The emotion of anger evoked through the image of the horns on the primary mask was woven into the phony mask that Aunt Willie wore to hide her angry grimace. Her sisters wore a similar mask on their faces.

To the untrained eye, their public performance appeared authentic, but I knew differently. Everything had been carefully orchestrated including each woman's wardrobe, make-up, hairstyle, and speech by Aunt Willie. She led her tribe of Turkish coffee-colored automatons in a satin-trimmed black tuxedo suit with black pearls on her ears and around her neck, right wrist, and right ring finger. A Cartier gold bracelet watch sat stoically on her left wrist. Her platinum princess cut diamond wedding ring was so large that I couldn't estimate the carat count. Offering an air kiss to my cheek, Aunt Willie slowly pronounced each word she uttered as she pretended to engage in polite banter. It showed no sign of her cussing sailor imitation that I experienced the day before. "Karma, I am so glad you could make it. How are your mother and sister?"

"Good to see you Aunt Willie. Momma and Violet are fine."

Touching Ohnedaruth's hand, Aunt Willie gushed with emotion, "I don't need any introduction. I can tell from your facial features that you are Eugene's son."

"Yes I am. It's so good to finally meet you."

Hugging him, Aunt Willie emphasized, "We're happy to have you, nephew."

Aunts Lucille, Mabilene, and Elizabeth barely spoke a word to me before they stepped in front of me to hug Ohnedaruth. Caught up in their embrace, Ohnedaruth followed them into the wake. I tagged far behind trying not to laugh. A familiar voice called out, "Is that my niece?"

I turned around and saw Uncle Junius dressed in a black cashmere sport coat, black and white stripped cotton dress shirt, black worsted wool slacks and suede belt, and black loafers. All that black against his flax-colored skin and white hair and beard made him look so distinguished. His attire had a Northern California feel and could have easily come from Wilkes Bashford's eponymous flagship shop on Sutter Street in San Francisco. "In the flesh."

Hugging me, he expressed his condolences. "I know this must be hard for you. Wilson was so fond of you and your sister."

Uncle Junius was the best thing about Aunt Willie. As long as I have known him, he managed to steer clear of her family drama. He was a true diplomat who could easily negotiate peace in the Middle East. I wondered how he stayed married to the sister of the Wizard of Oz's wicked witch. The only answer I could come up with was: his love for her is blind. "So your aunt tells me that your brother Ohnedaruth is with you. You'll have to introduce me when the Francois women finish parading him around the room like their prize poodle."

"Come on Uncle Junius, let's be nice now."

"If you insist."

"So where is Ellis?"

"He's talking to the funeral home director about some last minute details. You know your aunt. She has made it into a full pageant. Ellis is being the good son and making sure her every wish comes true."

"Enough said. His plate must be full."

"Indeed it is. I tried to warn Ellis, but I learned a long time ago not to get in between that mother and son relationship. Willie worships him as the prince. He worships her as the royal highness."

"How do you put up with all that worshipping?"

"I don't pay either of them any mind. That's how."

"You're something else."

"I wouldn't say that. Just know that your uncle has bigger fish to fry in his architectural design business."

"So when are you planning to retire?"

"Never."

"Come on Uncle Junius, don't you want to kick back and relax?"

Joking, he replied, "If I did that, I might have to deal with your aunt and her sisters on a twenty-four basis. And we can't have that."

"No we can't have that."

Ellis approached us and abruptly interrupted our conversation, "Excuse me Dad. Can I talk to you for a minute?"

"Ellis, whatever it is it can wait until you properly greet your cousin Karma."

Ellis extended his right hand to shake mine. "Hi Karma. It's good to see you."

"This is your first cousin. You can do better than that."

Feeling his father's pressure, Ellis offered a fake hug. I played along. "It's good to see you too. Uncle Junius, I better catch up to Ohnedaruth and see if he needs me to rescue him from the Francois women."

"Okay darling. Don't you leave without introducing me to your brother."

"I'll be sure to do that."

As I walked away from Uncle Junius, I wondered what Aunt Willie did to transform herself so that she would be considered an eligible bride. From the stories that Daddy told me, they were from opposite sides of the track. When Aunt Willie left Lake Charles in the forties and migrated to St. Louis, she was a high school drop out and single parent with a toddler who never knew the true identity of her father. The only work she could find was as a domestic servant. Life for her was hard. Daddy said that it was so painful that she knew exactly what Langston Hughes meant when he wrote: *"life ain't been no crystal stair."*

Aunt Willie met Uncle Junius while she was taking classes to become a beautician at Poro Beauty Institute. He was apprenticing as an architect for the firm that built the Institute. His mother, Pelagie Turner, was a member of St. Louis' Black aristocracy and the great granddaughter of Pelagie Rutgers, the grand dame of St. Louis' Black high society in the 1850s. His parents were what you would call a mega Black rich couple for their time. They both came from old money and made sure to build upon their wealth so their children and children's children could enjoy it. Mrs. Turner expanded her family's wealth through her entrepreneurial efforts in owning a flagship chain of beauty parlors called the Black Pearl. They were located in large Midwestern cities such as St. Louis, Kansas City, Detroit, and Chicago. Somehow Aunt Willie won her mother-in-law's favor and ended up inheriting her beauty parlor empire.

I'd never tell her to her face, but I actually admire Aunt Willie's ability to hustle. She completed her high school education while she worked as a beautician, earned a bachelor's degree from Roosevelt College in business administration, expanded her mother-in-law's beauty parlor empire, secured membership into the Chicago chapter of the Links, and transformed herself into one of the grand dames of Chicago's Southside while educating her daughter, son, and younger siblings so they would not have to endure similar struggles. Aunt Willie is definitely a force to be reckoned with. I know Daddy would hate to admit it, but he probably married Momma because she reminded him of Aunt Willie in her need to achieve, control, and dominate the landscape of her life and everyone else who was attached to it.

By the time I caught up to Ohnedaruth, Aunt Willie was showing him off to some of her friends. As I approached the small huddle of people, I heard Ohnedaruth say, "I will be spending the holidays with my partner George in Oakland."

Aunt Willie proudly announced, "Did you hear that? My nephew is also a business man."

Ohnedaruth corrected her. "Aunt Willie, I'm not a business man. I was referring to my life partner George."

The small crowd immediately dispersed as Aunt Willie's polite demeanor began to unwravel. "Young man, did I hear you say your life partner is a man?"

"Yes."

Shaking her head in disbelief, Aunt Willie forcibly led Ohnedaruth to the front door of the funeral home. I trailed behind. "I can't have a faggot at my brother's funeral. The Bible speaks against how you're living. It is s sin. Don't you know that?"

Not knowing what to say, I stood by silently and watched Ohnedaruth handle Aunt Willie with kid gloves. "I'm sorry that you feel that way. I didn't come here to upset you. I came here simply to pay my respects to an uncle I never knew and meet my family."

"As long as you're living this sinful life, you aren't family."

"Unfortunately, your words cannot destroy the blood bond that we all share. Like it or not, I'm your family."

In the blink of an eye, Aunt Willie's sailor cussing alter ego returned. "You look here, you mutha fuckin' faggot, I want you to get the hell out of here. Don't even think about bringing your ass to Wilson's funeral tomorrow. Go back to where you came from. You're a damn embarrassment to your father. Stay the hell away from us. You ain't no Francois man, do you hear me?"

Aunt Willie's words were filled were with poison. I quickly closed my eyes and began breathing deeply to center myself. All the wisdom messages from Isabella's tarot card reading flashed before me. I remembered that I had the strength to move through this situation. My strength was God. So I prayed and asked what I could do to harmonize the situation. The memory of my morning practice inserted itself in my consciousness. I began silently chanting *Lokah Samastah Sukhino Bhavantu*. When I opened my eyes, I heard Ohnedaruth offer Aunt Willie a blessing. "May you have a peaceful evening."

Instead of responding in anger and creating death with his words, Ohnedaruth chose the high road and used words of life to bless the situation. Dumbfounded by his calm response, Aunt Willie walked away in silence. I smiled at the power my brother wielded in the face of extreme Francois drama. "You were amazing. How did you find the patience to deal with all of that drama?"

"As soon as Aunt Willie began cussing at me, I tuned her out and began chanting the last few lines of the Heart Sutra to myself."

"It must be filled with some mighty powerful words."

"It's one of Buddhism's greatest wisdom teachings. It sounds like this in Sanskrit: *Gate Gate Paragate Parasamgate Bodhi Svaha.* The English translation is gone, gone, gone over, gone fully over. Awakened. So be it! I began using it years ago so I could surrender my ego and need to respond in anger."

"Smart move. It obviously worked."

"Beyond it being a smart move, I like to use it as an affirmation to remind me to let go of all things within me … all emotions, attachments, judgments, and dualities that separate me from the oneness of God in all people and all things."

After we gathered our coats and began walking out of the door, I touched my brother's hand and whispered in his ear, "You are pure divinity."

"So are you."

In the core of my spirit, I felt his words to be true.

CHAPTER 33

▼

"With all humility and gentleness, with patience, bearing with one another in love, making every effort to maintain the unity of Spirit in the bond of peace."

—Ephesians 4:2-3

For the first time in a long time, I woke up with a peaceful mind. Pulling back the quilt covering the bed, I found a comfortable place to sit. After I placed a pillow underneath my sitting bone for support, I stretched out my legs. Bending my left knee, I placed the sole of my left foot against my right thigh so that my heel touched my perineum. I did the same thing on my right side by bending my right knee and putting my right heel against my pubic bone. Sitting comfortably in *Siddhasana*, I inhaled a deep breath and brought my palms together. My thumbs rested lightly on my sternum. As I pressed my hands firmly together, I bowed my head slightly and drew the crease of my neck toward the center of my head. I began to feel the energy flowing from my hands to my heart. It spread throughout my body. I repeated the divine love mantra one hundred and eight times before beginning my warm up exercises and *Surya Namaskar* sequence. Before I ended my practice, I prayed that the fruits of my practice inspire the Francois family to bear with one another in love, making every effort to maintain the unity of Spirit in the bond of peace.

Aunt Willie pulled out all of the stops for Uncle Wilson's funeral and leveraged it as her social event of the year. The service was held at Apostolic Church of

God because that was Aunt Willie's church. She hired one of New Orleans' oldest funeral homes, Charbonnet-Labat Funeral Home, to carry Uncle Wilson's casket in an antique black horse-drawn hearse service. His casket was escorted to the church in a New Orleans jazz-style funeral with a street parade filled with a brass band.

In an effort to avoid any family drama, we sat in the car until it looked like most people were inside the church. Thinking that we had escaped the drama, we casually strolled through the first set of doors. When we reached the second set, Ellis stood guard as Vivian hung out in the background. As I reached for the knob to open the door, Ellis firmly grabbed my hand and warned, "Look, I really don't want any trouble from you. My mother thinks it's best that you not attend the funeral."

I calmly expressed my position. "I'm sorry your mother feels that way, but my brother and I have a right to attend our uncle's funeral."

"Unfortunately, you don't have that right today."

"Look Ellis, I'm not going to argue with you."

"I told you Karma, my mother doesn't want you here. So go back to your hotel."

"We can't do that."

Raising his voice, Ellis insisted, "Yes you will. Take that bastard faggot brother away from here."

Ohnedaruth spoke up, "Ellis, we would appreciate it if you would move out of our way so we can pay our respects."

"I can't do that, you little bastard bitch."

Much to my surprise, Vivian charged her brother and pinned him against the wall. Although Ellis was a few inches taller, she was able to hold her own despite her being almost thirty years older. "Stop calling him a bastard, you little momma's boy."

Ellis was Aunt Willie's menopausal miracle baby. She had him in her late forties.

Ohnedaruth begged Vivian to release Elllis. "Thank you Vivian for your concern, but please release your brother."

"I'll do it if he apologizes immediately."

"Vivian you're no better than he is. You're a crazy bastard bitch. Let me go."

As she tightened her grip, Vivian chastised Ellis, "Not until you apologize to both of us for calling us out of our names. Can you do that?"

Whining, he replied, "I can do it. Please let me go."

"Okay, say you're sorry."

"I'm sorry."

"Don't be a smart ass. We each deserve an individual apology."

"Okay, okay, okay … I'm sorry Ohnedaruth for mistreating you and calling you out of your name. Vivian, I'm sorry to call you out of your name."

"That's much better."

"Let me go now."

"Not until Karma and Ohnedaruth are inside the church."

We both thanked Vivian and walked through the second set of doors. I felt a surge of energy tingle up my spine. Maybe it was a sign that the Francois family was beginning to reflect signs of healing.

Uncle Wilson's funeral lasted four hours. Aunt Willie was the self-appointed Mistress of Ceremonies. She took an hour to welcome everyone. The next hour allowed for personal greetings from a star-studded cast of Chicago local celebrities. The third hour was dominated by a poorly delivered sermon given by Aunt Mabilene's newly ordained son-in-law, Walter. He never looked up at the congregation as he read each word of his sermon. He was slower than molasses. Ohnedaruth fell asleep on my shoulder. My mind drifted into a series of unanswered questions. What would make family turn on family? Why can't our differences be overlooked? Where is the love that we claim to wear as a badge when we embrace and call ourselves kin? Why do we change the way we treat each other when we learn of our differences? Where is the open heart? Are we not capable of acceptance? Why must we perpetuate what appears to be a cycle of pain? When will we choose to heal ourselves instead of hurt those who also bear our family name?

The wisdom from my tarot card reading weaved itself into the threads of my psyche, creating one single message: the only way you are going to live a full life is to demonstrate your strength to forgive your family for its drama. In that moment, I knew it was my turn to answer my own prayer.

CHAPTER 34

▼

"Daughter, your faith has made you well; go in peace."

—Luke 8:48

On the morning of my last day in Chicago, furiously wild winds brushed against the windowpane. My ears caught the echo of their rustling like a dream catcher catches a dream. Without regard for my need to sleep, the sounds of nature awakened me. My eyes opened into the darkness. I glanced at the alarm clock sitting on the nightstand. It registered three a.m. Intuitively, I knew what my wake up call was all about. God was trying to get my attention about forgiving myself and my family members. I came into *Balasana* in the middle of the bed and began my morning discourse with God. "God, I know that I'm being asked to forgive myself and everyone, but I'm not so sure that I can do it so quickly. I don't want to lie and pretend that I can do something when I can't. I also don't want to disregard your will. So I'm asking for your guidance. What would you have me do?" I continued to rest in the pose for several minutes. When my knees needed to be stretched, I came out of the pose and lied on my belly. Within the hour, I fell back to sleep.

When Ohnedaruth and I arrived at the offices of Antoine Lafayette, Uncle Wilson's attorney, we were surprised to see Guadelupe sitting in the reception area along with Aunt Willie. Without thinking, I grabbed Ohnedaruth's hand and turned back around towards the elevator. "Karma, what's wrong?"

"We need to say a prayer."

Hugging me, Ohnedaruth agreed, "Splendid idea."

Smiling back, I realized how much I love my brother's spirit. How could I hold a grudge against his mother and our father for creating him? I may not like how it was done, but I can't ignore the beauty of his spirit. As I opened my mouth to share a prayer, I surrendered and allowed God's voice to speak through mine. "Let us enter this experience with forgiving hearts. Let us forgive what we can and allow God to do the rest. Let us be patient with ourselves in this forgiveness process. Let us take it one step at a time. With each step, let us release any barriers within us that prevent us from fully embracing our family. Let us shine love and light in our thoughts, words, and actions. Let us be peacemakers, healers, and lovers of all our family members. Amen."

God's words were the answer to my morning prayer for guidance. Now all I had to do was follow it.

Mr. Lafayette's secretary greeted us before we could exchange pleasantries with Aunt Willie and Guadelupe. She informed us that everyone had arrived for the reading of the will. I blurted out, "What happened to everyone else?"

Aunt Willie boldly responded, "I'm the official representative of the Francois family."

A part of me wanted to respond sarcastically to her comment, but I let it go and politely greeted her. "Good Morning Aunt Willie." My greeting was met with dead silence and eye rolling.

Ohnedaruth made a second attempt. "Good Morning Aunt Willie."

His attempt invited her special blend of poisonous venom. "Look I don't want anything to do with you and your faggot ass ways. So don't speak to me."

Not giving Ohnedaruth a chance to answer, I quickly uttered, "Aunt Willie, God bless you."

She rolled her eyes and turned away. Guadelupe began speaking to us both. "So how are you doing this morning?"

Ohnedaruth remarked, "Lovely."

"My mother told me that she had a great time visiting with you both yesterday."

"Your *mum* is quite the hostess."

I added, "She is full of surprises."

The voice on the intercom sitting on the secretary's desk paused our conversation. "Alana, please send in our guests."

"Mr. Lafayette is ready to see you. His office is the first door on your left."

Aunt Willie and her floor length mink coat rushed to the door. Guadelupe, Ohnedaruth, and I politely stood by and watched her almost bump into a small bookcase outside of Mr. Lafayette's door. When she opened the door, I heard familiar music. It was Bach's *Air* from *Suite No. 3 in D Major*. Behind a mahogany desk sat a conservatively dressed and clean-shaven, bald headed elderly man with smoky quartz skin. Mr. Lafayette was dressed in a navy blue three-piece suit with a white shirt and grey and blue-stripped tie. The best phrase to describe him was old school GQ elegance.

Behind his desk, I noticed two framed diplomas hanging on his antique white walls. One was from Grambling State University. The other was from Southern University School of Law. A purple and gold coffee mug with the Greek letters of Omega Psi Phi Fraternity sat on the right side of his black telephone. A black and white framed photo sat on the left side. Aunt Willie walked over to Mr. Lafayette's desk and damn near forced him to stand before he was ready. "Antoine, thank you so much for being here for our family and taking care of my dear brother's estate."

As he hugged Aunt Willie, Mr. Lafayette introduced himself in a deep southern accent. "Willie, everything is going to be just fine. Let me introduce myself to these young folks. My name is Antoine Lafayette."

"It's a pleasure to meet you sir. My name is Ohnedaruth Shankar. This is my sister, Karma Francois and Guadelupe Rodriguez, a family friend."

"The pleasure is all mine. Son, I have known your family for ages. We all grew up together in Lake Charles."

"Antoine, I don't have time for small talk. Let's get down to business," Aunt Willie rudely commented.

"In due time Willie."

"I said I don't have time to waste."

Losing patience, Mr. Lafayette raised his voice, "Now you lookahere woman, you're not running this show. I am. We will get to the reading of the will. So settle down."

To my surprise, Aunt Willie found her seat and shut her mouth. Mr. Lafayette calmly explained, "Before I read the will, Wilson asked me to play a classical music recording and share a letter that he wrote in his final days. He wanted the music to relax you. The recording is Claude Debussy's *Reverie*. It was four minutes of peaceful content. I could feel Uncle Wilson in the room. Mr. Lafayette paused for a few seconds before reading Uncle Wilson's letter.

"Dear Loved Ones,

If you are hearing this letter, then you know that I have made my transition. Know that I am with you always. Know that I love you all. Deciding how to distribute my assets was one of the easiest decisions I have made in my life. It was easy as breathing air and loving you all. You may be surprised to learn that my estate is pretty substantial. God has been good to me. Now I want to be good to others. You should know that I have already made significant financial donations to my church, South Side Community Art Center, DuSable Museum, Mexican Fine Arts Center Museum, and Chicago State University's Gwendolyn Brooks Center. I wish to leave the remaining amount to you because I think that you will benefit the most from the money. Some family members and close friends may not understand my desire to bless you all, but don't fret one minute about their concerns. I want you to use your inheritance to live rich, passionate and fulfilling lives. Explore the world. Make your dreams come true. Love what you do and who you share your lives with. The will that Antoine has prepared spells out the details of my bequest, but I wanted to tell you what your gifts are. So without further adieu, let me begin by saying that I am saddened that I won't have the opportunity to know my brother's son, Ohnedaruth Eugene Shankar. Nephew, I have loved you since you were born. May my gift of $250,000 add beauty to your life. To my favorite nieces, Karma a/k/a Belle Violette Francois and Violet Belle Francois, may you each enjoy my gift of $250,000. Violet, yes you both get $250,000 each. I said that because I know my niece and how she thinks. Use this gift to expand your horizons. Guadelupe Rodriguez, you are the surrogate daughter I never knew I wanted, but was able to enjoy for so many years. You are a shining light. Use my gift of $250,000 to illuminate the world with your talents. Karma and Guadelupe, I want you both to work on a project together. It is the renovation of my home. I want you to transform it into a community museum that houses Afro-Mexican history and the achievements of Chicago's African American and Mexican communities. Antoine will share the details of my plans. Last but not least, I wish to leave my sisters some words of wisdom. All my life you have struggled to make your lives better. I have watched you become bitter, controlling, and angry women. May the prayer that I have said on your behalf for many years become your reality. Mother, Father, God, help my sisters heal and know that they are loved and divinely protected."

Ranting and raving, Aunt Willie yelled, "This is bullshit! These three misfits don't deserve anything. They weren't here to take care of my brother. Hell, they barely knew him. He wasn't in his right mind."

Mr. Lafayette calmly responded, "I haven't finished reading the letter."

Aunt Willie stood and put on her mink coat. "I don't give a good got damn what the will says. I don't need to sit here and listen to this nonsense. I'll contest the will. Antoine, you'll hear from my lawyers by the end of the day."

"Willie, you need to know that Wilson was mentally competent at the time he dictated this letter and signed his will. He also had a psychologist verify his mental state."

Her slamming the office door was her response to his comment. While Mr. Lafayette continued reading Uncle Wilson's letter and will, I sat quietly praying that Aunt Willie find the peace she was looking for. For the first time, I actually felt genuine concern for her well-being. The anger and hurt that I had felt previously had been replaced by peace. My faith in God was the only reason that I could feel this way. Then I heard a voice within me say, "Daughter, your faith has made you well; go in peace."

PART IV

▼

"The soul should always stand ajar, ready to welcome the ecstatic."
—Emily Dickinson

CHAPTER 35

▼

"I am my beloved's, and his desire is for me."

—Song of Solomon 7:10

Immediately after our appointment with Mr. Lafayette, Guadelupe, Ohnedaruth, and I parted our separate ways. Guadelupe had to get back to work at the Mexican Fine Arts Center Museum. I had to catch a cab to make my one o'clock flight at O'Hare Airport. Ohnedaruth had to return the rental car and catch a two fifteen flight from Midway. We all hugged and agreed to talk in a few days. Right before I boarded my flight to Washington, I called Ohnedaruth and left him a voicemail.

"Hi. This is Karma. Yesterday, I wasn't able to tell you what happened during my reading with Isabella. The wisdom messages from the tarot cards left me speechless. A lot of the things that she shared actually made sense and happened. I'm still processing everything. When I get home and settled, I'll give you a call to share more. Thanks for being here with me. I'm blessed to have you as my brother. Travel safely."

As the plane landed at Reagan International Airport, I sat comfortably in my seat and experienced an inner and outer stillness. I liked the way it felt. It was new for me. It allowed me to hear the sound of my life. The sound was pure goodness. Walking through the airport gave me a chance to embrace each step I took. It became a walking meditation that caused me to smile at each person who crossed my path. I knew my life was better.

A note taped to my front door welcomed me home. It was written by my new neighbor in apartment 203. She had received several of my packages. While I was fiddling with my keys to unlock my door, the door to #203 opened. Standing inside the entrance was a slender golden topaz-colored woman with shoulder length fuzzy black hair. She introduced herself. "Hi. My name is Alexandra. You must be my neighbor."

"Pleasure to meet you. My name is Karma. Welcome to the building."

"I have your packages."

"Yes I know. I just read your note. Thank you for keeping them."

"Let me get them for you."

While Alexandra was retrieving the packages, I opened my front door and stored my suitcase inside. When I returned, she stood in the hallway holding several envelopes. Three medium-size cardboard boxes were stacked against my door. As she handed me the envelopes, I noticed the return addresses on the shipping labels. They were from George, Ohnedaruth, Branford, Ming, and Francis. The first box was from the Baptiste Family. The second one was from Aunt Nina and Uncle Gary. The third was from Toys in Babeland. What was I doing getting a box from Babeland, one of the most popular self pleasure stores for women? "Thanks so much."

"I couldn't help but notice that one of your boxes came from Babeland. My sister and I love that place. When we lived in Newark, we made regular trips. My favorite vibrator is the Rabbit Habit. It drives me completely wild. Those rotating pleasure pearls, fluttering ears, and swiveling heard are awesome. Did you get one?"

Pausing to determine how I should respond to this unusual conversation, I contemplated how Miss Manners might address my new neighbor's vibrator inquiry. No answer came. So I relied on Momma's southern belle etiquette: avoid answering the question with a polite response and quick exit.

Stepping back into my apartment, I politely stated, "Thank you so much for keeping my package. It's been a long trip. You have a nice afternoon."

"You too."

Mission accomplished. After I closed the door, I sat in the kitchen and opened the envelopes. The envelope from George and Ohnedaruth contained two books, *Dreaming Me* by Jan Willis and *being black* by Angel Kyodo Williams. The card inside explained the gift.

"Dear Karma,

These books are something we think you will enjoy because they invite you to give yourself the gift of self-acceptance. The authors share how they learned to give to themselves without expecting anything in return. We both found the books to be helpful in our journey to accept the things we like and dislike about ourselves with loving kindness. We're still both working on accepting ourselves. Our prayer is that you accept all of yourself with love and compassion. Enjoy your birthday and know that we love and adore you sister.

Love your brothers, Ohnedaruth and George"

Branford's envelope was simple. No card. No note. Just a day spa gift certificate to Paris Alexander's on 18th Street. He knows me so well.

Inside of Ming's envelope, I found a card and book entitled, *Coming Out of the Wilderness* by Estella Conwill Majozo. The card read,

"Dear Karma,

Happy Birthday Cuz! Champs thought you would enjoy reading about the life journey of a Black female artist. Her book club read it a few months back. It's supposed to be really good. Enjoy!

Love, Ming and Champs"

Francis' envelope was a purple handmade card with a lotus flower on the front. Her message was short and sweet.

"Happy Birthday Karma,

Keep waking up to your true self!

Blessings, Francis"

The box from the Baptiste family was filled with an African-inspired birthday card from Kuumba Kollectibles and an assortment of CDs. The card was decorated with a picture of a brown woman with medium-length black locs. She was wearing an Egyptian scarab around her neck. I could tell that Aunt Jo picked the card and wrote the message.

"Happy Birthday Dearest Karma!

This year, we all wanted to brighten your days with some of our favorite music. We have organized the CDs into several sets with labels indicating who selected them. Enjoy.

Love your Baptiste family down the street."

The first set was from Millicent. She included four CDs: Jazzyfatnastees' *The Once and Future*, Amel Larrieux's *Infinite Possibilities*, and Maxwell's *Urban Hang Suite* and *Embrya*. Charlie's jazz CDs were included in the second set: Sting's *Mercury Falling*, Christian McBride's *A Family Affair*, and Roy Hargrove's *With the Tenors of Our Time, Approaching Standards, Moment to Moment*, and *Cristol Habana*. Aunt Jo's CDs were on the spiritual tip: Suresha Hill's *Oceanic*, Sista Shree Regina's *Sacred Sound Volume I* (Sanskrit mantra chants) and Rickie Byars Beckwith's *I Found A Deeper Love*. Uncle Charles' was pure New Orleans jazz: Wynton Marsalis' *At the Octoroon Balls* and *The Marciac Suite*. Colin's collection were all new to me: Marcus Johnson's *Chocolate City Groovin'*, Ravi Coltrane's *From the Round Box*, and Joshua Redman's signature CD—*Joshua Redman, Timeless Tales,* and *Moodswing*. Chase's CDs were African classical, U.K. spoken word and hip hop, and Afro-Latino music: *Lamentation* by Tunde Jegede, *Dark Tales from Two Cities* by Katch 22 (featuring HKB FiNN), Omar's *This Is Not A Love Song, Nuyorican Soul* and Mongo Santamaria's *Our Man in Havana*. Cane's music was all neosoul: Julie Dexter's *Peace of Mind*, Fertile Ground's *Spiritual War* and *Field Songs*, and a new songbird's self-titled CD, *Who is Jill Scott?*.

I decided to listen to Fertile Ground's *Spiritual War* as I opened the box from Aunt Nina and Uncle Gary. Their box was filled with a small gift card, seven t-shirts, and a collection of sixteen affirmation cards.

"Goddaughter,

When we saw the Andinkra OM t-shirts and affirmation cards, we immediately thought of you. One of the yoga teachers at Ming's church was selling them. Her company is called Andinkra OM.

Love,

Aunt Nina and Uncle Gary. "

The t-shirts each contained an Andinkra symbol. I was most attracted to the t-shirt with the Sesa Woruban symbol. It represented life transformation. The affirmation underneath the symbol spoke to my heart: Through the power of Spirit, I transform my life. I couldn't wait to put it on. So I slipped it over my head. Before I could get it over my head, my phone began ringing. I let the answering machine catch it. "*Cherie*, this is your mother calling to check in with you. When you have some time, give me a call on my cell phone."

I walked over to the breakfast bar and glanced down at the answering machine. I had seventeen new messages. Instead of listening to them, I decided to lie down and take a much-needed nap. When I woke up, I opened the Toys in Babeland box. It contained a card taped to a large basket of erotica. The card read,

"Happy Birthday!

Every woman deserves to experience and enhance the power of her own erotic pleasure.

Happy Self Pleasuring!

Love Sista7."

I gotta hand it to my sistaloves. This is probably the most unique gift I have ever received in a long time. As I unwrapped the basket, I discovered that I was now the proud owner of a Yab-Yum bronze sculpture, Deluxe Rabbit Pearl wireless purple vibrator, heart-shaped Magixx panty vibrator, Golden Ben Wa Balls, vibrating egg bullet, Kama Sutra Lover's Paint Box, Beginner's Anal Pleasure kit, and collection of DVDs including Toys for Better Sex and Soulmates Volume I and II.

After taking a shower, I decided to play with my heart-shaped panty vibrator. To set the mood, I lit a ginger patchouli candle in my bedroom, played Maxwell's *Urban Hang Suite* CD, and turned out all of the lights. I found myself sitting naked on my bed with my legs straight out in front of me. I inhaled and grabbed the vibrator from my nightstand. As I exhaled, I bent my knees and pulled my heels toward my pelvis. Then I dropped my knees out to the sides and pressed the soles of my feet together before laying my torso flat on the bed. As I relaxed into one of my favorite yoga poses, *Supta Baddha Konasana*, I breathed deeply several times before turning on the vibrator. With one click, I escaped into an orgasmic heaven filled with powerful vibes that massaged my clitoris nonstop. Maxwell's song, *Sumthin Sumthin'* kept me company as tingling sensations bombarded me. I couldn't help but voice a series of audible screams that let me know that I was experiencing my own version of what the woman in the Song of Solomon felt when she uttered "I am my beloved's, and his desire is for me." Self-pleasuring allowed me to become my own beloved. I never knew it could be so good!

CHAPTER 36

▼

"A time to mourn, and a time to dance."

—Ecclesiastes 3:4

I met the new morning on my yoga mat with my mala beads at six o'clock. Sista Shree's *Sacred Sound—Volume 1* CD guided me through my practice. Track 7 entitled *Bolol Muna Mere—Om Namah Shivay* was a blast from the past. Devi used to chant *Om Namah Shivaya* during my yoga teacher training classes. At the time, I wasn't a big fan. By the end of my practice, I was sitting in *Sukhassana* chanting the mantra one hundred and eight times with my mala beads. After yoga, I decided to take a walk in Malcolm X/Meridian Hill Park. As I entered the park at 16th Street and Florida Avenue, I saw Ma'at walking around the reflecting pool. I called out to her, "Good Morning Ma'at!"

She yelled back, "Girl, I didn't know you were back yet."

I walked over to where she was standing and gave her a hug. "I just got back yesterday."

"So how was everything?"

"I'm still processing it all."

"So it was that deep?"

"Deep is probably the best word for now."

"Well, whenever you're ready to share, just let me know."

"I will. So what brings you out so early?"

"Just trying to clear my head."

"About what?"

"Life stuff."

"You feel like sharing?"

"Only if you feel like listening."

"My ears are all yours."

"Last week, I found out that either my ex-husband or one of his wives stole my identity."

"How did that happen?"

"Apparently they decided to open up several credit card accounts in my name after I moved from Philly."

"So how did you find out?"

"From my credit report. A few weeks ago, my friend Drew introduced me to his financial advisor Judy. I liked her vibe. So I made an appointment. During the appointment, Judy asked me about my assets, debt, and credit rating. I admitted that I didn't know what my credit rating was. She suggested that I order a credit report. When it came in the mail, I noticed all of these unpaid credit accounts that I hadn't opened. Judy reviewed it and told me that I needed to report that I had been a victim of identify theft."

"So how did you trace it back to your ex-husband and his wives?"

"Their address was used for all of the accounts."

"Did you confront them?"

"When I called the old number, I learned it had been disconnected. I made a few calls to some friends in Philly and they told me that they had left the Ausar Auset Society and were no longer living in the city."

"So how will you track them down?"

"Drew and I were talking about it this morning. I was telling him that I don't want to focus my energy on trying to go after them. My time for mourning the past is done. I have worked too hard to let go of that part of my life. They'll have to deal with the consequences of their actions. I trust the universe to handle everything."

"Ma'at, that's incredible. Most folks would go after them."

"I can't lie and say that I wasn't angry. Girl, when I first looked at my credit report, I was on my way out of the door to Philly to kick some ass."

"What stopped you?"

"Drew's phone call. He let me rant and rave. Then he asked me to think about my life and the journey I have been on. I realized that I am in a new season. I have come through so much to get to the place of accepting and forgiving myself. Going to Philly would only create negative energy in my life. So I decided to focus on something positive and constructive like cleaning up my credit rating by working with Judy to contact the creditors to request that those charges be removed from my credit report."

"Would you recommend Judy as a financial advisor?"

"Totally. She works for American Express Financial Services. Drew and his parents have been clients for a long time. Do you want her contact information?"

"Most definitely. I have some family financial business that I need help sorting out."

"I'll call and leave you a voice-mail with her information later today."

"Who is Drew?"

"I met him at Grant's party."

"Yamuna's Grant?"

"Yes that's the one. Drew is one of Grant's frat brothers."

"I see Yamuna and Grant are playing matchmaker for the single Kappas and Sista7 members."

"Well, thank goodness for me. Drew is a wonderful guy."

"So tell me about this wonderful guy."

"Can we do it over chai tea at Teaism?"

"We sure can."

After breakfast, I came home to two more messages. Both were from Momma. Instead of listening to them, I dialed her phone number. "Good Morning."

"Hi Momma. This is Karma. Sorry I have't called you back."

"It's so good to hear your voice, *Cherie*. How did everything go?"

"It was exhausting and illuminating all at the same time. There was a lot of drama with Aunt Willie and the rest of the Francois sisters, but Ohnedaruth and I managed. We left with no hard feelings on our part. I can't say the same for them. Uncle Wilson left Violet, Ohnedaruth, and I $250,000 each."

Instead of pressing me for details, Momma offered, "*Cherie,* whenever you're ready to share more details with me, know that I'm here for you. Let me know if you need my help with anything."

"Momma, I have to say that I expected you to play twenty questions."

"Karma, I realized while you were gone that it's time to leave all those things in the past. We all have to move forward. I refuse to waste my life away stuck in some perpetual mourning state. It's time for your mother to dance with joy in the life she has. Besides, my life doesn't need anymore of the Francois sisters' drama."

"You're so right, Momma."

"So what's next for you?"

"I have to contact Violet to let her know about the inheritance. Have you talked to her recently?"

"I have left your sister numerous messages, but she hasn't called me back."

"So do you think I should try and call her?"

"It couldn't hurt."

"Then I'll call her later today."

"Do you have anyone helping you to invest your inheritance?"

"I'm going to call a financial advisor this morning. My friend Ma'at recommended her."

"If you aren't satisfied with her, call your Aunt Jo and find out the name of her financial advisor."

"I will."

"*Cherie,* I'm running a little late for a brunch date with my friend Henry. Can we talk when I get back from Wilmington later today?"

"Sure Momma."

I sat at my breakfast bar wondering who Henry was. What is my mother doing with him in Wilmington?

CHAPTER 37

▼

"A time to be silent, and a time to speak."

—Ecclesiastes 3:7

The neck-snapping energy of the tambourines, trumpet, and piano on *Loose Duck* from Wynton Marsalis' *The Marciac Suite* CD, kept me company as I fixed a cup of Yogi ginger tea. I always loved reading the spiritual messages contained on each tea bag. Today's message reminded me to let my heart speak to others' hearts. I was sure that it would come in handy. As I sorted through my mail and returned phone calls, my ears fell in love with *Marciac Moon*. It reminded me of the childhood adventures that Violet and I shared without five Baptiste cousins during summers spent at Highland Beach. Those were great times filled with late night ghost stories on the beach and adventures to make believe haunted castles in the woods. With seven different personalities, we all managed to get along. I was always amazed at how Violet and I seemed to treat each other better when we were around our cousins. Our visits to Washington were probably the only times we displayed sisterly affection. Since I was thinking of Violet, I decided to call her at her office. Maybe she might answer.

"Good Morning. Violet Arquette's Office."

Hearing Violet's married name announced so officially paused my response. Violet's secretary repeated her greeting. "Good Morning. You have reached Violet Arquette's Office."

"Hi. This is her sister, Karma Francois calling from D.C. Is she in?"

"Yes she is. Shall I connect you?"

"Could you do me a favor and tell her that it's a surprise?"

"Ms. Francois, I'm sorry, but Mrs. Arquette is not a big fan of surprises. She prefers to know who she is speaking with before she takes a call."

Politely, I asked, "What's your name?"

"Lydia"

"Lydia, I know how my sister is, but I want to surprise her. If it helps I will assume the blame for any fallout."

"Okay I'll do you this one favor."

"Thanks Lydia."

"Violet Arquette. How can I help you?"

"Hey Violet. This is Karma."

Sounding like the Queen of Bitchiness, she questioned, "To what do I owe this phone call?"

Remembering my tea bag message, I tried to soften my response with a sweet tone. "Happy Belated Birthday. Congratulations on your marriage."

"Like you really care. Look Karma I don't have a lot of time for social calls. What do you want?"

"Violet, I'm calling to let you know that Uncle Wilson left you, me, and Ohnedaruth $250,000 each."

"You're a little late on giving me the news. I heard from Uncle Wilson's attorney yesterday."

"Oh"

"So is there anything else you'd like to say before I end this call?"

"Look Violet, I know things haven't the best between us, but I thought I'd call and see if we could start over."

"You're right things between us haven't been good for many years. They'll stay that way as long as you continue pursuing a relationship with that bastard child."

Trying desperately not to go off on her, I pleaded, "Violet, you have every right to be upset with Daddy, but I beg you not to take it out on Ohnedaruth and I."

"Karma, I don't have time for this drama. I need you to listen to me. As long as you are pursuing a relationship with that bastard, I don't want you to be a part of my life."

The moment didn't call for me to speak. So I remained silent and said a prayer hoping that one day Violet's heart would hear my heart speak with love.

"Karma did you hear me? Don't call me anymore."

Before I could respond, Violet hung up the phone. I sat whispering into the silence, "I'll respect your wishes."

CHAPTER 38

▼

"A time to embrace."

—Ecclesiastes 3:5

After Violet's call, I decided to check in with Francis. Luckily, she had an opening in her schedule and agreed to see me at noon. On my walk to her office, I listened to Suresha Hill's *Oceanic* CD on my walkman. Her voice was peaceful and soothing. The lyrics for the song, *Sound of Peace,* echoed in my soul. They affirmed my truth. I don't need to struggle anymore because I'm exactly where I'm supposed to be. And where I am is a place of peace.

Peeking through the door, I glimpsed Francis enjoying a power nap on her couch. Not wanting to wake her, I quietly took a seat next to her. With her eyes closed shut and a chuckle in her voice, Francis greeted me. "So you thought you could just sneak up on me, did you now?"

Leaning over to touch her shoulder, I laughed, "Now how could I outwit my all-knowing therapist?"

"You know I have eyes in back of my head, don't you."

We both giggled. Opening her eyes, Francis smiled, "Well, my dear, it's been awhile since we last met face to face. How are you doing?"

"Honestly, I have to say that I am peaceful."

"That's a new one for you."

"I know."

"So what brought on this peace?"

"I think it was everything I learned about myself and family during my trip to Chicago."

"And what did you learn?"

"That I needed to let go of the past and forgive."

"Sounds like you hit the jackpot."

"Being with my brother and watching his responses to some very hurtful experiences opened me up to my choices in how I live and interact with others. I realized that I didn't want to live with the anger and drama that my Francois aunts have chosen to live with. I saw how much pain it causes. And life is just too short to go through it with pain. So I opted to forgive what I could forgive and ask God to help me forgive what I couldn't."

"What a wise woman you are to listen to your own inner counsel."

"I'm not sure if I would call me wise, but I'm taking my time to check in with my inner voice before I speak and act."

"So how are things with your mother and sister?"

"Momma and I are communicating better. I can see signs of healing. My relationship with Violet is in God's hands now. This morning, I called her to try and open up space for us to start over, but she wasn't able to receive what I had to say. She was angry that I am pursuing a relationship with Ohnedaruth. She asked me not to call her anymore."

"How did that make you feel?"

"Not too good, but I realize that she may need time to heal. So I'm going to honor her wishes and continue to affirm that she open her heart one day to my words."

"Karma, you should really be proud of yourself in how you have been facing your issues head on."

"I'm just doing what I need to do."

"Yes you are, but I want you to take some time to embrace the beauty of all you have come through and become."

"Embrace how?"

"By celebrating all of the hard work you've done. Don't take it lightly. You've made remarkable progress. That's something you need to really see and celebrate for yourself."

"Should I throw a party?"

"If that's how you choose to embrace your growth, then throw one. Whatever you do, I want you to honor where you have come from and where you are now. You have walked so far and through so much. You have acquired an arsenal of emotional and spiritual tools that you can use throughout your life. You don't need me anymore. My dear one, you are flying brilliantly with your own two wings."

Sounding a bit panicky, I asked, "What does that all mean?"

"It means that I think we have completed our work together for now."

"Are you sure?"

"I can't answer the question for you. You have to know it for yourself."

"I'm not sure."

"I think you are. You just may not be able to admit it yet."

"Can I still come and see you?"

"My door is always open, but before we see each other again, I want you to take some time to really reflect on all you have learned and let go of since the last time we talked. I think you'll find that you have been standing on your own two feet."

"Should I journal about it?"

"Karma, if you think it will help you, then write in your journal. Do whatever you think will help you reflect. Seek your own counsel."

"Francis, it sounds like you're trying to get rid of me."

"Beloved one, that's not the case. I work to empower people, not enable them. I want you to seek out what your spirit needs for emotional and spiritual harmony."

"Do you think I can do that on my own now?"

"I think if you look closely at your life, then you'll see that you have been doing it for quite some time without my assistance."

"Can you give me some examples?"

"No my dear, I want you to find them for yourself. You have everything you need to live peacefully. Embrace this as your truth and allow your life to enfold."

CHAPTER 39

▼

"My soul is satisfied as with a rich feast, and my mouth praises you with joyful lips."

—Psalm 63:5

On my walk back from my appointment with Francis, I decided to drop in on Aunt Jo and Uncle Charles. Momma met me at the door. "*Cherie*, you must have ESP. I just tried to call you at home to let you know I was back from Wilmington. So how are you?"

"Good."

"You look well rested."

"Jo, look who popped up?"

Aunt Jo came into the living room. "So my long lost niece is finally home. How are you, sweetheart?"

"I'm good."

"Your mother told us all about your Chicago experience."

Giving Momma a sly look, I commented, "Did she now?

"Well, you know your mother. She is not one to hold onto news for too long."

"Is Uncle Charles here?"

"No he's at the hospital with Colette."

"How is she doing?"

"A lot better. The doctors think she will be able to transfer to a rehabilitation hospital after Christmas."

"That's great news."

"God is working miracles for this family."

Momma chimed in, "Yes he is."

Somebody's cell phone started playing Marvin Gaye's song, *Let's Get It On*. I was shocked when I saw my mother reach for her purse to answer it. "Hello. Did you make it back okay Henry? That's good to hear. Karma is here with me. Can I call you later? Okay. Talk with you soon."

"So Momma, who is Henry?"

"A friend."

"Come on Momma. Who is this man?"

Trying to avoid answering my question, Momma started another conversation with Aunt Jo. "Jo, my own daughter is interrogating me."

"Hy, I am gonna leave you two Francois women alone."

"Yes, Momma, let's discuss your life. So who is Henry and what were you doing in Wilmington?"

Pretending to be coy, Momma replied, "Didn't I tell you?"

"No Momma, I think I would have remembered my mother having a friend."

"I met Henry a few weeks ago. He was in town visiting one of his relatives at Howard Hospital."

"So now my mother is picking up strange men in hospitals."

"*Cherie*, please."

"I'm just kidding. Finish your story."

"We had a few conversations in the hospital cafeteria and went out twice before he left town. Then he started calling me. Our conversations were quite enjoyable. During one of them, he invited me to come up to Wilmington to attend one of his Monday Club dinner dances, but I hesitated before answering. I talked to your Aunt Jo about it and she convinced me that I should go and have a good time. So I went."

"What is the Monday Club?"

"It's the oldest African American men's social club in Delaware."

"Why did they name it Monday?"

"When the club was founded in the late 1800s, its members worked as butlers, cooks, coachmen, janitors, and chauffeurs for wealthy families. Monday was a special because it was their day off."

"So what did you and Henry do after the dinner dance?"

"We talked and had some wine."

"Uhhhum…. and where did you stay?"

"In a hotel."

"With Henry?"

"No indeed *Cherie*. I just met the man. I stayed at a hotel. And he stayed at his house."

"Momma, you're a grown woman. You do know that you can stay anywhere you please."

"Okay, this is where the conversation ends. Remember I'm the mother. You're the daughter."

"Wait a minute Momma, is Henry your boyfriend?"

"We're just friends. Two mature adults enjoying each other's companionship."

"Yeah right Momma. That's why your face was all lit up like some smitten teenager while you were talking to him."

"That's it. I will not have you talking like that to me."

"Oh Momma, I am sorry. I was just playing. I didn't mean to disrespect you or make you feel uncomfortable."

"Karma, your mother has entered a new phase in her life. It's one that I hadn't expected or prepared for. It can be a bit scary and nerve wracking at times, especially with meeting men. I'm taking things very slow. Your father was the last man I dated. And that was forty something years ago."

"I'm just happy that you are meeting people."

"Thanks for saying that. It helps to know that my daughter is okay with it."

"Why wouldn't I be?"

"Well, I was married to your father for so long. You might think I didn't love him if I started seeing men."

"Momma, you are a vibrant, beautiful woman who deserves to be happy. So do your thang. Daddy would want you to be happy too."

"You know I actually think he would."

Hearing my mother talk about this new phase of her life satisfied my soul with a rich feast of happiness. All I could do was give God thanks and praise.

CHAPTER 40

▼

"When they had prayed, the place in which they gathered together was shaken; and they were all filled with the Holy Spirit and spoke the word of God with boldness."

—Acts 4:31

Christmas Day was spent with Colette and the Baptiste Family in Room 12 on the north side of the fourth floor at Howard University Hospital. Millicent's decorating frenzy extended from Colette's room to the nurse's station and the patient rooms along the 4 North Corridor. A pine wreath covered with a light dusting of snow and red berries hung from each patient's door. An African amaryllis plant and a Christmas tree shaped rosemary plant in red earthware pots sat on each patient's nightstand as a gift from The Baptiste family. A six-foot pine Christmas tree with gold, and burgundy blue ornaments stood at attention in the space between the waiting room and nurse's station. An oversized snowflake with thirty-six miniature lights sparkled on top of the tree. Gold and burgundy wrapped packages in varying sizes lied comfortably on top of a burgundy velvet tree skirt trimmed in gold. The far end of the nurse's station counter was decorated with African amaryllis plants and a botanical assortment of Christmas tree shapes made from pinecones, walnuts, seeds, and dried leaves from a variety of trees. Burgundy velvet stockings hung from a makeshift mantel on the front of the nurse's station.

Colette's room was a tastefully pink winter wonderland. The three-foot artificial Douglas fir Christmas tree stood on a table near Colette's closet. A collection of rose-colored glass ornaments blended perfectly with a strand of tiny pale pink blinking lights. A curly wire tree card holder containing pink cardstock cut into holiday ornaments, stockings, ginger bread men, snowflakes and stars was mounted on the wall facing Colette's bed. Her bed was covered with a beautifully crocheted blanket featuring a green holiday tree with rose-colored ornaments. A vase of pink roses sat on the nightstand near her bed.

Colette was in rare form. She was alert and able to recognize everyone. Her speech was pretty clear and conversation upbeat. Her appetite was excellent. She was able to eat solid food: baked codfish, carrots, green beans, and applesauce. Everyone took turns sitting in her room in groups of four. When we weren't sitting and talking to Colette, we amused ourselves in the waiting area with jokes and family stories as we ate the catered dinner that Aunt Jo and Uncle Charles ordered from Mango's Caribbean Restaurant.

Right before most of us were about to leave, we received two surprises. The first was news from Colette's doctor, Dr. Oluyemi. She informed us that Colette was strong enough to move to a rehabilitation hospital next week. Everyone embraced, creating a prayer circle around Colette's bed. She uttered the words, "Thank you God for my doctors, nurses, and family."

Aunt Jo added, "Good and gracious God, the place in which we stand is shaking with your love and power. You have given this family the greatest gifts this holiday season: the presence of your Holy Spirit and the ongoing healing of our beloved Colette. Each of us is filled with your Holy Spirit. With this power and presence, we speak your word of praise with boldness. Let the Baptiste family say Amen."

The entire family yelled, "Amen."

CHAPTER 41

▼

"I thank you, Lord with all my heart, before the gods to you I sing. I bow low toward your holy temple."

—Psalm 138:1-3

Right before Momma and I were leaving the hospital, her friend Henry appeared with a surprise winter bouquet of red roses, white calla lilies, red hypericum sprays, green button pom, silver dollar eucalyptus, cedar fronds, and curly willow. At first glance, I began comparing him to Daddy. Henry was a little taller than Momma. I'd say about five foot five inches with a stocky frame. There's no doubt that he was much shorter than Daddy's six foot physically fit frame. His snow-white thick hair was cut very close. It shaped his oblong clean-shaven face. Daddy always wore a "Cornel West" Afro with a mustache and beard. Henry's black tourmaline skin was much darker than Daddy's red jasper skin. The four things that they seemed to have in common were neatly manicured hands, tailored clothing, great taste in flowers, and Momma's attention. Her entire face lit up when he greeted her with a peck on the cheek. It was interesting to see Momma interact with him. "Merry Christmas Hyacinth."

"My goodness Henry. This is quite a surprise. I hadn't expected to see you until …"

"Until New Year's Eve. Yes I know, but I couldn't help myself. When I saw this beautiful bouquet of flowers, I knew they had your name written all over them. So I brought them to you."

"Well, I don't know exactly what to say."

"You could say thank you and introduce me to this young woman who bears a striking resemblance to the picture of the daughter you have shown me several times."

Momma blushed. "Karma, this is my friend Henry."

Taking my hand and kissing it, Henry responded, "The pleasure is all mine. Karma, your mother has told me so much about you and your sister Violet."

"Oh hush Henry."

"No it's true. Your mother is one of your biggest fans."

Winking at Momma, I answered, "I'm one of hers too."

"So am I."

Not wanting to rain on Momma's man parade, I put her escape plan to spend some one-on-one time with Henry in motion. "Momma, if it's alright with you, I'm gonna head over to my friend Ma'at's house for her holiday party?"

"*Cherie*, I didn't know you had plans for the rest of the evening. I thought we were going to have a slumber party at your apartment."

"Oh I forgot to tell you. Ma'at called me earlier today and invited me. I guess it slipped my mind."

Raising her left eyebrow and sounding suspicious, Momma questioned, "Karma, it sounds like ..."

"It sounds like I have a life and so do you. We can have our slumber party tomorrow. Henry, it was nice meeting you. I'm sure that I'll see you again.

Momma, have a nice time with your friend. Call me tomorrow when you have some free time."

As I walked out of the hospital, I heard Momma's tone change. "Young lady …"

I turned back around and blew her and Henry a kiss.

The next morning, Momma's seven-thirty phone call marked the beginning of my day. Before she could read me the riot act for giving her some time with her new man, I reminded her that it was Umoja, the first day of Kwanzaa, an opportunity to seek and show love to everyone including a smart—ass daughter who wants see her mother have fun.

"*Cherie*, thanks for doing a disappearing act last night. Henry and I had a great time. We spent the entire evening sipping coffee drinks at the Four Seasons bar in Georgetown. Afterwards, we went to an all night place called The Diner on 18th Street. I'm just getting in."

"Sounds like you're having a great time with your new friend."

"Marvelous would be the word."

"Oh so now it's marvelous. Do tell?"

"There's really nothing to tell."

"Well, then please tell me something about this man that has my mother saying words like marvelous to describe her evening."

"What do you want to know?"

"Come on Momma. You know. The 411. Where's he from? What does he do?"

"Henry was born in Terre Haute, Indiana. He moved to Wilmington when he was a teenager. He served in the Korean War. Henry met and married his wife, Eunice in Seoul. She was a nurse. They returned to Wilmington and raised two children. His wife died of lung cancer five years ago. Let's see, he used to be very active in the Republican Party in Delaware, currently serves as an associate minister at Bethel A.M.E. Church, and has been retired from the post office for a few years. He loves to play golf and is active in the Monday Club."

"Momma, I can't believe you are keeping company with a Republican. What will people say back in Oakland?"

"First of all, I'm not keeping company with Henry. We're just friends."

"Sure you right, Momma. A friend drives two hours to bring his friend a bouquet of flowers."

"Yes, that's what friends do, young lady."

"Okay so what's the next event you and your friend are planning to attend?"

"If you must know, I invited Henry to go with me to Boston for the Diva's Uncorked gala."

"An overnight trip. That sounds romantic."

"Please Karma. We have separate hotel rooms."

"Okay Momma, but are you coming back for the Kwanzaa celebration in Annapolis?"

"Most definitely. Henry and I will fly back in the afternoon on New Year's Day. You know I have to get back in time to see your Uncle Metoyer and Aunt Daphyne."

"So Henry's coming to Kwanzaa?"

"Yes he is."

"That's huge."

"Karma, please stop making such a big deal. Henry is my friend. Of course, I invited him. Can we change the subject now?"

"Sure thing. When do you want to have our slumber party?"

"Tonight would be good for me."

"Then tonight it is."

Later that afternoon, I journaled about my experiences and how I managed them during the past year.

I realize that everything I have come through is because of God. So I thank you God with all my heart for sending me the divine right people and experiences ... Francis, Aunt Jo, Ohnedaruth, Branford, Lawrence, Momma, Ming, Aunt Willie, Vivian, Daddy, Devi, and Violet. They brought me to this place where I can bow low to your holy temple within me. They all worked together for my highest good. I didn't really know they would when I was dealing with my stuff, but now I can see the truth. All the things Francis tried to get me to see and accept made sense when I watched Ohnedaruth interact with Aunt Willie, Vivian, and Ellis. The key for me was that I had to know in my own heart and spirit that it was okay to surrender my will and ask for help in forgiving myself and others. I had to know that I was ready. Now I know that I am.

CHAPTER 42

▼

"A time to love."

—Ecclesiastes 3:8

My slumber party with Momma was cut short due to the early arrival of Uncle Metoyer and Aunt Daphyne. When they heard the news about Colette, they decided to fly in a few days early. They were staying at Aunt Jo and Uncle Charles' house. Momma and Aunt Jo organized a family dinner. Chase and Colin were working late. Cane, Millicent and Charlie promised to stop by for dessert. The last time I saw Uncle Metoyer and Aunt Daphyne was at Daddy's funeral. My tummy fondly remembered the great food they cooked for Daddy's repast. It was five star just like the meals they served in their Crescent City Jazz Restaurant in Los Angeles. Their son, Gus was missing in action. He decided to stay in New Orleans with his grandmother and girlfriend for the rest of the holiday season before returning to Xavier University. It was hard to believe that little Gus was a junior.

During dinner, Aunt Daphyne discussed her new favorite pastime, yoga. "Last year, I started having pains in my lower back. At first, I would wake up with a slight stiffness. The stiffness matured into a reoccurring pain that made it difficult to stand for long periods of time. You know that is the kiss of death in our business."

Uncle Metoyer laughed, "I had to tell Dee that she was getting old. You know the former UCLA cheerleader didn't want to hear that."

Aunt Daphyne teased, "Shut your mouth Metoyer and let me finish my story. You see how he is. The man is always butting in on my stories."

"The floor is all yours, dear."

"One of our waitresses is a yoga teacher. She suggested that I take her kind and gentle yoga class. I checked with my doctor and found out that yoga would actually help relieve some of the pain. I signed up the following day and immediately felt better after the class. Now I go twice a week and practice at home."

Momma joined the conversation. "Dee, when do you practice at home?"

"I like to do it first thing in the morning."

"Me too."

"Hy, I didn't know you practiced too."

"You remember my girlfriend Nina, Karma's godmother. Well, she dragged me to my first class right after Eugene died. The breathing exercises really helped me relax and release a lot of the stress."

"Didn't Eugene practice yoga?"

"Yes he was a yoga enthusiast. For most of the time we were married, he tried to convince me to take a class, but I resisted. You know Karma has been teaching for several years. She's teaching at a women's center. Karma, tell your aunt about your classes."

"Aunt Daphyne, I teach three classes at Our Womanist Center. Aunt Jo actually hooked me up with the gig."

"What type of yoga do you teach?"

"Hatha."

"That's the same kind that I practice. What are your classes like?"

"I teach beginner's level classes that focus on helping students get in touch with their breath and bodies. It is kind and gentle yoga."

"Are you teaching any classes this week?"

"I have a class tomorrow morning and a special one on New Year's Eve morning."

"I don't think I'll be able to make the one tomorrow because your uncle and I are going to spend time with Colette at the hospital. After that your aunt is taking me to see her loctician at City Kinks. What time is the New Year's Eve class?"

"It's at ten o'clock."

"That's doable. Hy and Jo are you planning to come?"

Aunt Jo replied, "Unfortunately, I'll miss the class. Charles and I will be at the beach with Cane getting the house ready for Kwanzaa."

"*Cherie*, I don't think I'll be able to come since my flight to Boston leaves at eleven."

"That's okay Momma."

Aunt Daphyne asked, "Karma, where's your class located?"

"It's further down 16th Street. About a fifteen minute walk from Aunt Jo's."

"Do you mind stopping by to pick me up before you walk to class?"

"Sure. Just so you know I need to be at the Center an hour before class begins. That means we will need to leave by eight forty-five."

"It's a date."

After dinner, I came home and started listening to my birthday CDs as I planned my yoga classes. I decided to build the class around the fire chakra—the solar plexus. It will help people increase their metabolism, prepare for the New Year by seeing their lives clearly, and release any holiday blues. I created an Afro-Latino inspired CD for the class that featured Roy Hargrove's *Una Mas* from the *Cristol Habana* CD; Eddie Palmieri's *Taita Caneme* and *Habriendo El Domiente* from the *Nuyorican Soul* CD; *Jamaicuba, Viva La Felicidad, Yeye-O for Ochun,* and *Ochun Mene* from Mongo Santamaria's *Our Man in Havana* CD; and Willie Bobo's *Fried Neck Bones & Some Home Fries* from the *Uno, Dos, Tres* CD.

My morning class was smaller than usual. Kalahari and Serengeti were among the five students present. My normal class size is fifteen. Having a smaller group allowed me to spend extra time assisting each person. Everyone seemed to enjoy the music. We even had some impromptu Salsa moments led by Kalahari. When we finished the class, Serengeti and I met in her office to discuss the Center's plans for the new art exhibition space. A cinnamon candle was burning on the right side of her desk. The left side of her desk was home to a beautiful shooting star hydrangea in a tapered square earthware pot with faux-silver leaf finish. Holiday cards were thumb nailed to her bulletin board. "Karma you look fabulous. Whatever you've been doing, keep doing it."

"You think so?"

"Yeah sista. You have this glow about you."

"I had a lot of healing moments."

"Ain't nothing wrong with that. So long as you can see yourself and life more clearly."

"Amen to that."

"While you were away, Kalahari, Greer, and I brainstormed a bit about the exhibition space. We thought we should create an airy minimalist space that incorporates feng shui concepts. Greer recommended Savoy and Sons, an architectural design firm to help us design the specs. She mentioned that she thought your cousin Colette was dating one of the Savoy sons."

"Yes she is. It's Julian."

"Small world. How is Colette doing?"

"A lot better. She is moving to a rehabilitation hospital this week."

"That's great news. Let her know that we will keep sending her love and light."

"Will do."

"Before we sit down with the Savoy firm, we thought we'd solicit your ideas about the space. Are you free to meet with Greer, Kalahari, and I the day after New Year's?"

"What time?"

"It would have to be after six in the evening because Greer has a client job she is wrapping up this week."

"You wanna make it for seven. Where?"

"Greer suggested Mocha Hut on 14th Street. Are you familiar with it?"

"I've been there a few times with my Aunt Jo. It's one of her favorite spots to spend one-on-one time with Uncle Charles. Vernal, one of the owners, is Uncle Charles' former student."

"What a small world."

"Have you and Kalahari been there?"

"No. It will be our first time."

"I'm sure you'll enjoy it."

"Excuse me for a moment. I need to call and leave Greer a voicemail before I forget."

While I waited for Serengeti to call Greer, my eyes noticed a flier advertising the Center's Black History events. The flier read,

Come celebrate Black February with Our Womanist Center.

Meditation on Loving Ourselves and Each Other—On February 1, come honor yourself, ancestors, family, and community by spending an evening in meditation about the power of love.

Community of One Love Circles—Join a community of colored folks on February 8 as we celebrate the spirit of Bob Marley's music by dialoguing about why we need to learn how to love our differences (gender, sexual orientation, class, socio-economic status, education, and age).

Healing My Holy Temple—Learn how to use reiki-healing touch to cleanse your spirit, mind, heart, and body on February 15.

In the beginning was the Word—Participate and/or listen to the creative energy of spoken word artists and musicians on February 22. Featured artists include: Doria Roberts, W. Ellington Felton, Tim'm West, Monica Mcintyre, Terri Knox, J. Scales, K'alyn, Queen Sheba, and Original Woman.

"I see you discovered the draft flier for Black February. What do you think?"

"I like what I see. Are you planning to offer any community yoga classes?"

"That depends on you. Can you put together some African-inspired classes for the month?"

"When do you need class descriptions?"

"By next Thursday."

"I can teach two community classes. I'll e-mail you the descriptions tomorrow."

"Do you have a class name and theme?"

"I am toying with Andinkra OM."

"Brilliant. Where did you get the name from?"

"My godparents gave me several t-shirts and an affirmation card set called Andinkra OM."

"So will you be using Andinkra symbols as part of your class?"

"The symbols will shape class themes. Right now I'm planning to use a symbol to shape the theme of my New Year's Eve class. It is called Sese Woruban and represents life transformation. I even have a t-shirt with the symbol on it."

"Sounds divine. I can't wait to take your class."

"For the Black February event, I think we should offer four classes. One per week. I suggest we focus on themes such as God's presence is everywhere and in everyone, the power of love, humanity's oneness, and patience and understanding,"

Serengeti's phone rang. She put the person on hold. "Karma, I need to take this call. It's from the Center's financial advisor, Mr. Allure."

"Okay. I'll see you in class."

On my walk home from the Center, I realized that I hadn't called Judy to schedule my appointment to discuss how to invest my inheritance. She was the first person I called when I got home. I got her answering service. "Hello. You've reached Judy Weathers, Financial Advisor for American Express Financial Services. I'm sorry that I can't take your call. Leave a message with your name and telephone number. Please know that I'm out of the office until January 16. I'll return your call after January 17. Make it a great day!"

So I left her a voicemail. "Hi Judy. My name is Karma Francois. My friend Ma'at referred me to you. She said you would be a great person to talk to regarding my recent inheritance. Please call me back when you return to the office. My number is 202.555.7249. Have a blessed day!"

I spent the next few days handling details for Howard's art gallery, discussing plans for Uncle Wilson's home renovation with Guadelupe, organizing my New Year's Eve and Black February community yoga classes, and making notes about the Center's art exhibition space. Cane added one more task to my list of projects when he stopped by to request my creative assistance in planning our family Kwanzaa celebration. *There's Nothing Like This* by Omar, the U.K. godfather of neosoul music was playing when Cane entered my apartment. He immediately started hand dancing with me. When the song was over, we hugged and laughed. "Cuz, what's up with all of the CDs on the floor?"

"I'm sampling music for my New Year's Eve yoga class CD."

Picking up Omar's CD, Cane smiled, "I know you're going to include my boy Omar, right?"

"Most definitely."

"What about Fertile Ground?"

"They're included too."

"Which tracks?"

"I selected *Be Natural* and *Peace & Love* from the *Spiritual War* CD."

"Who else are you featuring?"

"Julie Dexter's *Peace of Mind*. Sting's *Let Your Soul Be Your Pilot*. Roy Hargrove's *Always and Forever*. Rickie Byars Beckwith's *I Found A Deeper Love*. Joshua Redman's *Body and Soul*. Ravi Coltrane's *Between Lines*. Marcus Johnson's *Morning Light*. Christian McBride's *I'll Write A Song For You*."

"Sounds like the Baptiste Family's musical gifts are being put to good use."

"They are. I really dig all it."

"Any thoughts about music for Kwanzaa?"

"I hadn't really thought about it. I figured you had all of that organized since you are King Kwanzaa."

Looking at me with puppy dog eyes, Cane whined, "With everything that's been going on with Colette, Dad and I haven't had a chance to put things in motion. I was hoping that you could help me out."

"Come on Cane. What about Colin and Chase?"

"Those guys aren't as creative as you are."

"Did you check with Millicent?"

"Mom said not to bother her since she took care of Christmas decorations at the hospital."

"I didn't hear Charlie's name."

"He's swamped at work. He doesn't have any extra time."

"Okay so it looks like I'm your girl. What do you want me to do?"

"First off, it would be great if you could help me develop the program and music"

"From scratch?"

"Not exactly. I thought we'd use the program that I created for my school's Kwanzaa celebration. We used an Andinkra symbol to represent each Kwanzaa principle. Then we created an affirmation and asked each child to reflect on what it meant to him or her."

"That sounds easy enough."

"Since our family is celebrating Imani, the seventh principle of Kwanzaa, I thought we could use the Andinkra symbol called Nyame Nte. It represents faith in God."

"What does it look like?"

Pulling a folded piece of paper out of his back pocket, Cane uttered, "My bad. Here it is."

"I like the simplicity of the tree design."

"I was thinking we could just keep everything nice and simple this year. Mom suggested that we make the ceremony more of a reflective time for everyone. No elaborate production. Just a libation, calling on the ancestors, lighting the candles, sharing what's in our hearts regarding faith, a short reading, and a prayer at the end. She offered to say the prayer. Dad volunteered to do the libation and call on the ancestors. I thought we could both share the responsibility of lighting the candles and asking people to share their thoughts about faith."

"Sounds like you already organized everything."

"I didn't mean to sound like everything is written in stone. I'm open for suggestions."

"Cane, nothing is wrong with your program."

"Okay, but if you want to make some changes, just let me know."

"Everything sounds great. Who is gonna do the reading?"

"I was thinking about reading an excerpt from a poem in Dr. W.E.B. Du Bois' book, *Darkwater: Voices from Within the Veil.*"

"I knew we couldn't have a celebration and not get some deep Black history lesson out of it."

"You know that's how I roll. I gotta keep feeding y'all hungry brown folks with soul food."

"So what's the poem called?"

"You probably know it because it's one of your dad's favorite poems."

"Is it *The Riddle of the Sphinx*?"

"The one and only. I love how it begins, *'Dark daughter of the lotus leaves ...'*"

"Are you planning to read the entire poem?"

"Just the first ten lines."

"Cool. So do want me to select any music?"

"Nah, I got that covered."

"Then why did you ask for my opinion earlier?"

"That was just a line I used to get your attention."

"You ain't slick."

New Year's Eve came so quickly. The number of students in my morning yoga class shocked me. Twenty-five women squeezed themselves into space that comfortably accommodates twenty persons. Sista7 members were present and accounted for. They greeted Aunt Daphyne and officially made her an honorary member of our group. I spent most of the class encouraging everyone to relax and let go of whatever limitations they were carrying. Everyone appeared to enjoy my life transformation theme and the yoga poses that opened the crown and third eye chakras. I gave reiki-healing touch with peppermint oil during *Savasana*. At the end of the class, I invited everyone to join me in chanting *Om Namah Shivaya*. We closed our practice with three long-winded Oms. Aunt Daphyne and I stopped at Bua Restaurant for lunch. While we waited for our entrees to arrive, she asked me, "So what's going with you?"

"What do you mean?"

"Well, I know you have a pretty full life with rebuilding your career. Are you dating anyone special now?"

"Uhhh."

"Karma, if I've overstepped my boundaries, let me know."

"No it's okay. I don't mind talking about my nonexistent dating life."

"Is it nonexistent because you have chosen not to date?"

"Well kinda."

"What does kinda mean?"

"To be honest, I had to take a sabbatical from the dating scene because of the unhealthy patterns I noticed."

"What were those patterns?"

"I learned through therapy that I consciously chose emotionally unavailable men as partners."

"Now that you recognize your past choices, what are you doing differently?"

"I'm not dating."

"Are you still on sabbatical?"

"I'm not sure. I just don't trust myself in choosing the right kind of men."

"Well, honey, when are you going to test the waters to see if you can choose healthy partners?"

"I don't know when."

"Karma, I know how you feel. I spent my twenties and early thirties in a series of bad relationships. You see this skin. I thought because it was the color of hematite that I didn't deserve to be treated right by men. I settled for less than what I deserved."

"That's hard to believe because you are so confidant."

"It took a lot of work to get to this place."

"How did you do it?"

"Like you, I found a therapist. I worked with her for over a decade on my self-esteem issues. Once I cut through those barriers, I had to build myself back up. It wasn't until I attended church at Agape International Spiritual Center and heard Reverend Michael Beckwith preach about the power that each of us has within us. I started taking classes at his church. One of my good girlfriends kept telling me that your uncle was interested in me, but I paid him no mind. Like you, I was scared and didn't trust my ability to choose healthy relationships. Plus your uncle looked like the typical man I went after. Tall, light-skinned, hazel eyes, and Creole features. His looks alone marked him as the wrong candidate for me."

"So what changed your mind?"

"One day I realized that my divinity was the foundation for my divine right to have a loving, healthy, and fulfilling relationship with a man who loves and honors me. I also had to surrender my fear of choosing the wrong mate."

"Did Uncle Metoyer make a move on you after that?"

"It was a year later. By then, I had opened myself up to the dating world and gotten to know some gentlemen. I needed that time to show myself that I was capable of choosing the right man."

"How did you and Uncle Metoyer eventually connect?"

"That same girlfriend who was trying to play matchmaker had a party for Valentine's Day dinner for all of her single friends. Your uncle and I were the only ones who showed up. So we had dinner with her and her husband. Afterwards, we went out for coffee and have been together ever since."

"That's a nice story."

"Yes it's nice, but it takes a lot of work. I want you to know that you can have a fulfilling relationship with a loving partner whenever you are ready to. All you have to do is surrender your fears and allow God to guide you."

"I hear you Aunt Daphyne."

"I know you do, sweetie."

I decided to spend New Year's Eve alone listening to some of my new music. Amel Larrieux's *Infinite Possibilities* CD kept me company as I wrote a poem in my journal about what love looks like in my life.

What does love look like in my life?

Part One

In my life, love looks like a lotus flower in the center of my heart

Within the center of this lotus flower, lies a pink and green jewel shaped in the image of the Star of David

In this sacred place, I hold the love energy of my life

It is funneled through an equation that Stevie Wonder wrote about in the liner notes of his 1976 classic *Songs in the Key of Life*:

love + love - hate = love energy

In my everyday life, this equation manifests in my thoughts, words, actions, choices, creativity, and relationships when I choose to allow it

When I make this choice, my heart opens to loving my spirit within, and everyone and everything in the universe

Part Two

In my life, love looks like me celebrating all of me

surrendering to the sweetness of life

claiming my beauty

Love looks like the trees, flowers, nature, Mother Earth, great goddesses and angels watching over me

Love looks like me

embracing the light

living healthy

making time to pray and meditate

opening a journal to write my thoughts

creating art

putting more massage, music, and movement in my life

relaxing with candles and drinking tea

practicing yoga with kindness, gentleness, compassion, and acceptance of my body for what it can and cannot do in the present moment

knowing myself and being able to be at peace with who I am

Part Three

Love looks like the feeling I get from being connected to God and everything in the universe when I listen to John Coltrane's *A Love Supreme*

It looks like art, fruit, nature, and living in the light

It feels like when I remember and accept that God and I are one at all times

Part Four

Love looks like

my life purpose

me caring for myself

the most powerful thing I can give myself and the universe

flowing with the vibration of all life

honoring the divinity in all things and people in the universe

After writing the poem, I sat rereading it a few times before falling asleep. Several hours later, my phone rang. I glanced at the clock. It registered 12:03 a.m. Momma was calling from Boston to wish me a Happy New Year. She sounded so bubbly and happy. After we spoke, I made a cup of blackberry tea and returned to my journal.

Love is like an incredibly elastic umbilical chord that is never cut even after we emerge from our mothers' wombs. It started way before we were even thought of much less conceived by the folks who came together to create our physical existence. Just that thought alone allows us to know how special we are. It is the reason we are affectionately called God's beloved. And because God is love so are we ...

Love is an energy. The soul food we need to live in this life and the next. When we choose to open our eyes and wake up to the truth of our identity, we can see that love extends into the empty spaces of the universe following us wherever we choose to go. Its reach is endless. Its power is amazing. Its essence continuously reveals itself to be much more than we thought it was yesterday. It teaches us to live in the present moment by surrendering what we think it should be and accepting what it is while allowing it space to evolve into its highest and most radiant form.

Love carefully plants its seeds in our lives with one request: that we nurture and care for them as they grow in and around us. Love's seeds grow in the thoughts we think and the ones we discard, the words we say and the ones we allow to remain silent, the actions we choose to take and the ones we decide not to, the dreams we welcome and the ones we allow to die, the connections we maintain and the ones we let go, the experiences we celebrate and the ones we bury.

In all of our growing, love calls us again and again. Sometimes we can get so tangled up in what we define as love that we work ourselves into frenzies. Instead of allowing love to shape itself in our lives and relationships, we try to control it. Our desire to control is really rooted in our fear of the manifestation of love's power and impact in our lives and relationships. For some us, if not all of us, love sometimes feels so big and vast that it is too much for us to bear. So we cringe, crumble, and allow fear to dominate our decisions. Our perspective is shaped by short-term desires instead of long-term needs. The short-term desires that we choose to embrace have us living beneath our divinity. Everything that we think, say, and do is covered by an odor that smells like a perfume or cologne called less than our authentic selves. We walk around proudly parading the canvas of our lives, relationships, and experiences as good and wonderful things rooted in love. And mark my word for awhile they all look, smell, and feel like good and wonderful things, but the appearance slowly fades away and reveals the truth that we have voluntarily hidden from love, an act of surrendering all of who we are for a higher will than we currently know.

Love as an act of surrender is a present moment experience available whenever we want to accept its invitation in our lives, but we have to accept it as it is. Most of us want to control it. It's human nature. For some of us this reality may be hard to see much less accept and claim as our own. Trust me most of us do it. The thing we have to always remember, become comfortable with, and accept is that love cannot be controlled. It is organic fluidity at its best. So I surrender to its flow and become who I was created to be: Karma, one of Love's Troubadours.

CHAPTER 43

▼

"May the God of hope fill you with all joy and peace in believing, so that you may abound in hope by the power of the Holy Spirit."

—Romans 15:13

Our family's Kwanzaa celebration was a small, intimate gathering with family members and Momma's friend, Henry. My favorite part of the evening occurred when everyone shared their definition of faith. Uncle Charles delivered an eloquent speech about watching his mother and her two sisters use faith as a tool to navigate their lives. He called them faith finders. Uncle Metoyer shared how they insisted that their children form strong bonds with their cousins. Since he and Uncle Charles were the only male cousins, they forged an immediate bond. He told us about his struggles to build a thriving business and the supportive reminders he received from Uncle Charles who always instructed him to turn to God as his source of faith. I felt called to testify about my first year in D.C. I shared the details of my personal struggles with my family for the first time. I admitted that Ohnedaruth was my greatest faith teacher because he showed me how to have faith in God's power to heal all things through love.

After the ceremony, Cane and I talked. "Cuz, I had no idea that you were going through so much. Why didn't you tell me?"

"Cane, I could barely understand what I was going through. I just didn't have the words to share with a lot of people."

"I'm not a lot of people. I'm your cousin."

"Yeah that's true, but I didn't want to burden you."

"Karma, did you hear anything that Dad and Uncle Metoyer were talking about?"

"Yes, I was sitting right next to both of them."

"But did you understand what they were saying about us being adamant about maintaining our family connections?"

"I got that part."

"Well, if you got that part, then you should understand why I want to know what's going on in your life. You aren't a burden to any of us. You're family."

I hugged Cane. "I hear you loud and clear."

"Good. I want us to be close again. You're like my sister. If something is going on with you I wanna know. I want us to spend more time with each other. Do dinner. Grab a movie from time to time. Visit a museum. See a play. Hey, since you like the neosoul music I gave you as a gift, I thought we could hang out at a few concerts. Fertile Ground is coming in February. Eric Roberson, this cat that I went to Howard with, is coming in April. I think you'll really like his CD. I'll drop it by this week."

"Sounds amazing."

2001 was off to a great start. Branford came down for the King Holiday weekend. We were able to spend an afternoon together without me feeling attracted to him. When he shared his excitement about his new long distance relationship with his partner Derrick, I was genuinely happy for him. I even agreed to meet them for brunch on Sunday.

By the time I got home from hanging with Branford it was six thirty. That meant I would be fashionably late to Yamuna and Grant's party. Normally, I would be rushing to get to my destination on time, but tonight's party wasn't something I was really looking forward to. When I first received their invitation, I was really excited. My excitement died when Yamuna told me that she and Grant identified several gentlemen callers that I could interview on the sly at the gathering. There was one in particular that she kept raving about ... Sy something. What kind of name is that? It's not that I'm against brothas. I'm just not trying to hook up with anyone now. 1999 and 2000 were just way too much for a sista. My mantra for 2001 is no more man and family drama. I just want to do me.

Last night, Yamuna left me a message emphasizing that I should come ready to meet someone special. What's that supposed to mean? I couldn't help but call her back to ask for clarification. When I told her politely that she and Grant shouldn't try to hook me up with someone, Yamuna quickly mumbled "uhum girl." Translation ... I don't care what you said, I'm gonna do what I said I was gonna do from the get go!

Six thirty quickly moved to seven fifteen. I still wasn't close to getting dressed. Saturday evening found me sitting at my kitchen table drinking a cup of ginger tea. Thoughts about my workload for the upcoming week at the gallery and the Center filled my head. Passionate excitement was the best phrase I could find to describe my joy. I think the Sufi poet Rumi wrote something that said we should let the beauty of what we love be what we do. Being able to curate art the way that I want to is what I love. It's a blessing to be able to return to this work.

Seven forty and still no shower. Guilt finally set in. I quickly showered, tied my locs in an upsweep, applied a touch of MAC "O" lip stick, and slipped on my denim dress, turquoise earrings and matching necklace, and camel boots. Looking in my bedroom mirror, I gave myself the once over and critiqued my appearance as "casually dressed ... definitely in chill mode."

Eight thirty nine is the time the World Cab dropped me off in front of Grant's row house on 7th Street in Brookland. Solomon, Yamuna's son greeted me as I entered the house. As I was taking my coat off, I noticed three men huddled in a corner near a cracked window. At first glance, you might disregard their presence, but not me. I could feel their vibes from across the room. These brothas weren't your ordinary brothas. But then are there ever any ordinary brothas? Suddenly my interest was peaked. Yes, me the sista formerly known as not interested in meeting new men. I was beginning to think that Grant and Yamuna's match-making might pay off.

There was something about these cats that drew me in. Perhaps, I was mes-merized by their physical features. Each one had the same shaped bald head and wore the same style of mustache and neatly trimmed goatees. What a sucker I am for men with Isaac Hayes' bald heads, linebacker bodies standing five foot eight to five foot ten, Yoruba-etched eyes and noses, and butterscotch skin! There was no denying that they were some kind of kin. Silently, I nicknamed them triplets.

Finding it hard to dismiss the triplets' masculine mystique, I made my way over to their corner. A table with hors d'oeuvres became my haven. As I filled my plate with raw vegetables and ranch dressing, my ears plugged into their conver-sation. The one dressed in a black turtleneck with gray wool trousers that had those fancy cuffs I have always been fond of was spittin' some crazy intense verse about Franz Fanon. "If we wear white masks to decorate our black skins, we betray our ancestors. If we betray our ancestors, we speak a language that is not our own. If we speak a language that is not our own, we forfeit the basic impor-tance to the phenomenon of what it means to speak in the ways we were born to communicate. If we aren't careful, our forfeiture could be passed from one gener-ation to the next, creating an absence of wisdom and understanding of what it means to grasp the morphology of our ancestral language. Our negligence could be the death of us, if we don't wake up and change. The only thing we'll have left is morphological confetti."

He sounded like the spoken word artist Saul Williams. His words reminded me of something Daddy might say. The shoe freak in me couldn't help but notice his incredibly shiny black Johnson and Murphy tie ups. Hey can you blame me. The one closest to the table stood at military attention in his urban prep blue denim shirt, tan khakis, and sharp as a tack sienna square-toed boots. They looked very Kenneth Cole-ish. The other triplet leaned against the wall in his col-orful dashiki, faded denim jeans, and blond Timberlands. They made me feel like I had died and gone to fine ass brotha heaven.

My gaze deepened as I leaned in to hear Spoken Word triplet. An unknown hand lightly touched my shoulder. I looked up and it was Dashiki Triplet. Black Turtleneck Triplet stopped reciting his poem. Yes I had to name them according to their clothing. Black Turtleneck Triplet and Urban Prep Triplet stared into my face as Dashiki Triplet spoke. "Queen, you look like you might want to join our conversation."

Slightly embarrassed, I smiled and politely nodded with the grace of a southern debutante.

Dashiki Triplet continued. "Allow me to introduce myself. My name is Baraka. These are my two brothers, Baldwin (Urban Prep Triplet) and Biko (Black Turtleneck Triplet)."

"Wonderful to meet you all. My name is Karma."

Baldwin remarked, "Karma. Cause and effect in Sanskrit. Interesting name."

Biko questioned, "So Karma where are you from?"

"Oakland, but I've been living in D.C. for two and half years. What about you?"

"We're all from Americus, Georgia. My brother Baldwin and I currently live in Atlanta with our wives and children."

Silently, I made a mental note that two were married with children. That meant that one might be available. "Americus. Isn't that the place where three dozen Black female teenage freedom fighters were taken to an abandoned Civil War era prison and held against their will in 1963?"

Baldwin chimed in, "The girls were from Americus and taken to Leesburg Stockade which is twenty miles from Americus. Our family knows the story well because our eldest sister Betty was a part of that group."

"That must have been an awful time for your family."

"Awful doesn't begin to describe that period. None of us boys were born yet, but our parents and older sisters made sure we knew what Betty went through. She was only twelve years old. Our parents had forbidden her to participate in a civil rights march down Cotton Avenue, but she had a mind of her own. Betty still does."

"Where does she live now?"

"Betty lives in Atlanta."

"What does she do?"

"She's a civil rights attorney in private practice."

Baraka interjected, "Yeah our big sister is committed to the struggle."

Baldwin asked, "So how did you develop an interest the Americus story?"

"It started with my father. He was a Black history professor who archived every single issue of Jet and EBONY. Daddy made my sister and I write reports on the events that we read about in both magazines. I wrote one of my sixth grade reports on the Americus incident."

"My wife and I will have to keep that one in our mental library for our new-born."

My question was answered. None of them were available. Oh well. I'm not really interested in men anyway. "So you are all having a male bonding week-end?"

Baldwin answered, "Yes indeed. We love our wives and children, but some-times brothas just need to go on road trips, sit back, and talk. Take me for instance. I've been married to Edwina for almost eleven years. We're two sons deep into our family. Edwina is my rock, lover, and soulmate. She's my bliss. Our two boys, Elijah and Isaiah, represent all the love we share."

Biko shared the same passion for his wife and daughter. "I feel you man. Rachel and I got a real live *Love Jones* thing happening. Me and that woman been through the fire and have consistently risen from the ashes into a beautiful phoe-nix. We ain't perfect, but we are perfect for each other. Together, we've been able to raise a healthy thirteen year old daughter, Ann Marie, our pride and joy."

Baldwin commented, "So you see we had to come up here and get renewed in order to love our women and children at full force. Plus we had to give our baby brother some last words of wisdom before he and his lady Ratu have their first child."

"Ratu. That's a unique name."

Baraka responded, "It means love in the Sotho language."

"Do you know what you're going to have?"

"We told the doctor that we wanted to be surprised."

"Any names?"

"Stephen Michael for a boy. Kindred Grace for a girl."

"I love those combinations."

Blushing, Baraka praised his wife. "My baby Ratu is really the mastermind behind the names. She has a way with words. I'm just the honey who does what she wants me to do."

"That's so cute."

"Is it so obvious that my wife got me sprung and wide open?"

"Yeah, but what's wrong with that?"

"Nothing. I wouldn't have it any other way. I been like this since the day we first met as freshmen on the campus of Savannah State College. That beautiful plum-colored, fast talking, wide-hipped walking woman knows I'm hers for a lifetime."

"Well, I wish you both the best."

"Thanks. We need all the well wishes we can get."

Hearing these men talk about their wives and children made me feel proud about the power of Black love. It was also so refreshing to hear them confess their feelings.

Biko questioned, "So Ms. Karma, how do you know Grant?"

"Yamuna introduced us after they started dating. We're good friends. So what's your connection to the happy couple?"

"We're Grant's cousins. Our father and his mother are siblings. Grant is like our fourth brother. He spent summers with us when we were growing up. The city cousin visiting his country cousins."

"My twin sister and I used to do that with our cousins in D.C."

"Twins. Is it true what they say about twins?"

"And what's that?"

"That you can both feel when something is wrong with the other."

"Violet and I would definitely prove that theory wrong. We are day and night."

Baraka concluded, "It sounds like you and your sister are not that close."

"I'm closer to my brother, Ohnedaruth."

"Now that's a unique name."

"It was John Coltrane's Hindu spiritual name. In Sanskrit, it means compassion."

"Your parents were deep into the Sanskrit names with you and your brother."

"Karma is a nickname that my father gave me when I was a little girl. My given name is Belle Violette."

Baldwin exclaimed, "Gentlemen, we have before us a genuine southern belle."

Biko initiated the next phase of interrogation. "What's your story, Ms. Southern Belle? You married?"

Baraka called attention to my left hand. "Man, look at her ring finger."

Biko continued his line of questioning, "Now if you're not married, I know a beautiful sista such as yourself is surely attached to a brotha."

"Currently unattached."

"I find that hard to believe. So what's the dealio? You just playing hard to get or what?"

"There's no dealio. I'm just taking time for myself."

"Okay I know what that means. What's his name? How did he hurt you? You want the West brothers to teach him a thing or two."

Laughing, I said, "Thanks but no thanks. I'm just taking some time to work on me."

"As long as you aren't planning to quit on us brothas."

"I could never do that."

"Good to hear."

"Can you point me in the direction of the bathroom?"

Baraka teased Biko. "Man, look what your interrogation tactics have done. Now Karma is trying to escape our company."

"No I'm not. I just have to make a pit stop. I'll be back."

"In that case, the bathroom is upstairs on the left."

On my way to the bathroom, I saw Yamuna and Grant walk through the front door. "Girl, I'm sorry I wasn't here to greet you. Grant and I had to make a run to Whole Foods and the liquor store."

Giving me a kiss on my left cheek, Grant welcomed me. "Karma, it's so good to see you. Let me apologize for my frat brother. Sy is missing in action tonight. He left me a message earlier saying he wasn't feeling well. Yamuna and I will have to plan something next week so you can meet each other."

"That's really not necessary."

"Karma, yes it is. We really wanted you two to meet. I think he could be your Mr. Right."

"Hold up girl. You know I ain't ready for Mr. Right."

"Well, it doesn't hurt to meet Mr. New Friend."

"Yamuna, you're persistent as the day is long. I just want you to have what Grant and I have."

Grant wrapped his hands around Yamuna's waist and tenderly kissed the small of her neck. "Yeah Karma, can you blame your girl?"

"Not one bit."

"I can't wait to make this woman my wife."

"So have you set a date?"

"If it were up to Grant, we would marry tomorrow. Justice of the peace and all."

"What's wrong with that?"

"Sweetie, what's right with it?"

"Karma, let me show you that I am husband material. You're so right dear."

I congratulated Grant on learning lesson one. A wife is always right. "Smart man."

"I know who is running this show. She is."

"It's not like that. We compromised and picked the first Saturday in May."

"I'll mark it in my calendar."

"Write it in red and start shopping for a red and white dress. You have to come Kappa correct."

"Girl, don't pay this man no mind. We're still negotiating the colors."

"Karma, get a red and white dress."

"Y'all are funny."

Grant unwrapped his hands from around Yamuna's waist and took the groceries into the kitchen. Yamuna walked me upstairs. Curious about the absence of our sistacircle, I asked Yamuna, "So where's the rest of Sista7?"

"Serengeti and Kalahari are in Madison visiting Reverend Ayo and her partner. Tomorrow, Serengeti is participating in a forum discussion at Reverend Ayo's church about the Center's lesbian, gay, bisexual, and transgender anti-violence campaign work. They sent us a beautiful floral arrangement. Ma'at and Drew were the first ones to arrive."

"That's nice that she is hanging with Drew."

"He's Ma'at's new man. They're an official couple. They left about an hour ago to see Drew's sister. She is having a house warming party. Greer came for awhile, but she had to leave to meet a client. That girl is working her behind off on this huge job in Chevy Chase. Sunee said she would be coming later when things at the restaurant slowed down."

I hugged Yamuna. "I really miss seeing my sistas."

"Me too. The good news is that we are all supposed to get together next week at Mocha Hut for a personal finance seminar with Ma'at's financial advisor. That's when I am planning to tell everyone about the wedding date. So can you keep it a secret until then?"

"Not a problem."

As I excused myself and walked into the bathroom, I realized how much I needed to be in the presence of people engaged in good loving. They represented a community of Love's Troubadours. It felt like God's hope was filling me with joy and peace to help me believe that this kind of love was possible for me.

CHAPTER 44

▼

"A time to seek."

—Ecclesiastes 3:6

I arrived at Mocha Hut an hour before we were scheduled to meet with Judy for the sole purpose of ordering a soy chai latte and reading my new book, *being black*. Unfortunately, the only thing that I did was eavesdrop on the discussion of a small group of people comfortably huddled around a table located a few feet from where I was sitting. Their physical presence as a group was striking. They came in a variety of colors, shapes, sizes, and genders. Their attire was colorful like a carnival on a Caribbean island. Bright blues, sunny yellows, joyful oranges, passionate reds, exciting pinks, luscious greens, and stunning purples.

They rested on seats made of faux leather. A medley of tea and coffee drinks decorated their table top. The aroma of hazelnut and vanilla coffee, early grey tea, apple cider, and hot chocolate filled the air. The group's tone was upbeat and intense as they shared pieces of banana bread, oatmeal cookies, and blueberry scones. Their facial expressions alluded to confidential banter being exchanged. I think they thought nobody was listening since there were only a few of us urban dwellers taking up space on a rainy evening.

The main speaker sat in the middle of her comrades. Her full Afro-puff ball flopped up and down and grazed her yellow citrine skin as she dramatized her words with hand movements. Her performance was so enticing that I decided to bookmark the page I started reading. "There are no formulas to follow when it comes to loving yourself and others. You have to ask yourself what do I need and what must I do to love myself? What do others need and what must I do to love them? Sometimes the answers to these questions are surprising. Sometimes in managing my own energy, I have been directed to seek a healthy emotional and spiritual balance by intentionally keeping physical distance from others and choosing to send them love and light from my spirit to theirs. The physical distance serves as a boundary that allows me to maintain detachment or interaction in the physical realm. It also reminds me that sometimes no matter how much we love others, the best thing we can do is let them be without any involvement or interaction. Then there are times, when I'm also called to accept that my choice in loving others influences the triangular connections I have with folks who are connected to all parties involved. That's not an easy one to do, but sometimes it just makes more sense to step aside and let the connections go. New connections will fill the space of old ones. Life will move forward. I will grow. Maybe there'll be days when I look back at the choices I've made and wonder did I do the right thing. No matter the answer, I'll be called to accept it all and live in the present moment."

The second speaker was a vanilla almond-colored man who wore a long black braid down his back. "It sounds like you are describing what I call the elasticity of love. The process by which you gently open your heart a little more each day to embrace the divine spark within yourself, others, and the universe. It makes you a little more grateful each day for a heart that is opening wider."

The third speaker was a man with a thick unshaped reddish brown Afro that framed his sandalwood face like a halo. "When we make the decision to embrace another as our partner, do we ever ask ourselves if we have the emotional and spiritual maturity to be in a relationship? Do we realize that the purpose of relationships is twofold: spiritual and emotional healing? Are we really willing to do the work to heal ourselves in relationship and support our partners in their healing process? Are we honest about our strengths and weaknesses? Do we know how to resolve conflict? Are we willing to learn how?"

I missed the next response because Ma'at introduced me to Judy. Greer and Sunee arrived five minutes later. Yamuna, Kalahari, and Serengeti called to say they were running late. That gave me an opportunity to talk with Judy one-on-one about my inheritance. She asked me to describe my personal finance goals. I told her that I wanted to learn how to manage my income, pay off debt, and invest my inheritance wisely. She applauded me for having personal financial goals and investing the time to identify a financial advisor. I liked the way Judy took the time to find out about me as a person. She helped me see that my decisions were important steps in my journey to become healthy. We agreed to meet in a week to discuss how we could work best together.

I woke up in the middle of the night wondering about the statements that the folks in Mocha Hut made. I realized that the only way I was going to find out if I could have a healthy relationship was to test the waters. Glancing around my kitchen, I wondered where I could find an eligible pool of bachelors at two thirty in the morning. Out of the corner of my eye, I saw my laptop sitting on my breakfast bar. *Voila.* Love@AOL. Yamuna had success with it. Why not give it a try? My fingers pressed the on button. I logged onto my AOL account and visited the women's ads to get ideas for my ad. I decided to call my ad "SBF Seeking New Friendships." I had a good time writing it without censor.

It's a new year. A time for new beginnings … new opportunities to connect with new people. I am a thirty something SBF with a creative spirit, honest heart, and open mind. My spirit, health, creativity, and relationships are the things I cherish the most in life. I'm passionate about art, music, yoga, theatre, laughing, reading, meditating, spending time with family and friends, playing scrabble, learning *Chaturanga* (an Indian game that is the mother of chess), and taking walks in nature. I currently live in D.C., but spent several years in New York. I'm originally from Oakland, California with some serious Louisiana roots. If you are an honest, open-minded, spiritual, health-conscious, and fun-loving single man of color, send an e-mail. Please include a photo. Enjoy your new year!

I wasted no time in posting my ad. AOL sent me a message it would be approved in twenty-four hours. Let the game of seek and ye shall find a few good men begin.

I waited two days before checking my e-mail. A part of me was afraid that no one would respond to my ad. When I finally broke down and checked, I learned that I had nine potential suitors.

Ad #1—JazzOrinthologist@aol.com

Hi Ms. Lady! I wish I had your name to use instead of Ms. Lady. I hope that title meets with your approval. I figure you have to be a lady by the words you used in your polite, well-mannered ad. My name is Evan Murphy. I am a Kansas City native, single (divorced; married once), relatively healthy, and 47. I came to D.C. to attend Georgetown and stayed to work in the federal government. Sunday through Sunday, I am the proud father of two pre-teen sons and one self-sufficient adult daughter. Monday through Friday—9 to 5 … I am an economist in downtown D.C. I live in Silver Spring. I am a jack of many trades … my favorite trades are jazz ornithologist and wordsmith. Are you familiar with the meaning of the term ornithologist? Just in case, the wordsmith in me would like to explain. An ornithologist is a zoologist who studies birds … a birdwatcher. Now I'll share my definition of a jazz ornithologist: a person who passionately studies and appreciates the music of Charles Christopher "Yardbird" Parker, Jr. and lives life as free as the birds. Hence, I'm attracted to female ornithologists … a five dollar word that defines down to earth brilliant, bold, beautiful, bronze-colored women who live life as free as the birds. Traveling, music, yoga, reading, and learning new things are some of my interests. I am seeking to establish friendships with female ornithologists. If you think that you might be one, contact me. My photo is attached. It was taken at my son's piano recital in November.

Evan

Ad #2—tbond007@earthlink.com

Hello. Let me start by saying that you are gorgeous. I had to get that out of the way. Recently, I relocated to this area due to my job. I'm single, 34 and Jamaican. I don't have any kids. I have never been married. I'm college educated with an advanced degree. Education is important to my family. I enjoy current events (CNN junkie), spicy food, dancing, swimming, art galleries, concerts, biking, soccer (World Cup fanatic), and spending time with someone special. Your ad sounds very pleasant and down to earth. I would like to meet someone who is down to earth, nice to talk to, and who is familiar with this area. Friends describe me as being spontaneous. I'd agree. I think that character trait helps to keep the intensity in a friend/relationship going. I have attached a photo that was taken during my last visit home to Kingston. The man in the picture is my father. He was celebrating his seventy-fifth birthday.

Travis

Ad#3—Chocolatecityman@verizon.com

You look like a woman who could easily become my baby's momma. Sike. I knew that you would get your attention. My name is Phil. SBM 41, divorced with four children. I work as a plumber. I am a D.C. native with a lot of Chocolate City humor and flavor that needs to be shared with a special woman. I'm not one for this e-mail thing, but I thought I would give it a try.

Phil

Ad#4—Ajohnson1976@aol.com

I am a SBM, 32. My name is Abe. I'm a pretty basic person. I work at Home Depot in the painting department. Motorcycles, football, boxing, hip hop, and spending time with my special lady are important to me. I'm feelin' you something hard. You know what I mean. I'm not a good writer, but I think you are pretty and might be the one for me. Hit me back on my pager. 703.555.7726.

Abe

Ad#5—Taurusman2000@hotmail.com

God did a wonderful thing when he made you. I'd love to talk with you in person sometime. My name is Boyd. I'm a 35 year old, Black man with no children. I'm married, but things are falling apart. I think we will be separated soon. If that doesn't bother you, e-mail me.

Boyd

Ad#6—diehardredskinsfant1965@yahoo.com

Hey. I thought I would drop you a line to say hello. This is my first time responding to an ad. So excuse my virgin behavior. My co-worker suggested that I try online dating. My name is Dewayne. I'm a 29 year old southern man from Charleston, SC. I have been in D.C. for five years. I work for the post office. My work as a postal carrier is pleasant. I like meeting people in the neighborhood that I serve. Sometimes the cold weather is challenging, but I love my job. When

I'm not working, I am working out, playing pool with friends, watching the Redskins play football, barbecuing on my new deck (townhouse in PG County), or attending Bible Study or church at Ebenezer Baptist Church. I am looking for a partner in life. I was married and went through a pretty bad divorce. Right after that, I started dating Black women, but I found their attitudes were just way too much for me. My ex-wife was a Black woman. No offense, but I was just tired of dealing with demanding, know it all sisters. So I moved on to dating white women. I found them to be more accommodating. Even though I like white women better, I still want to be married and have a family with a nice submissive God-fearing Black woman. The kind I can take home to my mother. So if you are interested, write me back.

Dewayne

Ad#7—david.thomas@hotmail.com

Online dating is a journey in itself. My name is David. I am a single, white, 39 year old professional living in the Mount Pleasant neighborhood. I enjoyed reading your ad. I thought it was refreshing. Art, running, music, dancing, and traveling are some of my interests. I'd love to chat more with you. My photo is attached.

David

Ad#8—prhombre@aol.com

Here it goes. I am not really comfortable with e-mail, but your ad made me get comfortable. So I'm breaking down my own barriers by writing this short note to a beautiful lady. My name is Cesar. I am from Ponce, Puerto Rico. I am single, 28, and have never been married. I have one son who lives in Ponce with his mother. I work as an analyst for the Department of Defense. I live in Reston. I own my own home and also sale real estate on the side. It makes for an interesting life. Sports, traveling, amusement parks, eating at different restaurants, movies, working out, and playing scrabble are some of my interests. If you think you might be interested, send me an e-mail.

Cesar

Ad#9—talentedtenth@aol.com

My name is Albert. I am a 34 year old, single man of African descent living in Landover, MD. I was born on the Eastern Shore, but raised in P.G. County. I have never been married before and do not have any children. Right now, I am working on my Ph.D. in history at Morgan State University. I'm close to defending my thesis. Let me just come out and say that your ad stopped me in my tracks. I think you might be someone I should meet. You sound like that you understand your nature as a Dark Daughter of the Lotus Leaves. If you like what I have shared so far, can smile back at my photo, and understand what I am talking about when I refer to the talented tenth, drop me a line.

Albert

Deciding who to write back was easy. The guys who did not attach a photo were immediately removed from list of eligible bachelors. That group included Cesar, Phil and Abe. I didn't feel like corresponding with faceless men. Boyd, the married man and DeWayne, the Black woman hater were nixed from my list. Too much drama. That left Evan, Travis, David, and Albert. Travis' picture was the most promising out of the bunch. Everyone else was decent looking. I wrote them all the same message and filled in their names.

Hi!

Thanks for writing me. My name is Karma. I would love to chat with you more. Let me know if you're open to having a telephone conversation this week. If yes, send me your telephone number. I feel more comfortable calling you first. Enjoy your day!

Peace, Karma.

Requesting a phone conversation felt a bit aggressive, but I didn't wanna waste time playing e-mail tag when we could talk by phone to determine whether we might want to meet in person. I gave them my cell number instead of my home number just in case any of them were problematic. To my surprise, they all responded with their phone numbers.

David and I played telephone tag for nine days before I abandoned ship. It was just too hard to connect with him. Travis only wanted to talk about himself for an hour. He was too self-absorbed for me. Albert wasn't a talker. I found myself struggling to create conversation tidbits just to keep the discussion moving along. That left Evan. We ended up having several great conversations and agreed to meet at Caribou Coffee on 17th and L on February 1st.

When I walked into the café, I knew immediately that I wasn't physically attracted to him. He was too skinny for me. I was polite and stayed for thirty minutes before making an excuse to leave his company. Walking home, I wondered if I'm too shallow or expecting too much in the physical appearance of a man. My conscience answered back, you just like what you like. That's all. Even though my first attempt at online dating didn't produce Mr. Right, I learned more about myself and the type of men I'm attracted to. So nothing was wasted.

Valentine's Day 2001 was pretty quiet. Momma called to wish me a beautiful day. Ohnedaruth sent me a Hallmark e-card. Sista7 members left me some cute voicemail messages. Cane surprised me with Thai takeout from Bua and India.Arie's *Acoustic Soul* CD. India's music was new to my listening ears. We sat up eating *Pad Thai* and dancing to India's music. I fell in love with *Video* and *Strength, Courage & Wisdom*. Both songs reminded me how far I have come in my journey of self-discovery. After Cane left, I cleaned up and did the moon salutation as my evening practice. I closed my practice by chanting *Aham Prema*. In my gut, I knew that divine love was my true identity.

EPILOGUE

▼

"A time to keep."

—Ecclesiastes 3:6

It was the third month in a new year. The first day of March was born. I celebrated its birth knowing that my heart was healed. Coltrane and Ellington teased my mind. I was in a sentimental mood looking to the possibilities of the present. The groove got better with Miles Davis. His composition, *Blue in Green* filled my face with a smile. With this newfound energy, I decided to take another plunge into the online dating world. This time, I chose my gentlemen callers.

Love@AOL offered me numerous ads to sort through. After an hour, I found one: Spiritual Black Man. I was intrigued to say the least. I clicked on the photo and saw a vibrant soul brotha who reminded me of the actor Courtney Vance. He had coffee-colored skin, a bald head, goatee, piercing eyes, jazzy black glasses that reminded me of some Italian designer whose name I can't remember, and full lips that held a smile I would be happy to have shining in my world. His physical attributes were short and simple: athletic, toned and five feet and eleven inches. A nice tall glass of water that a sista could use right about now. His geographical location was D.C. His vitals matched what I was looking for: single, never married, and very interested in having kids one day. A non-smoker and social drinker. His interests were varied: laughter, Eastern philosophies, coffee, conversation, cooking, dining out, sports (Redskins and NY Knicks), movies (*Love Jones* and *The Matrix*), museums and art (Romare Bearden), eclectic music

(John and Alice Coltrane), concerts, traveling, volunteering with a local fraternity, and wine tasting. Spiritual Black Man's personal statement left me speechless.

We live in a world filled with a myriad of opportunities to explore new terrain. Each day offers us a fresh start. How we approach it begins with our choice. And I choose to live fully and freely in the present moment. In this present moment, I invite you to read my words. Feel their texture. Allow their vibrant colors to shine radiance in your life. Perhaps they will become an interlude of impromptu poetry that pauses your day. Perhaps you will be called to ask yourself every few minutes if they create an interest far beyond just inhaling what my mind, spirit, and heart have expressed. Perhaps the end result will be an electronic encounter of a magical kind. Caveat emptor and strap yourself in as you prepare for the ride. Follow the wisdom of Emily Dickinson and allow your soul to stand ajar, ready to welcome the ecstatic.

Sincerity is the best word to describe my character. That hasn't always been the case, but life has taught me its importance. I'm a work in process. Can you dig that? If you can, travel with me into my world. Brooklyn is my birthplace. Cuba is the land of my *Mami*. I'm an interesting blend with untapped and unknown southern roots from Richmond. I take pride in my cultural diversity. It makes me who I am.

Enough about me. Let me get down to what you probably want to know. First and foremost, I am seeking a woman as a friend. She should have an open mind to all of the possibilities that might unfold between us. She should be someone that has a spiritual center, clear vision of her relationship values, and flexibility in discerning who works best in her life. She is a lady with an intuitive understanding. This lady might be you. You are a natural beauty with a *phat* smile (*phat* meaning *phabulous*), juicy personality, humor, wit, openness, confidence with zero arrogance, and intellectual curiosity.

I wanna take it slow and easy when it comes to building a strong and grand friendship. If we stay open to all possibilities, it may lead to a spiritual union. Let's take it slow and exchange e-mails. If the e-mails flow, let's move to the telephone. And if the telephone conversations create an incredible urge to meet, well let's just do that. Perhaps we will sit face to face among the twin tables of a local cafe. Our conversation could be the birthplace of us becoming friends. If you are adventurous, join me. Let's see where the possibilities take us. Optimistically awaiting your reply.

Spiritual Black Man's whole vibe reminded me when Miles gave birth to cool. I was so smitten that I crafted a stream of consciousness response in lower case letters.

good morning to you. happy march. my name is karma. i wanted to take a few moments and share how much i enjoyed reading your words. your profile appeared in my online search this morning. lately, i've been busy with projects at work. today, i needed to just switch gears. so i put on stevie wonder's *songs in the key of life. love's in need of love today* is actually playing now. when i clicked on your profile, i was moved to write a few thoughts. i may ramble so watch out. that's just me. kreative with a k. i'm a groovy chica sistalove in chocolate city. i was born in oakland, the same place that the black panthers called home. and yes, i do have a rebel kinda spirit. i rebel against boredom and limitations. i am a firm believer in surrendering myself to the beauty and blessings of the universe. i have learned about that thing called surrender in the past year. i spent several years in nyc after college. dc has been my home for almost two years. i'm doing my best to live fully in dc. i enjoy the cultural scene, nature in malcom x park, walks along 16th street, yoga, and dancing. they are some of the things i love to do. i'm passionate about peace, love, joy, art, creativity, health, family, quiet time, traveling, music, learning, and being open to the blessings of each day. i am an alice and john coltrane fan. stevie wonder and fertile ground too. they are incredible. i love walking down the street to whole foods on 14th and p as much as dancing at habana village with my girlfriends. the hardest thing i have ever done is tell myself the truth and then love myself afterwards. i'm still working on that one. it's a life-long process. okay so what else can i say. you write with words that paint pictures of possible conversations that i would like to have with you at local places in my u street neighborhood i can feel your vibe (... that sort of thing that makes me say huuuuuuuuuummmmm i should send an e-mail and see what happens with this brotha). this e-connection has me feeling a vibe. you are a witty wordsmith who has released something unique into my online dating experience. it has me sharing my thoughts about all kinds of stuff like how i'm about to eat some hot apple sauce with raisins. how does a rambling artista chica yogini sistalove wrap up an e-mail to a spiritual black man? where do i put my last period? hhhhuuu-uummmm ... pause.... pause.... pause.... let's see ... a poem to mark the occasion is probably one way ... let's see if it fits....

electronic encounters

his witty words tickle my brain
spark my imagination
and stop me from sipping my soy chai latte
that in itself is a miracle
cuz' me love me some soy chai

as i pause i wonder if an electric encounter
has the power to make me shine a *phat* smile

i wonder if it will enhance my natural beauty

perhaps it will flatter my juicy personality

well whatever the answers are
my curiosity about the world in which he lives in
has increased
so i surrender to the beauty of the moment, step out on faith, and push the envelope of life beyond its comfortable boundaries by wrapping my words in an
e-mail correspondence with the passion i have for living a fun-filled life

i begin with an introduction that may be a bit off the cuf
did i spell the word "cuf" correctly?
the rest of me disregards the question and frolics in the mere joy of the present
moment
my need to censure dies

i reach into places and share
my flow is flowing at least i think it is as i type thoughts that fly across the computer screen
i share what comes to mind
it keeps coming
then it stops on its own
i press the send button
with hope and satisfaction that an electronic encounter has been made.

hey thanks for reading. if you are interested in connecting, drop me a line. if not, i understand. it was fun chatting.

peace, karma

I selected a photo taken during our family Kwanzaa celebration and attached it to the message. It reflected passion at its best. It was enchanting to the viewer and invited him to come closer and enjoy my spectrum of rainbow shades. The message was finally complete. So I clicked the send button and allowed the journey with Spiritual Black Man to begin.

A few days passed, leaving my e-mail in-box empty. Impatience would not let me move on. I wondered why Spiritual Black Man hadn't replied. Perhaps it was the fullness of Mother Moon. Maybe Mercury was in retrograde. All I knew was that I had caught a nasty case of the royal blues that transformed themselves into azure and indigo blues.

My jiggie stopped jigging. I felt stuck in the universe. Some folks might call it a rut. I wanted to scream for help, but the words wouldn't come. So I sulked alone in my apartment, dragging the would haves, the could haves, and the I don't knows around for a couple of hours. They finally sat down on my unmade bed. I found a small corner of the bed to rest my head. I woke up with a burst of newfound energy. I couldn't remember the dreams but they sure made me feel good. They left a residue of jasmine and clover … a sugar candy warmth that only comes from a spring lover.

My laptop looked lonely. So I opened her up and checked my e-mail hoping to receive a nice surprise. She delivered what I needed: a witty response from Spiritual Black Man. It included his real name and telephone number. Symon Allure. 202.555.1018. I took a deep breath before closing my lap top and heading to my phone to call Symon.

"Good evening."

"Hi Symon. This is Karma. We've been exchanging e-mails on AOL."

"Hey. How are you doing?"

"Good."

"It's really good to hear your voice."

"Yours too."

"So what are you doing this evening?"

"I'm just taking care of a few odds and ends."

"It's laundry night for me."

"You have a lot to do?"

"Not really. I just have two loads. They're mainly sheets, towels, and gym clothes. Pretty boring for a Wednesday evening."

"So what made you send your telephone number?"

"Your poem. It was so creative. It left me speechless. You have some real skills."

"I try."

"Do you read at any places locally?"

"I'm supposed to read a few pieces this month at Our Womanist Center's spoken word event."

"That's funny. The Center is my client. I'm serving as their financial advisor."

"I work as a yoga teacher there."

"Then you must know Serengeti, Kalahari, and Yamuna."

"Wow, this is a small world. They are some of my best friends."

"Yamuna is the reason I was able to secure the Center as my client. She's engaged to my frat brother Grant."

The pieces of the puzzle all came together when he mentioned Grant's name. Symon is the man Yamuna and Grant have been trying to hook me up with since November. "Symon, you're not going to believe this, but I think Yamuna and Grant have been trying to get us together for the past several months."

"Wait a minute. Were you supposed to attend Grant's football party in November?"

"That would be me."

"Okay, yeah I know who you are. Grant got on me pretty bad for not showing up at the little get together he and Yamuna had in January. He said there was a young lady there they wanted me to meet."

"Well, I guess fate had different plans."

"Speaking of plans, what are you doing in an hour?"

"Not a thing."

"It's still early. Do you wanna meet for some tea and dessert at the 18th and U Duplex Diner?"

"I'm down for it if you are."

"I live at 15th and Swann. I should be there at eight fifteen. Where do you live?"

"You will not believe this. We're neighbors. I live at 16th and U."

"Let's just walk over together. Meet me outside of your building at eight o'clock."

"That's a date. Buzz me when you arrive. My apartment number is 201."

My phone rang at eight o'clock on the dot. It was Symon announcing that he was downstairs awaiting my presence. Butterflies filled my stomach. I had a queasy feeling like it was my high school prom night. I tried to play it off, but I couldn't. I closed my apartment door and walked down stairs. When I opened the front door of the building, a man with a smooth jive cool grin extended his hand and tenderly touched the small curve in my back. We stared at each other for a nanosecond until I hugged him closely. I knew right then that our connection was one to keep. He returned the embrace and whispered, "Let a brotha court you."

I surrendered and the evening took flight.

About the Author

Ananda is a registered yoga teacher, certified reiki practitioner, artist, and writer. She owns and operates Kiamsha.com, LLC, a company that allows her to share her healing arts gifts. Currently, she works as an artist-in-residence for Smith Farm Center for Healing and the Arts at Howard University Hospital. As an artist-in-residence, Ananda engages patients and medical staff in creative expression, guiding them to tap inherent creative and cultural roots through breathing, relaxation, and reiki healing touch exercises; and a variety of mediums including visual arts, music, storytelling, and creative writing.

Since 1995, her mixed media collages, wire sculptures, and paintings have been exhibited in the Washington D.C. metropolitan area, North Carolina, and Kentucky. The Women's Collective and Howard University Hospital own Ananda's wire sculpture collections dedicated to communities of color living with HIV/AIDS. In 2001, her artwork was featured in Heart and Soul Magazine.

Ananda's poetry is featured in *Beyond the Frontier: African American Poetry for the 21st Century* edited by E. Ethelbert Miller. She has also self-published several books of poetry and women's creativity workbooks.

In addition, Ananda has facilitated expressive arts and self-care workshops for women of color living with HIV/AIDS; cancer patients, their caregivers, and health care providers; interfaith communities attending the Washington National Cathedral's women's spirituality conference; children with unique learning styles; and lay ministers.

She is a graduate of Morgan State University (B.A. in French, 1986), Howard University School of Law (J.D., 1989), and Georgetown University Law Center (LL.M. in Securities and Financial Regulation, 1991). Ananda's memberships include the Yoga Alliance, Mid Atlantic Yoga Association, Washington Buddhist Peace Fellowship, Society for the Arts in Healthcare, Cultural Alliance of Greater Washington's Business Volunteer Program, Sigma Gamma Rho Sorority, Inc., All Souls Unitarian Church, Insight Meditation Community of Washington's People of Color Sangha and All Souls Sangha, and Results Gym. She lives and plays in Washington, D.C.'s historic U Street neighborhood.

For more information, contact kiamshaleeke@yahoo.com or visit www.myspace.com/lovestroubadours. To purchase Love's Troubadours apparel and products, visit www.cafepress.com/kiamshacom.

978-0-595-44081-8
0-595-44081-9